PRAISE

SUM

"Heartfelt but devoid of flower-child sentimentality, hard-nosed without being cynical. Certainly not the last real word on the subject, but arguably the first."
—Norman Spinrad,
author of *Pictures At 11*

"A fine novel packed with vivid detail, colorful characters, and genuine insight."
—*The Washington Post Book World*

"Just imagine *The Terminator* in love beads, set in the Haight-Ashbury 'hood of 1967."
—*Entertainment Weekly*

"A remarkable second novel . . . the intellect on display within these psychedelically packaged pages is clear-sighted, witty, and wise."
—*Locus*

"Mason has an astonishing gift. Her chief characters . . . almost walk off the page . . . and the story is as significant as anyone could wish. This book will surely be on the prize ballots."
—*Analog*

"[An] honest yet generous picture of an era slipping quickly into history."
—*The Plain Dealer,* Cleveland

"[Mason] is astonishingly good at conjuring up the sights and sounds of that much-missed era."
—*The Vancouver Sun*

The Golden Nineties

LISA MASON

BANTAM BOOKS

NEW YORK
TORONTO
LONDON
SYDNEY
AUCKLAND

THE GOLDEN NINETIES
A Bantam Spectra Book
PUBLISHING HISTORY
Bantam trade paperback edition published November 1995
Bantam mass market edition / November 1996

SPECTRA and the portrayal of a boxed "s" are trademarks of Bantam Books, a division of Bantam Doubleday Dell Publishing Group, Inc.

Library of Congress Card Catalog Number: 95-18211.

ISBN 0-553-57307-1

Published simultaneously in the United States and Canada

Bantam Books are published by Bantam Books, a division of Bantam Doubleday Dell Publishing Group, Inc. Its trademark, consisting of the words "Bantam Books" and the portrayal of a rooster, is Registered in U.S. Patent and Trademark Office and in other countries. Marca Registrada. Bantam Books, 1540 Broadway, New York, New York 10036.

PRINTED IN THE UNITED STATES OF AMERICA

RAD 10 9 8 7 6 5 4 3 2 1

For Tom Robinson

Contents

TENETS OF THE GRANDFATHER PRINCIPLE

DEVELOPED FOR TACHYPORTATION PROJECTS BY THE
LUXON INSTITUTE FOR SUPERLUMINAL APPLICATIONS

TENET ONE:

YOU CANNOT KILL ANY OF YOUR LINEAL ANCESTORS (PRIOR TO HIS OR HER HISTORICAL DEATH), INCLUDING YOURSELF.

TENET TWO:

YOU CANNOT PREVENT THE DEATH OF ANY OF YOUR ANCESTORS (AT THE POINT OF HIS OR HER HISTORICAL DEATH OR THEREAFTER, IF APPLICABLE).

TENET THREE:

YOU CANNOT AFFECT ANY PERSON IN THE PAST, INCLUDING AIDING, COERCING, DECEIVING, DETERRING, KILLING, OR SAVING HIM OR HER (EXCEPT AS DEFINED AND AUTHORIZED BY THE PROJECT DIRECTORS).

TENET FOUR:

YOU CANNOT AFFECT THE NATURAL WORLD IN THE PAST.

TENET FIVE:

YOU CANNOT REVEAL YOUR IDENTITY AS A MODERN PERSON TO ANY PERSON IN THE PAST, INCLUDING YOURSELF.

TENET SIX:

YOU CANNOT REVEAL THE PERSONAL FUTURE OF ANY PERSON IN THE PAST, OR OF HIS OR HER IMMEDIATE FAMILY AND DESCENDANTS, TO THAT PERSON, INCLUDING YOURSELF.

TENET SEVEN:

YOU CANNOT APPLY MODERN TECHNOLOGIES, INCLUDING TACHYPORTATION, TO PAST EVENTS OR PEOPLE, EXCEPT WHEN THE RESULT CONFORMS TO THE ARCHIVES, AND, IN THAT CASE, YOU CANNOT LEAVE EVIDENCE OF A MODERN TECHNOLOGY IN THE PAST.

THE CTL PERIL:

YOU ARE CAPABLE OF DYING IN THE PAST, INCLUDING YOUR PERSONAL PAST (BUT SEE TENET ONE). IF THIS OCCURS, THE TACHYPORTATION IS TRANSFORMED FROM AN OPEN TIME LOOP (OTL) TO A CLOSED TIME LOOP (CTL). *YOU ARE TRAPPED IN A CTL.*

OUT IN FRISCO

There is lots of time to burn
Out in Frisco;
Native customs you will learn
Out in Frisco;
In the famous French cafés,
With their naughty little ways,
That's the place where Cupid plays,
Out in Frisco.

The red light is contagious
Out in Frisco;
The ladies' conduct is outrageous
Out in Frisco;
When the bloodred native wine,
Mixes up the clinging vine,
She will call you "Baby Mine,"
Out in Frisco.

When you finally cash it in
Out in Frisco;
And you end this life of sin
Out in Frisco;
They will gently toll a bell,
Plant your carcass in a dell,
There's no need to go to hell,
You're in Frisco.

—Anonymous
Circa 1895

JULY 4, 1895 ▼ ▼ ▼

Independence Day

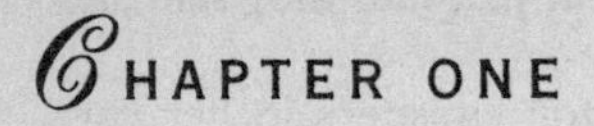

CHAPTER ONE

Fortune Cookies at the Japanese Tea Garden

Out of a tense and arid darkness she steps, her skirts sweeping across the macadam. Her button boot wobbles on the bridge over the brook in the Japanese Tea Garden. "Steady," the technician whispers. The shuttle embraces the ancient bridge in a half-moon of silver lattices. The air is susurrous, tinged with menthol, cold. The shuttle hums. High overhead, the dome ripples in a fitful gust. Zhu Wong listens for final instructions; none come. She closes her eyes. Anticipation quickens her pulse. She waits for the moment it takes to cross over.

And then it's happening: the Event sweeps her across six centuries.

Odd staccato sounds pop in her ears. The Event transforms her into pure energy, suspending her in nothingness. Then the Event flings her back into her own flesh and blood, and she stands, a bit unsteadily, her button boot poised upon the bridge over the brook in the Japanese Tea Garden. A brand-new bridge, the fresh scent of cut wood.

"Muse?" she whispers to the monitor. Fear stains her tongue like a dash of lemon. A peculiar tension gathers behind her eyes. Her skin feels fragile. Heart batters her rib cage, lungs clench. *Now* she feels the Event just like they said she would. Again, "Muse?"

"I'm here, Z. Wong," the monitor whispers in her ear. Muse nestles between scalp and skull behind Zhu's left ear, burrowed in her neckjack. "We're here." Muse automatically checks points of reference. Alphanumerics dance in Zhu's peripheral vision: coordinates confirmed. "We're fine."

But she's not fine. The tension moves to Zhu's sinuses. A soft ache commences.

She opens her eyes. The dappled sunlight shocks her, the azure sky dazzles. Birds cheep, foliage rustles. Sights and sounds seem magnified, amplified, as though she has returned from the dead. Musty scent of eucalyptus infused with overpowering floral perfumes. The tension, the ache transform into throbbing congestion. She sneezes; again, violently. Eyes spurt tears. Sultry heat dampens her armpits.

Bang, bang, bang! Odd staccato sounds? Now earsplitting blasts, the stink of gunpowder.

Gunpowder! Zhu falls to her knees on the macadam, evasive action instinctive at the sound of gunfire. Her breath rasps in her throat. Her fingers twitch, reaching for the handgun she kept strapped beneath her right arm for so many years it was like another limb. Its absence now, an amputation.

She fights panic. No gun, no decent cover. An easy target, perched on the arching bridge. She wipes her eyes with her sleeve and tries to rise, but she's stepped on the skirts, the slip. Stumbles; she moves as if hobbled. The ankle-length layers of silk and cotton have cushioned her knees against abrasion, but not impact. Pain shoots through her kneecaps. There will be bruises.

"Be calm, Z. Wong," Muse whispers. "The loud abrupt sounds suggest combustible explosives, not projectiles aimed at you."

"What?"

"It's the Fourth of July. Independence Day; United States of America."

Zhu crouches, uncomprehending.

"Those are fireworks. The people of San Francisco always celebrated the Fourth of July in Golden Gate Park. The park was public then. Correction: public now."

"Independence Day, of course." Zhu has never celebrated America's Independence Day. She had never been to America at all till she was chosen for the Golden Nineties Project.

"This is long before the parkland was acquired by private cosmicist interests and placed under the dome." Muse's whisper in her ear does calm her. Confirmation coordinates continue to match like winning numbers in a gambling game.

She glances up, squinting. Recalls the milky PermaPlast dome rippling overhead as she stepped into the tachyonic shuttle surrounding the bridge. How wonderful to see the sky with no dome! "But the dome is old, too, isn't it?"

"Been in place since the 2100s when the stratosphere had thinned so dangerously that undomed lands were ruined by excessive radiation," Muse says. "This is 1895."

1895. She bows her head, struck with awe. Then it's true. They did it: she's six hundred years in the past.

"Please, Z. Wong," Muse says. "You haven't much time before the rendezvous. Get up. Walk around, stretch your legs."

Zhu frees skirts and slip without ripping the fabric. How can women tolerate these long dresses? Standing, she sneezes again. "Muse, what's wrong with my sinuses?"

"Unknown. An allergic response."

"I'm not allergic to anything."

"Pollen?"

"No, never."

Muse pauses. "Perhaps a response aggravated by the Event. I will analyze. In the meantime, you've got a cotton handkerchief." Helpful Muse becoming impatient. "Please; you have less time now."

Zhu finds the handkerchief in her leather feedbag purse. Hands shake. Rattled; can't get over the impression someone was shooting at her as she stepped through the tachyonic shuttle. She looks around. The shuttle was installed at the historic site they called the Japanese Tea Garden in New Golden Gate Preserve. Smiles; secretly glad the shuttle is gone.

Zhu never liked it: photon guns aimed like assault weapons at the arrays of pretty calcite crystals; banks of blinking microframes slaved to vast offsite mainframes. The maw of the macrofusion chronometer, savage hooklike heads of the imploders. The whole thing militaristic, foreboding. The shuttle instituted-consummated the awesome technological feat they called the ME3 Event. And the Event is what has instantaneously translated the matter of her body into pure energy and transmitted that energy faster than the speed of light.

Flinging her body and soul from July 4, 2495, to July 4, 1895.

She honks into the handkerchief. Hard, curving stays of the corset—slender strips of steel covered in black satin—dig into her ribs. Quickly, before anyone can see, she flips up skirts and slip, examines her knees. No blood leaks through the heavy black cotton stockings, but the bruises will be colorful. She smooths back the slip, the skirt, the overskirt, the traveling cloak. All in shades of pearlescent dove gray.

"I beg your pardon, miss, but may I be of service to you?"

Zhu glances up.

A young man. He stands, startled, at the crest of the bridge, wringing his large mottled hands and staring open-mouthed at her calves. His bright blond muttonchops and clean-shaven chin transform his face into a funny square shape. His equally bright yellow hair is combed back over his scalp and falls to the shoulders of his black frock coat. A scarlet polka-dot tie throttles his starched wing collar. His straw porkpie hat tilts at a rakish angle. The navy blue vest is carelessly unbuttoned in the heat of the afternoon. Quite the dandy. Bawdy grin, stink of gin. Gets his way with ladies.

But his expression of concern closes up like a door slamming shut when he glimpses Zhu's pale golden complexion, black hair, wide cheekbones. Her slanting eyes, the irises gene-tweaked green.

"Why, thank you, sir." She extends her hand. Gray lace

mitts cover her palms, wrists, forearms, but leave her fingertips bare.

The startled young man does not take her hand. He frowns, turns without another word, and strides swiftly away. Glances over his shoulder, eyes of ice.

"Too bad, Muse," Zhu says tartly to the monitor. She pulls the veil down from the brim of her straw Newport hat. Ties the veil under her chin, shielding her face from the sun. From other prejudiced eyes. "I guess he didn't want to help a lady."

"You're not a lady, Z. Wong." Muse suddenly as cold as the startled young man's glance. "You're a fallen woman."

❘ ❘ ❘

A fallen woman. She certainly was. In the golden nineties, six centuries in the past. And in her day, too.

It was late June, 2495, when her lawyer barged into the central women's prison facility at Beijing and roused her from an exhausted sleep. "A deal?" she said wearily. "What kind of deal?"

"We don't have all the details, but I think they'll reduce the charge from murder to manslaughter," the lawyer said and shoved a petition in her face.

"*Attempted*," Zhu reminded her. "Attempted manslaughter. I didn't mean to do it." Too tired to read the tiny print. "And he's not dead yet. At least no one's told me so."

The lawyer was court-appointed, since Zhu had no money. One of those bleary-eyed, pasty-faced public defenders perennially overworked and underpaid. A heart attack waiting to happen at ninety-three years old with an inflamed neckjack beneath her ragged crew cut. Theoretically the people had equal access to due process, but it didn't happen much in Socialist-Confucianist China. The lawyer glared at Zhu, distaste curving her mouth. Despised all her clients, especially Zhu.

Attempted murder. The charge could be upgraded to murder if the victim died. Sick at heart, Zhu had asked the guards every day after her arrest, "Is he alive?" No answer. "Please tell me. *Is he alive or dead?*"

It was crazy. *Never* supposed to happen this way. As she lay in the cell, sick with forced detoxification, waiting to be charged with attempted murder, she herself had trouble believing the campaign could have gone so wrong. How she could have done such a thing: the atrocities, the Night of Broken Blossoms. She was a Daughter of Compassion, dedicated to the Cause. The Daughters were comrades who fought for a sustainable future in mother China. They were allies of the World Birth Control Organization, supporters of the Generation-Skipping Law. They weren't murderers. She wasn't a murderer.

Was she?

Since the arrest, she had trouble remembering exactly what had happened. The door to the room; had it opened to the left or right? One sentry or two? She remembered a crowd, other times only a few people. When had she pulled the handgun from beneath her right arm? The astonished look on the woman's face: because Zhu had a gun or because she was left-handed? Memories of that night flashed through her mind, vivid and horrifying, then abruptly dimmed, and rearranged themselves. On the morning the lawyer barged in with the deal, Zhu was beginning to wonder if she were going mad.

They had beaten her after the arrest, of course, ripped off the black patch, and forced her through detoxification in a matter of days. Jacked her into an interrogator that had yammered at her day and night.

"Name?"

"I am Zhu Wong."

"Age?"

"I am thirty."

"Occupation?"

"I am a comrade with the Daughters of Compassion. I am dedicated to the Cause. I believe in the Cause. I never meant to hurt. . ."

Jolt of electricity in her neckjack, and the interrogator had started all over again. "Name?"

The lawyer said, "They want to send you on a tachyportation."

"A tachy what?" she asked. They never shut the lights off in the women's facility. She was sore all over. Dizzy from the interrogator, nauseated and addle-brained with withdrawal from the black patch. The insides of her eyelids felt as if coated with sand. *Tachyportation;* she rolled the unfamiliar word around in her mouth like a spicy candy.

"The techs will explain," the lawyer said, taking out a neurobic, popping the bead open, and snorting. Zhu watched wistfully. Sadist. "They're going to ship you to the States. San Francisco. Place called the Luxon Institute for Superluminal Applications. The LISA techs will tell you all about it. Sign here."

"I don't know," Zhu said.

"What do you mean, you don't know?" the lawyer said.

"I can't agree to something before I know what's involved." She had heard stories. Jacking convicts into the computer-constructed reality called telespace for strange experiments. DNA editing, brainwaving, testing new drugs. Political prisoners were especially vulnerable. The lawyer herself suggested the Daughters of Compassion had been politically harassed; maybe an extenuating circumstance. "I have my rights."

"Rights! Be grateful they came to me with this deal, Wong," the lawyer said, flicking the neurobic onto the floor. "Do you have any idea how bad you and your comrades make the organization look?" Said "organization" in capital letters. The World Birth Control Organization inspired all manner of passions; so did the Generation-Skipping Law. "Frankly, I don't give a damn if they jack you into a rehab program and make you compute actuarial margins for twenty years."

"Thank you, counselor."

"Do you have any idea how your crime affects the Cause?"

"Yeah," she said. Burned with guilt and shame. The lawyer didn't need to remind her. It was the last thing in the world the Daughters of Compassion had ever wanted: to harm the Cause. She had dedicated her life, it was crazy, *crazy* . . .

"But what's a tachyportation?" she insisted.

"Way I understand it, they want to send you six hundred years into the past," the lawyer said. Coughed.

Zhu gaped. "You mean . . . send me . . . *physically*?"

"Physically, yeah. With less than a picogram of loss, whatever the hell that means," the lawyer said. "Like I said, the LISA techs will explain. It is strange, I admit. The institute doesn't conduct t-port projects anymore. You can ask the techs about that, too. I remember when they shut down the tachyonic shuttles and discontinued tachyportation. All very hush-hush. Must have been a couple years after you were born."

"Six hundred . . . *years*?" A prickle of excitement, of wonder and delicious anticipation had pierced her foggy exhaustion. They wanted to t-port her six hundred years into the past? Was it dangerous? What would she do there, six hundred years in the past? A thousand questions tumbled through her mind. She trembled, a strange sensation coursed through her blood, and suddenly the conversation seemed familiar. As if she'd heard it before, just exactly like this. As if she'd always sat there, on that seat of shame, and the pasty-faced lawyer had always sneered at her as she was sneering now. "Why me?" she finally managed to ask.

"Beats the hell out of me," the lawyer said, "after what you've done. But you're the one they want, Wong, and I say take the deal. They're raring to go. They call it the Golden Nineties Project."

❘ ❘ ❘

Zhu strolls out of the Japanese Tea Garden through an enormous red gate and stands before the shallow bowl of Concert Valley. "Beautiful." She's never seen a landscape like this: shaggy palm trees, aloe veras as high as her waist, glossy dark pines, flowers blooming brilliant pink and gold. "So fresh and new!" After the cracked old domes and barren concrete, the unforgiving fields of the village of Changchi where she had spent her life, Golden Gate Park, 1895, is a wonderland.

Alphanumerics flicker in her peripheral vision. Muse

downloads a file and scans it. The monitor carries a one-gigabyte Archive. "The California Midwinter International Exposition was held here in 1894. This is what's left. Over two million people attended the fair."

"Two million?" Zhu cautious after the monitor's cool rebuke. "What's the population of San Francisco?"

"Three hundred thousand." Muse amiable again, the eager guide. "The two million came from all over the country on the transcontinental train. The park itself is the result of John McLaren's horticultural hand. Did you know this place was sand dunes less than two decades ago?"

"Doesn't seem possible," Zhu says. Such trees, lawns, flowers. "A cultivation like this would take half a century."

"They call McLaren 'Boss Gardener.' He was the first to discover that Scotch sea-bent grass would hold to the sand in the ocean winds long enough to establish a subsoil in which other plants could thrive. Perhaps we'll see him."

"Oh!" Zhu glances about. John McLaren might stroll right by her!

"The cosmicists who own New Golden Gate Preserve in our time revere McLaren. His love of ecosystem, his understanding of plants, his perseverance and dedication." Smug tone in Muse's whisper.

"Ah, yes, the cosmicists," Zhu says. "How lovely for the cosmicists. Only they and their friends can enjoy this place in our time. I would never have been permitted inside the preserve at all if I hadn't been chosen for the Golden Nineties Project. Isn't that true?"

Muse silent.

"But is it right, Muse? Do you think that's correct, that a public place has been privatized and withheld from the people?"

"'The people,'" Muse says. "All twelve billion of them?"

"I thought cosmicists were democratic, egalitarian," Zhu says, venturing down a walk leading into Concert Valley. "That they believe in equal rights according to True Value. At least, that's the line handed to me at the Luxon Institute for Superluminal Applications."

"Egalitarian?" Muse a little exasperated. "The cosmicists

believe in equal sacrifice to the Great Good. Human interests do not necessarily take precedence over nonhuman interests. The hyperindustrial era and the brown ages taught us that only too painfully. In short, cosmicists believe in privatizing natural resources when 'the people' can't or won't properly care for them."

"Oh, I see," Zhu says. "The cosmicists know better?"

"Well, yes. The brown ages were long before your time, Z. Wong. You have no notion of the devastation, the panic. Once the dome went up, no one was permitted into New Golden Gate Preserve. If it makes you feel any better, the owners don't spend much time there, either. The animals and plants and insects have it all to themselves."

Zhu quells further argument. The cosmicists; abundantly clear who programmed Muse. She sneezes, tears welling in her eyes again.

"That barnyard smell is from the horse manure gathered by the street cleaners downtown." Muse wry. "Boss Gardener has it spread all over the grounds. That's what makes the lawns—as you put it, Z. Wong—so fresh and new."

The labyrinth of macadamized walks is interspersed with charming snippets of boxwood and purple hydrangea. The De Young Art Museum stands to Zhu's left, the impression of Egyptian antiquity reinforced by two magnificent concrete sphinxes. The structure and its statuary were cobbled together in a few months before the fair. There is the Temple of Music, a huge sandstone arch in the style of the Italian Renaissance, flanked by Corinthian columns. The medieval castle with incongruous Arabian arabesques is the Administration Building. And at the center of the valley stands the Electric Tower, a smaller version of the Eiffel Tower adorned with a slew of international flags. The Bella Vista Café perches on the first mezzanine. A globe crowns the tower's peak. A life-size papier-mâché California brown bear balances on the globe like a circus performer, the Bear Flag clutched in its paw. The tower touts the newfangled energy source and Mr. Edison's electric lightbulb. Zhu won't see many electric lightbulbs. San Francisco is still mostly gaslit in 1895.

Zhu tours Concert Valley, circling back to the tea garden. Tightrope walkers have strung a wire between two trees in front of the Temple of Music, cavort with parasols and chairs. A fellow with an extraordinarily bushy beard and a shiny top hat cracks his whip over a ring of pedestals upon which two lively hounds leap about, while a forlorn-looking baboon in a yellow satin jacket occasionally deigns to perform a wobbly handstand.

A crowd promenades in Concert Valley. Somber suits of the gentlemen are relieved by the pale pastel colors of the ladies' dresses. Despite the heat, everyone wears layer upon fluttering layer of clothing, from buttoned-up collars to buttoned-down boots. And hats—everyone wears a hat, even the children. The ladies wear veils and carry parasols, scalloped edges drooping with lace or velvet fringe.

Zhu gulps. Her daily dress in Changchi? Jeans, a T-shirt, sneakers; a padded jacket in winter. These people would think her half-naked if they saw her perambulating in her jeans and shirt. Like most postdomers, she has always worn Block, the fine protective microderm protecting her skin from all solar radiation. Her complexion, though golden, is paler than that of these veiled ladies.

So beautiful.

Yet there: Zhu spies a frail woman. Cascades of cerulean silk. Yet the veil on her flowered hat barely conceals a battered eye. The blue ribbon tied around her chin does not at all conceal the bruise discoloring half her jaw. The burly husband towers over her, quick anger in his narrow eyes. And there: a gust blows off a woman's broad-brimmed hat. Straps at her chin, ears, forehead hold a translucent face glove. Her eyes, nostrils, mouth show through stitched openings. In the sunlight Zhu can see pustulic acne beneath the fabric of the face glove. The woman retrieves her hat and furiously pins it back on. There, too: a girl so thin she is nothing but satin skin over bird bones. She shuffles behind her sisters. Dark circles surround her eyes, skin tinged like pale celadon. She delicately coughs. Blood blooms in the handkerchief her mother impatiently thrusts into her fragile hands.

"Outta sight, you friggin' hoodlum!" shouts a portly man in a charcoal cutaway coat as he grapples with a fellow in a bowler and navy three-piece suit. Sweat pours down their flushed faces, staining high starched collars strangling thick necks.

"I'll take me knuckledusters to ya," the bowler shouts back.

Reek of whiskey. The cutaway passes a silver flask to the bowler, who swigs from it and slams the flask back into the cutaway's chest. Are they roughhousing or about to commence fisticuffs? Their violent conviviality makes Zhu's heart race. Men like this go down to Chinatown, set a house on fire just to see the flames. Men like this chase a Chink, string him up from a lamppost just for sport.

"My calculations show that your rendezvous is fast approaching," Muse reminds her, a little too loudly.

A woman turns and peers at her. Zhu adjusts her veil. That's all she needs: a disembodied voice hovering around her, she answering it. Muse is perfectly capable of communicating in subaud so that others cannot overhear. Why this exercise of Muse's projection mode when she hasn't commanded it? She'll wind up in Napa Asylum if she's not careful.

The rendezvous! Zhu gathers up her skirts and hurries back to the Japanese Tea Garden. She finds the elegant redwood pagoda, takes a place in the queue. A Japanese woman in kimono and clogs bows and smiles. Zhu returns the bow. The Japanese woman pours tea, sets the cup on a red lacquered tray.

"No more than a thousand Japanese in San Francisco," Muse whispers in her ear. Alphanumerics flash. "The staff is part of the attraction."

The concessionaire behind the counter is an exuberant Japanese man in a blue and white kimono and scarlet headband. "I am Mr. Makota, dearie. You will please try my cookie?" He proffers the treat, a wafer folded over like a half shell, fragrant with vanilla. He breaks the cookie open, extracts a slip of paper from the crumbs.

Zhu takes the slip and reads:

THERE IS A PROSPECT OF A THRILLING TIME
AHEAD FOR YOU

The concessionaire laughs at her startled expression. "You like my fortune cookie, dearie? I make them for the fair, number one first, but, oh my! how the Chinese copy me. Every Chinese restaurant in town have fortune cookie now. But I first!" He pops a piece of cookie in his mouth. "You try? Bake today."

"Thank you, Mr. Makota," Zhu says, taking her tea and a fortune cookie to a little table at the back of the pagoda. She unties her veil from beneath her chin, discreetly lifts the cup beneath the netted fabric, and sips. Hot sweet tea soothes her throat, calms her sinuses. The swirling, tenuous feeling—what the techs warned her about, a reaction called tachyonic lag—fades away. She smiles, encouraged, breaks apart the cookie, and takes the slip of paper:

YOU WILL ALWAYS BE SURROUNDED
BY LOVING FRIENDS

The girl. There she is.

Crouching behind the table, huddled next to the wall of the pagoda. So silent and still, a bundle of shadows barely breathing, that Zhu didn't notice her at first. Furtive motion; a skinny little hand darts toward Zhu's leather feedbag purse on the floor.

Zhu is quicker. She seizes the girl by her wrist, grabs the other flailing arm, and pulls her out from under the table. The girl is strong, much bigger and older than Zhu expected.

"*Oy ching, ching, syau-jye!*" the girl squeals.

"Please, please yourself, miss." Zhu stern. Deposits her captive on the opposite chair. "*Pa liao.*" Enough of this, settle down. "Trying to steal my purse, are you?"

"I not take purse," the girl says. Haughty thing. Sulky face filmed with grime. Hard to tell if she's pretty. Filthy, though, that's plain. Thick black hair coming out of its braid. She is clad in an apple green embroidered silk tunic held together with gold satin frogs. When she lowers her arms to her sides, the sleeves droop below her fingertips, making her look as if she has no hands. Too bad she doesn't keep her arms down. Dreadful fingernails, a sprinkling of sores across the knuckles. Green silk trousers fall to her ankles. Her straw sandals are threaded with more green silk and set upon thick platform soles. Big bare feet, long knobby toes. "I not take purse from *fahn quai*," she says with a toss of her head.

"*Fahn quai?*" Zhu says. "You think I'm a white devil woman?" She flings the veil up. "Look. No white devil woman."

The girl's eyes widen. Zhu has the same golden skin, same round face, same wide cheekbones as the girl herself. But the irises in Zhu's slanting eyes are a brilliant gene-tweaked green.

"*Oy.*" Perplexity clouds the girl's black eyes. "Jade eyes."

"I am Zhu." Smiles at the girl's wonder; touched. "Yes, jade eyes."

"*Oy,* Jade Eyes," the girl says. Pleading. "I not thief, Jade Eyes. This true. You must believe! Look." From some hidden pocket in her tunic she takes out a small carved rosewood box and sets it on the table. "I have jewel. My mama give me for dowry."

"Let me see." Zhu waits impatiently as the girl fumbles with the latch.

So the Archivists were right, after all. Amazing! The Luxon Institute for Superluminal Applications was not a pack of kooks, after all. And all that data, all those years. So much they didn't know about Chinese women in America, 1895. Still, the Archivists and their searchware had actually traced this girl—or someone like her. Had located reports of a runaway found in the Japanese Tea Garden on the Fourth of July.

They even knew the girl would have this box of jewelry. They knew she would possess the aurelia, the peculiar brooch made of gold, diamonds, and glass that they called the aurelia.

The girl lifts the rosewood lid. Zhu peers in eagerly.

Three bracelets of jade, one of ivory. A pair of filigreed gold earrings. A gold ring with a nice jade cabochon.

Zhu frowns, stirring the pieces, turning them over. "This is it? This is all you have?"

"All have? Mama give! This my dowry!" The girl's black eyes flash. "This jade, this gold." She proudly holds up the bracelets, dangles the earrings. "Real gold."

And for the second time since she stepped across the bridge over the brook in the Japanese Tea Garden Zhu feels a painful jolt of fear.

The aurelia; the girl doesn't have the aurelia.

❜ ❜ ❜

The aurelia, the aurelia. All this fuss over a trifle, a mere bauble, a piece of decadent jewelry. Was it possible the success of a complex application of arcane high technology turned on a piece of old gold? Even after the official explanation, Zhu had always been troubled by the aurelia.

Not that she was happy with most of what happened after the pasty-faced lawyer sprang her loose from the women's prison facility and promptly sent her in restraints with two copbots for company on a transcontinental EM-Trans to San Francisco.

"I'm just a country gal," she joked as the copbots hustled her down a series of high-speed escalators to the tubes. The copbots were mute. Either someone took out the voice chips or the bots were issued a gag order. Zhu had heard of EM-Trans, though she'd never personally seen the train, let alone ridden on one. Holoids didn't begin to capture its magnificence. The mag-lev train—the whole vehicle levitated over the narrow ribbon of track by the force of electromagnetism—looked like a gigantic black bullet, each end a monocoque wedge. The transcontinental train reached speeds of over a thousand miles an hour in tubes cut through global curvature. The ride lasted half a day, the trek up to the surface another hour or more. And then: San Francisco.

San Francisco! Zhu had heard that Hong Kong surpassed San Francisco in management of the coastal encroachment that threatened seaside cities two hundred years ago; that Tokyo surpassed it in modernity, New York in sheer upward thrust. But Zhu had never seen Hong Kong or Tokyo or New York, either. The entertainment districts glittering along offshore dikes, the leveed containment canals, the gardens planted over ancient traffic corridors, the magnificent cosmicist domes over New Golden Gate Preserve and central megalopolis districts, the estates of the wealthy, the spectacular skyscrapers literally touching the clouds; all these were nothing short of intimidating.

How isolated Zhu had been her whole life! How shamefully provincial! The countryside around Changchi where she and the Daughters of Compassion had focused the campaign was burdened with more crumbling concrete, polluting ground traffic, the daily detritus of too many people than this megalopolis of five million souls, which had managed to hide just about everything unsightly away. China's size and scale was horizontal. Zhu thought of the motherland as prostrate, huge and sprawling, only too plain to see. San Francisco was dizzyingly vertical, its gleaming surfaces concealing a million modern arcana.

But if San Francisco was intimidating, the Luxon Institute for Superluminal Applications was formidable. Once topside, the copbots dispatched her to the waterfront. From there a catamaran sped her to the silver monolith rising up out of north bay waters. Zhu had heard about hydroplexes: marine-based skyscrapers modeled on the ancient oil drilling platforms that had bobbed offshore in the days when the technopolistic plutocracy held a stranglehold on a world economy fueled by petroleum. South Honshu was mostly hydroplexes. South Cork, too.

Had heard about them. Now Zhu stepped into a hydroplex, feeling every inch the country bumpkin she knew she must appear, especially in her dirty blue prison jumpsuit. The hydroplex perched high above a polished gridwork harbor into which the catamaran navigated and docked. If the meticulously groomed denizens of this modern platinum palace were troubled by the ceaseless rocking and swaying, they gave no sign but hurried silently through hushed rose-hued corridors on what must surely have been urgent business. Zhu thought she was going to be sick.

When the red-haired man stepped out to greet her, suddenly she was sick. "I . . . long ride . . . detox maybe," she muttered and, much to her embarrassment, keeled over. How could she explain the vertigo that seized her, the dread that squeezed her into unconsciousness?

She felt a little better when she awoke, but her head was still woozy, her stomach sour. She opened her eyes. Found herself lying on a chrome and leather divan in a chamber swathed in gauzy pale fabric like the inside of a cloud.

The red-haired man sat watching her.

He gestured to a viewer perched in the corner like a predatory bird. "We're holoiding your instructions here today. The file, called *Zhu.doc*, will go in your monitor's Archive." He gave her a Coke, which tasted delicious, much better than the colas in Changchi. "I'm the one who offered your lawyer the deal." Fell silent, watching her again as though she were a specimen in a petri dish.

She should have been flattered someone of his stature had deigned to attend her. She should have been grateful, should have been cordial, should have been eager to please.

But she wasn't grateful or cordial or eager. Sharp dislike rose in her chest. She didn't like the red-haired man at all. She puzzled at her unruly emotions, then felt guilty. There was no rational reason for disliking him.

He had done nothing to her; she'd never met him before.

But she could not deny her resentment, as though she knew something about him but she couldn't say what. *Had* she met him before? Where? She swallowed her tumult as best she could, silently admonishing herself. She wasn't wearing the black patch for the first time in months, that was all. Her customary state of sullen discontent had simply reasserted itself.

He sat before her in an exquisite leather and chrome chair and steepled his fingertips, scrutinizing her. "I am Chiron Cat's Eye in Draco," he said at last.

China's people had a thousand different faces, but people of the West were a crazy quilt, variegated colors of hair and eyes and skin. And this man; this man was different from anyone Zhu had ever seen. He was tall and slim, skin as white as bone. His hair and eyebrows were the astonishing color of pomegranates, a rare fruit Zhu had found at the farmers' market just one time years ago. The astonishing hair fell over his shoulders and trailed down his back. His eyes were as clear and blue and deep as the sapphires she had seen only in a natural history holoid. Young, perhaps in his fifties.

"We want to tachyport you to 1895," he said. Voice modulated, precise. "Do you understand what that means?"

"I'm giving you all such a hard time, you're sending me six hundred years into the past," Zhu joked. What was wrong with her? She struggled to be polite.

"It's not meant to be a punishment, Zhu. Tell me. You find that difficult to believe, don't you?"

Zhu considered. "Mister . . ."

"You may call me Chiron. Or Chi."

"Chiron, I'm a comrade with the Daughters of Compassion. I'm a devotee of our patron goddess, Kuan Yin. I've been dedicated to the Cause since I was fifteen. I've worked in the fields, in the processing plant, in the recycler. All I care about is survival of the motherland. The survival of my China. China has struggled with poverty and famine and oppression of her women for over two thousand years. Politicians come and go. Social theories come and go. Campaigns, reforms, platforms, regimes; they all come and go. We struggled years ago. We struggle now." She shrugged. Old sentiments but the words tasted fresh. "The Mars terraformation and orbital metaworlds and telespace and hyperpoetry; those things are all right. Every kid dreams of getting morphed, getting a neckjack, linking with telespace. But you know what? I just don't care."

"But you do have a neckjack," Chi said.

"Sure, because Changchi had three seasons of prosperity when I was in lower school and the first thing the administrators did was morph the kids for telespace. So we could keep up!" Zhu touches the neckjack installed behind her left ear. "You think computer-constructed reality did a damn bit of good when the rains didn't come in the fourth season, and they couldn't get the clouds seeded or herd a storm down from Siberia?"

"We all owe much to telespace," Chi said. "The technique for herding storms was developed using telespace models."

"That's fine. But my eyes keep looking at the mud that won't yield enough peas, not at telespace or the stars. You want to tachyport me six hundred years into the past? No; sorry. It doesn't make any sense to me."

"Then listen carefully."

He told her about the genesis of tachyportation technology. The Luxon Institute for Superluminal Applications was a venerable cosmicist think tank that had long devoted its private resources to the study of the Cosmic Mind and the nature of spacetime. The LISA techs had been experimenting for decades with luxons—particles that travel at the speed of light—when one of the physicists made a quantum breakthrough: Ariel Herbert proved superluminal correlation of information by tracking tachyons—particles traveling faster than the speed of light.

At the same time, other LISA techs mastered a phenomenal technology: translating matter to its energy equivalent and back again with less than a picogram-picosecond of loss. Translation technology was driven by a process known as the Matter-Energy Equivalence Equation—the ME3 Event.

Coupling superluminal correlation with the ME3 Event meant the LISA techs could translate matter into energy, transmit that energy superluminally—faster than the speed of light—and retranslate the energy into its original form at a specific destination. The piggybacked technologies of translation and transmission—each enabling the other to carry out its function—were bundled together and called tachyportation: t-porting.

"The Event is created within an installation called a tachyonic shuttle," Chi said. "At first, we used t-porting to translate-transmit personnel and materiel to Mars for the terraformation project. The two-year transit time was eliminated. It was tremendously efficient! I believe the Mars terraformation could not have succeeded without tachyportation.

"Then we discovered paradox: when we transmitted a packet of energy to a destination superluminally, the energy arrived at the destination *before* the transmission began."

"Could that be?" Zhu said.

"We knew theoretically that could be," Chi said. "A mathematician, Fritz Pirani, conjured up the paradox centuries ago. Imagine three people seated in a triangle, playing a game of faster-than-light Post Office. When Alice sends a superluminal message to Bill and Bill sends the message to Carol and Carol superluminally returns the message to Alice, mathematically Alice receives the message before she sends it to Bill. Still, imagine everyone's surprise when the Pirani paradox proved true!"

"How did you discover this?"

"We t-ported three laborers to work on Mars," Chi said. "They found themselves on Mars before they stepped through the tachyonic shuttle on Earth."

From there a past-travel application was developed, and t-porting to the past began.

"And have you t-ported, Chiron?" Zhu asked, unsure whether she was awed or appalled. Changing people into energy packets and back again! Shooting them around like human cannonballs in some premillennium circus—only faster than the speed of light. It was pretty weird.

"Yes, I have," Chi said and smiled wistfully. "I t-ported to San Francisco, 1967. To a space and time called the Summer of Love."

"But how," Zhu said, wrestling with these concepts, "could you go to the past if the past has already happened?"

"That's where the Archives come in," Chi said.

The Archives were the repository of all known information about the world, preserved, recorded, and uploaded into telespace. Using telespace technology and some very fancy searchware, the Archivists could analyze moments in the past.

"Analyze them at a level of detail unknown to historians before," Chi said somberly. "The Archivists began to realize that the closer they examined any given moment, the less they knew about the *complete* reality: the intimate details, the smells and sounds, the thoughts people carried in their heads, their emotions, their memories.

"The Archivists also discovered that certain moments contained historical ambiguities. They found gaps in the data, gaps they called dim spots.

"Theory and practice and philosophy intertwined. The cosmicists believe in a cocreatorship of reality between humanity and the Cosmic Mind, the force of Universal Intelligence. As physicists pondered the question of how you could travel to a past that already exists, cosmicist philosophers and Archivists came up with a quick and simple answer that was consistent with paradox itself: If you've traveled to the past, you have already done so. You *must* do so.

"Please understand, we cosmicists are conservationist," Chi added. "We believe in the mandate of nonintervention: nonaction is as vital as action. We scorn the aggressive, exploitative pursuit of new technologies that so typified the technopolistic plutocracy at the turn of the millennium. We approached tachyportation cautiously. Bearing the mandate of nonintervention in mind, we formulated the Tenets of the Grandfather Principle for the proper conduct of t-port projects."

He produced a sheet of hardcopy. "We'll want you to know the tenets intimately before you t-port. It is essential that you make every effort to observe them."

"All right," Zhu said, taking the hardcopy. Sighed; didn't know there'd be studying.

"I admit with hindsight that the Archivists' answer to paradox was solipsistic, self-perpetuating, recursive." Chi steepled his fingers again. "You must understand the atmosphere of sheer excitement then. It was contagious! The LISA techs asked the Archivists to find evidence that a modern person had been to the past. Dim spots turned out to be the most likely candidates for such evidence. The Archivists found that where data supporting the reality of a moment were incomplete, you could construe the evidence to suggest that a t-porter had been present. Further, if sending a t-porter to the past created a new probability in the timeline, then sending that person to a dim spot was less likely to disturb reality as we know it."

"Create a new probability?" Zhu said. She was sure she was over being amazed, but she wasn't. "Excuse me?"

"We cosmicists believe that humanity is always cocreating reality with the Cosmic Mind," Chi said. "If you view reality as a multiverse—a set of probabilities, a set of multiple realities, which is a notion long supported by quantum physics—there is no terrible flaw in that."

"No, you want to do more than cocreate," Zhu said accusingly, "you want to take over the Cosmic Mind."

He gave her a sharp look. "That was never our intent," he said and fell silent for a long time. Brows furrowed, he stared over Zhu's right shoulder and tapped his fingertips to his lips.

"Then," Zhu said, uncomfortable, "you're really serious? I've already lived in 1895? Before I was even *born*?"

Chi nodded. His sapphire eyes bored into her.

"But how can that be?" she protested, flinching under his gaze. "I don't remember!"

"You don't remember because you haven't experienced it yet within your personal timeline. Your personal consciousness is a forward-moving experience. You haven't yet experienced what will happen to you in 1895. You won't remember that time till we t-port you there."

He stared at her again in a way that made resentment boil up in her heart. She shifted on the divan, clutching her prison blues. "Why me?"

He nodded, expecting the question. "There's evidence suggesting that you—or someone like you—were there."

"Really! What evidence?"

"Well. . . You're a Chinese woman."

Zhu laughed out loud. Was he a racist after all, this sophisticated cosmicist? "Sure, just me and about several billion others."

"You've got a neckjack. Doesn't matter if it's primitive, it'll work. We want to install a monitor in your jack."

"A monitor?" *Here we go,* she thought. Strange experiment time.

"An artificial intelligence that will carry an Archive of relevant files, make sure you get where you're supposed to go, keep you informed about your environment. It will have full holoid capability, in case you need it. I took a knuckletop on my t-port," Chi said. "Looked like a man's ring. Carried files, had holoid capability, too. Your device is much more sophisticated. It can talk to you on a subaudio level or project its voice, as you wish."

"I'm going further into the past with better equipment than you had?"

"Odd, isn't it?" His smile faded. "There isn't much time to train you, I'm afraid. The shuttle will be ready in another day or two."

"Another *day* or two?"

"Because of the unfortunate incident at Changchi," he said, choosing his words carefully, which instantly raised her hackles again, "the monitor will also ensure you're fulfilling the object of the project."

"Because I am an accused criminal."

"I trust you don't think we are trying to take advantage of your situation," he said.

Now that this manicured cosmicist raised the point himself, Zhu wasn't so sure.

"You've got other qualities, as well." Chi hurried on. "You're educated. You've got some gene-tweaking. Nice eyes, by the way. And you've got no family responsibilities."

"I'm a Daughter of Compassion, Mr. Chiron."

"Yes. Just Chi is fine."

"And I'm a skipchild."

"I'm a skipchild, too," he said.

"Yes, but you're Chiron Cat's Eye in Draco." She waved her hand at the room like a cloud. "You're part of all this, isn't that true?"

He inclined his head.

"I thought so. My skipparents got tired of playing mommy and daddy. I was abandoned to the state when I was fifteen."

"The Generation-Skipping Law can be harsh." Chi was fumbling, a condition that looked odd on him. "Look, Zhu, we've researched the project. And we've chosen you. *I've* chosen you." He plunged on, shying away from touchy issues. "There isn't much information on Chinese women in San Francisco in 1895. Mostly they were smuggled into the city to become slaves. Immigration authorities never knew who they were. Their masters changed their names, falsified family relationships. When they died, they were buried in anonymous graves."

"So their identities are lost to the Archives," Zhu said. An unexpected pang of sadness clutched her heart. "Then that's a dim spot."

"That's right." Chi smiled, a real smile at last, warm and encouraging. "We've constructed an identity for you."

"And who will I be?"

"The runaway mistress of a British gentleman. That will explain your presence in San Francisco and your proficiency in English."

The resentment swelled again. "I told you, I'm a Daughter of Compassion. I will *not* be some white man's mistress!"

He laughed. "Of course not. You'll go to a home in Chinatown established by Presbyterian missionaries expressly for women and girls like yourself. You'll stay there, work for the director. It's all women. You'll like it. I understand the place is not unlike the compound owned by the Daughters of Compassion."

"I guess that sounds all right," Zhu said slowly.

Suddenly, Chiron searched his pockets. Incongruously, like an old-timey stage magician pulling a dove from his sleeve, he produced something shiny and commanded, "Look at this."

His actions startled her. An odd prickly feeling rose in her throat. "What is it?"

It was just a piece of jewelry. "We call it an aurelia," Chi said in a low voice. "A golden butterfly."

But the thing was not exactly a golden butterfly. A fantastic Art Nouveau brooch, its elaborate wings were crafted out of swirls of gold set with marquise-cut diamonds and bits of multicolored glass that caught the light like tiny stained glass windows. Instead of an insect, the body of a tiny, graceful woman cast in gold stood at the center, her outstretched arms bearing the fabulous wings. Her shapely legs were poised as though she were about to dive. Heart-shaped face of a classic Gibson girl: large eyes, full cheeks, delicate chin and mouth. Her hair was swept up in a sort of futuristic hood. Her expression was impassive, yet charged with hidden passion.

"Fancy," Zhu said and reached for the aurelia. "For me?"

But Chiron held the aurelia away, as if teasing her, though his expression was anything but teasing. "This is an artifact of 1895. The style and materials date from that year. This is a point of reference for you, Zhu. You must look for this artifact in 1895."

"Look where?" How the gold had glinted! The glass sparkled like gems.

"*She* will have it."

"She?"

"The Chinese girl you're supposed to meet. You'll know she's the one because she'll possess the aurelia. That's the object of your project: once you have found and identified this girl, the two of you will go to the home. She'll live in safety there, eventually meet a Caucasian man, and bear a child. A daughter, in fact."

"Don't tell me," Zhu said, "I'm this girl's great-great-granddaughter."

"No, the Archives establish that your lineage is based in China." Chiron tucked the aurelia into some hidden pocket. "The object of your project is simple, then. You'll meet the girl, verify that she's got the aurelia, win her confidence, and take her to the Presbyterian home on Sacramento Street. Meet the new director—a remarkable young woman named Donaldina Cameron—and take a job with her there. Make sure the girl settles in. We want you to stay at least till Chinese New Year in 1896. That's when the dim spot closes and we have data supporting the existence of the daughter. Then you'll t-port back. Okay, Zhu? Sign here."

She took the petition he offered, thought about it. The

project did sound simple. Exciting, even. After the wearisome campaign at Changchi, an adventure! She was sick to death of prison. "And then what?"

"We'll see about handling your trial. By then, we ought to know what the charge is."

"You mean the status of the victim." Hard for her to say it. "*My* victim."

"Yes."

"Is he alive or dead?"

Chiron turned away. Didn't like being reminded of the despicable incident, apparently, any more than she did. "We've arranged for a delay in your arraignment."

They'd arranged for a lot of things. Zhu congratulated herself. It wasn't just a matter of reducing the charge against her. Perhaps this was a chance to redeem herself. She had not known how badly she wanted that till now. Of course, she would tachyport to 1895. Sure, she knew what she was doing.

▼ ▼ ▼

"What do I do now?" Zhu mutters to Muse as she hauls the girl by her elbow out of the Japanese Tea Garden. "She doesn't have the aurelia. She was supposed to have the aurelia, and she doesn't have it. She doesn't have it!"

"Stay calm," Muse whispers. "You're attracting too much attention."

"Calm? I'm panicking!" Must sound like Zhu has got two voices coming from her throat, one answering the other. Truly a devil woman. She can sympathize when the girl howls, fear, puzzlement, and dismay screwing up her face. "Muse, you will switch to subaud mode *now*."

"Assume she is the contact," Muse insists, still blasting in projection mode. "She was there. Take her to the home, and we'll look for the aurelia."

"Look for the aurelia! Look where?"

"I not go! I not go!" the girl wails.

"I don't know." Muse flustered. "I will analyze. Why don't you ask her name? We believe she was called Wing Sing."

Zhu takes the girl by her shoulders. She is *much* bigger than Zhu expected, as tall and thin as Zhu. Attract attention? But no one promenading in the park pays any attention to a woman dressed in Western clothes taking forcible custody of a scruffy Chinese girl. "What's your name?" Zhu asks.

"I Wing Sing," she says. "I go home, Jade Eyes!" She points toward the Pacific Ocean.

"Wing Sing," Zhu says, "thank goodness." She expels a breath. "Yes, home. That's exactly where we're going. We're going to the home. The nice home on Sacramento Street." She points downtown, in the opposite direction.

"Not go to *fahn quai*!" Wing Sing cries, struggling. "I die first!"

"You're going to be just fine." Alternately pushing and pulling, Zhu wrestles the girl to the station of the Park and Ocean Railroad where they can catch the steam train downtown. Zhu puffs, sweat drizzling beneath her corset. The stays gouge her rib cage, making her breath catch. "When is the next train?" she asks the conductor.

Now people in the passing crowd begin to take notice of her struggle. A buxom blond woman watches them shrewdly. The woman wears elaborate pink flounces and a grotesque hat studded with the carcasses of Brazilian hummingbirds. A scruffy black brougham drawn by two lathered geldings waits at the curb. The driver notices Zhu and Wing Sing, too.

"Well, miss." The conductor, a well-whiskeyed fellow in a rumpled uniform, clicks open his watch and checks it with drunken precision. "I reckon it'll get here when it gets here." Zhu catches his small gesture to the driver. The driver knocks his whip handle on the brougham's door. The conductor pockets the watch. He turns a gold coin through his fingers.

What's going on? A chill runs through Zhu. She picks up at once the covert communication between the conductor, driver, and whoever waits in the brougham. All of them, on the lookout.

Three Chinese men leap out of the brougham. Dressed entirely in black, they wear queues tightly braided, oiled, and wrapped in buns at the napes of their necks. Black slouch hats are pulled low over their foreheads, black slippers on their feet. One is a wiry little fellow with tattoos covering his hands, a curved knife tucked conspicuously in his belt. The second is a fat man, diamond rings on every finger. Silent and steely-eyed, he surveys the crowd. The third is tall and gaunt, a black eyepatch over his left socket. Beneath his black overcoat bandoliers are slung across his chest, two pistols visible in his belt.

The eyepatch spots Wing Sing first. In an instant, the men in black surround Zhu and the struggling girl.

"Highbinders!" shouts the buxom blond woman. "Hey, fellas!" she says to the white men standing about. "You gonna let them highbinders ruin our Fourth of July?"

The men laugh nervously and look away. Chinese business is Chinese business.

"Z. Wong, please exit immediately," Muse whispers. "These are hatchet men. Enforcers for a tong."

"*Boo how doy*," Wing Sing whispers, going limp.

Alphanumerics flicker in Zhu's peripheral vision.

"Queues coiled left," Muse says, opening a file. "Chee Song Tong."

"I say, fellas!" says the buxom blond woman. "What kinda lousy cowards are you, anyway? You gonna let them highbinders trouble a lady?"

"I've no quarrel with you," Zhu says to the eyepatch, boldly staring into his eye. "Let us go."

"This our girl," the eyepatch says. "We pay gold for her. We take now."

"I don't think so," Zhu says, circling her arm proprietarily around Wing Sing's shoulders. "She's mine." The girl huddles passively, eyes cast to the ground.

"Z. Wong, preservation of your person is the first priority," Muse whispers. "Please review 'The CTL Peril' subsection of the tenets." Muse posts the text in her peripheral vision.

"I don't think I'm going to review anything right now, Muse," Zhu says, jerking away when the eyepatch puts his hand on her shoulder.

"Our girl," the eyepatch says.

"Chee Song Tong," Muse says, "sponsors slavery and assassination. These are assassins, Z. Wong."

"What about the girl?" Zhu says.

"Let them take her," Muse says.

"Damn it, Muse, she's the reason I'm here!"

"It appears you have no choice," Muse says.

"It's a goddamn shame!" the buxom blond woman yells at the crowd. "You all oughta be ashamed!"

"Please step away, Z. Wong," Muse says. "They don't want you. I said go!"

"Too late," Zhu says.

The wiry fellow and the fat man seize Zhu's elbows. The eyepatch smacks Wing Sing across the face with the back of his hand.

"Jade Eyes," Wing Sing whimpers.

Heart pounding, Zhu shoves the hatchet men away, goes to Wing Sing. She clutches the girl. Anger parches her throat.

The girl clings to her, murmuring, "Jade Eyes."

The eyepatch stoops and stares at Zhu, peering intently at her. He flips up her veil. His eye widens in surprise when he sees her gene-tweaked green.

The hatchet men hustle them into the brougham. The driver yells, whipping the horses.

With a lurch and a jolt, the brougham speeds away.

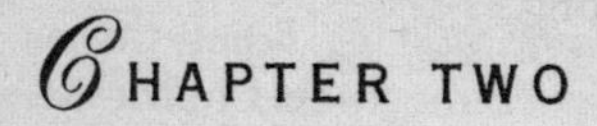

A Toast to the First and Last Chance Saloon

Daniel J. Watkins taps out another ciggie, lights it, takes a drag as the Overland train bound from Saint Louis speeds down the last miles to the Port of Oakland, California. He plays with a miniature Zoetrope: a little drum that whirls on a spindle. He peers at slits cut in the cardboard side of the drum all around its circumference through which he can see watercolor drawings rendered in a sequence. The sequence merges through the persistence of vision, producing the illusion of continuous motion. Typically a toy like this shows a parrot on the wing or a peasant in country dress capering about. The clever fellow who marketed this toy in Paris painted a whore drawing black stockings up her bare legs and down again. Up and down, up and down.

But even the Zoetrope—which usually fascinates him—cannot cheer him. The infusion of nicotine does little to stave off the throbbing in his head. Bloody train—the Overland was a very fine train till he ran out of whiskey early this morning—lurches and rolls from side to side like a ship in a restless sea. His stomach rolls in sickening counterpoise.

Daniel drags the ciggie down in three great gulps, stubs it out. He tucks the Zoetrope in his ditty bag, finds and lights another ciggie. Hums the waltz from *Sleeping Beauty* in a scratchy tenor. Poor Tchaikovsky kicked the bucket in Mexco, '93, from that vile pox called cholera, which they say is contracted through filthy water. Tchaikovsky had not been an old man. Daniel has resolved to drink nothing but bottled fluids during his sojourn through the West. Wouldn't you know that Father—the eminent Jonathan D. Watkins of Saint Louis, London, and Paris—believes the waltz is the work of the Devil. An inspiration for lurid passions among the young and impressionable. By God, how eminently true. He hums more vigorously. Daniel adores works of the Devil.

In the dawn sometime after Daniel discovered his grievous shortfall of potables, the Overland had stopped in Sacramento to pick up passengers. But the stopover wasn't long enough to scare up a little hair of the dog. By the time he'd roused himself to a functioning consciousness, they were on their way again. Daniel pulls frantically on the ciggie. Is he to arrive in San Francisco on vital family business shucked out, half-crocked, and airing his paunch like some overindulgent schoolboy? He is nearly twenty-two, after all, heading for old age and senility by swift and sordid leaps and bounds. Indeed, he is a gentleman, occasionally a scholar.

This will not do, sir, no it will not. Daniel stands, groggy as a dog, and surveys the passenger car. He roams the narrow aisle. Spies the old cowboy who's ridden the Overland out of Saint Louis, the same as Daniel. A grizzled coot in rustic togs that apparently have never been sullied by soap and water. Nor has the old cowboy bothered to shave since their departure from that thankfully distant city. Skinny bowlegs sprawling, he hunkers down in his seat, talking to himself, cackling, conferring with an invisible companion now and then. Oh, yes; and nipping at something under his greasy topcoat.

In a word, the old cowboy looks promising. Daniel barges in gregariously, grinning like all get-out with what he knows is a manly mustachioed face that charms the ladies and the gentlemen. Oh, he charms them all. He wastes no time in giving the old cowboy a wink and a ciggie, a pat on the back.

"A long haul, sir?" Daniel says, leaning back on the leather seat, lighting another himself. "But I suppose you've seen longer hauls. Harder ones, too. I suppose you've knocked about across this great continent of ours by harder means than the Overland train. In the good old days, eh?"

"Them was the days," the old cowboy agrees, accepting the ciggie without acknowledgment, lighting and drawing on it.

"The glory, the wild glory, eh? Knocking about like that. Ah, yes. Yes, and I don't suppose you've got a drop to spare of that libation you've been nipping at?" Daniel grins when the old cowboy squints up at him with a bloodred eye, openmouthed that a total stranger has discovered his closely guarded secret. "I'm dry as a bone, sir, and we've just about reached the coast."

" 'Tain't somethin' fit to drink fer a young gent like yerself," the old cowboy grunts, swiftly taking in Daniel's gray gabardine suit and starched ivory collar, the blue checked silk vest and tasteful French blue necktie, his British bowler of brushed felt. " 'Tain't fit fer a bear, if truth be told."

"Fit to drink? Sir, I have imbibed the Green Fairy herself."

The old cowboy examines him more closely with that painful-looking eye. "What in damn hell is the Green Fairy?"

"Absinthe, sir." Daniel sighs. What he would give for a gold-green bottle of Pernod Fils, a sugar cube, a perforated spoon, a lovely bell-shaped glass. What he would give to be back with Rochelle and the gang at La Nouvelle-Athènes sipping rainbow cups, flirting with poetry, lust, and death. "*La fée verte*, the Green Fairy. The sacred herb. Holy water. A finer, eviler brew has never been concocted. One hundred twenty proof and reeking of wormwood. *Tremblement de terre*."

"Tremblin'?"

"Earthquake, sir, that's what we call absinthe."

"Haw. Well, you'll find you some o' that in Californ', young gent." The old cowboy is unimpressed.

"Just a hair of the dog." Daniel offers another ciggie, cajoling the coot. The old cowboy takes the second offering—fine

Virginia weed machine-rolled to perfection—without a blink. "Come now, what have you got?" Daniel says with a persuasive, if edgy, smile.

"Hunnert twenny proof is a cinch, young gent." The old cowboy cackles. From beneath the topcoat, he produces a scummy fifth, a neat piece of glass with flat sides that fit against the chest and do not extrude indiscreetly. The fifth is down to the last four fingers, but that should last till they reach the Port of Oakland. "This here's puma piss."

"Puma piss?"

"Home-brewed rotgut, tobacca juice, an' a dose o' white lightnin'. What some call rat poison."

"By God, strychnine?"

The old cowboy nods. "Yep, hunnert twenny proof is a cinch, but ye can't prove it by me." The old cowboy consults with his invisible companion, cackling and nodding.

Puma piss! Daniel will have to remember that! "Let's have a taste. Just a drop, sir." With sunlight gleaming off his teeth, he offers a third ciggie. Damn bloody coot! But Daniel can purchase more machine-rolled cigarettes in San Francisco. The American Tobacco Company is spread out all over the West. He can get anything he wants in San Francisco, or so they say.

But right now, right *now*, what he needs is a drink.

The old cowboy hands over the fifth.

"It's a cinch," Daniel says and winks and tips the scummy fifth to his lips.

Vile cannot approach the taste of stagnant well water infused with putrefaction, but the needle-sharp fangs of newly distilled grain alcohol mangle the inside of his mouth, his tongue, so that taste becomes swiftly irrelevant. He knows the stuff is liquid, but the sensation in his throat is of a scorching fire and fangs, fangs, the fangs of a raving beast.

In less than an instant, his heart begins to beat like a lunatic desperate to escape his chains. Pure vertigo seizes him and whirls him around. A black satin curtain drops over his eyes; unconscious, blinded? Oh, no! Sometimes home brews steal sight as well as sanity. The black satin curtain is abruptly whisked away.

And he stares at the golden brown hills of California, curving like the bodies of women. Brown women reclining in the poses of whores, golden breasts and hips and swooping waists. The ill-starred Sioux, perhaps, or the Apache. Or the fabled Celestials, the Chinese. Women harried and driven by brute forces of rape and slavery and murder till they have fled, disguised themselves, mysteriously reincarnated into the landscape itself. He *sees* them, sees their awful transmogrification, their anger parched and mute save for the testimony of the hills, the golden brown hills in which a man could get lost and die. Hears them screaming now—oh God!—feels them reach for him, reach and lurch. They mean to tear him limb from limb with curved fingers of thorn, they mean to drive him mad with anguish only he can see and hear.

That high rending sound: only the whistle of the train.

Daniel shuts his eyes. The black satin curtain falls again, but the blackness is so dizzying his lids pop open at once. Now the landscape changes as he speeds toward his destiny. The hills grow greener, studded with shrubs and sturdy trees. Abundant palms that are the rage in fashionable houses grow wild by the track bed. Shameless flowering bushes raise up pink and purple thunderheads, and huge twisted succulents are so vibrant and filled with a peculiar presence that they seem like living creatures in some cunning disguise, waiting in ambush for the unwary. Waiting to pounce like pumas do.

And Daniel feels the hand of destiny spinning him round like a Zoetrope. Does he only go through the motions of his life, inexorably, a pathetic little painted figure? The tracks clack below him. The lunatic again, he's rattling his cage. A great fate awaits him—he *feels* this in his heart—unlike anything he has ever confronted before. Not in Saint Louis, not in London or Paris. Perhaps he will live, perhaps he will die in San Francisco. What does it matter, what does anything matter? We're all just painted figures spun round by the hand of God.

Grief wells up inside him, squeezing the frantic beat of his heart. Well, Mama died. People do. He had seen three grandparents meet their Maker before he was ten. It was not as though family had never passed on before. Mama died in late spring, in the fecund heat of incipient summer. A time he himself always thought of as a sick time, rife with disease in the air, poison in the water, rotting food. He should not have been surprised. She'd been dying for a long time. But why did she wait for him? Why did she have to wait? He did not want to see her face, pale and beautiful as always. Her eyes—what she called her deep sea eyes—beseeching him. Her question, always her question, even on her deathbed, "Danny, haven't I been good to you? Haven't I been good? Haven't I always loved you?" And his answer, always the same answer, "Yes, Mama. Of course, Mama. I love you, too, Mama."

He takes another taste of puma piss, swallowing the grief. "Ish a shinch," he says, handing the fifth back to the old cowboy with as steady a hand as he can muster. A gentleman must observe the niceties of sharing a drink.

"Haw." The old cowboy grins, broken brown teeth through neglected whiskers. His invisible companion apparently adds a trenchant comment. Daniel himself can almost see the companion. Yes, there he is: a hand from the good old days, long dead and still lively in the old cowboy's eyes.

"Thank you, shir. Mush oblished." Daniel stands, the vertigo fading, his pulse slowing. A nice feeling of arousal courses through his veins. As soon as his stomach settles down, his feelings turn to another part of his anatomy that he has too often abused. By God, sir, his heart.

There are ladies on this train. He vaguely recalls two fine ladies who boarded the Overland at dawn during the stop in Sacramento. How could he have ignored them for so long? What a cad he's been! He should go pay his respects, find out if they're bound for San Francisco, too, and, if so, what in heaven's name is their address? The pilgrim seeks the comfort of fellow travelers, that is the natural way of the world, is it not? He staggers to the dining car, newly filled with the spirit of amorous adventure, tapping out a ciggie. Where are they, who are they?

They sit at a table set for tea. The thin, small girl with a narrow mousy face, protruding bright eyes, and an overbite interests him not at all. She is dressed in gray leg-o'-mutton sleeves and a plain gored dress. She chatters and chirps in ugly broad vowels. She is much too American and much too thin. No, her companion, an elegant lady with a high-cheeked face, rose-kissed skin, lovely mouth with full lower lip, huge soft eyes; she interests him. A startling streak of white accentuates her burnished brown pompadour. A lady getting on in her years. Perhaps in her late twenties? Yet still with the spark of youthful passion, he can see it in her eyes. Perhaps more passionate than her younger companion either because she's experienced more of the world or less than she had always longed for.

She is well dressed, too, a quality in ladies for which Daniel has the highest admiration. The young companion wears proper traveling togs. But her. The elegant lady wears a full skirt the color of French burgundy. An ivory silk blouse with abundant lace spilling over the chinchilla collar of a short cashmere coat belted tightly about her waist. A gay hat, piled high with ribbons and flowers, perches upon the pompadour. A voluminous veil is drawn over her face and pinned at her throat with a glittering Art Nouveau brooch. And gloves. The elegant lady wears immaculate gloves that accentuate her long fine fingers, the white cotton unsullied by mundane contact. Her fingers twitch in her lap as if longing to touch a man.

"Good afternoon, ladies," Daniel says, carelessly tossing himself on the chair next to her. She's tall, he can see that. Tall, with a long slim body beneath the coat, the skirts, the bodice, the corset. Rochelle was tall, too, and her long legs literally went up to her throat when she danced the cancan at La Nouvelle-Athènes. Of course, Rochelle was a whore. But this one, this one. He is smitten. What a marvelous land, this Californ'!

"Good day, sir," they murmur and recommence their conversation about some sort of charity work.

"But, Evie darling," says the elegant lady, "the Young Women's Christian Association puts up dozens of these Chinese girls every month. Every month! And still dozens more are defiled in Chinatown. Defiled, imprisoned. They are literally, Evie, quite literally sold into slavery!" Her melodious voice quivers. "Can you imagine that our dear Jesus Christ should allow this abomination?"

"Well, they are heathens," says the mousy girl.

"In San Francisco, Evie! Young girls! Oh, our Christ would surely die all over again to see it."

A Holy Roller, Daniel thinks, uh oh. A Bible thumper. Jesus this, Christ that.

"And here we are, celebrating the one hundred and nineteenth anniversary of our nation, Evie," the elegant lady says, nearly in tears. "The shame!"

Indeed it is the nation's anniversary, why, it's the Fourth of July. He's lost all track of the days in his trek west. The elegant lady glances at Daniel. Big dark eyes, yes! With the depth of intelligence, the sheen of passion. Clearly, passion! Passion in a lady is a far different thing than the depraved opportunism of a whore. His heart assumes a more frantic pace.

"That is why our dear Christ has sent for you, Dolly," the mousy girl says, not altogether with approval for her friend's passion. She darts an even more disapproving look at Daniel and sniffs loudly.

"In point of fact, Miss Culbertson sent for me, Evie darling." The elegant lady corrects her with refreshing logic. "When the directress of our mission at Nine Twenty Sacramento Street invites one, one goes. One goes gladly, to serve our Lord."

"But I'm so worried for you, Dolly. We've got so many parties planned for the season. And San Francisco is so dreadful."

"I'll stay at the mission only a little while, I promise. But perhaps we should not speak of such things in front of this gentleman."

"You may speak of anything you like, dear ladies," Daniel says. "The sound of your sweet voices is all I crave."

"Dolly, he's stinking," the mousy girl whispers. "Perhaps we should find another table."

"Yes, it's true, I'm quite drunk," Daniel says. "I confess all, you need not whisper." He observes their startled eyes. Now there's a fine line for a couple of Holy Rollers. He congratulates himself. He reaches for the mousy girl's paw. She snatches her hand away. He pantomimes having seized her hand anyway and proceeds to kiss the air in his palm. "I confess! I confess I'm drunk on your presence, ladies, drunk with wonder at this marvelous land. I've been away too long. Yet, hark, I have returned, your true native son. At your service, madame." He slides off the seat and kneels before the elegant lady, taking her hand between his two, clasping the whole package upon her knees, and breathing deeply of her fragrance. She's a hummer, all right.

The mousy girl gasps at his impropriety, but the elegant lady smiles indulgently and neither reclaims her hand nor casts him off her knees. Smitten by him, too? Better and better! "And who might you be, sir?"

Encouraged, Daniel does not press his luck just yet. He springs back up, regains his seat. He tries to catch her eye. Once he catches a lady's eye, he more often than not gets the rest of what he wants, regardless of her station. But the lady casts her eyes to the floor, evading him.

"I might be the Devil, but in fact I am Daniel J. Watkins of Saint Louis, London, and Paris. May I inquire who you are?"

The mousy girl gasps again, perhaps appreciating at last his inestimable attentions to what are, after all, chance acquaintances on a train. London and Paris? She widens her eyes and blushes, adding a modicum of charm to her sallow face. "Why, I'm Evie Brownstone, Mr. Watkins, and this here is Miss Donaldina Cameron. We all call her Dolly."

Dolly! Yes, a Dolly! Very much a Dolly! Daniel eagerly leans forward.

"Or Donald," the elegant Miss Cameron says, frowning at the impertinence of her friend. "Or Dodo."

Donald? Daniel slumps back. *Dodo?* He bows a little stiffly. "Miss Cameron."

"Dolly is one of the MacKenzie Camerons." Miss Brownstone rattles on, uncertain how she has offended her friend or him. "Of Scotland, New Zealand, San Francisco, Oakland, and the San Gabriel Valley!" she says proudly, yet with a small doubtful look at Miss Cameron.

Daniel rouses himself. "You know San Francisco, Miss

Cameron? You know Oakland? Still the mud hut frontier, this town, is it not?"

Oakland glimmers behind the windows of the Overland train. After golden brown hills and rustic flatlands, he has not expected this: a shimmering lake, a stylish city. Three-story Queen Anne mansions rim the littoral shore, with astounding gardens and sprawling lawns, carriage houses and small parks set with classical sculptures wrought in marble as white as a lady's cheek. Daniel spies fine carriages driven by liveried coachmen trotting down well-worn lanes bordered by more of the astonishing cacti and palms, broad swooping oaks with odd reddish-green leaves unlike anything he's seen back East.

A gaily colored open wagon crowned with a weird curlicued contraption hooked to sturdy lines overhead chugs upon a single wheel on a track choked with purple wildflowers. Solemn men in bowlers or top hats perch upon the benches inside, while giddy boys in vests and stockings hang off the running boards.

"That's Mr. Casebolt's cable car bound for Berkeley," Miss Brownstone cries, pointing. "Isn't it a daisy?"

Miss Cameron coolly regards his surprise. "We call Oakland the continental side of the bay, Mr. Watkins. Evie herself attended Snell's Seminary."

"Snells?" Daniel thinks of escargot in garlic butter.

"*The* finishing school, of course."

The sliver of a headache pokes behind Daniel's eyes. "Did you go to finishing school in Oakland, too, Miss Cameron?"

"Heavens, no," she laughs. "My finishing, such as it was, was accomplished in the San Gabriel Valley. But we did live here in Oakland once." She gazes out the window, shifting into a pensive mood. "The good people live in Oakland. People who love books and art and sculpture. Aesthetes, Mr. Watkins. Birders, scholars, astronomers, entomologists. Dr. Merritt lives here, and the Peraltas, and Joseph Knowland the publisher, and Judge Sam McKee. Mr. F. M. Smith, who discovered all that borax in Nevada. His ballroom accommodates hundreds; his gardens are legendary, of course."

"Of course."

"The houses in Oakland have telephones, Mr. Watkins. Do you know the telephone?"

He laughs indignantly. "Why, of course, in London and Paris . . ."

"Oaklanders own more telephones than San Franciscans," Miss Cameron says, growing animated. "They've got more electricity in their houses than anyone."

"Mother's got a system of electrical buzzers to summon the servants," Miss Brownstone says breathlessly. "Like Mrs. Winchester, the rifle heiress."

"And electrical lights," Miss Cameron says. "Oaklanders employ Mr. Edison's genius to good advantage, Mr. Watkins."

"I never said you didn't. . . ."

"Mother's got hot water for my bath," Miss Brownstone yells, getting into the spirit. "Pumped right into my rooms on the third floor!"

"You say you've seen London and Paris, Mr. Watkins," Miss Cameron says imperiously. "Well, the McPhail mansion was designed by Californian architects, and do you know what those clever fellows did? They installed a chute in the wall that opens up in the mistress's boudoir upstairs and goes all the way down to the washerwoman's tubs in the basement. No one has ever seen anything like it."

"All Mrs. McPhail does is toss it in!" squeals Miss Brownstone.

"Have you ever seen such a thing in London or Paris, Mr. Watkins?" Miss Cameron says, her flowers and ribbons quaking with civic pride. Before he can respond properly or even crack a joke about tossing it, she snaps, "I thought not, sir! We are modern in California. We are striding forth into the future. And we are in the height of fashion. *And* don't you forget it!"

The two ladies rise and storm out of the dining car, leaving Daniel dazed.

| | |

The Overland train pulls into the station at the Port of Oakland. Daniel collects his bags and trunk. After midday. A languor settles over the port. Sunlight filters through a high haze, a breeze whips in from the bay. Clang of ships' bells, slap of waves, squeak of tightly drawn rope around wood. Ah, London, how he recalls those sounds, his night walks along the piers. Some of these fisherman are already homeward bound. Fished since long before dawn, no doubt. He sees holds heavy with flopping salmon, black speckled oysters.

By God, his head aches. He lights a ciggie, inhales deeply. His stomach rolls over. Another shot of puma piss would put him right. But the old cowboy has vanished as surely as his invisible companion. "Porter," Daniel calls, extracting coins from his coat pocket. "Where's the ferry bound for San Francisco?"

"You'll be wantin' the *Chrysapolis*, sir, and a lovely steamer she is, too," says the porter, a stringy old man in a cap and rumpled uniform. He flashes an abundance of gold teeth. A failed prospector? If the stringy porter had been a youngster during the gold rush—and many forty-niners were just kids—he could very well have scratched about those golden brown hills and panned the streams. Taking only a taste of fortune with him: a mouthful of gold teeth.

"Let's go," Daniel says. He scowls, his headache deepening. He can see it: the stringy porter's years of searching, the endless frustration, his ultimate failure. Perhaps the porter wasn't so stringy then, perhaps he'd once been a robust young man like Daniel. That's what failure did: wrung you out, plucked your bones, sucked you dry. It was revolting. A failed man is a loathsome thing. And Father? Why, the eminent Jonathan B. Watkins, he's a failure, too.

"Sir, she doesn't depart till half past three," the porter says apologetically, unsure how he may have offended the young gentleman.

"Half past three! What in heaven's name am I to do till then?" Daniel demands.

"If you please, sir, the sights are quite nice along the promenade." The porter points to where Miss Cameron and Miss Brownstone are strolling next to rocks strewn on the steep grade of beach.

"I think not," Daniel says, still stung. Holy Rollers, indeed.

"Then a gentleman like yourself might seek some refreshment?" the porter says, voice quavering. He points in the opposite direction, where seamen slouch about the docks and boats and the murmur of distant merriment can be heard.

Refreshment; exactly. Daniel hands more coins to the porter. "Then you shall watch my bags while I seek refreshment. And you shall come and fetch me when the *Chrysapolis* is ready to depart. Do you understand?"

"Yes, sir. Very good, sir. That way, sir. That way!"

Daniel stalks along the waterfront, loosening his collar and the blue silk tie. Get hold of yourself, sir. Why should he be so disquieted by some porter? There is no such thing as equality, his friends in London say. You Americans are deluded if you believe in such nonsense. There are those who are superior, those who are inferior, and that is that. Yet the porter—if he truly is a failed prospector in more than Daniel's imagination—is no different from Father. No different at all. In the whole scheme of things, they are equals.

Father fancied himself so clever. A friendship with a rich British lady during one of Mama's many illnesses enlightened him. Father realized that America's rebellion could be turned to his advantage. This was the New World, replete with land and resources, cheap labor and huge ambitions. Funds were all the aspiring grubbers lacked. And funds, capital, gold could be secured from the old merchant families, royalty, continental capitalists hungry for higher returns, all eager to exploit the peasants and criminals and reprobates who'd beat out a life for themselves in this New World. Consider the beauty of it. You loan the wretches money against their homes, their land, their businesses. Let them think they've won their freedom, then reinstate their servitude not by force, king, or country, but by debt.

This was all part and parcel of Father's insidious propaganda. If strident communists and clamoring workingmen infesting Europe are worrying you, then bring your gold to America where entrepreneurs are making a killing. Did you know about property values, he would whisper to yet another British widow or a German dowager. Have you any notion how property values increased during the gold rush in a backwater boom town like San Francisco? Any notion at all? Why, a little commercial front on Portsmouth Square with a bar slinging shots of rotgut and a rouge-et-noir game in back was bought for six thousand dollars and sold but a few years later for one million. One million dollars, madame. El Dorado House, the first bohemian restaurant in the city serving hard-boiled eggs for five dollars apiece, leased its premises for twenty-five thousand a month. These anecdotes were hardly apocryphal. Father would produce documents setting out the numbers.

Oh, Father had them coming and going: the dreaming settlers, the idealistic farmers, the ambitious shopkeepers scraping out a life in the cow towns, dead ends, tenderloins, and Chinatowns throughout the West. And the scheming capitalists, the jaded merchant dynasties, the indolent royalty of Europe hungering for more profits, for greater cash flow.

The eminent Jonathan B. Watkins became a mortgage broker and from 1888 to 1892 extended twelve million dollars, mostly in European capital, in loans on real estate throughout America, mostly in the West. He put Daniel on H.M.S. *May Queen* on New Year's Day 1892, bound for London and Paris. This was the time when for once Father had favorably regarded his son's good looks, quick charm, and easy manners. Hobnob, those were Daniel's orders. Ingratiate yourself to all those charming British widows, those diamond-studded German dowagers, those plump Dutch blue bloods. And hobnob Daniel did. So what if he ended up in Paris, drinking absinthe with whores and poets at La Nouvelle-Athènes? He scratched up plenty of capital for Father's schemes. Removed from Father's stern ambit, he found he cared little for business, moneygrubbing, the power of gold. He kept his bohemian life to himself and dreamed of pictures on a strip of painted paper whirling in a Zoetrope.

Then the panic struck America in '93. Banks failed, capital dried up in a financial drought the like of which no one had seen in a decade. Businesses collapsed. Angry gangs of unemployed men roamed towns and cities with sticks and knives and guns. Needless to say, property values plummeted, especially in the West where the economy was still so fragile.

By 1895, the eminent Jonathan B. Watkins found himself with twelve million dollars of outstanding debt, debtors who could not or would not make payments, and property securing all that debt worth next to nothing.

What could he do? Father declared bankruptcy and recalled his son from Europe. Daniel remembered the telegram. What excitement to receive a telegram, quite the rage. Brand-new telegraph wires looped all over the streets of Europe.

> "DANIEL STOP WE'RE DONE STOP COME HOME AT ONCE STOP FATHER." Then, as an afterthought, "MOTHER NEEDS YOU STOP."

Daniel hadn't understood the full import of the message till he reluctantly returned home, dragging a bag filled with scandalously decadent paintings and four bottles of Pernod Fils. *We're done?* What did *that* mean? That Father had decided upon a new strategy? A more lucrative way to become a millionaire besides lending the money of strangers to other strangers?

No. Jonathan B. Watkins was a failure, just as surely as the stringy old porter with his gold teeth. Bankruptcy was as evil as moral turpitude and as far-reaching as extrafamilial indiscretion. Sins of the father? Daniel was doomed.

Daniel kneads his brow. Refreshment. Indeed, sir, some refreshment is just the thing.

He quickens his pace along the waterfront. The seamen stare at him, poke each other in the ribs, guffaw or mutter half-heard obscenities. Daniel tips his bowler, keeping his spine ramrod straight. He's got the accoutrements any gentleman should possess when sojourning through the West: a Remington double-barreled derringer stuck in his waistband and a jumbo Congress knife with a two-inch blade. He's strolled among dives and joints before. He can walk into any accursed place he cares to. The sound of merriment loudens.

He spies a crude, one-room establishment: a tiny building of unfinished wood, two plain windows, a strictly functional front door. A converted bunkhouse in which oyster fishermen once slept. The place is plain as a pig, relieved of any frill or indulgence, yet possesses a rustic charm, a sort of barbaric purity. The odor of many a previous drunk teases his olfactory senses. Beneath the eaves, emblazoned in red letters across the weathered boards, he sees:

HEINOLD'S
FIRST AND LAST CHANCE

Daniel steps into the smoke-choked caucus. A potbellied stove glows red-hot in one corner. An assortment of rickety chairs and tables, none of a matching set, are jammed onto the sawdusted floor, together with retired packing barrels and tumbledown stools. Men sit at these or stand at the bar. Ropes and buoys are slung on the planked walls, along with a couple of brass lanterns thick with the patina only years of heavy salt air can render.

A wizened beerslinger stands behind the bar, sucking on a stogie. Deep lines crease a tanned forehead made high and wide by his receding hairline, and what's left of his hair is slicked straight back from that. Elephantine ears protrude as though Nature has thus equipped the beerslinger the better to hear each customer's request over the din of those previously served.

"Johnny, hey Johnny!" calls out one of the patrons. "Got any aspirin?"

"Back right up, an' you can get some ass burn," the beerslinger says, nodding at the potbellied stove.

"How much?" Daniel says.

"A nickel for the beer, a deener for the whiskey," says the beerslinger, "nothin' for the ass burn."

Beer is peasant's fare, a heavy sour taste Daniel has never much cared for. But he finds this beer is fruity and clean, thick with malt. The beer chases the whiskey down his parched throat just fine and settles his stomach. The whiskey is smooth, mellow, and eases the ache in his head admirably.

Daniel throws coins on the bar and looks for a place to sit. A vacant stool set before a barrel looks promising except for the table crowded with rowdies directly next to it. Two men and a tawdry lady barge in the front door. Daniel seizes his opportunity. The stool it is.

"Say there, little brother, now can you tell me what is a brick?" says the huge rowdy seated next to Daniel. The rowdy sports long wild yellow hair, an enormous mustache, a bush of a beard beneath a broad-brimmed Stetson hat. A cape of thick mangy fur that looks and stinks like bearskin is draped about the shoulders of his bright blue Prince Albert coat. Instead of a necktie, the rowdy wears a black leather cord with some sort of crystal cabochon containing the preserved remains of a scorpion. His bright red flannel shirt is splashed here and there with drink.

"What is a brick?" Daniel says.

"Why, there are bricks of gold, and silver bricks, bricks without straw, and bricks to be hurled at mad dogs. Ergo, bricks!" The rowdy slaps his suede chaps. One trouser leg is tucked into a fancy-stitched high-heeled cowboy boot. The other isn't. He toasts Daniel and triumphantly tosses a shot of whiskey down his throat, pleased at his pronouncement.

"Joaquin, you are living proof that American poets have yet to master the English language," says his gaunt companion. The companion smiles dreamily, sipping at his beer. He wears a sea captain's cap over his mop of dark curls, though from his pale aristocratic face, pale elegant hands, and foppish bow tie, he is clearly no sailor. "Sir, may I introduce the great Californian poet, Joaquin Miller, also known as Cincinnatus. And a very fine poet he is too, if only he could make a lick of sense."

"Ergo, bricks," Daniel says. "Actually, I think I'm drunk enough to understand Mr. Miller. Bricks made of stardust, bricks without wormwood, bricks to be juggled by a beautiful lady. Ergo, bricks!"

"Another boilermaker for the young gentleman," roars Joaquin Miller. "And may I introduce George Sterling, who might one day amount to a great Californian writer if he could only give up carousing among the redwoods long enough to write something. Carousing, I might add, with fair maidens, sir, clad in togas! Do you know what a toga is? A drapery, in the Greek style. A mere drapery, I say, under which the maidens in question wear nothing but their . . ."

"Gifts from God," says George Sterling. His gaunt face is expressionless, but his eyes twinkle at Daniel. "I wear a toga, too, sir."

"To togas," says Daniel, toasting Mr. Sterling with another boilermaker.

"Try an alligator pear, sir," says the third member of their party. He offers Daniel a plate filled with thin slices of some pale green fruit sprinkled with salt and pepper. He's a handsome blond fellow dressed like a dandy in the height of European fashion: a fitted burgundy topcoat, canary yellow waistcoat, and spats. "The greasers call them avocados. You must try a dish called guacamole at Luna's in North Beach." He leans forward confidentially. "You've just come from the Continent, then?"

"Indeed, I have, sir," Daniel says, trying the green fruit, which has a strange oily texture and is not sweet at all. "Is it so obvious?"

"Frank's been over and again himself, isn't that so, Frank?" says Joaquin Miller. "Verily and thus, and thus verily it is."

"Name's Frank Norris," says the blond fellow, shaking Daniel's hand. "I haven't been to Paris since college. Haven't the time. The novels must come first."

"By God, sir, you write novels?"

"Certainly. Title of the first book is *Blix*. A romance, with tequila. Got another in mind, going to call it *McTeague*. Inside joke. A tragic one, that. Fellow beats his pretty wife to death."

Daniel is enchanted. Marvelous Californ'! Grizzled old cowboys and failed prospectors and Holy Rollers; these he expected. But poets and novelists? Dreamers like himself? Oh, hand of destiny! That merciless hand does not oppress him now. Yes, a great fate awaits him, live or die. He raises his glass. "To the First and Last Chance Saloon!"

"To our dear, dear, near and clear, to our dear, dear watering hole." Joaquin Miller wipes a tear from his eye.

"To the Fourth o' July!"

"To Johnny Heinold!" call out several patrons.

"Hear, hear!"

The beerslinger grins and lights another stogie.

A startlingly handsome but rough-looking kid with a broad sunburnt face and hands to match charges into the saloon. He finds a spare barrel and rolls it to the table, nodding to the company.

"My name is Daniel Watkins, and I'm looking for lodging in San Francisco," Daniel says to his new friends when the room calms down. "Could you recommend a place?"

"Try the Palace Hotel," says the rough kid sarcastically. His quick eyes flick over Daniel's suit. Filthy fisherman's togs, that's what the kid is wearing, stained with mud and blood and who knows what else. His thick curly brown hair spills over his ears to his collar. "That's the dive for you, mister."

Daniel has heard of the Palace Hotel, the first luxury resort on the West Coast. They say the Palace boasts eight hundred rooms and rivals the finest hotels in New York or Paris for amenities. "Can't afford that," Daniel says mildly, sensing the kid's antagonism. He offers the kid a ciggie, which the kid seizes and lights. No, he cannot afford such luxury. Not anymore.

"Yeah, I see," says the kid. "Only a rich capitalist can afford a fancy joint like the Palace. I guess you're no rich capitalist. I guess you're no tramp, either, mister."

"Leave him alone, Jackie," says Frank Norris. "He's all right."

"Yeah?" says the kid, eyeing Daniel's bowler. "When the revolution comes, it's the property-owning class that will be stamped out. Stamped out, I say, by the working classes. The working classes are the vanguard of the future. Without 'em, the rich capitalists couldn't survive. And with 'em, the rich capitalists won't survive, because the working classes will have a revolution. It won't be long. Won't be long at all before the revolution comes. Even as we speak, the United States of America is embroiled in a class struggle between those with property and those who labor in the service of those with property. A class struggle, and there's no denying it. What do you say to that, mister?"

"I say have yourself a beer, Jack," says Joaquin Miller. "Studying books all day has fevered your poor young brain."

"Even as we speak, mister," the kid says, continuing to fix Daniel with a baleful stare as he gulps a mug of beer.

"That's fine, Jack," says George Sterling, handing the kid a shot of whiskey. "This fiery young fellow is Jack London, Mr. Watkins. Jackie's studying at the University of California. He may amount to some kind of writer one day, don't you think so, Frank?"

"If he stays in school long enough to graduate and doesn't get thrown in the calaboose first," Frank Norris says.

"I fear no jail," Jack London says contemptuously. "I've seen plenty of jails."

"What sort of lodgings are you looking for, Mr. Watkins?" Joaquin Miller says. "You a churchgoin' man?"

"Hardly," Daniel says, thankful to be off the subject of revolution. He's not sure anymore where he stands when it comes to politics. In truth, he never thought much of Father's schemes. But perhaps he has only arrived at that conclusion after Father's bankruptcy. How would he feel if the family were still worth twelve million?

"Ah. You're wanting a quiet sort of place to rest your weary head?"

"Mr. Miller, I have journeyed many miles from Saint Louis, which is as deadly quiet a place as you can imagine."

"Ah ha. You like the theater, then. The opera, perhaps? The Tivoli is the place for you."

"The opera is all right," Daniel says. "I can take it or leave it."

"Leave the opera to the dogs," advises Jack London.

"What's your preference then, Mr. Watkins?" Joaquin Miller says.

"My preference?" Daniel considers. "Sir, I have spent many months past imbibing the Green Fairy at La Nouvelle-Athènes while whores danced the cancan and poets as fine as yourself labored to express their desire to achieve ecstasy or die. I suppose you could say I'm . . . lonely."

The company guffaws. Jack London snorts, but Frank Norris slaps Daniel on the back.

Joaquin Miller stoops to whisper in Daniel's ear, though his voice still manages to boom throughout the saloon. "Then you must try Number two sixty-three Dupont Street, Mr. Watkins. Tell the lady there, a fine proprietress name of Jessie Malone, that Joaquin sent you. You'll be in the thick of things, Mr. Watkins. The very thick of things, I assure you."

"Sir, sir!" The stringy porter pokes his head around the door of the First and Last Chance Saloon. "The ferry to San Francisco, sir. She's about to depart. Hurry!"

"Thanks!" Daniel says to his new friends, much refreshed by the boilermakers. "By the way," he points to the banner hung above Johnny Heinold's head behind the bar that reiterates the sign outside. "Last chance before what?"

"Last chance for a taste if you're going to Alameda," Frank Norris says, pointing south. "They're dry as a bone over there."

"And first chance?"

"Why, if you're going to San Francisco, this is your first chance to get pickled, dipsy, pie-eyed, dead blue, and, I say, loaded, Mr. Watkins," shouts Joaquin Miller. "Verily, and lackaday, tell them Joaquin sent you, sir!"

Marvelous Californ'!

❘ ❘ ❘

A magnificent double-deck steamboat, that's the *Chrysapolis*. All black and white with a huge smokestack spewing charcoal-colored clouds. The willful bay would fling a lesser boat about, but the *Chrysapolis* plows through wave and tide, speeding the passengers on their way. Some are pilgrims from the Overland train, some citizens of genteel Oakland or Contra Costa bound on business in the city on the other shore.

Daniel waves to Miss Cameron and her dreadful little friend, but the ladies snub him. Perhaps he does reek too much. They're ladies, after all, not whores. Well, hell with them. What does he need with a couple of Holy Rollers, anyway? What he needs are new accommodations from which he can commence his business operations. Father holds mortgages on several parcels upon which Daniel means to collect outstanding payments or foreclose, rousting the rascals out and repossessing the property. Two parcels are empty lots out on the periphery of the city in a place called the Western Addition. Of the two others, one is a commercial building on Stockton Street in the heart, Father warned, of Chinatown. The other is a shack in the red-light district of Sausalito, a little port north of San Francisco across the bay. Daniel grimaces when he thinks about this business of collection and foreclosure. By God, is he cut out for it? Hobnobbing was one thing. Strong-arming recalcitrant debtors another. He would much rather study his Zoetrope.

As he ponders these dark controversies, he suddenly realizes someone is hovering behind him. Alarm heats his blood. Damn Jack London with his talk of revolution. He is more vexed by such talk than he cares to admit. For a moment, he fancies the golden brown devil women have conspired against him, their fingers of thorn reaching for him, grasping, seeking revenge for all the wrongs done them by man.

Daniel whirls. A lovely little bird stands next to him in a pale blue summer dress set with snippets of lace. She is petite, with an astonishingly tiny waist. An ivory-colored veil is flung over her face from a dainty hat perched upon her curls. Her topskirts swirl in the turbulent breeze, very much like wings of some tropical bird. Yes, a little blue canary! She presses her fingertips, hands sheathed in ivory lace mitts, to the base of her slender throat and moans.

"Please, miss, may I be of assistance?" Daniel says. Of course he is a man of nice sensibilities, quite sympathetic to the trials and tribulations of the weaker sex. Miss Cameron was barbaric in her shoddy treatment of him.

"Oh, thank you, sir," the veiled bird says in a quavering voice. "The ferry makes me ill. I'm so sorry."

"No cause for apology, miss. There, there, now." Daniel takes her elbow, places his hand on her tiny waist, caressing the small of her back. He braces her as the *Chrysapolis* pulls into the Port of San Francisco.

The steamboat slams into the dock with a mighty *thump*! The veiled bird turns toward him. She wraps her arms around his chest and clings to him like a child.

"Ooh," she moans louder and leans against him.

He can feel her corset, the stays, her heaving breast. The image of her satiny skin beneath the layers of fabric and whalebone rises up in his mind's eye, making his breath catch. Come now, sir, this will not do. Still, it's been hellishly too long since he shared carnal knowledge with a lady. He tightens his grip. She's so frail! Perhaps he can persuade her to dine with him?

The crew of the *Chrysapolis* scampers about, tying up the fore and aft. A plank is lowered. The passengers descend. Miss Cameron and her dreadful mousy friend trip down regally, lifting their skirts only just enough to find their footing, but not enough to let anyone glimpse their ankles. Daniel snorts. He's seen whores pose nude, splayed and shameless, in the studios of artist friends in Paris and London. Truly, do these ladies believe men are not acquainted with every detail of their anatomy beneath the silks and cashmere? Yet Daniel finds himself peering at the elegant Miss Cameron, craning his neck for a glimpse of her ankle. What sort of shoes does she wear, anyway? What color are her stockings?

"Ooh, sir," moans his veiled bird louder still, clinging to his waist pathetically. "Will you help me down the plank, and then I'll trouble you no longer?"

"Heavens, miss, it's no trouble at all," he says, gesturing at a strapping young porter to take his bags and trunk. "Tell me your name. Would you care to dine with me?"

She shakes her head in weak assent, clutching her throat wordlessly.

"Do you live in San Francisco, then?" Daniel says. "Have you an address where I might call upon you?"

"May I take your card?" she whispers.

Of course; why should she impart personal information to a stranger? He peers through her veil, getting only a glimpse of the curve of her lip, her wide-set eyes that stare at him more boldly than he would have expected. He gives her the business card he's used in Europe. "That's my name, at least," he says. "Daniel J. Watkins of Saint Louis, London, and Paris. I haven't settled upon a residence yet, but I shall be here a while to settle my father's accounts. When can I see you again?"

"Soon, I'm sure, sir," the veiled bird says as they step off the plank onto the dock.

Though she had clamped quite a grip on him, and he on her, she manages swiftly to extract herself and slip away. In less than an instant, his veiled bird disappears into the crowd milling about the dock. Such a tiny waist!

Never mind. San Francisco! San Francisco, at last! Daniel breathes the salt air, relishing the cold clean tang of it. *Bang, bang, bang!* He starts, then laughs at the smoke and the stink of gunpowder. Small boys leap about the dock, lighting some sort of red tassels and flinging them to the planking. A Chinese man—a coolie, they're called—clad in pajamas made of indigo denim, straw sandals, and a wide-brimmed conical straw cap chases after the boys, shouting and gesticulating. A boy tosses a silver coin onto the dock where the boards are pocked and uneven. The coolie dives frantically for his coin before it drops to the water below. Daniel smiles wryly. Cruel kid, but after all, the coolie is little better than a dog, isn't he?

He strolls through the ferry building, a portion of which is under construction, the wood skeleton laid bare. A long, narrow trade sign below the eaves announces destinations proudly, if ungeographically:

CLOVERDALE, REDDING RED BLUFF,
NAPA, CALISTOGA, YUMA,
PORTLAND OR, ST. LOUIS, SAN JOSE,
SACRAMENTO, LOS ANGELES, CHICAGO

Billboards advertise land auctions in Berkeley. The strapping porter trots after him, hauling his bags and trunk. Daniel's boots clatter on the cobblestones outside the ferry building. Horse-drawn wagons and cable cars and gangs of men mingle chaotically on the street. A green and red cable car with "SIGHTSEEING" emblazoned down its sides waits on a track. The cable car is much like the trams he's seen in Europe, only bigger and wider and grander, more

American. They say Mr. Hallidie, the brilliant Scotchman who invented, designed, and built the first cable car line on Clay Street with twenty thousand dollars of his own life savings, is a multimillionaire now. There's a business for a young gentleman to consider. Daniel wonders if he should try to buy a street-railway franchise and lay in a new cable car line.

Bang, bang, bang! A brass band strikes up a rousing tune. A gigantic parade promenades up the street.

"What's that?" he points to the avenue before him.

"This here's Market Street," shouts the strapping porter, flushed with excitement. "It's the Fourth of July parade, mister! Ain't it grand?"

Regiment after regiment passes by, men in uniform, some on foot, some on horseback, some in carriages or open wagons. Gold and silver braids crisscross coats of blue and maroon, deep green and violet. There are high-peaked caps, caps with brims like wings, plumed helmets. Feathers flutter, tasseled ropes swing. The men bear their pistols and rifles proudly. Banners and flags flap in the brisk sea breeze. Daniel peers at the scores of trade unions. So many affiliations, from railroad workers to garment workers; are they truly fomenting a revolution? The United States Army and Navy march next, then the Coast Guard, the California Club, the Schuetzen Club, the Scottish Clan, the Native Sons and Daughters of the Golden West, the Camera Club with their tripods set up in surries, snapping photographs of the cheering crowd. The Cycling Club wheels past. Three men in tight bicycling togs wobble precariously on old-fashioned high wheelers while the rest of the club—including ladies in bloomers!—clips smartly along on modern bicycles sporting low wheels of the same size rimmed in sterling silver, huge silver bells, and fish horns with which they produce a terrific racket. Grizzled Forty-Niners totter past in rustic buckskin and bandits' hats. The Rifle Club struts with gleaming firearms; the Whist Club saunters in tuxedos, smoking cigarettes.

Vehicular traffic congests Market Street, navigating around and through the parade. A fine brougham pulled by gorgeous matched horses with plumes in their bridles. A hansom with an elegant blue body, green and carmine striping, and plenty of scrollwork in gold and silver leaf nearly collides with an ice wagon bearing on both sides a fine reproduction of Emanuel Leutze's painting of George Washington crossing the ice-choked Delaware. More coolies in wide-brimmed caps and pajamas dash across the boulevard, their baskets heaped with vegetables or fish and slung on yokes that they bear over their shoulders. Daniel spies the magnificent Palace Hotel itself looming eight stories high and taking up the whole block amid other elegant commercial buildings wrought in an intricate style more flamboyant, more exuberant, more baroque than any architecture he's ever seen. The street lamps are crafted of beveled capiz shell and stained glass.

Ladies in their summer dresses and gentlemen in top hats and checked vests snack from picnic baskets right on the street corners and uncork bottles of champagne. A crowd of common people have congregated around a tall fountain, the base of which is made of openmouthed cherubs carved in gray marble with that vaguely lascivious air such creatures always evoke. The crowd dips cups and glasses into a boozy sparkling fluid that spouts from the cherubs' mouths.

"What is it?" Daniel asks.

"Help yourself." A gentleman with a face blooming scarlet dips his hand. "Happy Fourth of July!"

Daniel scoops a palmful of cheap champagne from the fountain, astringent bubbles tickling his nose as the wine slides down his throat. The strapping porter grins and stoops and sucks, plunging his face right into the champagne cascading from a cherub's face. Equality in San Francisco, Daniel thinks, means champagne for all.

A ferocious clanging cuts through the celebratory din. A spectacular red and black fire wagon with bright brass fittings, a gigantic brass cask of water, and intricate pumping equipment thunders by, pulled by wild-eyed blowing steeds whose prancing hooves show off their skills at negotiating city streets beyond the capabilities of the ordinary nag. Boys cheer and whoop and chase after the frantic fire wagon.

"Happens every Fourth, mister," says the strapping porter with a malicious grin. "Somebody lands a rocket on somebody's roof—for spite or sport or maybe sometimes just for fun—an' the whole friggin' joint burns down. Ha, ha."

"Burns down!" What about Father's commercial building on Stockton Street? Sometimes for spite? Daniel suddenly wonders if Father's tenants have any inkling he's here. But how could they? Father felt that taking them by surprise was best. After the last plea for payment he had wired no one. Still, suddenly Daniel feels uneasy. It's the noise and confusion, he tells himself, the smell of gunpowder, the lingering aftertaste of puma piss. He finds a handkerchief, wipes sticky champagne off his palm as best he can. "Let's get going."

"Sure, mister." The strapping porter stops dead in his tracks and extends his hand. "But first, that'll be two bits for unloadin' you from the ferry."

"Oh, very well." Daniel searches his coat pocket. Blew too much cash at the First and Last Chance Saloon, that's a fact. But he's got more. Reaches into his vest, fingers searching for the smooth Moroccan leather of his boodle book. Got a few treasury notes, but Father warned him no one honors paper currency in the far West. A gentleman needs coins, gold preferably, and he's got several dozen in the coin pocket of the boodle book. Now where is the thing? Seems to have migrated someplace.

Daniel searches, puzzled, searches and pats himself, reaching here and there into all his pockets. Nothing. Nothing! "Damn," he mutters.

"Something the matter, mister?" Malicious grin again.

With that awful sinking feeling of sudden defeat, Daniel knows the boodle book and its contents are long gone. "Seems I've lost my dough."

"Cashed in your chips on the trip out, did you, mister?"

"No, I haven't gambled since. . . No. That bird. The little one I left the ferry with."

"Oh, her?" The porter grins. "Yeah, I seen her. I seen her lots a times. Good ol' Fanny, she's a hummer, ain't she?"

"By God, she's a dip?"

"Fanny Spiggott? Ha, ha. Faintin' Fanny, that's what we call her. Every fool knows Fanny. Of course, a smart young gentleman like yourself wouldn't fall for her racket, now, would you, mister?"

Daniel stands aside, fights the anger and disgust welling up in his chest while the strapping porter sticks his mug into the champagne cascade for another guzzle. Of course, he didn't carry his whole kit and caboodle in the book. He's not some bumpkin, after all. There are a few more gold coins stashed away in his ditty bag. There's the trunk with his deeds and papers, a bit of art he acquired in Paris. He's not wiped out.

Still! Still! The lousy bitch, he could take her little neck in his hands and twist. . . . Women! They'll steal your soul if you give them half a chance.

The strapping porter reels up from his guzzle, flushed and shiny-eyed. He has drawn his own conclusions from Daniel's sudden dejection for he proclaims, with high spirits, "Hell with the two bits. Where you goin', mister? It's the Fourth of July. Welcome to San Francisco!"

"Thank you, sir," Daniel says humbly.

"Next time, mister."

The strapping porter lugs the trunk, Daniel takes the bags, and together they fight the festive crowd up Market Street. Dupont Street appears to the north at last. The porter turns right up a gentle incline that might as well be an Alp, for all Daniel cares. By God, his mouth is dry. Thank heaven Father can't see him in this predicament.

They enter another part of town, and the traffic, the sounds and the smells, the mood and the light change. A saloon stands on every street corner, four per intersection, sometimes more if another proprietor has got the story up. Daniel has never seen so many saloons and resorts crowded together in such proximity. Music blares from the doorways, inviting him in. Men guffaw and shout. Glasses bang on bars or crash together in toasts. The stink of gunpowder is infused with the powerful smells of whiskey, tobacco, roasting meat, and an odd indefinable sweet sickly scent. A few women drift about, in and out of the saloon doors, but mostly on the streets, lingering on the corners. Daniel approaches a young girl who skips gaily in a sailor's costume, a fluttering navy and white topcoat over charming bloomers, striped stockings, little button boots. A jaunty straw boater is pinned over her shiny yellow curls. She sidles up to him, curtseys charmingly. He gapes at the wrinkles creasing her face, the heavy white powder over peculiarly grainy jowls, her withered lips beneath the mouth drawn on in red paint. She frowns at his startled look and skips away, tittering.

The strapping porter laughs nervously. "Here's as far as I go, mister." The porter unceremoniously plunks the trunk down. Perhaps his throat is as dry as Daniel's.

Daniel glances about. Something dangles above him, thrown over the telegraph wires. Lace and ribbons, straps and stays. A woman's undergarment dangling from the telegraph wires? His eyes travel from the garment to a window, where a young woman sits. Half-dressed she leans out, seizes a string of the corset, and reels in the undergarment like a hooked fish. But she does not attend too closely to her task. No, her eyes—are they blue?—are trained right on him. He looks over his shoulder, to the right, to the left. She throws back her head and laughs, her bare throat throbbing.

Heat rises under his belt, under his collar, in his face.

He drags his trunk a step further. Damn that porter! He finds himself in front of a huge house with square-cut bay windows, angular battens, geometric decorations. The house is painted a conservative pale gray with bronze green trim, sable brown doors and vestibules. He should think it a perfectly respectable house except that another lovely young woman leans out of the window above him. Her hair is disheveled, her robe falls lazily open over her shoulders. At least she dangles no corset.

Daniel checks the address. What luck! The strapping porter didn't abandon him, after all. He climbs up the stairs and pulls the door bell at Number 263 Dupont Street. The bell chimes within. The young woman in the window exclaims and withdraws from her perch. Flurry of activity behind the heavy beveled glass. He pulls the bell again. The door swings open.

"Good afternoon, sir," the young woman says. She breathes shallowly from her sudden exertion. "How may we help you?"

Daniel steps into the foyer of Miss Malone's Boardinghouse for Gentlemen.

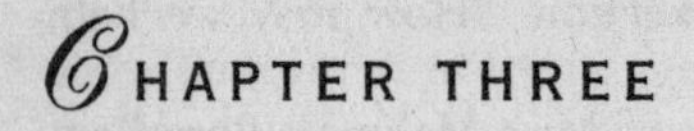

CHAPTER THREE

Miss Malone's Boardinghouse for Gentlemen

"Jar me, I'll not have my Fourth of July cooked," says Jessie Malone to the sympathetic gentleman as he negotiates with her in the downstairs smoking parlor. "And on a Thursday, too, which is, I'll have you know, my most magnetic day."

"Magnetic day?" says the gentleman, feigning surprise. Jessie knows that his wife, who also consults with famed spiritualist Madame De Cassin, surely possesses tons of magnetic days herself. You don't blow it in on magnetic days. Still, if Mrs. Heald was more of a slut and less of a shrew, Mr. Heald might not be speaking so earnestly with Jessie right now. "What the devil is your 'most magnetic day'?"

"Sure and it's the day I always speak with the sweet spirits," Jessie says.

Mr. Heald twirls graying tufts of his tremendous mustache and smirks. How transparent men are. Plotting how he can convince her otherwise. He would not dare broach the topic he hinted at this morning of the small increase in the civic contribution he delivers for her to certain persons in the mayor's office. Not when he wants to dip his wick. The biz is the biz, no less and never more when it comes to Mr. Heald. Sure and Mr. Heald is such a dear friend from the days when she was the toast of the town and the special gal of the Silver Kings.

"Now, Jessie," he says. "Hell with the spirits and your magnetic days. Hell with the Fourth of July."

"Mr. Heald! I thought you were a patriot!"

"You've had your breakfast and your outing. Now I want to go upstairs like we agreed. Didn't we agree?"

Jessie smooths the feathers of the pressed hummingbirds decorating her Caroline hat. Brushes dust from the ruffles and bows on her bodice. She spies a clot of horse manure clinging to the hem of her pink topskirt, gives the silk a good shaking. "No, I'm all done in. Good day, Mr. Heald."

"Now, Jessie." His tone deepens alarmingly, though he's more or less sober. Mr. Heald takes her wrist in hands that have been known to throttle a man. She does not struggle. Merely lifts her face to him and raises her eyebrows. He lets go, but her wrist throbs. He broke it once. When was that? Years ago, so many years ago, perhaps not long after she was a mermaid at Lily Lake. Was it really dear Mr. Heald? Never mind. She's lost track of time, of men.

"If truth be told, Mr. Heald, I cannot abide that ruckus. It's made me weary." Cannot abide? She is outraged at the affront she witnessed in Golden Gate Park.

How she loves her traditional Fourth of July outing! A fitting tribute to the United States of America, this great and marvelous country that has allowed her, Miss Jessie Malone, once a penniless orphan, now a woman of nice sensibilities and simple desires, to amass a humble fortune. And all on her own. Her custom on the Fourth of July is to take breakfast with a roast turkey, champagne, and a gentleman. Then on to Golden Gate Park for a promenade through Concert Valley. A breath of air, a shot of sunlight, the company of the fine, upstanding citizens of San Francisco. How she loves to see the little children skip and run, to admire the ladies in their frocks, to nod to gentlemen she scarcely ever sees in the broad day. She feels positively patriotic, righteous, even honest, though her liver aches beneath the stays despite a dose of Doan's Pills.

There's a goddamn war among the tongs these days, as if a woman of her sensibilities didn't know. They're gangs, of course, organized crime despite the excuses of the Six Companies, Chinatown's official liaison. The tongs deal in coolies, slaves, opium, weapons, extortion, murder-for-hire. They've got codes and signals. Each tong man wears a special coil in his queue, a particular cap, an earring, a snip of embroidery on his jacket. There must be thirty tongs operating in San Francisco, with rivalries and feuds bloodier than thirty cockfights. Lately highbinders have been hacking each other to bits right under the very noses of the bulls running this burg. The stories Jessie's heard. But that's Chinatown, not Golden Gate Park on the Fourth of July. What's the city coming to?

The front bell rings. Li'l Lucy, housecoat slung over her corset and bloomers, flies out of her bedroom on the second floor and hurtles down the stairs.

"Li'l Lucy," Jessie calls as she passes the parlor.

"Yes, Miss Malone." Li'l Lucy skids to a halt. A pastry of a girl, all buttery and plump, but the plumpness is beginning to lose its firmness. Li'l Lucy is under contract at Jessie's Sutter Street resort, the Parisian Mansion. She'd gotten in the family way for the second time. Has spent the past week recuperating after her medical treatment. She does not look proper, housecoat flapping about. Not here at the boardinghouse, which is a respectable establishment. Jessie frowns.

"Why aren't you dressed, Li'l Lucy?"

"I still ache, Miss Malone," she says.

Jessie seizes the ties of Li'l Lucy's housecoat, wraps them around her waist twice, secures the ends in a bow over her stomach. Wets her forefingers, smooths Li'l Lucy's eyebrows, vigorously pinches her cheeks, the fullness of her lips. Tender skin blooms with pain and color. The bell rings again. Jessie rearranges curls of Li'l Lucy's yellow hair across her forehead, smooths strands down her plump neck. "There," she says. "You gotta get back in the habit of grooming, Li'l

Lucy. That's what gentlemen expect. Now you may answer the door."

"Yes, Miss Malone. Thank you, Miss Malone." Li'l Lucy gazes up at her like a starving bitch dog given a thimble of cream.

Jessie still frowns, watching her go. Li'l Lucy has begun to be more trouble than she is worth.

"Now, Jessie," Mr. Heald says. Takes the liberty of nuzzling diamonds dangling from her earlobes. Diamonds that beat anything Mrs. Heald owns. "You can speak to the sweet spirits later, can't you? Right now, my . . . my own angel, I thought we would go up upstairs."

His mustache tickles, oh, she likes mustaches well enough. Upstairs is her own private parlor. Doesn't have to live at the Parisian Mansion anymore. She can afford door maids to handle the traffic when she's not there.

"I have a caller, Mr. Heald."

"Jessie. You know how I adore you. Have pity on me."

Pity. Jessie kneels in the smoking parlor. Sure and she shouldn't have to do this anymore, really she shouldn't, but there's the boodle for certain persons in the mayor's office. Perhaps Mr. Heald, being such a dear friend, can persuade these persons that Miss Jessie Malone makes an adequate civic contribution. She tugs at the buttons on his trousers.

Gentleman, pah. Like most of his Snob Hill associates, Mr. Heald is a fool and a coward. A deadbeat when it comes to the behavior she expects of him. Allowing tong men to carry on in full view of law-abiding citizens. Tong men—hatchet men, highbinders, the *boo how doy*—it's all the same. She knows why they made a fuss, all right. The ragged Chinese girl is likely to be worth up to two thousand in gold, if she's fifteen or sixteen. Well, the biz is the biz—for the Chinese, too. Jessie doesn't give two hoots about that. The outrage is hatchet men troubling a consumptive-looking lady in a veil and a smart gray dress. A lady, on the Fourth of July! Jessie trembles with anger, but she finishes her work. Mr. Heald is done quickly. She glances up. He's got that sagging look he always gets through the jowls. She finds and dabs a handkerchief to her lips. He helps her to her feet. Suddenly weary of him, him and all the johns. They're not even men to her anymore. She needs a drink.

"That'll be the usual for the pleasure of my company, Mr. Heald," she says.

Not a moment too soon. She hears the murmur of voices, Li'l Lucy conversing with the caller at the front door, he answering. A man, of course. Jessie checks her face in one of the mirrors, peers around the corner. Glimpses gray gabardine, a blue vest, a bowler. He inquires about something in a charming accent. She spies a hefty trunk, a small collection of baggage that the caller is vigorously stacking in the foyer. Sure and he's vigorous. She can see it from here. Young and vigorous, brown curls tumbling down his neck.

"Now, Jessie," Mr. Heald says, pulling her back. "If truth be told, I thought this was for friendship, not the usual."

"If truth be told, it's always the usual, Mr. Heald."

Jessie whips out her pink lace fan, stirs a bit of breeze before her flushed face. A drink, a drink. She runs to the window, leans out, and yells, "Mariah!" The maid is on the roof, keeping a lookout for rockets with a broom and two pails of water. On the Fourth of July in '93, a stray rocket landed on the eaves of Hunter's Resort on Water Street in Sausalito and damn near burned down the whole business district. Jessie has no intention of losing this house, a very fine three-story Stick-Eastlake with extra gingerbread and a proper paint job that cost an arm and a leg. "Get down here, Mariah, we've got company. And bring me some champagne!"

"Ah, I see. You're still angry about those Chinee hoodlums?" Mr. Heald says, loosening his collar. "Now, Jessie. Chinee business is no business of ours. Why, you should know. You're the Queen of the Underworld. Why should a little discombobulation like that put you off your feed?"

"The Queen of the Underworld is never off her feed, Mr. Heald."

"Well, then. I expect such tenderheartedness from my . . . that is, from ladies. Not from the Queen of the Underworld." Mr. Heald's eyes glisten at Jessie's self-proclaimed title, which is as much a flattery to her as a titillation to him.

"Oh, you expect, do you? Well, the Queen of the Underworld says there is a place for sin and a time for sin. And that time and that place is not during my Fourth of July promenade in the park!"

Jessie gasps for breath, she is so distraught. Then she does her act. She breaks out into tears, great fat raindrops of tears, the kind that really get to Mr. Heald and the likes of Mr. Heald. She fans herself furiously, peeking through the deluge at his mortified face.

"Now, Jessie," Mr. Heald says gently. "I had no notion you were such a patriot." Fumbles in his vest, pulls out a fistful of double eagles. He spills them on the table for the pleasure of her company.

"Darlin'." Jessie permits herself a smile.

How she loves double eagles, her favorite of all the gold circulating in San Francisco. So pretty. Madame De Cassin says the American eagle is really the phoenix, the mythical bird that never dies. He just hatches over and over again and lives for all eternity. Jessie adores that idea. The phoenix is like the soul, dying and being born in the Summerland. Like her Betsy, her sweet innocent Betsy who speaks to her from the Summerland through Madame De Cassin's expert auspices. Double eagles. Jessie wouldn't think of taking anything else, let alone that worthless paper money. Government certificates, pah. You can't even bite them.

"Let's forget about those hoodlums," Mr. Heald says, watching her as she turns the coins over in her palm, fingering them, stroking them. "Let's forget about the Chinee, and the park, and all such argle-bargle, shall we, my angel? Say, I'd like a drink. How about going upstairs?"

Jessie snaps the fan shut and smartly slaps the ivory rib of it against his cheek. "Forget about the highbinders? I should say not! You're a coward, Mr. Heald. I'll entertain no cowards today. Mariah!"

She shouts out the window again as the maid descends the fire escape, black skirts billowing about her black ankles. Not some auntie or chippy is Jessie's Mariah, oh no. Mariah is a prize, one of the Negro maids hired straight out of the Palace Hotel for a pretty penny. Mariah takes as high a wage as a hotel chef, since she can cook something grand, keeps the boardinghouse spotless, and keeps her mouth shut. Mariah knows how to behave around the likes of Mr. Heald. She demurely draws her skirts through the window and glares at the gentleman with so evil an eye that Mr. Heald blanches visibly.

Jessie is in distress. Her liver positively throbs. She cannot see another caller in this condition. "Get me my Scotch Oats Essence, Mariah. I feel faint."

Mariah scurries for the medicine and a spoon made of pure gold. How Jessie loves gold! And how she loves the pale green bottle filled with precious medicine. The label shows a buxom, apple-cheeked mother stirring brew in a cast-iron cauldron while a bevy of bare-assed cupids flutter all around her on pink wings. Mariah expertly slides a dose through Jessie's lips. Jessie feels absolutely healthful in a trice. The delicious bitter tonic slides down her throat with a somber burning sensation. Swells her head with a sanguine joy that assures her she will live forever, despite the ache in her gut.

She slides the fan into her sleeve, peers in the mirror again. She always looks so much better after a dose of Scotch Oats Essence. "Not bad for forty," she tells her reflection. Forty years old? Can it really be? She finds and smooths some ruby-colored balm over her pursed lips. Mr. Heald watches her, his mouth falling slightly open, his eyes glazed. He likes to watch, a lot of men do. Them Snob Hill ladies never use face paint, which Jessie learned about from her pal, Maggie Colton, who played Lady G. in *A Box of Monkeys*. That's why them Snob Hill ladies look so plain, despite their fancy togs.

"You don't look a day over twenty, Jessie," Mr. Heald says in a ragged whisper.

"Nor am I, darlin', before the sweet spirits and my simple heart," she tells him. He is so eager, he'll pay double the usual when she gets around to entertaining him again. Jessie turns to him with wide blue eyes. "Nor am I."

❜ ❜ ❜

"Joaquin Miller sent me," the caller tells her. He leaves off brushing the dust from his coat and politely bows, pulls out a smoke and lights it.

Li'l Lucy gazes at the caller as if he were a shot of fine aged bourbon and she a-dyin' of thirst.

Jessie enters the foyer regally. Mr. Heald ambles behind her, like a courtier at her beck and call, his respectable appearance enhancing her own prestige. The caller examines them curiously. Jessie likes making an entrance like one of them Snob Hill ladies.

"Joaquin Miller!" she says. "Now, there's a good egg even if he is an odd bird. Says he gimped that leg of his fighting the wild Cherokee, but have you noticed he never limps on the same foot twice? I'm Miss Jessie Malone, proprietress and landlady. What's your name, buster?"

"I'm Daniel J. Watkins of Saint Louis, London, and Paris."

"Paris! You just blew in from Paris?" Jessie whips out her fan, concealing her excitement behind the lace. "Are they still wearing bustles in Paris, Mr. Watkins?"

"Oh no, Miss Malone. Mr. Worth has eliminated the bustle in the latest creations, which I for one approve of. Now one can observe the long, slow sweep of the hip. Don't you agree, sir?" he says to Mr. Heald.

Mr. Heald stares, stupefied.

Li'l Lucy turns beet red with excitement and begins to giggle like a lunatic.

Jessie shushes her but she can barely contain herself, either. A gentleman who can yap about Paris fashions! Mr. Worth's latest creations! Can you imagine? But her suspicious nature kicks up. Is he one of those birds who goes to drag parties? She's been to drag parties. There was one on Snob Hill where the whiskey magnate demanded she lace up his corset extra tight. The long, slow sweep of the hip, indeed.

"Sure and aren't you an outspoken young gentleman?" Jessie saunters over, making a show of brushing dust from the back of his coat. She runs her hand down the long, slow sweep of his back. Young and vigorous, with some little gun tucked in his belt. It'd be a crying shame if he turned out a fairy. "You have an interest in ladies' fashions?"

"Only when they're being discarded."

Li'l Lucy presses her palm to her mouth.

"Oh yes," Mr. Watkins says, "they've widened sleeves in Paris and the front of the skirt. Tightened the waist and added fullness to the bosom, pardon me, miss," he says to Li'l Lucy, who is beside herself with giggles, "so that a lady like yourself, Miss Malone, will show the perfect figure. Like an hourglass, is how they put it."

What gentleman in this burg hasn't flattered her so shamelessly, can anyone tell her that? Jessie tosses her head and stands back, trying to size him up. Is Mr. Daniel J. Watkins of Saint Louis, London, and Paris a little too smooth? What is he, anyway? A gambler or a tool? She's been scammed and chiseled before. She'll tolerate no deadheads in *her* establishment.

"Tightened the waist?" she says forlornly, kneading her aching liver through the corset.

Mr. Watkins circles her, staring blatantly, inspecting her. "I fear you'll have to nip it in, Miss Malone."

Jessie hasn't blushed in fifteen years. The heat in her cheeks must be a sudden fever. "Jar me, we can all stand some improvement." Frowns. The Queen of the Underworld has a skin as thick as buffalo hide, but she is stung by this pup's insolence. Seizes a heavy brass ashtray, presents it to him. "Smoking is permitted only in the smoking parlor, Mr. Watkins," she says. "I loathe the demon weed."

He stamps out the smoke and shuts his trap. A wary look of utter exhaustion crosses his face. It occurs to Jessie that young Mr. Watkins looks a tad green about the gills. She glares at Li'l Lucy, who stops giggling at once. She sniffs, detecting the stink of choke-dog beneath the tobacco.

"What brings you here and what can I do for you, sir?" She crosses her arms and taps her toe, looking him up and down with a thundercloud on her face.

"Miss Malone, I'm merely looking for a suite of rooms to let. I'd prefer my own water closet and a bath, if this fine establishment boasts such things. I'm told you may have something available?"

Jessie considers the possibilities. Li'l Lucy will have to add two weeks to the term of her contract for her medical treatment and resting-up time at Dupont Street. High time for Li'l Lucy to get back to work. "Mr. Watkins, this fine establishment boasts many things, and a suite to let with a water closet and a bath is one of them. This young lady was just about to move out, weren't you, dear? Get packing, Lucy."

She stares meaningfully at Li'l Lucy, who cringes and dashes back up the stairs. Li'l Lucy is getting long in the tooth and dim in the noggin. She is nineteen. Jessie watches her go. If Li'l Lucy suffers another medical problem, Jessie will have to move her to the cribs on Morton Alley, and that's that. The biz is the biz.

"There's just one problem, a minor one, I'm sure," Mr. Watkins says with a lovely smile beneath his lovely mustache. He pats his pockets for a smoke with the blind gesture of habit, finds one. Recalls her injunction, twirls the ciggie mournfully through his nicotine-stained fingers.

Jessie sighs. Young and vigorous. And insolent *and* on the make. "Sure and you can't pay me right away."

He looks up, fraudulent innocence, cunning, and genuine desperation aging his face into an odd sort of mask. As though a wholly different person stands before her for a moment.

Jessie's breath catches in her throat. Fireworks pop and crackle overhead. She starts, heart fluttering.

But then a horse clatters on the cobblestones, and the spell is broken, and poor Mr. Watkins looks like nothing so much as a sick, lost kid.

Through the window, she can see Madame De Cassin outside. What a fine lady she is, too! Jessie smiles as the dashing spiritualist leaps off her black stallion, ties him to the hitching post, and stomps up the stairs. She bursts into the foyer without ringing the bell, splendid in her billowing black cape, black riding habit, and tall black boots. She always smells of horses, leather, and lavender oil. Madame De Cassin surveys Mr. Watkins with a piercing glance and, without hesitation, says, "Well, give him a room, but he'll want to watch his step. I'll wager you're born under the sign of Aries, sir, is that correct?"

Jessie fairly bursts with joy. Madame De Cassin is the

most respected, most sought-after expert in matters of the occult in this burg. Surely the spiritualist has never laid eyes on Mr. Watkins before. "You see, Madame De Cassin knows *everything*!"

"Aries, yes?" says Madame De Cassin. "The headstrong ram."

"I wouldn't know, madame," Mr. Watkins says and lights his smoke with trembling fingers, despite Jessie's admonishment. Mr. Heald pats perspiration off his forehead and grins tightly at the new arrival, who looks him up and down. The spiritualist *has* laid eyes on Mr. Heald before.

"Well, I know *this*, my dear," Madame De Cassin says to Jessie, tossing her whip on the side table, together with her black riding hat with its jet beads and black plumes. She flexes her hands, which she always keeps gloved in the finest black kid, and imperiously surveys them all. "I know it's a fine time to call upon the sweet spirits."

"Li'l Lucy! Mariah!" Jessie calls. "Get the sitting room ready."

Madame De Cassin struts up to Mr. Watkins and boldly stares in his face. "Are you a believer, sir?"

"Believer in what, madame?" Mr. Watkins stares back.

"In communication with the dead." She moves on to Mr. Heald. "How about you, sir? Have you ever spoken with the sweet spirits? Indeed, have you ever spoken truthfully with your wife?"

Jessie is too excited to pay much attention to Mr. Heald's scarlet face and sputtering breath. "Sure and we have enough for a séance, don't we, Madame de Cassin, if we include the gentlemen and Li'l Lucy? Have you ever sat at a séance, Mr. Watkins?" she says, taking his arm. "Mariah! Bring us the sherry."

❙ ❙ ❙

Jessie's sitting room is a small inner chamber with no windows, one door, and one low-burning brass gaslamp left unpolished so that a dark green patina has mottled the metal. The walls are heavily draped in black velvet. Even in the middle of this bright, sunny day, the sitting room completely lacks natural light. A large round wood table stands dead center, surrounded by eight plain wood chairs. A single brass candlestick containing a squat black candle thick with wax drippings juts up from the table.

Jessie breathes the scent of old candle wax. How that scent transports her, makes her dreamy and sad. Though she has meditated upon the Summerland for many years, she has never liked speaking with the spirits in rooms other than one like this: a room of her own. Perhaps it was that awful Mr. Oleander in '77 who put his hand on her knee. Perhaps it was Senora Cortez, a dreadful fake who couldn't identify Betsy, let alone convey her voice clearly in English. In time, Jessie became adamant that her consultations should occur within her own residence where she need not contend with secret panels and hidden confederates. When other spiritualists declined to indulge her, insisting upon the magnetic powers of their own sitting rooms, Madame De Cassin readily agreed, stipulating only how Jessie should outfit her room. Jessie had followed the spiritualist's instructions to the letter, and, for three years, Madame De Cassin has visited her every Thursday afternoon with unfailingly gratifying results.

Li'l Lucy busily rearranges five of the chairs about the table, scraping three chairs into corners. Mariah lights the black candle, holds a flame to incense burners slung on brass chains mounted on the wall among the folds of black velvet. The room is heavy with the scent of lavender oil and incense.

Next Mariah sets out sherry in a crystal decanter and five heavy crystal tumblers. She scowls with disapproval, black eyes flickering. Turns down the gaslamp, makes the sign of the cross over her breast, then flees.

Madame De Cassin generously pours out sherry. "To the sweet spirits," she solemnly toasts the group as they sit and settle in. She seats herself, swirling her black cape over her shoulders.

"Well, now. Didn't know they nipped a tick before the mumbo jumbo," Mr. Heald mutters to Mr. Watkins with a wink. "No wonder the wife goes in for it."

"To the sweet spirits," says Mr. Watkins enthusiastically, tossing his sherry down his throat and reaching for the decanter.

Li'l Lucy noisily slurps her sherry, burps, and giggles.

"To the sweet spirits," Jessie says passionately, ignoring the others' disrespect. They'll see. Madame De Cassin insists on ritual imbibing of spirits—spirits for the spirits, you see. The spiritualist supplies this particular sherry to Jessie for this sacred purpose and this purpose only. The sherry establishes a certain sympathy with her contact, Chief Silver Thorne, who during his life on earth much favored the beverage. Jessie happily gulps the smoky-tasting liquor, which warms her just as the medicinal benefit of Scotch Oats Essence was beginning to fade. This particular sherry makes her head spin unlike any other. "I want to speak with Betsy, Madame De Cassin."

"Of course you do," says Madame De Cassin. She sets her tumbler down, staring severely at the sitters. Even Mr. Watkins gets the hint. He reluctantly relinquishes his tumbler. Madame De Cassin makes long sweeping motions with her gloved hands, clearing the magnetic energy over the table. Her handsome face goes slack in the candlelight. Her eyelids flutter. Her pupils roll up, showing the whites beneath them. "You will all join hands," she says in a harsh whisper.

Jessie takes the spiritualist's left hand and Mr. Watkins's right hand. Her heart begins to pound. Head whirls in the perfumed darkness.

Mr. Heald sits next to the spiritualist on the right. Li'l Lucy blinks nervously between the two gentlemen. They join hands, and the circle is complete.

Madame De Cassin wastes no time. She begins to moan and sway, keening louder and louder till she leans over the black candle and, with a chilling screech, blows out the flame.

"Chief Silver Thorne?" she calls. "My dear friend, my dear chief, where are you-oo-oo?"

A shudder rocks the spiritualist. Jessie trembles with fear and excitement. She grips the spiritualist's gloved hand—heavens, her hand is so hard and firm from equestrian activities. Jessie can't see a thing in the darkness. Suddenly a ghostly caress tickles the back of her neck. "Oh, I feel him," Jessie says, dread rushing deliciously up her spine. Shapes blacker than the darkness reel and totter before her eyes.

Mr. Heald makes little yelping noises from the other side of the table.

Madame De Cassin lets loose a bloodcurdling yell. A horn bleats softly just above Jessie's ear. Then a bizarre masculine voice spills out in the vicinity of the spiritualist's mouth. "I am here, Rebecca." The voice has a strange accent.

The spiritualist's cloak rustles as she sways and lurches. "Chief Silver Thorne, we have strangers with us today."

"Yes, I sense their presence," Chief Silver Thorne answers irritably, cutting off Madame De Cassin's statement. "Two gentlemen who do not support woman suffrage."

Mr. Heald sputters and says, "I'll be a fiddler's bitch."

Mr. Watkins says, "I hadn't thought much about it."

Ghostly caresses patter all over the back of Jessie's head. "Please, Chief Silver Thorne," Jessie pleads. "Let's not discuss woman suffrage again. You know I don't approve of it, and my employee is here."

"Yes, my dear chief," Madame De Cassin interrupts. "Miss Malone wishes to speak with her beloved Betsy."

"Very well, Miss Malone," Chief Silver Thorne says. "I will see if I can find Betsy if you will promise to treat Lucy with kindness. She has been ill, Miss Malone, has she not?"

Jessie clucks her tongue. Chief Silver Thorne is forever going on about equality for women, rights for Negroes and the heathen Chinese, and showing kindness toward her girls. Why should a Sioux chief who lived two hundred and fifty years ago give two hoots about woman suffrage? Sure and she wishes Madame De Cassin would find another spirit guide who isn't so damned self-righteous.

"Has she not?" Chief Silver Thorne repeats.

"Yes, it's true, sir, I still ache," Li'l Lucy whispers.

"All right, she has," Jessie says. Serves her right for including the girl on her most magnetic day.

"And you will promise to treat her with kindness?"

"I promise," Jessie says. She's *still* sending Li'l Lucy back to the Parisian Mansion today.

"I can't hear you, Miss Malone."

"I *promise*." But perhaps the Morton Alley cribs can wait.

"Betsy," Chief Silver Thorne begins to call in a cloudy voice that seems to come from the ceiling. "B - e - t - s - y?"

"Betsy?" Madame De Cassin says briskly in between the spirit guide's exhortations. "Betsy?"

The high, clear voice of a young girl emanates from the ceiling. "Jessie? Oh, is that you, Jessie?"

Grief spills through Jessie like it always does. The sharp, deep yearning for her Betsy, for Lily Lake lost so long ago. Jessie grips the hands of Mr. Watkins and the spiritualist even tighter as tears, real tears, spill down her face. "Betsy? My beloved Betsy?"

"I'm here, Jessie."

"Are you all right?"

"I'm fine, Jessie. And you, darling?"

"I'm fine, Betsy."

"Have you gone to see the doctor about that pain we talked about last time?"

"No. I . . . I've been busy, Betsy."

"You really must go, Jessie. I feel that something may be wrong with you. You must see a doctor, Jessie."

"Never mind about me. Betsy, I saw a lady today. She was attacked by them hatchet men in the park. I can't get her out of my mind! Can you tell me if she's all right?"

Betsy hesitates, and Madame De Cassin says, "Betsy has been picnicking in the Summerland today, Jessie. She's been enjoying her own Fourth of July, and she may not know . . ."

But Betsy says, "Someone has come. Someone else is here with me. Someone who has crossed over in recent days. A lady. A pale, pretty lady with such a sad face. Such deep sea eyes, swimming with tears, always swimming with tears."

Mr. Watkins inhales sharply as though someone has punched him in the gut. Whispers, "By God—Mama?"

"Yes, it is Mama," Betsy whispers. "Mama says . . . Mama says, 'Beware, my son. Beware, you are in danger.' "

"Yes, it's true! A dip pinched my boodle book on the ferry from Oakland!"

Betsy whispers, "Mama says . . ."

Suddenly a freezing wind whips through the sitting room with an eerie whistling sound. Jessie's teeth begin to chatter, a sour taste pools on her tongue. The stench of rotgut wafts over the table. A snippet of honkytonk music blares in her ear. The utter darkness turns blindingly white—stark white for an eye blink—then flips into darkness again.

"Jar me, what is it?" Jessie turns toward Madame De Cassin.

The spiritualist snatches her hand away and leaps to her feet. Jessie hears something clatter on the floor. Madame De Cassin stoops, whirls, and sprints across the room. Light blooms. She stands at the gaslamp, turning it up. Her face is drained pale, her brown eyes wide. Jessie has never seen the spiritualist look like this before.

"It's true!" Mr. Watkins says, flushed with excitement. He looks around. "Mama?"

Li'l Lucy's teeth chatter audibly. Mr. Heald looks pinched.

"My mother died just over a month ago!" Mr. Watkins says. "And that strange presence, did you see it, did you feel it? On the Overland train, I felt a strange presence, too. A strange presence, I tell you, a vision that changed all the world for a moment. She said 'beware, my son.' She said 'beware'!" He seizes Jessie's arm. "What does it mean?"

"Sure and what does it mean?" Jessie demands, turning to Madame De Cassin.

"Let's go downstairs," Madame De Cassin says. "All of you, come on." She herds them out of the sitting room. The others go as Jessie turns off the gaslamp, crushes the smoldering piles of incense in their burners, and plunks a silver snuffer over the smoking candle. The spiritualist takes Jessie by the arm and resolutely closes the door to the sitting room behind them.

"What was it?" Jessie whispers as they climb slowly down the stairs.

"My dear," Madame De Cassin says, "there is a strange time coming."

❛ ❛ ❛

Madame De Cassin assures Jessie that evil spirits, or whatever the strange presence was, departed from the sitting room when she turned up the light. But the unflappable spiritualist looks unsettled herself. Jessie pays her the usual fee out of the gold Mr. Heald gave her, plus twenty dollars extra, and begs her to come back and make sure the sitting room won't be haunted. The spiritualist agrees, consulting her little black leather appointment book, scheduling another visit.

"Madame De Cassin, tell me what to do." Mr. Watkins confronts her as the spiritualist pins on her riding hat.

"Beware," she says. "Beware of others. Mostly beware of yourself, sir." She stomps out the door.

Mr. Heald hurries out the door, too, without another word about going upstairs. Sure and it's just as well. Jessie is hardly in the mood for biz. But an anxiety grates at her. Truth be told, she must admit Mr. Heald is a nice gentleman, a dear friend after all, and always flush. The diamonds swinging from her earlobes were paid for by all the Mr. Healds. Mr. Heald is no worse than most and better than some. She makes a note in her head: She'll have to invite him to the musicale on Sunday night at the Parisian Mansion, stand him a bottle of champagne. She can't afford to lose the patronage and goodwill of Mr. Heald. There's the civic contribution he delivers to certain persons in the mayor's office. What was the increase he mentioned?

A séance usually refreshes her. Not this time. She can only be glad that her Betsy is still doing so well in the Summerland after life cheated her so cruelly. That bittersweet thought instantly hardens her heart, and she finds Li'l Lucy lingering in the foyer with Mr. Watkins.

"Pack your things," she orders the girl before she can protest. "Off to Sutter Street with you."

"But Miss Malone," Li'l Lucy says, "I still ache. And Chief Silver Thorne said . . ."

"Never mind Chief Silver Thorne. Be quick about it." There, you see? Never mix employees in her personal affairs. Oh, give them an inch! The biz is the biz. "And clean the place up, Li'l Lucy. I'm letting out those rooms today." Smiles at the young gentleman, who is definitely looking the worse for wear. "Mr. Watkins, let's talk. Will you come up to my parlor? Will you have a drink? I'm thirsty as a camelopard myself."

"Gladly. I'm dry as a bone myself, Miss Malone, but I do believe you mean a camel. Nasty beasts that run about the desert. Spit and bite and smell, dreadful things. A camelopard, on the other hand, is a lovely creature with an extraordinarily long neck who lives on the plains far south of the desert and nibbles charmingly on jungle foliage."

"A scholar, then," she says.

"And a gentleman." He shows sparkling white teeth. "Please excuse my poor manners. I just got off the Overland train from Saint Louis. I'm beat."

Bang, bang, bang! Firecrackers pop in the street. "I'll show you. . . ." Two bruisers commence a brawl in front of her door, fists swinging, pals cheering them on. "Heeeey, biff 'im one, Johnny!" "I'll smash yer face."

Never has Jessie seen such a Fourth of July!

"We're all a bit rattled today. Mariah! Let's go upstairs, darlin'. Let's have some champagne."

❜ ❜ ❜

Huffing and puffing every blasted inch of three flights up, stays cutting into her liver at every stair, Jessie shows Mr. Watkins her private parlor on the top floor. "Got to look into one of them elevator contraptions that the swells use in their downtown skyscrapers," she tells him. Sure and this is her pride and joy. A room of her own design, not at all like the sitting room for the sweet spirits and Madame De Cassin.

When Jessie bought the three-story Stick-Eastlake mansion with the intention of securing her personal residence above, private boarders below, the place was plain, the paint peeling to shavings. Since the seventies, lower Dupont Street has become a tenderloin. Respectable folk fled the old city as the poor of every nation flooded in, tainting once-genteel streets with vice and sport and crime. Yes, and also with the mere presence of the poor, their flapping laundry and cooking smells and rowdy children. But the rooms are huge, the architecture sound, the views superb. And views cost a pretty penny. To the southwest, she can see the top of the Palace Hotel and Lucky Baldwin's showplace. Due south, the whole panorama of Market Street, the Cocktail Route, all the delights of the old city. To the northwest, the exotic curved roofs of Chinatown like another little country. Purple hills rise behind that: Nob Hill, Russian Hill, Pacific Heights. Northeast, the scruffy dome of Telegraph Hill—"dirty awld smelly awld Telygraft Hill"—the German castle barely visible at its crown. And when she throws open the wobbly glass of the east window and leans far out past the scarlet velvet curtains, she can glimpse the whole crawling heap of the Barbary Coast. Beyond that, the bobbing masts of great clipper ships, the steamers and fishing trawlers, the blue-gray bay that sparkles, when the sun falls just so, like a sack of diamonds spilled at her feet.

It is a beautiful house, and Jessie has covered the bare walls with the finest rose-colored damask she ever did see with an intricate rose-of-Sharon pattern. That's for starters. She has hung every single window with scarlet velvet curtains that sweep up and back and dangle yards of tassels and thick furry fringe. Had an ironwork grille made for the entry, a swooping black metal arch bordered all about by spiderwebs and sunbursts and starbursts and blooms. Sometimes she entwines dried herbs and dock through the iron curves. And she has laid Persian carpets down on the maple plank floors, layer upon layer till the floor is a patchwork of arabesques and medallions in astonishing burgundies and blues. She has put in good furniture, some wood, some wicker, some French gilt stuff. A profusion of ferns potted in massive Chinese vases stand in every sunlit corner. And gold, lots of gold: a gold tea set, gold dinnerware, gold lamp sticks, gold embroidered doilies, gold statuettes of Venus with their arms and heads intact. Jessie cannot abide Venuses without their arms and heads. The long mirror is framed in pure burnished gold, encrusted with birds and foliage in pale gold and silver. A gold-plated spittoon is set out just for show, since Jessie abides no chaw in her private parlor. Gilt frames surround every piece of art.

Oh, the art! Jessie prides herself on her private collection, which covers nearly every square inch of that pretty damask except for one strip by the door that she leaves bare just to show the rose-of-Sharon design. She's made them Gump boys richer than thieves in their import business. One of Gump's best customers, that's what Jessie Malone is, more than two of them Snob Hill ladies rolled up into one. She's got fauns playing flutes, plenty of cupids on the wing. But mostly Jessie collects nudes. The female, in all her glory.

Nudes recline on couches. Nudes stroll through fantastic gardens and forests. Nudes are sold into slavery with their hands bound behind their pearlescent backs. Nudes pose in the bedroom, in the bath, in the stables.

Mariah brings in tall fluted goblets, the gold-plated ice bucket. Jessie frowns. Should have got the solid gold bucket, not this cheap plate, but her horse had lost at Ingleside that afternoon, and she balked at the expense. She pops the cork with a smile nonetheless, a smile she wears well as she splashes champagne. The young gentleman sits. Studies her collection, his mouth inscrutable beneath his mustache.

"Miss Malone, you've got an Aubrey Beardsley!" Mr. Watkins exclaims over the photomechanical reproduction of an odd line drawing Jessie has never much understood except that it's wicked.

"A gambler whose name you would recognize gave it to me," she says.

The drawing depicts denizens of the night: a masked clown, a depraved ballerina, a devil-eared satyr with a huge erect penis and cloven hooves.

"Is it true Mr. Beardsley slept with Oscar Wilde?" Jessie hands Mr. Watkins a glass. Smiles at his surprise at her frankness. She follows the international gossip as best she can.

Heard that after the glory of his play, *The Importance of Being Earnest,* Mr. Wilde has been imprisoned for having his way with young men.

"I cannot vouch for Beardsley, but we do call him Awfully Weirdsley," Mr. Watkins says. "Poor fellow is a wreck with the consumption. They say he won't live out the year."

"So young and talented. It's a shame," Jessie says. Clinks her glass with his. "That's why I say eat, drink, and be merry, for tomorrow we die." They drink. Madame De Cassin's sherry always makes her thirsty for bubbly. She refreshes their goblets. "Mr. Watkins," she says, "you're not a queen, are you?"

"No," he says, not missing a beat, "but I've a few pals who've hoed that row." He downs his second glass, holds it out for another. "Have you read Mr. Wilde, then?"

Jessie pours again. Loves to see a man who can guzzle the bubbly. "Of course I've read Mr. Wilde. Why, I've read them strange French poets, Baudelaire and Verlaine." Jessie takes her copy of *Salon* from the sidetable where she keeps naughty magazines like *The Pearl* and *Boudoir*. Leafs through the pages, opens at random. Strikes a pose, hand aloft, and proclaims, "'Goddesses riding hippogryphs and streaking their lapis lazuli wings with the death agony of clouds.'" She slaps the book shut, slides it back on the sidetable. "Isn't it grand?"

"What in hell does it mean?"

"I don't know, but it makes my head swim!" Refills her glass. "This world can be such a cold, gray place. Look how life has changed. The romance is gone. Things aren't like they used to be. Them big ugly factories, and the millionaires breaking the backs of the unions, and the working folk suffering from booms and the busts, and the train taking people all over the land, and no one lives in the old hometown. No one knows what to believe in. Everything's a jumble! Maybe strange writers give us back the romance and the wonder. Maybe they can tell us what the world is like, or used to be like, or will be like, better than the newspapers. Maybe they tell us things no one else will, whether it's pretty as pink or black as death. What do you think of that, Mr. Watkins?"

"I think you're a remarkable woman," he says. "I had no idea."

Jessie whips out her fan warily. Acutely aware of his unspoken words: a remarkable woman for a whore. "A woman of nice sensibilities and simple desires has to keep up on the culture, Mr. Watkins," she says coolly. "These are modern times. We sporting women have got to amuse you men. You can't imagine how easily men get bored with sex." With a weary sigh, she lies down on her rose-colored satin divan, stifling a groan of pain. "You'd rather gamble or drink."

"Really." He stands. Comes over, stands over her as she reclines on the divan. Like a lord claiming his territory. Lord Watkins, is he? "Boredom," he says, "is the province of the unimaginative soul."

Jessie pulls herself up, though the pain is excruciating. "Look here, Mr. Watkins. I've been in the biz for damn near twenty-five years. In case you don't get it, I own the Parisian Mansion on Sutter Street and cribs on Morton Alley and this boardinghouse, which thankfully is my very own residence after many years in the saddle. And a respectable place. I own what I own, I'm a citizen of the United States of America, and I can drink any man in San Francisco under the table. I am the Queen of the Underworld, Mr. Watkins, and don't you forget it, sir."

He toasts her. "Tomorrow we die."

"That we do," she says, "and you must pay. Too bad about your boodle book being pinched. But how do you propose to pay, Mr. Watkins? Other gentlemen pay me two months in advance. The rent is twenty-eight dollars a month for the suite. Private water closet and bath. And your board."

"Miss Malone," he says, returning to his chair. "All the money I had was in that wallet. The porter said the dip who took me is known as Fanny Spiggott."

"Sure and the fainting pickpocket." Permits herself a mocking smile. Mr. Saint Louis, London, and Paris. "Bamboozles the best of them. That little chit."

"Then you know I'm not lying. Look, my father owns several properties here."

"How nice for you."

"The mortgagors defaulted during the '93 crash. I'm going to collect back payments and renegotiate the terms or repossess. It's as simple as that."

"But in the meantime, sir." She will permit this pup no slack.

"That trunk I'm lugging? When my mother died, she left me her junk. Father doesn't want the stuff. French and English antiques, dusty eighteenth-century bric-a-brac. Maybe some of it is worth something. Know where I can sell it?"

"Take it to the Gump brothers," Jessie says at once. "One thirteen Geary Street, near Union Square. But let me see it first."

"All right." Sly look. "As for your advance on the rent, I've got something else that might interest you." He leaps to his feet, clatters down the stairs. Clatters back up again, bearing a square of canvas tacked to wood stretchers.

"Have a look," he says.

A painting: a bare-breasted woman with haunted, dreamy eyes rises up from a frothing sea. She clutches a young man with her long-fingered hands. But wait. At her naked waist, the woman transforms into a sea creature with shining scales, an elegant fanned tail. A mermaid. A living mermaid, not a carving of stone, but a werewoman with pink and silver flesh, filled with strange passions and ambiguous intent. She is lust incarnate. She is death.

"Jar me," Jessie murmurs, "a mermaid."

"Do you like it?"

"I've never seen anything . . ."

"She's yours. Picked her up for a song on the Left Bank. She's not old. In fact, she's the latest thing. Symbolist."

Jessie calculates and calculates again. A modern French nude with an erotic fantasy theme? Sure and that's worth two months' rent at Miss Malone's boardinghouse for gentlemen. Not that she'd sell a mermaid, not for a minute.

"Done," she says briskly, taking the painting before he can change his mind.

But Mr. Watkins relinquishes his treasure readily. "And here," he says, handing her a stack of magazines. "I'll sweeten the deal. This is only to lend since I don't want to give them up. But if you like strange writing about other worlds . . ."

She takes the stack. *The New Review*, a British magazine from January through May, 1895. "What is it?"

"This fellow named H. G. Wells wrote a novel called *The Time Machine. The New Review* ran it in five installments. All the critics in London, even that curmudgeon Frank Harris, call Wells quite the genius. And it is wonderful, Miss Malone. The story goes like this: A fellow invents a machine that can take him far into the future and back again, all to tell the tale. Can you imagine such a thing?"

"Jar me. Do women have the vote in Mr. Wells's future?"

Mr. Watkins laughs. "I don't believe Mr. Wells touches on the subject. Which, now that you mention it, is probably a shame."

"Will this amuse my gentlemen callers?"

"I should say so, if they've half their wits!"

"Then I'll try it, Mr. Watkins." Jessie drains the bottle of champagne into their glasses. "Let's have a look at your rooms."

❜ ❜ ❜

Jessie shows him the suite, which Li'l Lucy speedily vacated, leaving only a hint of her scent. A parlor with some handsome rosewood tables, chairs, a chest, and a desk. A fireplace, a store of dry kindling. The bedchamber is larger, with a Belgian wool carpet in somber hues, a sturdy brass bed frame that Mariah polishes to gleaming gold. A water closet and a large claw-footed tub with running hot and cold water, though Mr. Watkins will have to schedule his bath with her other boarders, since the plumbing can tolerate only one bath at a time. Gaslamps cast a golden glow.

"Splendid," he says.

Jessie hands him the brass key. "Live up to my expectations, Mr. Watkins."

"I shall try my best, Miss Malone," he says and reaches for her, embracing her waist.

She turns away from his mouth. "I believe you've been

lonely too long, Mr. Watkins. You need to get yourself a filly."

"I never pay for whores, Miss Malone. Rochelle, my can-can dancer in Paris, gave herself freely, though I must say, I seldom touched her, if you understand my meaning."

Jessie understands exactly what he means. Mr. Heald is only too fresh in her memory and her mouth. Seldom touched her. As if the part of him that is pleasured by a woman is not a part of *him*, Mr. Daniel J. Watkins, the gentleman, the citizen.

"We'll see about that," she says. "Just between you and me, don't go gambling at the mansion. The games are rigged."

He laughs. "Thanks."

"You miss your mama, don't you?" she says softly, half hoping to hurt.

"She was a lady." He shrugs. Eyes glint for a moment and die out. "I'm starving, Miss Malone. Will you dine with me?" Turns away, crestfallen. "Oh, pardon me. I haven't got a red cent."

Tomorrow we die.

"Meet me downstairs in half an hour," she says. "I'll take you to the Poodle Dog."

She fairly flies up the stairs like a spring chicken. Dinner with a young gentleman at the Poodle Dog, where all them Snob Hill gentlemen go to dine on some of the finest French food in town. How tongues will wag when she strolls in with Mr. Watkins. She shrieks for poor Mariah, who has mounted her watch on the rooftop again. Mariah climbs down, softly cursing. Sure, Jessie knows them Snob Hill gentlemen. When they get a gander at her with the likes of Mr. Watkins hanging on her arm, they'll be panting at her door just to see what new tricks she's learned to charm such a handsome young foreign-looking man. If she's going to pay for his dinner, she might as well reap whatever harvest she can from his company.

"It's advertising," she tells Mariah, who helps her shimmy off the pink silk frock. "The American way."

"I'd watch out for that young gentleman," Mariah says, "if I was you."

"Sure and I'm watching him," Jessie says gleefully.

Tightening the waist? French ladies are tightening the goddamn waist? "Relace the corset, Mariah."

"Please, Miss Malone. Madame De Cassin says go see the doctor about the pain in your side."

"Relace the corset! Tighter! Tighter!"

Mariah does. When Jessie cries out, Mariah feeds her a dose of Scotch Oats Essence. Then they pour her into the mauve damask evening dress with lace festoons, garlands of pearls, and crystal pendants on the bust. She finds her blue diamond earrings and filigree necklace, pulls on opera-length mauve satin gloves. Stuffs her handbag with a thousand in gold. When Jessie Malone goes out on the town, she likes to go with plenty of cash. She goes downstairs to Mr. Watkins.

He's waiting, spruced and spiffy, in a black wool Prince Albert suit, an ivory silk shirt with a thin pinstripe, red silk vest, black leather boots. Slicked down his thick brown hair so that it falls behind his ears to his shoulders. The mustache is combed and groomed. He's donned a black silk top hat.

"You're a daisy, darlin'," Jessie says.

"You're a picture yourself," he says.

They step out the door of 263 Dupont Street into the dust, clouds of gunpowder, the stench of spilled rotgut. The frenzied celebration of the Fourth of July carries on well into the deepening dusk. Drunken brawls ring out from every corner. Squealing horses rear and bolt. Wives cry or plead with their husbands to come away. Men are passed out dead drunk on the street or careen in chortling packs, arms entwined over shoulders. The street hookers flirt furtively. Jessie sniffs. They are as many classes down from Jessie as Jessie is from a Snob Hill lady.

Jessie hails a hack as the elegant hansom of Mr. Jackson is trotting up Dupont Street. Abundant silver trim gleams on fine mahogany leather. Jessie hesitates, her idle flirtation with Mr. Watkins forgotten. Mr. Jackson is a good john, regular and always flush. An aging Silver King, he was a rival of one of Jessie's beaux once upon a time. He likes Jessie's parlor as much as the girls at Sutter Street, if only for revenge. Is Mr. Jackson headed her way?

Suddenly a scruffy black brougham careens through the

intersection, slamming broadside into Mr. Jackson's hansom. Horses shriek and kick. The drivers leap from their seats, seize the horses' bridles. Mr. Jackson himself dismounts from the hansom, takes his driver's whip, confronts the offending brougham and its occupants.

They spill out, three men dressed in black, queues coiled at the napes of their necks. Black slouch hats, black slippers. A wiry tattooed fellow with a knife tucked in his belt begins to berate Mr. Jackson in a high, excited gibber. A fat man with diamond rings surveys the gathering crowd. And a third man, tall and gaunt, a black eyepatch over his left socket, barks orders at his driver.

The hatchet men Jessie saw in the park! And there, crawling out of the brougham, is the tall thin lady in gray who was accosted in the park, towing the squalling Chinese wretch. Mr. Jackson's driver and the driver of the brougham begin to shout at each other, curse and argue. The driver swings at Mr. Jackson's driver, Mr. Jackson shouts at the hatchet men.

Jessie rushes over, her earlier outrage kicking up like a mule. A lady, a proper citizen accosted by tong men. What's the city coming to? What's next?

Jessie runs to the lady, takes her arm. The lady throws back her veil in the dusk. Jessie stares. The lady has pale golden skin, high cheekbones, long slanted eyes with the most amazing irises the color of shamrocks. A Chinese woman! In proper outing togs?

"They've been driving and driving, going all over town," the lady says, breathing heavily. "I can't think of what they were doing, except looking for where they could imprison us both." She looks at Jessie, beseeching. "They seem to think they own her, but they certainly don't own me."

For a moment, Jessie is sure she hears a tiny voice tinkling in the air over the lady's head. Something extraordinary about this lady! Those eyes. Without thinking twice, Jessie strides up to the tong man with the eyepatch.

"How much for her?" she shouts at him, pointing at the lady.

The eyepatch turns, surprised. He knows her. Sure and

everyone knows the Queen of the Underworld. His eye narrows. "That one?"

"Yes, the tall one, how much?" she shouts.

"Tall girl?" the eyepatch says. He spits something at the wiry fellow and the fat man, who withdraw from the confrontation with Mr. Jackson and his driver. The eyepatch nods at the wretch. "She ours."

Jessie isn't sure she understands him. Spills out eight hundred dollars in double eagles, which is probably way too much for the lady if she's consumptive or poxy. Still, she's got to get the lady out of here. She's got a feeling. "For *that* one," she says.

The eyepatch nods, grins, and seizes the gold. "She yours."

Jessie takes the lady's arm. "Come on, miss. Let's get away from here."

"Jade Eyes!" cries the wretch as the fat man wrestles her back into the brougham. "Don't go, Jade Eyes!"

"I can't leave that girl!" the lady says angrily. The tiny voice again—like a spirit.

Jessie pulls her away, out of the street. "Miss, please. There's nothing you can do for her." Jessie pats the lady's hard, thin arm. "Now you belong to me."

OCTOBER 12, 1895 ▼ ▼ ▼

Columbus Day

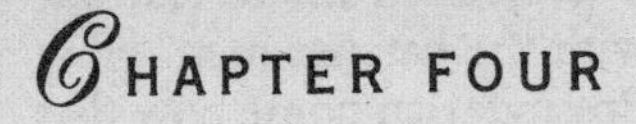

CHAPTER FOUR

Up and Down Dupont Street

This is the United States of America, 1895. Mr. Lincoln announced the Emancipation Proclamation thirty-two years ago. Casualties from the War Between the States have lain in their graves longer than Zhu Wong has been alive. Slavery is abolished in America. Every person here is free.

"Red wine!" Jessie Malone proclaims to Zhu, tossing back her cascade of blond curls. Unsatisfied with her natural endowments, Jessie pins hair switches from the Montgomery Ward catalog here and there in her tremendous coiffure. "You will go get me red wine, missy, and be quick about it!"

"Excuse me, Miss Malone?" Zhu says.

"It's Columbus Day. Don't you know anything?"

Deferentially, as is fitting for an indentured servant, "Excuse me, Miss Malone." Mutters to Muse, "Columbus Day? I can't keep these American holidays straight."

"Fourteen hundred and ninety-two," Muse whispers in her ear. "Ocean blue." Muse poetic?

Jessie looks at her askance. What must she look like, muttering to herself, rolling her eyes to the side to view whatever Muse has posted in her peripheral vision?

Zhu doesn't know what to expect from Muse since the

first day of the Golden Nineties Project when the monitor spontaneously communicated in projection mode and advised her to let the girl go off with the hatchet men. How can she secure a position in the Presbyterian home now that Miss Jessie Malone holds a two-and-a-half-year contract for Zhu's services and the madam intends to enforce it? The girl is gone, the aurelia never showed up at all, and Zhu is not virtuously serving the Cause. The Golden Nineties Project has turned out to be nothing like what the Archivists planned.

Yet she dallies at the breakfast table, overcome with a peculiar lethargy. Things always change moment to moment, don't they? At the most basic quantum level, reality is no static thing, but a flux, an incessancy, a great trembling. Spacetime spins; it ebbs and flows. In cosmicist theory, reality is One Day, existing for all eternity. Isn't that what Chiron said? Reality is a set of probabilities constantly collapsing into the timeline. Multiple universes coexist like motes of dust swirling in a sunbeam. Quantum physics has long supported this. Zhu chuckles to herself; quantum physics. You won't know the difference. You awaken in the multiverse, transformed: a self once contemplated yesterday, soon a self scarcely anticipated.

She yawns and blinks, drowsy in the morning, and hardly knows herself. Breathes the scent of red roses and champagne, peeled oranges, roast quail and butter. Who is this woman who lazes in a long silk dress at the opulent table of the Queen of the Underworld, conversing with the gentlemen boarders, sipping coffee six centuries in the past?

What a change!

Only three months ago, she stood accused of attempted murder. She, Zhu Wong, a dedicated comrade in the Daughters of Compassion. In jeans, a T-shirt, and sneakers, trudging through mud, a handgun strapped beneath her right arm, a black patch bonded to the back of her left knee. Devotee of Kuan Yin. A skipchild, a Generation-Skipping radical, supporter of the only sustainable future mother China could hope for.

Three months ago; six centuries in the future.

She tilts her head. There's music from the saloon across the street, where they've got a string quartet for the early-morning drunks. A lilting waltz, romantic and dizzying. She plays with her sleeve, the silk a luminous turquoise, the buttons on her cuff little mother-of-pearl nubs.

Only three months ago, she breathed the stink of petroleum fumes from the antiquated ground traffic Changchi had no funds to install underground. Breathed stinking air from fourthhand recyclers beneath the shabby dome over the compound where the Daughters of Compassion lived. Breathed the ever-present reek of compost, disinfectant, too many human beings living too closely together.

The perfume of red roses sends a shiver of pleasure through her.

The Night of Broken Blossoms is a distant nightmare, no longer looming over her every anxious moment. In three months, the Golden Nineties Project has taken on the quality of a dream.

Who is she?

She is Zhu Wong, of course, a modern Chinese woman. Tough, morphed for telelink, blocked for UV radiation, her eyes gene-tweaked green. Her fingernails were always caked with grit, with soil and oil, bits of plastic.

Yet she is Zhu Wong, the runaway mistress of a British gentleman, come to America by way of Hong Kong and Seattle with nothing but a feedbag purse and traveling togs in tasteful pearl gray.

Who is to say she is not that lady? Who is to say who she really is?

"In fourteen hundred and ninety-two, Columbus sailed the ocean blue," Muse whispers in her ear.

"Jar me, missy, you are a dreamy chit. I said, it's Columbus Day. The day that dago discovered America." Jessie issues orders as she polishes off her customary breakfast of five roasted quail stuffed with sauteed oysters washed down with three bottles of champagne. The madam drinks champagne from morning till morning. Her endurance is staggering, her contempt for sleep awesome. "Ten cases for the mansion, that should do the trick."

"Ten cases of red wine?" Zhu savors Mariah's thick black coffee, Colombian, strong and savory with a hint of chicory.

She reaches for the green leather account book for the Parisian Mansion that lies at her elbow on the dining table. Every morning she goes over the books with Jessie, setting out debits and credits for the madam's parlor, the Morton Alley cribs, and the boardinghouse. She doesn't mind. Finds the work oddly satisfying. Declines to use Muse's calculator. Likes to figure the numbers by hand. Checks her calculations three times.

"We've got fifty cases at the mansion," Zhu says, flipping through the account book. "Ten cases each of whiskey, rum, gin; two of champagne for the night, as usual. Do we really need red wine?"

"Of course we do!" Jessie declares with the expansive joy that always overcomes her after her first champagne for the day. She turns the bottle neck-down in the ice bucket. Mariah whisks bottle and bucket away. "I love them dagos, don't you? I told Ah Chong he's got to cook a spread at the mansion tonight. Minestrone, melon and prosciutto, yellow squash fried in butter. Veal parmigiana." Jessie's lips are still buttered from her breakfast, but her eyes shine with gluttonous anticipation. She knows of more different dishes than Zhu can remember eating in her whole lifetime. "Tortellini with pine nuts and heavy cream. Rigatoni in marinara sauce with shredded beef. Macaroni and cheese. Avocado salad and that bread they bake in North Beach dipped in olive oil. Macaroons and nougat, spumoni with candied cherries, baby rum omelettes. And red wine, missy; go get me red wine!"

Jessie pops the cork on another bottle of champagne. My fog-cutter, she calls her breakfast libation. When she comes to the table particularly haggard and groaning, she informs Zhu that a lady never feels good in the morning. Mr. Ned Greenway, tastemaker for the Smart Set, said so himself. Muse searched the Archives. It turns out Mr. Ned Greenway says a gentleman never feels good in the morning. Mr. Greenway does not approve of more than one glass of champagne for ladies. Jessie loves to twist the truth to suit herself.

Jessie splashes champagne into her glass, tops off Daniel's. Daniel usually starts his day with a half-pound of grilled bacon, an oyster omelette from the secret recipe Mariah pilfered from the chef at the Palace Hotel, and coffee laced with French brandy. Today Daniel and another boarder, one Mr. Schultz, a gentleman who books arrivals and departures for the Pacific Mail Steamship Company's China Line, have joined Jessie in quail and champagne.

Zhu studies them as they tuck into the food. Feels queasy just watching them. The only nourishment Zhu takes before noon besides black coffee is a glass of orange juice that she or Mariah squeezes fresh every morning. "No wonder you're skinny as a flea knuckle," Jessie complained, offended Zhu wouldn't try the quail.

"Go see Mr. Parducci on Union Street," Jessie says, issuing orders. "Chisel him down, he charges too much." Downs champagne with alarming speed. "Then check up on the mansion for me, missy. I've got errands to run before I make my appearance today."

"I hear the two-year-olds are running at Ingleside today," Mr. Schultz says, grinning.

"You hush," Jessie says, but Zhu already figured Jessie is off to gamble on the horses at the brand-new Ingleside Racetrack out beyond the Western Addition. Jessie's crazy for colts, shrewd at betting.

The front bell rings. A sweaty boy from American Messenger Service. Mariah brings in a letter for Daniel. He bestows a contemptuous glance at the letter and slips it quickly into his vest pocket.

Catches Zhu's furtive observation as he reaches for his champagne. She can feel her face burn, a pulse beat in her throat. Mr. Watkins is arrogant, rude, condescending, bold. Acts like he's entitled to whatever he wants. He's completely unlike any man she's ever met. He smiles at her discomfort. She casts her eyes down. Can just hear Sally Chou's sardonic laugh. "Think with your brain, kiddo, not some other part of your anatomy." Abruptly turns away and surveys the heaped table to conceal her fitfulness.

This table—beautifully set with china and crystal, linen

and flowers—is a foreign image to her. A museum relic. Zhu has never thought much about food. She finds the way Jessie and the others linger over their plates, discuss dishes, extol the virtues of taste and texture, to be odd, quaint, self-indulgent. Before the Golden Nineties Project, how often she tried not to think about food. Ignored the pounding in her stomach on many a long night, disregarded gritty water, nutribeads like chalk between the teeth, nutribars resembling the packaging in which they came wrapped—which in fact was digestible fiber you could nibble on after steaming off germs and grime and softening the bite. It's self-indulgent to dwell on food beyond your nutritional requirements; uneconomical and incorrect. The closest the Daughters of Compassion ever came to such communal feasting was the occasional surfeit of millet gruel, Mars candy bars for dessert while squatting round a trash fire.

She is not squatting round a trash fire now.

Zhu picks at a piece of toasted French bread, thickly spread with butter and honey, while Jessie regales the gentlemen with tales of betting on the ponies. Well, why not? Earlier tachyporters had not been as fortunate as Zhu. Chiron Cat's Eye in Draco had been forbidden to eat or drink during his tachyportation to San Francisco, 1967. An irony, since Chiron, a rich cosmicist heir, had been accustomed to elegant fare. A second irony, since food and drink in America during the Summer of Love were subject to modern regulations assuring quality and wholesomeness. Still, technicians at the Luxon Institute for Superluminal Applications had feared that Chi could be contaminated. The food could have contained some microbial toxin or innocuous parasite that didn't affect the people of the late 1900s due to exposure and natural immunities but could have jeopardized Chi, perhaps fatally.

"Do you know I had to carry filters and strain my water for drinking and bathing?" Chi had told her during her instructions session. "And prophylaks; I carried ten thousand with me to 1967. I had to wrap my hands every time I touched something or someone."

"What a nuisance!" Zhu had laughed

"You don't know the half of it! I wore a necklace of nutribeads. The calories were supposed to be enough to sustain me, but I was always starving. Took plenty of bellyache. Barely staved off the hunger."

But Chiron had disobeyed the injunction not to eat. He had tasted food and wine during the Summer of Love Project. "Sharing nourishment with the people turned out to be a communitarian experience that brought me closer to them," Chi had said. "Dangerously closer."

"Why dangerous?" Zhu had asked, troubled by his look.

"I got involved," Chi had said.

"Got involved," Zhu had joked. "What does that mean?"

"I fell in love."

Chiron Cat's Eye in Draco? The tall cool sophisticate, in love?

She eats the toast. Eyes drift to Daniel again.

"You hear me, missy?" Jessie says. "Jar me, maybe she needs to go back to bed."

"Maybe she does," Daniel says.

"What did you say, Miss Malone?" Zhu says.

"I said, you see that Li'l Lucy is off the booze. You stay off the booze, too." Jessie loves to be peremptory and demanding in front of an audience. Makes her feel powerful, in control. She knows very well Zhu never drinks.

Daniel watches sardonically, but Mr. Schultz pays no attention. Zhu is just the Chinese servant.

"I beg your pardon, but I never drink," Zhu says. The polite words stick in her mouth, false and gluey. Zhu is a modern woman. She is not deferential, frightened, shy, or weak. She does not possess the mentality of a servant. She does not need to play this game. Does not need to stay at the boardinghouse at all. She can run away any time she wants to.

❘ ❘ ❘

Jessie had bought her from the eyepatch. Just like that. How much was Zhu worth? Eight hundred dollars in gold. She should have been flattered. Since working as Jessie's bookkeeper, she'd seen the bill of sale from Jessie's Morton

Alley cribs recording the purchase of a cross-eyed girl for two hundred dollars, along with a quantity of silk underwear from Shanghai.

But at first Zhu had been furious, as well as frantic to find Wing Sing. Jessie had seized her by the elbow, taken her upstairs to the spare bedroom in Mariah's suite. Pointed out the decanter of brandy on the nightstand and promptly locked and bolted her in for the entire night.

Locked up in the room, Zhu had argued with Muse. "I don't understand you, Muse. Finding Wing Sing is the whole reason the LISA techs sent me on the project. How can you just let her go?"

"And what were you to do? Single-handedly fight three heavily armed hatchet men?" Muse reasonable. At first.

"I should have gone with her."

"And be forced into prostitution?"

"*Prostitution?*"

"What do you think Wing Sing is?"

"She's a teenage girl."

"Z. Wong, she's a prostitute," Muse had said.

Zhu could not accept that. "What's all this stuff about her dowry, then?"

"She was tricked. Her mother was probably tricked, too. But maybe not. Could have sold her. Parents did."

"Are you sure?"

Muse barely patient. "Z. Wong, I thought Chiròn explained. Most Chinese women and girls in San Francisco in 1895 were smuggled in to become prostitutes."

"He said slaves."

"Yes, household slaves when they're between the ages of five and eleven or twelve. Sex slaves after that."

"*Damn.*"

"Immigration authorities not informed, false names, et cetera. Would you like to view your instructions holoid? I will download *Zhu.doc* for you."

"No." Zhu had paced. Had smelled the sour odor of her own frustration. "Then who is this woman who 'bought' me?"

Alphanumerics had flickered in her peripheral vision. "My

analysis of the Archives indicates a high probability that she is a procurer. A madam."

"She runs a brothel?"

Muse blunt. "Correct."

"Is *this* a brothel?"

Muse had posted a line of tiny print. "I don't believe so. Appears to be a residence. The more successful madams lived off premises."

"Then *she's* going to force me into prostitution." Zhu had gone to the window, opened it, looked down. Maybe thirty, thirty-five feet to the ground. A fire escape at the next window over, nothing in between but ten feet of bare boards. No pipes, no gutter, no gingerbread. Nothing. Would have broken her damn neck if she had fallen.

All she had were the clothes on her back, a wealth of data in the monitor, a feedbag purse filled with antibiotics, antivirals, antitoxins, neurobics, and a very nice mollie knife. No rope. No pitons. Not even a tube of superglue. She had gotten out the mollie knife, torn the sheets off the bed.

"Z. Wong, please refrain from causing damage to these premises."

That was when a cold needle of fear had stitched down her spine. Why was the monitor so recalcitrant?

"Muse," Zhu had said. "I swore I'd fulfill the object of my project. I want to get the charges against me reduced. I *want* to serve the Cause."

"Be calm, Z. Wong," the monitor had said.

"I'm getting out of here, I tell you. I'll not prostitute myself. And I've got to find Wing Sing." Had felt terrible about abandoning the girl, for whom she felt a rush of protective loyalty. A prostitute? Tricked? She was just a kid.

"Steady, Z. Wong," Muse had purred. "This is the turn of events. I cannot verify your presence in this residence. But neither do the Archives refute it. This is the turn of events. Try some brandy. It's probably quite good."

"I don't drink," Zhu had snapped, outraged at the monitor's complacency. Almost as if Muse were encouraging her to abandon the project. Why? Was Muse testing her?

"You don't know San Francisco in 1895," Muse had

pointed out. "You could get yourself killed out there. Please review 'The CTL Peril' subsection of the tenets." Obstinate Muse. The monitor had posted the text in her peripheral vision again.

That had shut Zhu up. She had paced about the locked room while Muse had rattled on about the technopolistic plutocracy and how employment during the hyperindustrial era closely resembled slavery.

"Imagine taxes so high that income was halved," Muse had argued. "Imagine housing costs and personal costs so high that the rest of people's income was consumed in daily living expenses. That it was normal to assume debt in excess of one's personal resources. Imagine such an economic structure engineered by the same class, the same interests. *That* was the heyday of the technopolistic plutocracy. The woman who bought you is a small operator." Muse had added, "But she'll come after you if you try to run. She knows this town. She knows the police. She could get you thrown in jail. You don't want to go to jail, Z. Wong. Pest Hall, the jail for Chinese? Believe me, you don't. Besides," and this, Muse's final argument, had clinched it, "you're more valuable to her for your intelligence. Convince her of that, and she won't force you into prostitution."

In the morning Jessie Malone had unlocked and entered Zhu's room. Introduced herself. Splendid in a lavender shirtwaist and billowing skirts, reeking of patchouli oil and booze. She had Mariah bring in a tray with fresh-squeezed orange juice, coffee. The black maid had silently regarded Zhu with deeply sympathetic eyes.

"I got a feeling, missy," Jessie had said in a blunt manner that Zhu had liked in spite of herself. "There's something I see in you. Maybe you can tell me what it is."

Zhu had reprised her alibi, embellishing. Added a British education in Hong Kong. She had declared, "I didn't sell myself, Miss Malone. I have no intention of doing it here."

"Did it for love, what a shame," Jessie had said, circling her, appraising her as though she were a cut of beef. "Jar me, you are a skinny one. It's true my johns don't much like the skinny ones. No consumption? No pox? No syph? No plague? No worms?"

Chastened by her night with Muse, Zhu had quickly established that she was fit and capable. "My name is Zhu," she had said.

Jessie had tried it out. "Shoo? Zoo?"

"It means 'pearl,'" Zhu had said.

"Then I'll call you Pearl."

"Also 'pig.'" Zhu had laughed.

Jessie had liked that, too. "Jar me, I'll call you Pearls Before Swine."

"Call me Zhu. *Zzsh; Zzsh;* Zhu." She had demonstrated the buzzing noise. "Call me Zhu."

Zhu had proceeded to pull a copy of *Poems of Pleasure* by Ella Wheeler Wilcox off a bookshelf and read from it. She had set out a column of numbers, added them, and divided the result by five.

Jessie Malone had not missed a beat. She had produced a written contract, right then and there, crossed out some clauses, scribbled in others. The contract stipulated that Zhu agreed to work for Jessie as her personal servant for a term of two years, during which Zhu would earn back the eight hundred dollars in gold and reside at the boardinghouse.

"But what am I to live on?" Zhu had asked, amazed at the document.

"I'll feed ya. You got a bed."

"What about clothes? I've nothing but these. Medicine?" Zhu had cast about. She might need cash. If young women were so easily bought and sold, perhaps she could buy Wing Sing from Chee Song Tong. "Jewelry," she had tried again. "Books? Entertainment?"

"Now her highness wants jewels and the theater," Jessie had said.

"Come on, Miss Malone. Pay me a salary. *Some*thing."

Grumbling, Jessie had scribbled in a monthly stipend of fifteen dollars and added six months to the term.

And Zhu had signed. She had never held a pen like this before. You dipped the tip in ink. She had offered her hand. Jessie had taken it. And pulling herself together after the dreadful first day, the awful first night, of the Golden Nineties Project, Zhu had advised Jessie, with all due sympathy and a charm she herself did not know she possessed, that the corpulent madam should loosen her corset because the undergarment could be causing her internal organs to hemorrhage.

❙ ❙ ❙

Zhu scrapes back her chair from the breakfast table, strides from the dining room. Her face burns with anger. She will not tolerate abuse from Jessie in front of Daniel and Mr. Schultz.

Jessie chases after her, catches her in the foyer. "Hell, I'm sorry, missy," Jessie says, seizing Zhu's wrist. "I know you don't drink."

The gentlemen rise and drift to the smoking parlor. The madam's eyes pool with sorrow, contrition, a genuine perplexity. A jumble of passions plays across her face. Jessie is only forty years old, but she looks like a centenarian from Zhu's day. She slips a gold coin into Zhu's palm. "You know I like you. You're a smart kid. You're different from the rest. In the time you've been here, I've come to depend on you. I don't know what comes over me."

"I know what comes over you," Zhu says. "You want them to know you control me. It gives you pleasure."

Jessie's cornflower eyes light up. "Am I as terrible as that?"

"You are," Zhu says. Pockets the coin.

Jessie smiles at her bluntness. "I'm the Queen of the Underworld. I take crap from no one, no how."

"And I don't take crap from you, Miss Malone. I will order your wine, and I will check up on the mansion. But I am my own woman, and I have my own business in San Francisco. Don't you forget that."

Jessie's eyes turn dark, suspicious, then shrewd, all in a moment. "Never met a chit like you, Zhu," she says at last, plaintively. "You can't be more than sixteen. That's why I paid through the nose for you."

Zhu wants to say she's thirty. Wants to boast. She can expect to live to one hundred twenty or more. Her complexion is Blocked. Even a bumpkin like her from a jerkwater town like Changchi has been gene-tweaked, edited, morphed. But she swallows the boast. It is not Jessie's business how old she really is.

"I'm older than you know," she says.

❘ ❘ ❘

Zhu is climbing the stairs to the suite she shares with Mariah, intending to change her morning dress into suitable outing togs, when Daniel confronts her in the hall.

His suite of rooms is on the north side of the house. He has no business in the south hall. He smells of tobacco, liquor, a cologne evocative of some exotic spice. He does not hurry down the hall like the other boarders do. Purposefully steps into her path, his expression inexplicable.

"Good day, Mr. Watkins," she says. Attempts to pass him. The tension she always feels around him rises in her nerves, making her clumsy. She'd had a man friend once in her early twenties, but their relationship couldn't survive the rigors of the Cause, Zhu's dedication to the Daughters of Compassion. She is not ignorant of sex. Still, she cannot explain why his glance makes her heart lurch. "Mariah's not in. I believe she went out to the . . ."

"I'm not here to see Mariah. I'm here to see you."

"Is Miss Malone troubling you for the rent? I'm just the bookkeeper, there's nothing I can. . ."

"Miss Malone does not trouble me. You trouble me."

"Me?" She does pass him and hurries down the hall. "Why?"

Close behind her, he catches her wrist. "You're not who you claim. Runaway mistress of a British gentleman, by way of Hong Kong and Seattle? I think not. You're not who you claim to be at all."

Speechless. He stands over her less than a hand's breath away. She is acutely aware of his physical presence, bristling and insistent. Paranoia rushes through her. Her heart knocks.

He and Mr. Schultz are always regaling her with questions at the breakfast table. She isn't always sure her answers are correct. Damn the Luxon Institute for Superluminal Applications! Rushing her through training. *The shuttle will be ready in a day or two. A day or two?* Vital that she go at once, some hellish sum of International Bank Units spent on the project. *Muse will fill you in.* Yes, and Muse seems to have forgotten just exactly why she's here. *The Pest House, jail for Chinese. Believe me, you don't want to know.* She is a Chinese woman without family or real allies in 1895. A white American man could do so many things to her.

"I don't know what you mean," she says at last. Carefully, politely.

Daniel silent. Boldly examines her.

"Won't you tell me what you mean?" Embarrassment heats her face.

"Mr. Schultz works for the China Line. He says you don't know the proper name of the ship that supposedly brought you from Hong Kong to Seattle."

"Why, it was the *Wandering Jew*."

He shakes his head. "The *Jew*'s port of destination is Cuba, not Seattle."

She stares. How could the Archivists have been wrong about the name of her ship? They knew all sorts of details: that a runaway Chinese girl would seek refuge in the tea house in the Japanese Garden on the Fourth of July, 1895, for instance. What kind of a damn fool did Chiron take her for?

"In your room," he says. Knows he's got something on her. Knows she knows it. Immigration authorities would be very interested in a Chinese woman. Under the Exclusion Act, a woman like her is forbidden to enter the United States.

She produces her key, unlocks the suite. They enter the small parlor she and Mariah share. Mariah is as secretive as Zhu and considerate beyond the bounds of courtesy. She has created her own aesthetic in the homey room: handcrafted chairs of oak or maple, rustic rugs of braided wool, surprising wood carvings of farm animals, bold black iron tools before the fireplace, sculptural cactus and jade plants. The spare, elegant look will one day be considered as significant a form of interior decoration as Jessie's Victorian excess. But now, in this day, Mariah's parlor is merely provincial, proletarian, reflecting the taste and means of the American lower class. Zhu gestures to a chair.

"In your room," Daniel repeats. Barely glances at the parlor.

It occurs to Zhu that he's drunk. "We can talk here, Mr. Watkins. I told you, Mariah went out after breakfast. She won't disturb us."

"In your room," he says. He comes over, stands over her. Asserts his physical presence. Threatening her.

Zhu is no weakling. After years in Changchi, in the fields, in the factories, she has grown strong and muscular. During the campaign, the Daughters of Compassion insisted on self-defense training for all comrades. She could hold her own in a struggle with this man, despite his size and weight. Turns this assessment over in her mind, readying herself, bracing herself. He thinks he can push her around. Mr. Daniel J. Watkins, entitled to whatever he wants.

Poises her hands, takes a fighting stance.

He circles her curiously. She balances herself, shuffles to face him.

He seizes her wrist, faster than he ought to be after French brandy, and heaves himself at her, using the brute force of his size. The single-mindedness of his assault astonishes her. They stagger back together, she tripping on the damn skirt, he bullying against her like a locomotive.

She twists away and dashes to the door of her bedroom.

Daniel springs after her, catching her arm, her waist. He kicks the door open, flings her inside before him. She regains her balance, whirls, dives at him. Punching, pushing him out the door. But he's got his foot wedged between door and jamb. He pushes back, shoves inside.

"Fight me, mistress," he says. He laughs. "I know you don't want it. Fight me. A lady would fight me."

She gasps beneath the corset, fighting for breath. Lungs bursting against the stays. He shoves her back onto the bed, knocking the wind out of her.

And then something even stranger than the assault itself happens: the room goes black for an instant. Black, stark white, then black again.

Losing consciousness, oh *hell*!

But no, she's back. Finds herself lying in the tangle of her slip. Arousal flares up like a fever. The tussle excites her. *Wants* him. Seizes him, tearing at his clothes.

He contests her hands as though she still fights against him and not for her own pleasure.

How long since she's had a man? And it's crazy, *never* supposed to happen this way. . . . What does the Cause mean in this ancient day? She arches her back, uttering strange sounds. Rocks back, seeking her rapture.

He takes her jaw in his hand. "Don't move like that," he commands. "Only whores move like that."

She stares back into his dark eyes, startled.

"Be still. If you're a lady, you'll be still."

He rears above her, watching as she stills herself. She seizes the coverlet in both fists, grits her teeth.

Expects Muse's admonishment; none comes.

"No, you're not a whore," he whispers. "You hate it, mistress. Don't you know how much I adore you?"

❙ ❙ ❙

Zhu pulls the veil over her face and steps out onto Dupont Street, bound for the wine merchant's shop in North Beach. Thrumming with the sheer satisfaction of new sex while her own common sense assails her: *never supposed to happen this way.*

Daniel, oh Daniel.

Stop it. What has possessed her?

A trade wagon passes, the body built to look like a gigantic cigar set upon wheels, advertising Sloat's Smoke Shoppe & Sundries on Montgomery Street. Emaciated driver clad in tobacco brown. His narrow face disdainful, beaked nose raised in the quintessence of bourgeois snobbery. Whip and reins clutched in pointed little hands like a weevil perched on the end of the huge cigar.

A thin woman in a little girl's frock and stockings dawdles on the corner. Stained smile, cheeks chalk-white with pancake makeup. Zhu doesn't want to look too closely. Even from this distance, in the bright sun, she can see scabs and sores about the woman's mouth, crusted beneath her powder and rouge. No rain has fallen in nearly three months. Dust hovers over the street in a choking haze, dirty-smelling.

The funny cigar wagon turns the corner. Smythe's Sundries & Smoke Shoppe on Sansome Street. She chuckles in spite of herself. Advertising works. Doesn't smoke, but what clever sundries does Mr. Smythe stock? Perhaps she'll find some amusing . . .

Wait. The gilt lettering across the giant cigar said *Montgomery* Street, not Sansome. *Smoke Shoppe & Sundries,* not the other way around. *Sloat* not *Smythe*. The tobacco brown serge of the driver's suit bulges. Why, the man is positively stout. Soft knobby features of a Russian peasant.

What has come over her, tachyonic lag? The LISA techs warned about this side effect of a tachyportation. A disturbance of body and mind caused by superluminal drift during the ME3 Event. Could induce fatigue, disorientation, even hallucinations.

She swallows. Tastes French brandy on her tongue.

Wait! She drank no brandy with her breakfast, *never* does. Is it the taste of Daniel? But he didn't kiss her.

"Muse?" she whispers. "What's going on?"

Muse silent.

Come, now. The sign on the wagon. It's like the woman with the face glove in Golden Gate Park. The illusion of an immaculate complexion till the sun exposed her. Perhaps Zhu merely saw the other side of the wagon when the driver turned the corner, and the sign painter had fumbled his job. Perhaps two smoke shops employ this particular wagon.

Zhu runs to the corner before the wagon can clatter out of sight. On the right, she sees Smythe's Sundries & Smoke Shoppe on Sansome Street. Circles around. On the left, too. The stout driver smiles and tips his hat, pleased at her attention.

"Damn it, Muse," she whispers to the monitor. "What's happening to the cigar wagon?"

"I tried to warn you," Muse says. "He's a young man of 1895. A social Darwinist."

Zhu stops dead in her tracks at the monitor's non sequitur. "Excuse me?"

"I told you he was stalking you. Thinks he's entitled to whatever he wants."

"You said no such thing!"

"I told you to be careful. He cares nothing for you. You are less than an animal to him."

Offended now. "He says he adores me."

"He blackmailed you into having sex." Muse patronizing.

Deeply offended. "Why do you oppose me, Muse? You're supposed to monitor my progress with the project. You're supposed to *help* me."

"I am not opposed to you, Z. Wong." Muse polite. "I have only reminded you, when appropriate, of the object of your project."

Zhu strides north on Montgomery. "What about Wing Sing?"

Muse posts a calendar in her peripheral vision. "The package you ordered should have arrived at the mansion today."

Yes, the package. Perhaps what the package contains will aid her search for Wing Sing. "All right," she says, weary of Muse's recalcitrance. "But what about the cigar wagon?"

"What cigar wagon?" Muse says.

She trudges up the long slow slope, silent and troubled. Is the monitor deliberately being cruel?

How much more cruelty can she bear?

▾ ▾ ▾

The Generation-Skipping Law was cruel, but a population of twelve billion inhabiting this frail earth caused more cruelty. Depletion of ozone in the high sky, permitting leakage of excessive solar radiation through the atmosphere; that was only one consequence of too many people, too many pollutants flung into the air. Global warming had whittled rich coastlines. Waste clogged rivers and oceans. Salt water contaminated fresh. Fumes poisoned the breathing space. Chemicals, radiation, heavy metals degraded food and drinking water. Poverty crushed eight billion people. Disease wracked their lives. Hunger and thirst dogged their days and nights.

Yet still the population increased. A phenomenon of exponential growth. Fertility outpaced mortality in a cruel game of statistical tag.

At last the World Birth Control Organization held an emergency meeting and issued a mandate to the nations of the world: *control growth*. The cosmicists—the movement founded after the turn of the millennium by the first woman president of the United States—proposed a slogan: Live Responsibly or Die. Zero population growth—two children per couple—wasn't enough. One child per couple was still too many. The world needed negative growth. *Fast*.

In an unprecedented act of world cooperation and self-sacrifice by all of humanity, the Generation-Skipping Law was set into place. Under the law, two billion people were randomly chosen by lottery to forego having children within their lifetimes. They would skip a generation.

But countless people decried the plan. Charges of genetic discrimination were leveled; some suggested genocide. People everywhere were reluctant to forego all possibility of producing heirs, of continuing the family. So a compromise solution was offered: the law permitted lottery couples to harvest and preserve their genetic material. From their harvest, they could create a skipchild. Skipparents were arranged, youthful members of a younger generation. After the genetic parents died and a statutory period passed, the skipchild would be birthed in a laboratory or implanted in the skipmother and raised by the skipparents as their own.

Like all nations of the world, the People's Republic of China, under Socialist-Confucianist rulership, conceded to the law, and her people were charged with carrying out its terms. Chinese people had engaged in a one-child policy at the turn of the millennium, at times successfully, at other times less so. Chinese people felt they had already sacrificed to enforce the one-child policy long before the rest of the world.

Producing children—many children—was an honorable and ancient tradition in mother China. Children were wealth. Children were security. Children ensured proper care for the elderly. Despite degradation of the ecosystem, drought in the south, famine in the north, tradition had tarnished little over two centuries since the brown ages. Tradition had ruled with scant challenge over the droughts and famines and wars of the past two thousand years. Hadn't China always had drought in the south, famine in the north? What really had changed? In the megalopolises, the rich lived in luxurious domed estates, the poor lived on the street. In telespace, a chatboard, rather than the corner store, distributed pornography. In junk heaps, semiplast replaced plastic, which had replaced glass, which had replaced clay pottery.

Tradition: there were always intellectuals who decried tradition. And always people who clung to tradition. Many had rebelled against the one-child policy. Many more felt the Generation-Skipping Law was an attack on the family. Was unconscionable; an outrage.

Factions sprang up. The Society for the Rights of Parents organized a virulent opposition to the law and its local perpetrators. When Zhu was a kid, the Parents burned down and bombed World Birth Control clinics. Shot WBCO workers, hacked credits out of local accounts. Infected the huge and complex WBCO administrative files with viruses that turned data into chaos. The Parents had always been concentrated mostly in the south, but in recent years the movement had surged to the north, wreaking violence and terror.

Zhu Wong was born in the northern village of Changchi, an ancient place long inhabited by humanity. Undulating fields of millet and peas met the bleak concrete of superhighways and graceless processing plants. Old domes that stood over what was once wealthy real estate were now in the poor side of town. Chunky patchworked high-rises from the last building boom were nearly indistinguishable from long, depressing rows of barracks and community housing.

A skipchild, Zhu was entrusted under the law to her appointed skipparents, Yu-lai and Li Wong. Each a distant cousin in the families of Zhu's birth parents, Yu-lai and Li had been barely more than children themselves when they were chosen for their duty. They were in their early forties when Zhu was birthed in a Beijing lab and shipped to Changchi by express mail. Struggling with debts and a fierce desire to own property like so many of their sophisticated upclass friends in Chihli Province, yearning to escape community housing and the deadening life of agriwork, Yu-lai and Li suddenly found themselves saddled with a baby.

She was darling, of course. Her DNA had been carefully edited, her eyes were gene-tweaked green. A portion of her parents' life savings had been invested in equipping the newborn with intelligence, strength, physical beauty. She arrived along with a small inheritance—the other portion of her parents' life savings—provided for her care and rearing. A retrograde capitalist device nevertheless permitted in China as a reasonable means for carrying out the law, which might otherwise impose an intolerable burden on new skipparents.

Who were they really? Had they loved her? Had they ever considered her their own? Did those questions make any sense when the world groaned under the weight of twelve billion people?

Zhu remembered little about her skipparents. Recalled a few sentimental memories. A lavender kite in the shape of a fish. Her first bicycle, all silver and blue. Cultured shrimp for Saturday suppers. A trip to the Great Wall, which stood as it always had for what seemed like eternity. The excitement of her morphing for telespace when the schools of Changchi were flush with new money. Installation of a neckjack and telelink wetware. The promise of an international profession in Zhu's future. "Little face," Li would say, "why are you always so sad? Such wise eyes. What do you know?"

Sometimes Zhu allowed these memories to surface. But

mostly she remembered the day when—at the age of fifteen—she came home from school to the empty apartment. Ransacked drawers, scattered papers. Her mother's jewelry—her *real* mother—the bankbooks, the holoids; all of it, gone. Never forgot the humiliation when she went to school the next day and told the matrix teacher, "My skipparents left me." The shame and sheer perplexity kept her from tears. She didn't cry till she was twenty, long after she'd joined the Daughters of Compassion. A summer outing; someone had flown a kite shaped like a fish.

Yu-lai and Li Wong were prosecuted for abandonment, child endangerment, embezzlement, theft, skipchild abuse—a whole litany of local and international offenses. Due to her youth, Zhu was not included in the proceedings. There was a settlement. She never saw her skipparents again, but she sure saw their images splashed all over the media:

GENERATION-SKIPPING LAW IS SHAMEFUL
SKIPCHILD ABANDONED BY SKIPPARENTS WHILE
LOTTERY COUPLES CRY FOR THEIR OWN

It was when the Parents tried to make an example out of Zhu and publicized her case that she was first approached by the Daughters of Compassion. Orphaned once by the law, orphaned twice by her skipparents, rejected, harassed, and alone at a vulnerable age when everyone needs a friend, Zhu gladly fled to the Cause, to the rigors of comradeship. To contemplation of Kuan Yin.

A woman came calling as Zhu studied in the library for winter examinations. The village administrators had placed her in the custody of the cooperative to which her skipparents had belonged. Another shameful thing. Had to face neighbors and peers as a ward of the state. No longer a skipchild with a family, an inheritance, the likelihood of going off to the university. She was so depressed at the time she had actually considered taking her own life. A bona fide option according to fashionable international death cults.

The sharp-eyed wiry woman sat down next to her. Zhu glanced up from her workstation, the lesson hovering before her: an English translation of a spectacular holoid by the classic master, Magda Mira. An American writer praised for her celebration of the death force. Gory stuff, but Mira's work was as popular as rice chips. The woman was clad in a tight blue sweatsuit that showed off her astonishing biceps and well-built thighs.

"You're the skipkid?" the woman said.

She didn't need to elaborate. Zhu gathered up her bag and books, preparing to flee, although she'd waited sixteen days to get access to the workstation.

"Don't waste your time with that crap," the woman said, pointing to the holoid. "There's work to be done. Here, in our mother China. The Cause is more important than vulgar American entertainments. That has no meaning for *your* life."

"Mira praises the death force," she said automatically. Then, "The . . . Cause has more meaning?" Hesitated, despite the panic skidding through her.

"Hell, yes!" the woman said. "All the sacrifice and pain you've gone through as a skipkid means nothing if lottery couples are going to go off and have kids illegally. Let alone if parents with one kid—skip or natch—go off and have another. Talk about challenging the odds. Talk about *greed*. And they say Changchi will have another drought this summer. Don't know if they can herd rain from Siberia. *That's* the shame, ten times worse than what happened to you, Zhu Wong. Not that I'm saying you haven't been chucked one, kiddo. But the death force? That's much too easy."

Zhu remembered listening to all this with her mouth hanging open. She swallowed, her head buzzing like after a whiff of good neurobics. "You're talking about negative population growth."

"I'm talking about the Cause," the woman said. "I'm talking about enforcement of the Generation-Skipping Law, the finest gesture of civilized international cooperation ever witnessed in our sad and sorry history of the world. And the only hope for our mother China." Stuck out her hand, thick and square. "My name is Sally Chou. Born and raised in Chicago, but I came to the motherland with a bunch of Americans in the pilgrimage of '73. I'll not go back to America. I'm a Daughter of Compassion."

Thrilling pride. Zhu remembers her voice still.

"What are you doing after graduation?" Sally Chou lit a cigarette. Delicious scent of herbs, not tobacco.

When Zhu shrugged, Sally Chou said, "You're coming with me, skipkid. The Daughters of Compassion need you."

Needed *her*?

Zhu moved to the compound that the Daughters of Compassion owned south of Changchi. A wealthy Californian friend had repossessed the place after the local real estate developers defaulted on one of countless refinancings. Nothing in Changchi was particularly elegant, but at least the compound was cleaner than most, boasting a secondhand PermaPlast dome and air conditioner to match, plus the best water recycler and generator that could be procured in a provincial burg like Changchi.

"We must fight the Society for the Rights of Parents," Sally Chou said as she sat in a circle of women.

The wall-to-wall carpet laid over bare concrete had worn to the thickness of weathered silk. Zhu's skinny butt had not gotten used to the hard floor yet. She remembered shifting about, searching for a more comfortable position for her bones.

"We stand armed guard at WBCO clinics," Sally Chou said. "We chaperone clinic staff. We trace illegal fund withdrawals. We restore order in virus-plagued databases. There is no turning back for mother China. We must break the base of exponential growth."

"So what if another hundred thousand illegal babies are born?" someone said in back. "Who cares? Why should it matter?"

"Because under the principle of exponential growth," Sally said, "in a time when more people survive than die, another hundred thousand means two hundred thousand, four hundred thousand, a million six. A million six more people before we've reached our own middle age. Another million six people who weren't planned for in our little village of Changchi alone!"

"Can our fields feed another million six people when *we* don't have enough to eat?" someone else called from the back of the hall.

"Can our factories employ another million six people when we've got fifteen percent unemployment?" someone else said.

"Can our future sustain another three million people after *that*?" came a third.

Sally Chou was sweating and exhausted by the end of this rally. Zhu could not remember what happened to the heckler in back.

To the cadre, new campaigns were announced each spring at the long plywood tables, over bowls of millet gruel.

"Women must be the arbiters of what happens to their bodies," Sally Chou said. "Women must be the first to understand that having children—skip *or* natch—is a *privilege*, not a right. Women must sacrifice that privilege for the children. Not just for their own children, whom they may never see, but for all children. They must sacrifice a little part of their lives for a sustainable future. The cosmicists say, 'To give is best.'"

"Are you a cosmicist, Sally?" Zhu asked.

"We can learn from the cosmicists," Sally said, a little evasively. "We must all learn that a sustainable future rests on sacrifices we make now. Let us make those sacrifices gladly! Make them out of compassion! We must inculcate our women of China with that sentiment, they who have traditionally sacrificed so much over the millennia. They who have worked the fields like animals, subjugated themselves to the Confucian notion of family, bound their feet, and sold their bodies in the service of patriarchal institutions. All our women must sacrifice again, but not for the preservation of an exploitative state, for masculine pride, for dynasty. Now they must sacrifice for the future. *Their* future; *our* future; our *children's* future. We must win the hearts and minds of our women. All the world watches mother China. Our China must not fail!"

Our mother China. We, the women. These words and ideas thronged through Zhu like eagerly awaited guests invited to the banquet of her intellect and sensitive nature. Her own sacrifice and pain as a skipchild meant nothing if the Cause failed, isn't that what Sally said the first time they met? And if all the world watched mother China, then all the world watched her, too. Zhu, the abandoned skipchild, became a Daughter of Compassion.

The compound was comprised of scrawny gardens, a small fishpond, an ugly office high-rise, a mediocre clinic, a depressing dining hall, uninspiring recreation rooms, and a dormitory and baths for the live-ins like Zhu. Zhu thought the compound was the most wonderful thing she'd ever seen. Especially the shrine to Kuan Yin.

Kuan Yin: patroness of the Daughters of Compassion. Five-thousand-year-old goddess, a mystic presence, an intellectual principle, a metaphor, heroine of fables, source of aphorisms, focal point of philosophical thought. A political statement.

"Who is Kuan Yin?" Zhu asked as she sat on the hard floor, contemplating three images on the altar. The shrine was underground, cooled by an extra splice in the air conditioner, dimly lit, hushed.

Three images for three aspects: a seated woman in a cloak of celadon, lidded eyes closed, her left hand poised in a graceful gesture, her right hand holding a jeweled scepter. A standing woman, eyes wide open, a baby tucked upon her hip. And a crouching woman in golden armor, myriad arms raised in martial gestures.

Zhu was unsure which Kuan Yin she preferred: the virgin, the mother, or the destroyer.

"She is the bodhisattva of compassion," Sally Chou said. "She who hears all pleas."

Sometimes in fables Kuan Yin was androgynous. Sometimes she was a hunter, like the Greek Artemis, who offered women the spiritual life as an alternative to marriage. In one story, Kuan Yin was an innocent girl whose parents abused her, then sentenced her to death. Each time the executioner took pity on her, and she survived. Then, when the parents fell ill, she carved strips of flesh from her own arms and made meat soup, which nourished the parents and saved their lives.

Zhu was incensed by this story but Sally Chou whispered, "The Daughters of Compassion are strips of flesh. We are the sacrifice."

Zhu nodded and embraced the Cause gladly. Threw herself into the life of abstinence and discipline. But she never ate meat after that. Meat of any sort—red flesh, fish, or fowl—tasted too much like a sacrifice.

❙ ❙ ❙

Zhu gains the crest of Montgomery Street, still troubled by Muse and gasping for breath. The Archivists insisted she wear the corset for authenticity. A corset gives the female figure a distinctive look, even a woman as thin as Zhu. At her most anorexic her waist measured twenty-one inches. Wearing the corset, she's managed an eighteen. Perhaps she hasn't pulled the laces tight enough. The advertisements promise a reduction of up to five inches.

Runs her palm over her side. Remembers Daniel circling his hands around her corseted waist. Delighting in the bound portion of her body.

Not only does a corset restrict a woman's breathing, but the undergarment compromises her digestive tract, impinges on the bowels, uterus, liver, kidneys, bladder. The exoskeletal construction debilitates a woman's midriff muscles to the point that some long-term corset wearers cannot sit up or stand without the support of their whalebone stays. They become physically dependent upon the corset. "Braced for the day," Jessie says cheerfully.

Zhu sneezes at the corner of Montgomery and Broadway, where a procession of street sweepers bend to their task. Sneezes again. A man in a sombrero leads the way, listlessly driving a one-horse Studebaker wagon striped in red, white, and blue. Bolted to the plain flat body is a huge oak cask from which black cast-iron Niagara sprinkling heads protrude. The driver sprinkles water onto the dusty street, but without rain for three months, his efforts don't help much. Another Studebaker wagon follows, a huge cylindrical brush sweeping the refuse and dampened dust to the gutter. Still another wagon follows that, and a hunchback on foot. Clad in loose black trousers, the hunchback shovels horse manure, dust, and refuse, deposits his burden into the back of the wagon. The wagon buzzes with flies. Dust not captured by the sprinkling water rises over the street in a brown haze.

Zhu sneezes, pulls out antihistamine from her feedbag purse, as well as her freshly laundered handkerchief. Tears spill from her eyes, nose, mouth. Muse has managed at last to identify the source of her discomfort: powdered horse manure mingled with fly refuse. The fine particulate matter hovers in the air everywhere. Sometimes horses drop dead on the street and are abandoned. Along with feral dogs, the flies quickly descend there, too. It's the fly refuse that really gets to Zhu.

Zhu smelled plenty of compost in Changchi, but fly refuse was against regulations in the domes. Even the crudest air conditioner screened gross particulate matter. She's breathed plenty of carbon monoxide, carbon dioxide, and methane, but fly shit? Not till 1895.

Discordant blare of a brass band. A parade for Columbus Day wends its way up the avenue named for the discoverer, through the angled streets of North Beach. Leading the way on a prancing black stallion is the grand marshall, resplendent in a scarlet top hat and cutaway coat, scarlet sash and a blooming rosette, white breeches, high black boots. Fancy carriages follow with black leather hides and silver chasing. Members of wealthy Italian families ride within, decked out in bright silks and black gabardine, red, white, and green sashes slung over ample breasts. Nuns in crow black robes trudge solemnly behind, sacrificial victims called out on this honored day to look after their charges: little girls in white veils, each with prayer books embossed with purple crosses; little boys in black suits and green and red ties. The children sing—orphans, perhaps, Zhu thinks with a sudden pang—birdlike voices lost in the air. Jugglers follow, flinging silver balls, painted wood pins, flaming torches. Clowns costumed like the great Joey Grimaldi caper and prance, making the goggle-eyed children lining the street curbs scream with laughter. An emaciated brown bear with a muzzled snout snuffles and sways up the avenue. The unions follow, clubs and special interest groups from the Italian community, each with its triumphant spangled banner, caps and jackets, high-stepping drummers beating time to a measured strut.

Zhu follows the parade up Columbus Avenue to Union Street. In the lot next to Giovanni's grocery, a group of proper young men in boiled shirts and collars are throwing Parmesan cheeses. A fellow with glossy, close-cropped black hair carefully winds the round cheese with a piece of canvas tape. Hands the cheese to a contestant, who nestles the cheese on his forearm, charges madly, flings the cheese across the lot like a discus. The cheese whizzes through the air, bounces on the far side. Other fellows scramble to mark the end of the trajectory, chortling that the contestant failed to beat the previous one and insulting him vociferously.

"Throwing cheese," Zhu mutters. "How many nights have I gone to sleep with nothing in my stomach but a nutribar wrapper?"

"Context." Muse gentle. "You cannot judge them, Z. Wong."

Zhu turns right at the corner of Union, leaving the Columbus Day parade to promenade north to the waterfront. The street-cleaning procession has suddenly reappeared with its dreadful cart of refuse and flies. Zhu sneezes once, twice, three times. Her feedbag purse slides off her shoulder, her button boot slips on something slick.

Not spillage of the street cleaner's drudge, thankfully. No, the macadam is slick with squashed grapes, grape pulp, dark mottled juice. Zhu spots the wine merchant's address and steps inside.

The place is in a frenzy. Front counters of the retail establishment have been rolled back, revealing a warehouse of surprising size. Huge wooden presses are busily employed by boisterous flushed young men. Young women, hair caught in red and black bandanas, fill and cork green bottles as fast as they can. Racks of new wine bottled at the start of the season are stacked in front for ready sale. Other women fill great wooden casks with the rest of the runoff from the presses for proper aging. Bins bulge with blue grapes the wine merchant carted down from Napa vineyards.

"*Ciao, bella*," says the wine merchant, jovial, doused with juice and sweat. "Take a taste?"

New red wine will surely taste dreadful, and, anyway, she doesn't drink. "No, thank you, Mr. Parducci," Zhu says. "Let's talk about how much."

"Fifteen cents."

"Ten."

He's drunk. "Done."

Each bottle from Mr. Parducci, then, costs ten cents. Each drink from the bottle—and Jessie's girls will pour at least ten tiny drinks per bottle—will cost two bits. Jessie will be pleased no matter how the johns cough and gag. After two drinks, most won't notice. Jessie will make sure they imbibe at least two drinks.

"You work at Miss Malone's, *bella*?" the wine merchant asks, handing her a receipt. He's a handsome, graying man, though he's eaten too well over the years. Due for a coronary any day. Well, maybe not. They've proven wine consumption is good for the circulation. "You too nice." He surreptitiously hands her a coin as his dark round wife watches suspiciously. "Nice girl, you go find work in a nice house on the hill. You good washee washee, no?"

"Actually, no," Zhu says, surprising herself. "I am Miss Malone's bookkeeper and administrative assistant. Sometimes I negotiate contracts, as well. I am not her washerwoman, Mr. Parducci."

Cannot hide a smile—yes, of pride and triumph—as the wine merchant's jaw drops. Perfect English. He could not be more surprised if she were a talking dog.

"Happy Columbus Day," she says, oddly cheered, and signs the wine merchant's receipt. "*Ciao*."

Zhu supervises the wine merchant's driver as he loads the cases of red wine onto the wagon. She climbs up next to him, directs him to Sutter Street. The ride is welcome. The afternoon has warmed beneath the sun. Dust billows.

The wagon clatters up to the Parisian Mansion. A conservative brass plaque announces the moniker between two simpering but decently clad cupids. Such plaques have been the subject of dispute. Lucy Mellon, also known as Lucy Nelson or Miss Luce, caused a stir by mounting a plate on the door of her Sacramento Street house announcing "Ye Olde Whore Shoppe," but the bulls made her take it down. The Parisian Mansion's plaque is the most conservative item of its exterior. The large, flat-faced Italianate was abandoned by respectability some twenty years ago. Cast plaster cupids smile from every available newel post, archway, portico, and window hood. Jessie calls the paint job Pompeiian red. The elaborate gingerbread is detailed in ivory, eggplant purple, and a startling pale teal. The place is positively hallucinogenic. Zhu can't quite decide if it's dreadful or magnificent. Daniel only remarks, "How else does one paint a *maison du joi?*"

Zhu steps down from the wagon, carelessly swishing her skirts. Flash of her calf, the lace hem of her slip. She is completely swathed in traveling togs, collar tight against her sweaty throat. Still the driver—a dashing dark-eyed boy with olive skin and a mass of black hair—stares. She wears silk stockings of a pale pink hue. Gets them from Jessie. Far more comfortable than the heavy black cotton stockings ladies are required to wear.

The snippet of pink silk, however, is an unmistakable sign to the driver: homewrecker. A sporting lady, moll, owl, fallen angel, hooker. Whore.

Suddenly she is fair game.

"So, miss. How much?" Awful look; and such a dashing boy just a moment ago, chatting about the weather.

"You may take the cases round there." Zhu points to the trademen's entrance around the side of the Parisian Mansion down a well-swept narrow alley.

"I have time." Fishes a coin from his shirt pocket. "I have money."

"I *don't* have time. Please hurry up."

He steps into her path, slaps a fist into his palm. "What you think you are? I said I got money."

She waves the receipt at him and stamps her foot. "Take

the cases there or I'll speak to Mr. Parducci about you." Looks around on the street. "I'll call the cops."

"Cops ain't gonna help you. Whore." He spits. But he shoulders a case and follows her down the alley. Deposits her purchases in the kitchen, one by one, sweat and anger rolling off his skin.

She watches him, tapping her toe. Reaches into her feedbag purse for the mollie knife, closes her fingers over the smooth little shaft. The mollie knife is intended for healing, but she can hurt him with it if she has to. Was going to tip him. Says instead, "Get out."

And all over the glimpse of a pink silk stocking.

❘ ❘ ❘

Zhu steps into the kitchen of the Parisian Mansion.

"How you, missy?" Ah Chong, Jessie's chef at the mansion, abandons his huge cast-iron pot boiling with wide flat ribbons of lasagne noodles and comes to inspect her delivery. A wiry, shrunken fellow with a graying queue that reaches the backs of his knees when he unwinds it from around his head, Ah Chong's usual expression is dour. Now he positively scowls. "Miss Malone want me cook Eye-talian. I no cook Eye-talian. French my special!"

"I know, Ah Chong. But you know Miss Malone. Once she gets something in her head."

Ah Chong's scowl deepens. Even Zhu, Miss Malone's right-hand girl, cannot save him. He scurries back to his pot, cursing softly. Ah Chong is one of the best French chefs in San Francisco, hired away—Jessie claims—from Marchand's. Jessie covers her overhead at the mansion with the girls, but she makes her real profit from food and drink. The mansion has a culinary reputation. Ah Chong's specialty is terrapin in heavy cream, sweet butter, and sherry cooked in its own shell the way the Reception Saloon does, but with a certain herb Ah Chong will not reveal. Jessie traditionally serves Ah Chong's terrapin at 4:00 A.M., along with sentimental songs on the calliope, after the gentlemen are well soused and sexed.

"Five dollars for a tiny dish of turtle meat?" Zhu had asked, scandalized when she first observed this ritual. "Never mind that this species of turtle will be endangered in less than a century and never seen on menus again."

"In danger," Jessie had said. "In danger of what?"

"That must be a thousand percent markup, Miss Malone."

"Jar me, missy," Jessie had said, furrowing her brow, perplexed at Zhu's stupidity, "we gotta make a profit!"

Zhu inspects the large immaculate kitchen. Ah Chong's sideboard is already stacked with zucchini and yellow squash, Roma tomatoes, sacks of every kind of dried noodle known to North Beach, casks of olive oil, salmon and crabs dripping with bay water, a saddle of veal, a side of beef, fat garlic bulbs, bunches of scallions, bouquets of oregano and basil fresh from the farms in Cow Hollow below Pacific Heights, rounds of Parmesan like the ones the young gentlemen played discus with. Ah Chong can cook anything. He would be a celebrity in Zhu's day.

She goes to the parlor, takes one look. Hears tinny chords from the calliope, but everything is otherwise still and deserted. Not much business this time of day. Stale tobacco smoke clogs the room. Stink of spilled champagne, animal scent of sweat. Spittoons spattered and slick. Ashtrays overflowing.

Another busy night, apparently. No one has freshened the place up.

Zhu storms down the hall to the back bedroom where the parlormaid sleeps. The biz is the biz, as Jessie says. Jessie would be appalled at the mess. Zhu raps sharply on the door. "Myrtle." Silence. "Myrtle?"

Tries the door. The knob turns. Rustle of bedclothes, soft laughter. Myrtle a young black woman trained at the Palace Hotel. Zhu peers. Myrtle trying to hide another body on the bed beside her. Zhu doesn't want to know.

"You better attend to the parlor before Miss Malone shows up," Zhu says. "She'll have your hide."

Doesn't wait for an answer. Goes back out to the parlor. Red velvet curtains drawn over the windows, shielding all but a stiletto of sunshine. The lamp with the scarlet shade turned down low. The city has forbidden red lights over the doors of sporting houses, so Jessie—and every other madam in town—has resorted to placing the table lamp with its scarlet shade by the window, tossing lacy undergarments over the telegraph wires outside. The parlor is a dark scarlet cave. Gaslight much more flattering than sunshine or electricity.

"Hey, Miss Zhu," says Li'l Lucy. She sits at the calliope, staring at the keys as they depress and spring back. She's turned the volume down. People sleeping upstairs, or maybe she cannot tolerate loud noise. Her fingers curl around a jigger of whiskey. Raises the glass. "Drink?"

Zhu shakes her head. "You're stinking, Li'l Lucy."

She pouts. "Some Snob Hill gorilla hit me."

"It's barely past noon, kiddo."

"Day and night don't mean nothin' to me, Miss Zhu."

"Where is Daphne?"

"Jarred if I know, Miss Zhu."

Daphne is the door maid for this shift. She is supposed to manage the biz in Jessie's absence. Screen the men, serve drinks, take money, monitor the girls. Jessie will be furious.

Li'l Lucy's personal maid, Pichetta, drifts in. "There you are," Pichetta says coldly, eyeing Li'l Lucy with barely concealed contempt. Pichetta is a swarthy young Peruvian woman. Hint of a mustache over her lip. Her black and white maid's uniform fairly crackles with starch. "You need to get some sleep, Lucy."

"Ain't tired yet, Pichetta," Li'l Lucy drawls.

"Hmph." Pichetta surveys the parlor with disgust and commences emptying ashtrays, though that isn't her job. Myrtle bounces into the parlor. "Hmph," Pichetta says when she sees Myrtle. Together the maids carry off Persian carpets to the patio to be beaten free of ashes.

Li'l Lucy giggles. "You gonna tell Miss Malone?"

"I don't have to," Zhu says, raising her eyebrows at Pichetta's retreating back.

"Think she's a rat?" Li'l Lucy rises, stretches, finds the bottle, pours another round. She wears a thin, low-cut silk slip over her corset and garters. Large dark bruises stain her flabby thigh, her drooping arm, her thick neck. Large dark circles under her pouchy eyes. Even with her golden hair gleaming in the semidarkness, Li'l Lucy doesn't look good at nineteen years old.

"I don't think so, I know so," Zhu says.

"No," Li'l Lucy says. "I gotta pay her wage out of my draw."

Zhu shrugs. "She's hired to rat on you."

"Says who?"

"Says no one," Zhu says and finds a silk fan. She flips it open, circulates the stale air in front of her face. She knows; she does Jessie's books. That's the standard arrangement: each girl pays Jessie a flat fee per day—scaled to her marketability—to stay at the Parisian Mansion for the stipulated term of her contract. Each pays extra for clothing and personal effects and must take what Jessie supplies her. Such items are of the best quality and taste, and Jessie gets a discount for purchasing in bulk. Still, the wardrobe is expensive. Jessie pays six thousand dollars a month for all the dresses, undergarments, stockings, fans. Jessie demands the best, demands that everything be fresh and new. Each girl also pays for a personal maid, is required to keep one to groom and dress her properly. Jessie pays the maids extra for information. The maids don't have it so bad. Pichetta is probably thrilled Li'l Lucy has turned out to be a drunk.

Jessie is considered one of the fairest madams in town. A girl's fees and tips are all hers after expenses paid to Jessie. But Jessie does not tolerate deadbeats. She does not tolerate slovenliness or bad behavior. She does not tolerate any girl who doesn't earn out a pro rata amount of her expenses each night. The biz is the biz.

Zhu silent. Li'l Lucy is in trouble.

"Why in blue blazes"—Li'l Lucy laughs, pouring more whiskey—"would Pichetta rat on me when I pay her? Huh? That don't make no sense, Miss Zhu."

"Take care of yourself, kiddo," Zhu says. "Just take care of yourself." Under Tenet Three of the Grandfather Principle, she is not permitted to help Li'l Lucy, but Zhu doesn't really care about Tenet Three. No, in truth, she doesn't know what she can do for Li'l Lucy. Li'l Lucy walks down a destined path from which Zhu cannot dissuade her. "Did anything come for me by post?"

"Why, yes," Li'l Lucy says, stumbling to the foyer. There, behind the umbrella stand, is a package wrapped in string and brown paper. She picks it up. "You mean this?"

"Yes!" At last, the package Zhu has been waiting for. Muse was right, it's here!

Li'l Lucy shakes the package. Listens for telltale sounds. "Is it from a gentleman?"

"Give that to me!" Zhu grabs at it.

Li'l Lucy holds the package high over her head. Zhu lunges. Li'l Lucy ducks, giggling. She darts across the parlor, stops. Tries to read the label. Li'l Lucy hasn't had much more than a third-grade education. Parents just didn't care, who knows. Zhu doesn't know how Li'l Lucy got here from wherever she once came from. "Luh . . . lucky gold—see, I know gold, Miss Zhu—tray . . . tray . . . tray . . ."

"It says Lucky Gold Trading Company. Now give it here!"

"Why, that's in dirty ol' Chinatown. Did you order somethin' from a Chinaman's store? Oh, I bet I know. You got yourself some of those pink silk bloomers everybody's talkin' about. Can I see? Oh, please, please?"

"It's not, but would you like some?"

"Oh, yes, Miss Malone keeps promisin', but you know what a skinflint she is."

"Give me my package, and I'll get you some pink silk bloomers."

"You would do that for me?" Tears start in Li'l Lucy's eyes. "You really would?"

Zhu looks away, embarrassed. Li'l Lucy is like a beaten animal. The slightest kindness overwhelms her. "Is your bedroom empty?"

"Help yourself," says Li'l Lucy.

Zhu rushes upstairs with her package, finds Li'l Lucy's room, locks the door behind her. She dared not request delivery at the boardinghouse. If Jessie intercepted the package—and Jessie has to know everything that goes on at her private residence—she would never understand. Instead

Zhu told the clerk at Lucky Gold Trading Company to deliver the order in her name to the mansion. For a manservant employed there. She tears at the string, rips open the paper.

There, in crisp brown wrapping paper, is a pair of loose trousers made of soft blue denim and a long matching tunic. Specially cut—nice and loose—to her measurements. A *sahm:* the customary garb of the men of Chinatown. Cloth slippers with straw soles, too. She rips off her hat and veil, the cloak, the shirtwaist, the strangling collar, the skirt, the underskirt, the slip, the garters and stockings. Almost guiltily unlaces the corset, tears it off, breathes gratefully.

"You must maintain authenticity, Z. Wong." Muse stern.

"I don't need to wear a corset in these clothes." Zhu insistent.

But she cannot worry about Muse now. Slips everything on. Such freedom! Is this really the freedom she enjoyed three months ago before she stepped onto the bridge over the brook in the Japanese Tea Garden? Everything so loose and free. The sleeves of her new tunic hang inches below her fingertips, covering her hands. She unwinds her braid from her head, lets it hang down her back like a queue. Rummages in the package. Joy! The clerk didn't fail her. She picks out the soft felt charcoal gray fedora with a high crown and a broad brim. A Western-style hat commonly worn in Chinatown. Pulls the fedora down low, smooths the brim down lower, covering her brow and eyes. Rummages again. The final touch: a pair of spectacles with round lenses tinted a beautiful watery shade of sea green. She slides the glasses down her nose, perching the nosepiece at midbridge. Between the hat and the glasses she manages to conceal nearly half her face. Conceal her gene-tweaked green.

Stands before Li'l Lucy's mirror, slouching, lowering her chin. Tries on slump shoulders to go with the *sahm*.

Looks unspeakably crude. Looks like a slim Chinese man, any one of the tens of thousands who crowd Chinatown. Looks anonymous.

Zhu tucks her traveling togs in a corner of Li'l Lucy's closet. Silently pads downstairs. Slippers whisper on Persian carpets. Li'l Lucy sits at the calliope, the half-empty bottle at her side. Between Myrtle and Pichetta, the parlor is tidy again, fragrant with fresh roses and lilac water.

Daphne the door maid, a robust German woman with a harelip, has materialized. She sits on the couch, sipping a mug of beer.

The doorbell rings. Li'l Lucy leaps up, checks her face in a gilt-framed mirror, smooths tears from her eyes.

"Company, girls!" Daphne yells. Slaps Li'l Lucy's butt as she ambles for the door.

Three women stumble out of their bedrooms and down the stairs, cursing, pulling on silk chemises, hands fluttering at their hair.

"I ain't had more'n four hours sleep today."

"Honey, I ain't had more'n four hours sleep this year."

They laugh and groan, striding past. Someone bites into a clove. Zhu bends to examine a brass spittoon. The women pass her without a glance. As if Zhu were invisible.

Zhu goes back down Dupont Street to a completely different sector of this long thoroughfare.

From a block away she spies the Stick town houses huddled on narrow streets, the exotic jury-rigged rooftops. A pall hangs before the intersection at Dupont and Post streets—an invisible curtain, a wall, intangible but very real. The boundaries are so well marked—California to Broadway, Kearny to Powell—that when a tong war rages or bubonic plague breaks out the bulls simply barricade all the intersections like this one. The street sweepers never venture here with their Studebaker wagons, brushes, and Niagara sprinklers. The shadowed cobblestones are always slick with mud, butcher shop blood, fish juice, spittle.

Zhu steps across the intersection into Chinatown. What Chinese people call the City of the People of Tan: Tangrenbu.

Enters a peculiar silence. The sounds of the city—horses trotting, bootheels clattering—are suddenly hushed. Somber men stride by in blue denim *sahms*, straw or cloth slippers, queues wrapped tightly around their heads or trailing down their backs. They wear felt fedoras like Zhu's, brimless embroidered caps, or the coolie's broad straw cone.

She is overwhelmed at once by a distinctive stench: raw refuse infused with sandalwood, the spice of ginger, cloying incense. A sickly sweet smell mingles with scents of roast pork and frying peanut oil: opium. Opium is legally imported by those willing to pay the tariff, smuggled by those who would rather keep the extra twelve dollars a pound for themselves. Nowhere else has Zhu smelled such a unique blend of odors. The essence of Tangrenbu.

Chinatowns are scattered throughout the West, but only San Francisco's Chinatown is known as Tangrenbu. For decades Tangrenbu has been the primary port of entry. The bachelors who fled the war-torn, drought-ridden homeland in the 1850s came to California—*Gum Saan* or Gold Mountain—seeking their fortunes. They panned streams in the Sierras, found rich veins behind shafts deserted by impatient forty-niners only to be terrorized, cast from their findings, or murdered by gangs of white mountain men. They planted vegetables, coaxing lettuce, onions, and celery from soil abandoned by less diligent farmers. They set up small factories—dubbed sweatshops because they worked long hours for little pay—producing boots, trousers, or cigars. They willingly performed women's work—cooking and cleaning—and opened restaurants, or laundries of such efficiency that fine gentlemen along the West Coast no longer sent their shirts to Hong Kong for proper washing, starching, and ironing. The bachelors toiled for sixteen hours a day laying track for Mr. Huntington's transcontinental railroad, taking half the wage—a dollar fifty a day—that white workmen demanded. And when the Golden Spike was driven, the great task completed at last, they went back to their port of entry, to the home away from the homeland, to the only place they could go. They went to Tangrenbu.

To those with a poetic bent, the enigmatic industrious aliens—mostly young men who came without their families, wives, or children—were Celestials. To politicians and to white American laborers, they were the Yellow Peril.

Few Americans were feeling poetic in 1873 when Jay Cooke, who financed the Union army, squandered $15 million on five hundred miles of Northern Pacific track and failed to float a bond issue of $100 million to complete the job. Mr. Cooke announced that his bank could not pay depositors on demand. The subsequent bank panic caused a stock market crash. Debtors defaulted on loans, business owners slashed payrolls. Bankruptcy and unemployment were rampant. The ensuing depression lasted a grueling five years, and in its wake arose militant sandlot movements, angry mobs, violent gangs who roamed the cities seeking loot and revenge. There were riots, hangings, stonings, burnings. The unpropertied white male of European descent who dominated the American workforce welcomed no one new in an increasingly competitive job market.

The Celestials threatened not only white working-class European immigrants, but the wealthy and their politicians whose racism was based on new philosophical notions of ethnic superiority. For propertied white male intellectuals, Mr. Darwin's theory of evolution had exciting implications. Social Darwinism suggested that existing societal structures were the result of natural selection. Those who ruled did so because they were fittest. The poor, the unpropertied, women, and nonwhite people were destined for humiliation and servitude in the natural order of the world. It was inevitable, even proper, to continue their oppression.

Demagogues were quick to point out that the Chinese never intended to become true Americans. And there was just enough truth in that assertion to fuel flames of intolerance. Many bachelors *did* come to Gold Mountain solely to make their fortunes. Any fortune made, any profit however small, was promptly sent back to homeland and family. He who prospered well enough went back to the homeland, too. No one lingered who did not need to in Gold Mountain despite its mild climate, its rich soil, its teeming waters. The tug of tradition was powerful. Reverence for the homeland, for ancestors and patriarchy, was so great that the luckless ones who died in California had their bodies cremated and their consecrated bones carefully packed and sent back to China. No Chinese man wanted to be buried in Gold Mountain. There were clans in Tangrenbu who got rich on the funeral preparation and export of men's bones.

Zhu strides up Dupont, joining the throng. Men everywhere. She seldom sees a Chinese child or woman. The Exclusion Act of 1888 forbade the immigration of Chinese women and children. Men who through luck, perseverance, or happenstance had settled permanently in Gold Mountain could not send for their families even if they wanted to.

Did Daniel blackmail her? Or does he adore her? What should she believe?

Wandering along Dupont in her Western lady's clothes in the past three months, a shopping basket on her arm, Zhu had been a barely tolerated intruder in Tangrenbu. Yet, veil drawn over her face, passing for Caucasian, she never feared for her safety, either. Neither whore nor slave, she had been untouchable. The bachelors had given her a wide berth.

But she could not venture down certain alleys where the cribs are, where Wing Sing could be. The proprietors would always turn her away, block her path, or unceremoniously escort her clear out of Tangrenbu. When she had asked about a girl in apple green silk, all she got was a blank stare or a frown.

Now an anonymous bachelor, Zhu can go anywhere. No one turns her away from any place in Tangrenbu. Now hands beckon, shadowed doors swing open, secret smiles greet her as she hikes up the sloping block of Dupont Street.

"Well done, Z. Wong." Muse admiring. "Your disguise works."

Yes! For the first time in three months Zhu doesn't have to hurry through Tangrenbu, doesn't have to hunch her shoulders. She saunters at her leisure. She belongs. She ducks out of the pedestrian traffic, pauses on a street corner. Takes off the tinted spectacles so she can see past the shadows. Looks around.

A certain splendor adorns the heart of Tangrenbu. From the plain facades of the Stick town houses extrude elaborate balconies painted green or yellow. Bulletins of vermilion paper punctuated with ebony calligraphy cover every available wall, announcing local and international news. Gilt signs and flowered lanterns hang in doorways. Gleaming brass plaques of the T'ai Chi tacked on lintels bring good luck. Silk streamers tied to railings drift in the wind amid wind chimes made of abalone shell. Potted geraniums, stunted fuchsia, cineraria, starry lilies seek sun in stray nooks and corners.

Elaborate gingerbread, a curving roof, gilt balconies adorn a joss house—one of the multidenominational shrines in which those who worship any number of deities may stop, rest, contemplate. Zhu peeks into the joss house, sees the glimmer of the shrine tucked in back.

A few fancy shops can be found amid the vegetable stalls, fishmongers, and butcher shops. Zhu pauses. Windows display brocades and embroideries, jade and ivory carvings, painted porcelains, pearl and coral jewelry. She scrutinizes a rack of brooches. Is that the flash of multicolored glass on golden wings, the golden curves of a tiny woman's body?

The aurelia!

But, no. She rubs her forehead, pushes the fedora back. Eyes deceiving her. It's only an elaborate dragon, jade and gold. Lovely; but not the aurelia.

She presses on, turning off Dupont, striding freely through a labyrinth of alleys previously denied to her. Sees the wizened fortune-teller in his black skullcap and denim *sahm* crouching on the sidewalk with his low table, basket of bark, an oracular tome. He had summarily expelled the white lady. Now the fortune-teller looks up at the bachelor and grins, his mouth a black slash. He waves her on. This is the place Muse identified in the Archives: Spofford Alley.

She hears reedy voices, birdlike but ominously monotone, "Two bittee lookee, flo bittee feelee, six bittee doee." Tiny clapboard shacks line the alley, two or three cribs per shack. Each crib is six feet wide, set with sturdy narrow doors relieved only by small barred windows. Girls in black silk blouses stand at each window, beckoning and murmuring, "Two bittee lookee, flo bittee feelee, six bittee doee."

A skinny arm snakes out between the bars, seizes a handful of fabric on Zhu's sleeve. "China girl nice," the girl says. Pulls her blouse up to her shoulder with her other hand. Slack little breasts, a well-defined rib cage. Front teeth missing, bruised cheek. Hair pinned in a slovenly bun. Even white powder cannot conceal deep dark circles beneath her slit eyes. Consumption, probably. An old woman materializes out of nowhere, smacks the girl's arm with a stick. The girl whimpers, draws her arm back into the crib. Whispers to Zhu, "China girl nice. Five bittee doee."

Zhu recoils. Her blood boils. Inside her pocket, she rolls the mollie knife in her fingers. A vision: rip open these cribs, lead these young women to safety, to refuge, to the light.

"I'm sorry, Z. Wong," Muse whispers. Posts a page of text in her peripheral vision, scrolls down the tiny print. "Please review the Tenets of the Grandfather Principle."

The tenets. Under Tenet Three of the Grandfather Principle she cannot affect any person in the past, including aiding, coercing, deceiving, deterring, killing, or saving him or her, except as defined and authorized by the project directors. She cannot take out her mollie knife, cannot tear out these bars, cannot free these pathetic women from their bondage. Like Li'l Lucy, they are on their own.

"The tenets," she mutters to Muse. "You know what your tenets remind me of, Muse?"

"What?" Muse impassive.

"Your tenets remind me of social Darwinism," Zhu whispers. "People are where they are because that's where they belong."

"You're a tachyporter, Z. Wong," Muse says. "The Archives support. . ."

"The Archives," Zhu says, disgusted. She tours the alley, examining the unfortunate occupants at every barred window. Murmurs, "Wing Sing? Is Wing Sing here?"

"I Wing Sing!"

Zhu looks at the swarthy, broad-cheeked girl. Must be Mongolian. Definitely not the girl she met in Golden Gate Park three months ago. Three months! Yet Zhu has been so sure she would recognize her. Now with every strange new face her confidence falters. But this is definitely not the one.

A voice, "I Wing Sing!" And another, "I Wing Sing!"

"I'm sorry," she says, "no. No."

She flees Spofford Alley. The fortune-teller gives her a

reproving look, then shrugs. She trudges on to Bartlett Alley, to Brooklyn Alley, to Stout. Always the same shacks, barred windows, grim little faces poised in cribs reciting fee scales.

So many girls. But Wing Sing is nowhere in sight.

She rejoins the shifting throng on Dupont Street.

"Careful, Z. Wong," Muse whispers.

With a start she sees them before she can register what Muse means and her intuition, long honed by the Changchi campaign, sounds a warning: the wiry fellow, the fat man, and the eyepatch. *Hatchet men*. Hands purposefully tucked in their jacket pockets, they march behind an elderly gentleman with a gold embroidered cap and an air of self-importance. The boss. Other men on the street yield to the entourage.

Zhu stands back, too. She hesitates, drawn by curiosity. The eyepatch approaches, his good eye peering about with uncanny acuity. She tries to shrink into the shadows, but he zeroes right in on her. She yanks the fedora over her brow. Dons the tinted spectacles, brusquely pushes them up her nose so the lenses cover her eyes.

Too late.

He fairly pounces on her, backing her up against a shop window. "Jade Eyes," he says.

"Excuse me, sir, but I don't know you," she says. Tries to lower her voice. He stands so close she can feel the hard curve of the grip of the gun tucked into his waistband.

"You know me," he says. Taps the frame of the spectacles with a long fingernail. "Jade Eyes."

"Be friendly," Muse whispers in her ear. "Ask him where the girl is."

"We . . . we are all strangers here," Zhu says. Tries to smile. "All far from our home. You; me; Wing Sing."

"Yes," he says. Glimmer of surprise. Looks her up and down, checks out her *sahm*, the fedora, the spectacles. Shakes his head. An astute look springs into his eye.

She takes a deep breath. "I'm looking for Wing Sing."

"Why?" he says.

"I need to talk to her," she says.

"Why?" he says. The wiry fellow and the fat man gather behind him, look curiously over his shoulder. The boss waits, annoyance creasing his brow.

"I . . . She's my friend," Zhu says.

The eyepatch shrugs. "She our girl. We pay gold."

"I have money." Zhu fumbles with coins. Jessie gave her a double eagle after breakfast. Mr. Parducci gave her a bit. Odd reprise of her own encounter with the dark-eyed delivery boy. "How much for her?"

The eyepatch laughs when he sees her coins. His face grows taut, stern again. "We pay two thousand in gold, Jade Eyes. She sixteen. Pretty girl. Make much gold for Chee Song Tong."

Zhu gasps. Two thousand dollars in gold? She has earned exactly forty-five dollars over three months as Jessie's bookkeeper. What can she say? At last, "I . . . I miss her. I just want to talk."

"Talk of what?"

"Talk of mother China. Talk of family."

An unexpected sheen in the eyepatch's eye, though he frowns, tosses words over his shoulder at the others. Dismissed by him, uninterested in her, the wiry fellow and the fat man rejoin the boss, who resumes his promenade.

"You pretty girl, too, Jade Eyes," he says. "You should not wear rags." He hesitates, then reaches up, touches her cheek, her lip. "I should not sell you to Jessie Malone."

Suddenly aware of his fierce masculinity. And of the value—in gold—that he places on her femininity. He is one of the bachelors, too, after all.

"Where is Wing Sing?" Zhu says. "Please tell me."

"She not here," the eyepatch says. "You go to Selena's. You go to Terrific Street."

❙ ❙ ❙

"Muse," Zhu whispers as the hatchet men stride away, "check 'Terrific Street.' Check 'Selena's.'"

Alphanumerics flicker in her peripheral vision. Muse scans its Archives. Zhu watches the directory zoom by. Still makes her a little dizzy. All manner of file names in there, some with strange extensions like *.memory1025*. There is the instructions holoid, *Zhu.doc*, at thirty-five thousand bytes even. Muse locates and opens a file, *San Francisco.1895.geography*, searches the data.

"He means Pacific Street." Efficient Muse. "I believe he means a 'chop suey palace' on the border of Tangrenbu and the Barbary Coast. The women are Chinese or Japanese, maybe some Koreans and Filipinos, but the clientele is white. Your disguise may not work there, Z. Wong."

"I'm not a client."

Zhu hikes north on Dupont Street to Pacific, turns east. *Bang, bang, bang.* She whirls at the muffled sound of gunfire, crouches against a shop. Sniffs for gunpowder, but there's nothing. Must be a shooting gallery in a basement below the cobblestones, one of the cavernous illegal halls where white men mingle with Chinese men to practice their skill with firearms. Denim-clad bachelors in an uncharacteristically jovial mood stream in and out of another doorway set below street level and jingle coins in their fists while a sentinel stands watch at the door. Gambling den.

Again she approaches that invisible boundary between Tangrenbu and white San Francisco. Can no longer see the touches of colorful Oriental splendor. The distinctive stench fades, too. From here the Barbary Coast stretches down to the docks, a dense collection of dancehalls, saloons, gambling dens, opium dens for all races, hideouts, and bagnios.

Poised near the corner of Dupont Street and Columbus Avenue like a halfway house between Oriental and Occidental vice is the plug-ugly Stick Victorian with its brass plaque announcing, "Miss Selena." Neither the excesses of the Parisian Mansion nor the calligraphy above the cribs on Spofford Alley. The red lamp over the door is not lit. Miss Selena has not yet stationed a red lampshade by the window, but lace bloomers dangle from the ledge of a second-story window.

Zhu knows her way around a brothel. She pulls the fedora low over her forehead, pushes up the spectacles. Seizes the heavy brass door knocker cast in the shape of a rooster. Squares her shoulders, tries on a manly frown.

A middle-aged Chinese woman, golden skin tight over her

cheekbones and chin, peers suspiciously out the door. "What you want?"

"Miss Selena? I need to see Wing Sing."

"This place not for you, boy. You go to Tangrenbu. You go to Spofford Alley."

"No, I'm her . . . brother. Cousin; I'm her cousin from Shanghai. I have news of our family. May I speak with her?"

"Her time not free, cousin."

"I have money." Produces a coin.

Selena studies her contemptuously, then slams the door. Locks click. She brusquely swings the door open and stands aside.

Zhu enters a parlor far more elegant than one would suspect from the street. Rosewood furniture, painted porcelains, the usual red velvet drapes mixed with unusual swathes of silk. Chinese carpets with calligraphic and floral designs, more somber and muted. A relief from the gaudy arabesques of Jessie's Persians. Heady scent of plum incense. A musician sits in a corner on the floor, softly playing a moon fiddle.

The wall hangings and painted screens are also a departure from Jessie's obsession with female nudes. Here Oriental couples copulate on mountainsides, by brooks, in barnyards, in the midst of battlefields strewn with bloody corpses. European erotic art of this day seldom shows the Caucasian man explicitly engaged in carnal pursuits.

She hears whispers, a laugh. Slowly—feeling like a bumpkin—she turns from the pornographic screens. Golden-skinned girls lounge about in embroidered silk robes of scarlet or black. They wear thick white pancake makeup, glossy black eyepaint, vermilion lip paint so shiny it looks like lacquer. Dolls. Shiny ebony hair impeccably lacquered and styled in astonishing waves and winglike coiffures.

A black maid in uniform serves plum wine, coconut pastries, bits of meat or fish wrapped in won tons. A portly gray-haired gentleman relaxes in his shirt and vest on a scarlet divan, drinking and smoking, picking at hors d'oeuvres, making his selection from among the girls. Zhu glances quickly. Mr. Heald? Jessie will be miffed! She keeps her head down. He couldn't possibly recognize her, could he? She pushes the spectacles up her nose again and peers at the girls herself.

"Wing Sing?" she says in a husky voice. "I want to see Wing Sing," she repeats to Miss Selena.

"She there, cousin," Selena says sarcastically. The madam points. "Five dollar, please."

Zhu produces more coins. Anxiously studies the girl. White makeup is spread so thickly over Wing Sing's face, bright lip lacquer defines her mouth so falsely, her hair is so bizarrely primped that Zhu isn't sure for a moment. After the dirty little face, the disheveled braid? Not sure at all. The girl hardly looks human, let alone sixteen.

The cigar wagon; making love with Daniel; herself in a long silk dress. Dizzy for a moment, a *ping* behind her forehead. Zhu rubs her jaw.

"Wing Sing?"

The fantastic creature called Wing Sing shrugs disdainfully. The other girls giggle and whisper, eyes darting. The gray-haired gentleman—it *is* Mr. Heald—yawns, exposing big yellow teeth, and holds out his cup for more plum wine. Wing Sing dutifully takes Zhu by the hand and leads her upstairs to her bedroom. Lies down on the bed like a mannequin.

Zhu closes the door, takes off the fedora, shakes out her hair. Takes the spectacles off her sweaty face, revealing her eyes, her gene-tweaked green. "Remember me?"

The girl sits up, leans on an elbow. Her painted mouth drops open, her eyes widen. "Jade Eyes?"

"Thank goodness! Don't yell. Call me 'cousin,' okay? You *do* remember me?"

Wing Sing nods but fearfully glances at the bedroom door. "Okay, cousin," she says. Someone listening at the keyhole, apparently.

Surge of relief; she is the same girl. She *remembers* Zhu. "Don't worry, I paid Miss Selena. Are you all right? How are they treating you?"

"I do okay," Wing Sing says. In fact, she looks well-fed, healthy and sleek beneath the doll mask. No bruises, as far as Zhu can tell. No disease. "Chee Song Tong pay much gold for me." She actually glows with pride. "Miss Selena treat me nice for that. I sign good contract. Very lucky, Jade Eyes! I earn much gold. Then I go home."

Go home. Zhu has got to get this girl to the home, to the Presbyterian mission. But how? "How many johns do you see in a day?"

"Oh, ten, maybe. Maybe twenty."

"Wing Sing, ten or twenty? There's a big difference."

She only shrugs. Not the scared teenager anymore. Even to herself she's a commodity. "I earn much gold."

"Wing Sing, I thought you had a dowry," Zhu says, perching on the edge of a chair. "You still have your box of jewelry, don't you?"

The girl nods. She leans over, reaches under the bed, pulls out the rosewood box.

Zhu sucks in her breath.

Wing Sing flips open the lid, flashes the contents at Zhu. "This jade, this real gold."

Was that the curve of a golden wing? Zhu reaches to take the box. But Wing Sing claps the lid shut, promptly shoves the box under the bed.

"Let me see it," Zhu says.

"No." Suspicious look. "Why you want to see my dowry?"

Zhu sighs. "Well, with such a fine dowry you will find a husband, a man who will be happy to marry you. You will have your own daughter, your own place in life. Your own home."

Wing Sing stares, black eyes roiling.

"Wing Sing," Zhu says, "isn't that what you want?"

The girl's eyes dart away.

"I'm not trying to humiliate you."

The girl shifts uncomfortably, examines her nails, finds a file on the nightstand.

"Tell me. How did you get here?" Zhu asks, cajoling her. "How did you end up in the hands of Chee Song Tong?"

"I like all northern girls," she says, leaning back on the bed. "I my mama's girl. One day a man come to her. He want to marry me. She cry, but she say okay. She give me dowry, and I go. Then this man sell me in Shanghai to another man, who take me to San Francisco. It is the way; it is my fate. Same for many girls here." A little noise at the door. "Okay, cousin," Wing Sing calls out without conviction. "Listen, Jade Eyes. At first I scared. At first I want to run away. But now I see what I must do. I very lucky! I finish contract with Miss Selena. Then I go home. I get rich, Jade Eyes!"

"You're not going to get rich, Wing Sing," Zhu says. "If you stay here, you'll never go home. You'll never have your own daughter. You'll never have your own home."

Wing Sing's face darkens.

Zhu leans forward. "It's going to wear you out, Wing Sing. It's going to wear you out and make you sick and you will *never* get rich."

She sticks her fingers in her ears. "No."

"Twenty johns a day? How can you stand it? Don't tell me you like it. Did you bleed at first?"

"I . . . make . . . gold. . . ." Unplugs her ears, runs her fingers through her hair, dislodging the coiffure.

"You have a beautiful dowry," Zhu says. "Real jade, real gold. A dowry for your husband. Don't you want to take your dowry and get out of here?"

"No . . . no . . ." Starts to cry, carefully wipes the tears away before they ruin her makeup.

"Get out of here, Wing Sing. Get out before it's too late."

"How can I? Chee Song Tong kill me!"

"If I could arrange it," Zhu says, "if I could get you safely out of here and find a new life for you. Would you come with me?"

"I don't know, Jade Eyes. . . ."

"A new life, Wing Sing. Where you'll be safe from Chee Song Tong. Where you'll learn things and grow up like a normal girl. Where you'll eventually find a husband and have a family of your own. You want that, don't you? Don't you want that?"

Trembling, Wing Sing stares at Zhu as though she has just offered her the moon.

"Don't tell me you want to stay here," Zhu says. "I don't believe it!"

"Oh, Jade Eyes. Yes, I go. You really take me?"

"Of course!"

Someone knocks furiously at the bedroom door. Wing Sing shrinks back on the bed, huddling, curling up her legs. "Okay, cousin!" she yells in a quavering voice.

Zhu raises her hands: *Be calm.* "Not now. I've got to go get help. But I'll be back for you."

"You promise?"

"I promise."

"But I cannot run, Jade Eyes. You will carry me?" She stretches her legs.

And that's when Zhu sees her feet. In the Japanese Tea Garden, Wing Sing's feet were unfashionable peasant's feet, sturdy and whole. Made for days of standing while planting peas or millet, for walking across the whole country if she had to. Zhu clearly recalls the straw sandals threaded with green silk. Big bare feet, long knobby toes.

There is no mistaking the awful crippling inflicted on a young girl. The toes bent under the rest of the foot and brutally tied there with strips of cloth. The bone of the arch slowly bowed and broken over many long torturous years.

Wing Sing's feet are bound.

A Premonition

Selena barges into Wing Sing's bedroom. "Time is up," she announces and stands with her arms akimbo. Taps her toe, face taut with disapproval. "You go now, cousin."

Zhu hastily jams the fedora on her head. Panic skitters through her. Glances up from the impossible vision of Wing Sing's bound feet to the girl's face.

Wing Sing gazes back at her curiously, head cocked to one

side. A little smile curves her lips. The painted doll again, lacquered, masked. A stranger.

"I said go now, cousin," says Miss Selena, raising her voice. "Louie! Louie?" Calling the bouncer.

An eager young tong man with superb muscle tone shows up at the door.

"I'm going, I'm going." Zhu's mouth is dry. She fumbles with her spectacles. "Remember what I told you about home," she says meaningfully to Wing Sing.

But the girl merely purses her lips and shrugs noncommittally. Well, of course; she mustn't let on in front of the madam. Still, the girl's sudden contempt is too convincing.

Zhu stumbles downstairs and out onto Terrific Street. Midday sun slants down through telegraph wires, the lacy red foliage of a Japanese maple tree. Shadows dance and bob on the macadam. From the Barbary Coast a block away, sounds of men guffawing, a woman shrieking, tinkle of an ineptly played piano. A sulky reels down Pacific Avenue, the horse kicking clouds of dust into the face of the driver, whose livid complexion and dazed expression indicate an excess of drink. Zhu jumps out of the way, sneezing violently. Three burly white men stumble drunkenly out of a bar down the block, stand blinking in the day. One spots her and points. The others turn and stare. A lone Chink is what they see, somewhat out of his turf.

"Muse," Zhu says, "how do I get back down to Sutter Street from here without going through the Barbary Coast?"

Alphanumerics flit through her peripheral vision. "Go back to Dupont Street," Muse whispers, "through Tangrenbu."

I should not have sold you to Jessie Malone. "I don't think I want to go there, either."

"Take Columbus Avenue to Montgomery," Muse says. "Hurry."

The three drunks stroll toward her. Gleam of teeth beneath enormous mustaches, hands flexing. She practically sprints to the corner of Columbus and turns south, heading back downtown. At Montgomery, pedestrian traffic thickens. She loses them. Pauses at the stairwell in front of the

Wells Fargo Bank where a half dozen gentlemen have parked themselves for a smoke in the sun. Finds a secluded corner on a far step. Huddles on chilly granite. Pulls the fedora to the side, shielding her face. Cups her hand over her mouth.

"Muse," Zhu says, "the girl I just spoke with is not the same girl we located in Golden Gate Park."

"She is Wing Sing," Muse says.

"No! Not the same girl." Shiver of uncertainty at the monitor's nonchalance. "She isn't, is she?"

"She is as much the girl as any other." Muse infuriatingly calm.

"What about her feet?"

"She's got feet, hasn't she?"

"Damn it, Muse, you've gone buggy on me."

"She's got feet, hasn't she?"

Yes, she's got feet, bound feet. And Zhu is going to have a word with Chi about the monitor when she gets back to her day.

"All right," she says to Muse. "What about the aurelia?"

"Didn't you see it in her dowry box?" Muse says.

"No, I didn't see it."

"Did you *not* see it?"

Flash of gold, a gleaming curve. "I didn't *not* see it, either," Zhu says, exasperated.

"Then she is as much the girl as she can be."

"You make no sense!"

"I recommend that you review your instructions." Muse the stupid bureaucrat.

Zhu expels a breath. "No, no. I don't want to read pages of text. The print's too small."

The directory scrolls across her peripheral vision.

"You're giving me a headache, Muse!"

"I'm activating your holoid capability. Relax your left eye, please."

Zhu has not taken advantage of this feature Muse possesses, though the monitor has offered it on several occasions. Queasy feeling in her gut. A throb commences behind her left eye like the start of a migraine.

"Turn toward the building," Muse says, "please."

Data download through her optic nerve and project through her retina. And there! A tiny holoid field streams from the pupil of her eye, hovers in front of her face. The holoid field is a slim block of glowing blue light. Zhu can see Muse's directory in the holoid field. White and gold alphanumerics race by as several banks of files scroll.

Muse retrieves the file containing the instructions holoid and downloads it:

Muse:\Archive\Zhu.doc

Right, there it is: thirty-five thousand bytes even. Zhu blinks, straining to see as the field fades away and the holoid commences. But, wait. The file contains thirty-five thousand two hundred and forty-two bytes.

"Muse?" she says. "Wait a minute. It's not the right file."

But Muse does not hesitate, or perhaps the sequence is already invoked. The holoid pops up before her eyes: the room swathed in gauze like the inside of a cloud. The hydroplex housing the Luxon Institute for Superluminal Applications floating in the middle of the bay. Rose-hued corridors. The hush of wealth. Chiron Cat's Eye in Draco, tall and pale, his waist-length red hair, eyes like sapphires.

Shock of seeing herself—her old self. Just a glimpse, since the point of view of the holoid was over her right shoulder. Her ragged hair, ragged hands. Dirty blue jumpsuit, the prison uniform.

Ah. Her . . . self.

She had not liked him. She had resented him. She could barely bring herself to be polite.

"Please understand, we cosmicists are conservationists," he is saying in the holoid. Precise, modulated voice. Groomed hands, so elegant.

Anger chokes Zhu now as she watches the session, watches the two of them converse. Mostly watches herself watching him. He had done most of the talking. Had not liked him? No, she had loathed him! Took a deep and abiding dislike to the man. Instantly, as if she knew he were an enemy. As if—sudden realization—as if he were devious, scheming to lure her into some terrible plan hatched by the Archivists and the LISA techs, those haughty cosmicists in their modern platinum palace. A secret plan. And what was her role? She was not in on the secret. She is just an anonymous Chinese woman.

Zhu's left eye feels gritty. She rubs it. The holoid vanishes, then reappears as soon as she raises her eyes again.

But why would she hate the man? Had she hated him then? She had never laid eyes on Chiron before that moment, yet somehow she knew him. As if she had a memory, but not a memory. Could not be a memory, because she had no experience on which to base it. As if she had a premonition.

"There was a Crisis," Chi is saying in the holoid.

Zhu leans forward. Frowns. Does she remember this part?

"The Luxon Institute for Superluminal Applications," Chi says, "had been engaging in tachyportation experiments. They'd undertaken a project called the Save Betty Project. One of the preeminent physicists of t-port technology, a woman named J. Betty Turner, had proposed a project that had special meaning for her. When she was a girl, she had accidentally killed a woman. The tragedy had obsessed Betty her whole life. As she grew older she became depressed, agitated, even despondent.

"When it turned out the LISA techs could actually t-port someone to the past, Betty wanted to try it herself. She wanted to return to the day of the accident and save that woman. The Archivists researched the problem, found that no significant repercussions had been generated by the incident, and tendered their permission. They installed a tachyonic shuttle."

In the holoid Chi raises a small cigarette to his lips, inhales deeply.

Zhu starts, closes her eyes. Chi *smoking*? Then suddenly she recalls the smell, a lovely scent of cloves. He had offered her one, hadn't he? And she'd refused because she didn't smoke.

Opens her eyes. Scent of cloves; one of the girls at the mansion had bit into a clove. The holoid streams from her left eye, instantly materializing before her.

"No thanks, I don't smoke," she says in the holoid. Her voice muffled.

"Betty t-ported to the day of the accident," Chi says, blowing smoke rings, "but she did not return. She was the first recorded case of a Closed Time Loop."

"But . . . what happened to her?" Zhu says in the holoid.

"She died. She died in the past. Oh, the LISA techs and the Archivists were appalled, of course. When Betty didn't return from her t-port, everyone reviewed their research, their perceptions of the project. Some who knew Betty well saw her as cheerful and enthusiastic just before leaving. Others insisted she had been panicked that she wouldn't succeed."

"And that was the end of it?"

"Oh, no," Chi says. "The LISA techs sent another t-porter who brought Betty back into her personal Now so that the natural order of her life could be restored. But because we disrupted a CTL—which by definition has no beginning and no end—we tore a hole in spacetime. The Save Betty Project polluted all of reality. And one day, the fabric of spacetime itself split. And *another* reality, a dreadful spacetime like a corrupted version of ours, intruded into our reality. Entities from that reality, from that Other Now—entities we called demons—began preying upon our reality. And then the Archivists began to witness other peculiarities—data disappearing out of the Archives.

"We faced a Crisis—the annihilation of reality as we knew it.

"The Save Betty Project was never supposed to have had such a far-reaching catastrophic impact. But it did. Before all of the Archives unraveled and the Other Now could take us over, I was drafted to t-port to 1967."

On the cold granite steps, Zhu nods. Remembers this part. Pretty sure she remembers. "The Summer of Love Project," she whispers.

"The Summer of Love Project?" she says on the holoid.

Chi nods, his head wreathed in smoke. "The Archivists had always noticed the dim spots. After the Crisis, they began to witness wholesale disappearance of data that had once been there. They called these phenomena "hot dim spots." They traced one of the most radical hot dim spots to San Francisco, 1967, the Summer of Love. They targeted a girl."

A girl; again a girl. Zhu remembers her feeling of hostility had deepened. She might have been an accused criminal, but she was still a Daughter of Compassion and her hackles had risen. "Always a young woman, Mr. Chiron?" she says on the holoid. "Someone anonymous, dispensable, disposable? Is that how you cosmicists view women, after all?"

"No," he says, "cosmicism was founded by a woman. And the girl was by no means disposable. In fact, her life was crucial to the continued existence of reality as we know it. I was sent to protect her life and the life of her unborn child. She was supposed to be pregnant. And she had gotten pregnant over the summer but she'd had an abortion."

"So what did you do?"

"I arranged things so that she got pregnant again. That was my duty as a t-porter."

"You keep calling her a girl. I hope you mean she was a young woman. Like in her twenties or something?"

"No," Chi says. "She was a teenage kid."

"Did the father marry her?"

"No," Chi says.

"You made sure an unwed teenage girl got pregnant just because the Archives said she was supposed to be?"

"I never wanted anything bad to happen to her. I had come to love her. But when I returned to 2467, she was pregnant like she was supposed to be."

Zhu had been stunned by his story, she remembers that clearly. *Like she was supposed to be.* Some expression of outrage had risen to Zhu's lips. Her revulsion for this man, for all cosmicists, had simmered. Shooting people around like faster-than-light human cannonballs. Swooping in on people in the past.

But before she says anything in the holoid, suddenly—and of all the strangeness of their session, this was the strangest thing of all—Chiron searches his pockets. Incongruously, like an old-timey stage magician pulling a dove from his sleeve, he produces something shiny and commands, "Look at this."

Zhu stares at the holoid.

The aurelia. The decadent Art Nouveau brooch with

elaborate butterfly wings. Hadn't oppressed African laborers scraped that gold, those diamonds from mines owned by white colonialists? Didn't the bits of stained glass resemble the windows in churches that preached charity but extorted money from the poor? And the golden woman at the center. Her fatuous face, her exposed body. Her outstretched arms burdened by the wings. Her legs poised as though bound at the ankles.

"Why, it's horrible," she whispers.

But surely she hadn't thought that at first. She had been dazzled by the aurelia.

"It's horrible," she says in the holoid. Her hand reaches for the aurelia. "What a dreadful depiction of a woman! It's like she's being crucified. Crucified on the cross of beauty."

Zhu reaches into the holoid, fingers swiping through light.

Chiron holds the aurelia away as though teasing her and, with an imperious expression, slips it into his pocket.

"*She* will have it," he says.

Muse closes the file. The holoid disappears. Zhu pulls her fedora back on her head, lowers her hand, turns away from the wall. The men smoking on the stairs rise and saunter away.

Zhu's head throbs. Why all this fuss over a trifle, a mere bauble, a piece of decadent jewelry? It's not pretty at all. It's repulsive.

Bad taste in her mouth. *You chose a young woman, someone disposable, dispensable.* And on that first day of the Golden Nineties Project in Golden Gate Park, Muse had been more concerned about the aurelia than about Wing Sing. More concerned about a gold object than a young girl's life.

"Move along there, Chinaboy."

Zhu looks up. A swarthy young man stands over her. The wine merchant's driver, sweaty and belligerent. Working hard on getting loaded. His clothes are stained with a hard day's work. In his hand he's got a shot of something from the saloon across the street. By his side stand four equally muscular and belligerent pals.

"Look at 'im, Joey, he's got himself a pipe dream." The

driver kicks her thigh with the toe of his boot. "I said move along, Chinaboy. We want to sit here."

Zhu pulls her fedora down low and stands. Glances up at him through her green-tinted spectacles. Should she rebuke him for kicking a lady? Whip off her disguise?

But the driver's eyes are opaque with his loathing of Chinaboys. He doesn't remember the lady or the fallen angel. He doesn't see Zhu at all.

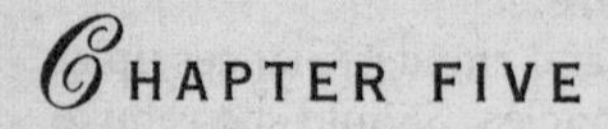

Strolling Along the Cocktail Route

"You going to get up, Mr. Watkins?" Mariah says. Disapproval strikes sparks in her ebony eyes. "Or you going to lie about all the day like a sick puppy?"

Daniel lounges in a sashed jacket on the satin settee in the smoking parlor. Lets loose a forlorn doggy howl for Mariah's benefit. Can't get the auntie to crack a smile. Has he ever seen her teeth? He grins fetchingly, hoping to inspire her, but she continues to glare at him, tapping her toe, holding the tray he ordered in arms that seem to bear just about any weight.

"Dunno," he concedes.

Will this flat feeling of oppression ever lift from his soul? Limp; every shred of ambition he might ever have possessed drained from his blood by this vampirish mood. Listlessness that refuses even to sharpen into something more severe against which he could at least rebel. The crudely scrawled letter from the messenger at breakfast lies half-crumpled at his feet. Stomach queasy; quail stuffed with sauteed oysters. No wonder Miss Malone is so well endowed. Should have had his usual omelette. Ah, but perhaps that's the cure? Something drenched in butter, would that settle his gut? Champagne giddiness, stiff douse of brandy; all of it worn away. Drowsy ache behind his eyes. Peculiar anxiety in his heart like a moth thumping on the glass of a lone lighted window. He needs a cure for that, too. His heart.

The servant girl, Zhu Wong. Chinese—one of the inferior races. But wholly unlike any coolie he's chanced to speak with. A woman; but unlike any woman he's known. Yet, a woman. A woman, surely.

They want to suffer pain, that's what Krafft-Ebing writes in his scholarly treatise, *Psychopathia Sexualis*. Sacher-Masoch's novels—not to mention those of the great Zola, the great Tolstoy—amply bear out these assertions. Women want to be taken. They are by nature masochists, hardly knowing their own minds, thus instinctively subordinate to men. Authorities like Lombroso, Ferrero, Schopenhauer, Proudhon, Michelet, Comte, Spencer—dare he go on?—have *scientifically* proven the feeblemindedness of women. Craniologists, too, the eminent Carl Vogt. Woman's skull is so different from the male that she might as well belong to another species. Smaller skulls, smaller brains.

Mama crying, always crying, muffled sobs in the night. He shivers. In the end all he remembers of her is pain. How her pain grieved him, Father's only child, a boy with the mother's beauty, her cheekbones, lips. Her weakness, too? A boy whose beauty his father had always observed with a scowl and a wary look in his eyes.

Yet pain was her natural province. He must remember that. Krafft-Ebing is quite explicit.

Rubs his eyes. He dwells too much on himself these days. Dwells too much on the past, which is dead and gone, never to be repeated, never to be remade. Too many memories now that he's away from the scowling father and the mother—*Wasn't I good, Danny? Wasn't I good to you?*—begging for his loyalty with her last breath.

They want to be taken, subjected to force. Schopenhauer has written extensively on the subject.

She—Zhu Wong, is not a whore. But the former mistress

to a gentleman, perhaps a man like himself. And thus tainted, not truly a lady. Of course *she* led him. Led him down the path. As much as she hated it, she wanted it. Knew how to get it. With every glance of her strange eyes, every languorous gesture, she'd spurred him on all these months. What could one expect in such close quarters?

Inevitable, what happened this morning.

She hadn't cried. Had to be all right, then, hadn't it? Authorities say so. Does she really hate what gives him such pleasure? Her hands on his shirt, unbuttoning. Or is she something other than the women he's known? Something other than a woman?

Listlessness closes over his soul like a fist. Krafft-Ebing warns against the spillage of bodily fluids. A man must protect himself, conserve his vitality.

"Over there," Daniel says.

Mariah bangs the tray down. Cup of black coffee, the last of the brandy in a smeary decanter, Miss Malone's bottle of Scotch Oats Essence, a spoon. She stands, waiting. Waiting for his command. As is proper.

For the balance of the morning and early afternoon, Daniel has been studying "The Lady of the Tides," the painting of the mermaid he gave to Miss Malone in trade for two months' rent. Whirling the Zoetrope before his bleary eyes. Thinking about that trick of nature: the persistence of vision.

He had gone to Gump's, as Jessie had advised. Importers, already formidable purveyors to the rich of San Francisco. Profusion of gilt and crystal, jade and Orientalia glittering beneath gaslamps, reflecting off ample mirrors. The Gumps themselves in immaculate black gabardine, patchouli wafting. What a gorgeous shop! Daniel had been deeply envious. This charming enterprise had survived the depression of '93. A worthy pursuit for a gentleman. But would Father ever entertain such a notion? No, Father had the aesthetic sensitivity of a toad. Daniel had sold all of Mama's junk for forty dollars. Nothing she had was noteworthy, well, he expected as much. During the transaction, he had described the mermaid painting to the younger Mr. Gump, who had removed and carefully wiped his spectacles. Poor fellow is nearly blind, the lenses of his spectacles as thick as the bottom of a brandy bottle. "I'd have to see it myself, of course," Mr. Gump had remarked, "but I'd say, offhand, the piece could be worth perhaps seven thousand dollars."

Seven thousand dollars! When Daniel informed Jessie of the true value of her new acquisition, she'd tossed her curls scornfully. "Sure and then make it four months' rent. And not a day more." Grinned like a minx. The biz was the biz. He'd traded her fair and square. She had him over a barrel and they both knew it.

Brilliant sun streams through scarlet fringe edging the curtains, making patterns of shadow and light. He spoons Scotch Oats Essence onto his tongue. A small breeze through the open window, and the patterns shift across the dizzying arabesques and medallions of Jessie's Persian carpets, creating an intriguing sense of depth. An illusion of reality. Like the persistence of vision creates the illusion of continuous motion.

Space and time. How to harness it?

"By God, so much to do, Mariah," Daniel says, studying the shifting patterns, "so little time."

Nice effect. Kinetic, that's the word, from the dear old Greek, *kinesis:* to move. Should brush up on the dear old Greek. Many a gentleman drinking on the Cocktail Route is a scholar. A hotbed of cultural discourse, the Cocktail Route. Thus, kinetic.

But how could one reproduce kinetic effect in an artwork? Not some trifle like the Zoetrope, either. How could one reproduce depth and motion in, say, the mermaid? Have the tart stretch, wink, and loll about, fishtail flopping. Right up there on the wall. The work ought to reproduce color, as well, the way a painting does. Yet remain flat like a canvas or a photograph.

For decades the best minds in Europe had pondered the question. Monsieur Roget advanced his theory of the persistence of vision back in '24: that the brain retains a visual image perceived by the eye for a fraction longer than the perception itself. Thus we gaze, oblivious to the hundreds of times we blink in the course of a day. We perceive space and time as a smooth continuous flow.

Then Sir John Herschel inflamed everyone when he spun a shilling, showing its head and tail at the same time. All manner of clever devices utilized the spinning-coin phenomenon, beginning with Dr. Paris's Thaumatrope. Plateau's Phenakistiscope, Horner's Zoetrope, Beale's Choreutoscope. Toys fit for the junk heap or the gypsy trade by now. Every fancy brothel in Paris sported some flimsy imitation of Rudge's magic lantern show. What things one could suggest in a mere seven phases of action. In the meantime, Eddie Muybridge in jolly old Californ' had proved in his rigged row of cameras that, at the height of a gallop, all four of a horse's hooves leave the ground. Photographic proof: the beast catapults into space. Muybridge won a $25,000 bet with old man Stanford. With a sturdy steed, sir, we defy gravity. We defy God himself.

Ah, but none of it, none of it is good enough. None of it captures the mermaid, her slick skin, her chatoyant scales, her coy eye. Nothing induces her to rise. To turn and smile. To splash across the wall and seduce that young man. By God, he wants to *see* it!

Scotch Oats Essence warms his head. Daniel lights a ciggie, picks up his toy. When you whirled the Zoetrope too fast, the images blurred. Yet the trick must be to speed up the sequence. Expand it, too. Make the flow continuous without sacrificing clarity. "So much to do and so little time, eh, Mariah?"

"Will that be all, sir?" Mariah says.

"In a hurry, are you, Mariah?"

"A young gentleman like yourself shouldn't be lying about all the day." For a person with no discernible mind of her own, she's awfully pesky. "Mr. Watkins, you ought to be ashamed."

"I am ashamed, Mariah." He grins agreeably. "Truly, you have no notion how ashamed I am."

"Thought you got important business in town. Your daddy's business."

"Ah, dear old Father and his dear old business."

Daniel had dutifully sent the eminent Jonathan D. Watkins a telegram once he'd settled in at 263 Dupont Street.

> "FATHER STOP ARRIVED STOP DANIEL" Then, just to get the old man's goat, "LOVELY LADIES STOP"

Lovely ladies. This town has cast an evil spell over the ladies. Look at 'em: Fanny Spiggot, a pickpocket; Li'l Lucy, a whore; Jessie Malone, Queen of the Underworld; even Donaldina Cameron, the lady who snubbed him on the train. A Holy Roller, which may be worse than all of the above. And Zhu Wong taunting him, leading him into sin.

Daniel draws the ciggie down, stubs it out. "Real estate. Do you have any notion what a lousy racket real estate is, Mariah?"

"I should think a young gentleman like yourself should be grateful to have the means to enrich himself handed over to him so graciously by his family," Mariah says. "No matter what he may think of his father."

"Indeed." He glances up at the auntie, astonished by this speech. As usual Mariah regards him and the world with the face of a wooden Indian. "Damnable plague, that's what real estate is," he says. "Interest rates, down payments. Defaults, bankruptcy—that's no laughing matter. Bankruptcy, Mariah, is a sin." He plucks the crumpled note from the floor, examines it.

> *Der Sir:*
> *Konserning yer rekwest I tern over key to bording haus at 567 Stockton I say damn you sir is mine an I ain't givin up nothin. Tis my haus & my borders. Yull git yer pownd of flesh. Sinseerly,*
> *Mr. Ekberg*

"Speaking of grateful, Mariah. Mr. Ekberg has enjoyed nearly a year's respite from all mortgage payments. And he sends me charming notes like this."

Daniel does not look forward to rousting Mr. Ekberg out of the commercial property on Stockton Street. A boardinghouse; dreadful piece of work. A crumbling Stick in dire need of a new roof and a paint job. Chinese tenants packed in like tinned fish. Mr. Ekberg a forty-niner, an old coot whose modest bonanza enabled him to purchase the house in the sixties when Stockton Street was white and Portsmouth Square was a gambling haven and dining resort. Now that Stockton Street is smack-dab in the middle of Chinatown, Mr. Ekberg's rents have plummeted, which is why he mortgaged the place in '90 to Jonathan B. Watkins & Son. Daniel doesn't want to manage the place himself. Chasing coins from those poor coolies every month?

He crunches Mr. Ekberg's note into a ball, tosses it across the room. Takes another fine taste of Scotch Oats Essence. Remarkable medication. Should get his own bottle. "Perhaps good old Karl Marx was right, after all. Perhaps Jack London is right. Perhaps private property is no damn good."

"Mr. Watkins," Mariah says, "the War Between the States was fought so that my people would not be someone else's property. So that my people could own their own property. Perhaps a privileged young gentleman like yourself should not be so quick to dismiss that which others have fought and died for."

By God, where does the auntie get her ideas? "The numbers, Mariah. Numbers make my head ache." At least Mr. Ekberg replied to Daniel's notice to quit. Mr. Harvey, the other debtor who has defaulted on the shack in Sausalito, has neither the manners nor the intelligence to reply at all. "Mortgages. Did you know that 'mortgage' means 'death pledge,' Mariah? It's a deadly business, all right. Deadly boring."

"And just how do you intend to pay Miss Malone her rent?" Mariah asks pointedly. "Lying about all the day?"

Thank goodness he has to pay Miss Malone and not Mariah. Airily, "Don't worry your little head about that. That lady up there"—points to the mermaid—"has paid my way around here for a while longer. Besides"—suddenly impatient with Mariah's interrogation; she's just the Negro maid, after all—"that's enough of your scolding, Mariah. My mother is in her grave. I don't need or want another."

Mariah casts her eyes down. "I'm sorry, Mr. Watkins. That's right, I forgot. You're grieving."

Daniel laughs sharply, dumps brandy into his coffee. Brandy sweetens coffee just fine. "Actually, Mariah, I believe I should refrain from champagne for breakfast. Knocks me flat on my prat all morning. I don't know how Miss Malone carries on."

"Miss Malone has got practice," Mariah says.

"Stick with whiskey in the morning, there's a proper drink for a gentleman. Whiskey gets me up and at it just fine."

He glances at Mariah. For a moment their eyes connect. Coal black irises, whites like aged ivory. High cheekbones, wide mouth, jaw like a battering ram. When Mariah looks at him like this, she seems to see right through him.

Sees more than she should. Herr Vogt's measurements prove that the Negress, in the physical configuration of her skull, jaw, and upper arm, retains such qualities of the simian as to convince the most skeptical doubter of Darwin's missing link. Damned uneasy, that's how Mariah makes him feel. He's not at all sure what goes on behind those eyes. How could he fathom the thoughts of such a creature, anymore than he could fathom what a horse thinks, or a dog? Indeed, the interior life—such as it might be—of women, Negro servants, carriage horses, and dogs is not a proper subject of speculation for an educated gentleman. Schopenhauer and Darwin would heartily agree.

"Thank you, Mariah," he says curtly, "you may go."

She goes without a word. Clatters upstairs to the suite she shares with Miss Wong, riffles about in there—no chance she could discover what went on in the second bedroom this morning, is there?—comes briskly out again. Bangs the front door so loudly the mirrors rattle in the smoking parlor.

Now and then he's heard Mariah mention to Zhu or Jessie something about "going to the meeting." No idea what sort of meeting a Negro maid would go to. A church meeting, perhaps, or, more to the point, temperance? Mariah is so sober it makes his teeth ache. He has never once caught so much as the slightest whiff on her breath. Or is there a union for house servants? Seems to be a union for nearly every occupation, avocation, and hobby. Is Jack London right? Is the revolution at hand? How about a union for drunks?

Ha! He'll start a union for drunks. The mustachioed senator and the great burly fellow who owns the bank on California Street and all the other fine gentlemen who stroll along the Cocktail Route will have quite a laugh. They'll march in the Fourth of July parade, a cask of fine whiskey set in a surrey. March in the Columbus Day parade, march in every parade the fine citizens of San Francisco marshal every month.

Coffee and brandy, down the hatch. Feeling so much better now. Buzzing like a bee. Four o'clock in the afternoon in golden San Francisco. Daniel stands, preparing to go up and change.

Time to stroll along the Cocktail Route.

His sinuses suddenly loosen. Touches a handkerchief to his nostril. Pristine cotton soiled, a blossom of blood.

He sniffs. What a puzzle; hasn't had a nosebleed since he was a kid. But he is feeling *much* better. Brandy battles effete champagne, emerging the victor. He goes to his suite, throws off the sashed jacket. Where is his shirt, his collar, his vest, his cutaway, his bowler, his boots, his tie? Where in hell is a pack of ciggies? He goes through two packs a day, more or less. Usually more, if you count the bums. A handful of silver bits, that'll get him going on the Cocktail Route.

The derringer, of course. The Congress knife. A red carnation from the bouquet Jessie Malone leaves outside his door every morning. What a pill, Miss Jessie. Remarkable how she runs her sordid little empire. Makes him laugh with her crackpot notions, her wild ways. Said she liked Mr. Wells's *The Time Machine* but the character of Little Weena reminded her too much of Li'l Lucy. Too trusting of strange men. Which is preposterous. Li'l Lucy is a whore, Weena a woman of the future. He tucks the red carnation into his lapel. Jessie says red carnations mean, "Alas, my poor heart."

And he's off. Steps out of 263 Dupont Street when a coolie barges in the front door.

"Hey, there!" He catches the bugger by the wrist, reels him in.

The coolie protests.

"By God." Daniel drops the wrist, peers. "Miss Wong?"

"Excuse me, Mr. Watkins," she—and truly it is *she*—says. She moves around him, makes for the stairwell and her room, but he seizes her again. Stares.

Shock like the time when he was ten and the horse threw him. A clanging in the nerves, head spinning. It cannot be true! He's only just won her. Only just gained mastery of her favors and already she has . . . degenerated?

He sinks into a chair. "What have you done?"

"What's wrong, Mr. Watkins?"

He points at her clothes, if one could call them that. The *sahm* of a coolie, a man's slacks, a tunic. And the hat! Spectacles in a weird tint, blending with her extraordinary eyes. *Sahm* cut so loosely that he cannot glimpse the curve of her waist, the swell of breasts or hips. The certainty that her body lurks beneath the ample rags is enough to make him ill. Is she wearing proper undergarments?

She laughs gaily. "You like my new togs?" Twirls before him like a mad child. "They're quite modern, really. Closer to what I used to wear every day than what you've seen me wearing. Perhaps I'll start a fashion trend. What do you think?"

"It's illegal," he says, scandalized.

"Illegal?"

"You're impersonating a . . . man."

"I'm comfortable," she says.

"You've become degenerate," he says.

"What do you mean, degenerate?"

"Max Nordau's treatise is quite explicit. You threaten all of human evolution with this bawdy display."

"Bawdy display?" She extends her arms, looks down at herself. Blue denim, hanging like a bag. "You see more of my bosom—such as it is—in those dresses."

"Nordau, the great Lombroso himself, are both very clear: if humanity has struggled out of indeterminacy into true manhood, then woman must become ever more feminine. For you to dress like . . . a coolie, for you to take on masculine qualities is sinking back into primal indeterminacy. In a word, devolution." He strikes his sweaty brow with the flat of his palm. "Is it something I did, mistress?"

"Oh, I am your mistress now?"

"Did I damage you this morning?"

His hands tremble. Needs a drink. By God, a drink badly.

She studies him with her bright, curious look like a bird cocking its eye at what the rain has brought up. "Not half as much as you damage yourself, Daniel."

He doffs the bowler. "Don't turn temperance on me, mistress. Go upstairs and change your clothes. I'm off."

Turns on his heel, goes quickly. She follows him out onto the street like a spaniel, dogging his heels. "Where are you going?"

"Got business to attend."

"You're going to the Cocktail Route," she says. "Haven't you had enough to drink today?"

Stops dead in his tracks. "The president of the Bank of California will probably take his usual at the Reception. He may be useful to me. I may need financing." As he lectures her, the nosebleed recommences.

She exclaims, offers her handkerchief. "Let me come with you, Daniel."

"Certainly not."

"Please."

"Only whores frequent saloons. You're not a whore, are you, mistress?"

She thinks. "Let me come like this." Plucks at the ridiculous tunic. "As your manservant." Grins. "Your coolie."

Protest burgeons, but the idea suddenly tickles him. Wouldn't Father be outraged by such a ploy? A young woman masquerading as a coolie?

"All right," he says, "but you cannot drink."

"I don't drink."

"You'll not be served free lunch."

"I don't eat much."

"You'll keep your head down and your mouth shut."

"Suits me. I'm an observer in this spacetime, anyway. The more invisible, the better."

"Hm." Spacetime? What the devil kind of a word is that? "Very well. But I want you to know, I do not approve, Miss Wong. I do not approve of this stunt at all."

"Yes, Mr. Watkins," she says. Giggles. Quite disconcerting.

"And don't go temperance on me."

"Yes, Mr. Watkins." Not so brightly.

Ah, but strolling along the Cocktail Route! Lovely tradition: promenading from saloon to saloon along Market Street, zigzagging up Montgomery to Sutter Street, then down to Market again along Kearny or Stockton. At least three dozen first-class establishments enrich the Cocktail Route, each place deserving of a respectful visit. Gambling resorts, sporting houses, and steam baths offer their delights in between. During the stroll—in which the important gentlemen of the city engage as a daily ritual—one encounters friends, acquaintances, associates, competitors, newcomers, occasionally a lady of certain charm. One hears Milton and Shakespeare quoted. Latin and Greek flow like wine. The latest political gambit, gossip, and rumors are mulled over, interpreted, adjudged. Business deals are discussed and consummated. No one cusses, guffaws, or tells lewd stories. Not along the Cocktail Route, sir.

Flit of shadows behind them. Zhu whirls. Anxiety stitches her brow.

"*Boo how doy?*" she whispers.

Daniel surveys the street. Couple of thugs roaming about, nobody he knows. No hatchet men, either.

"By God, mistress, why are you so skittish? What business have you with hatchet men?"

"None," she says, but continues to glance about anxiously.

"Fine," he says. Heartily disapproves of her propensity to dissemble. "We'll start at the Reception."

A block down, Daniel eagerly sweeps her through carved mahogany doors into the Reception Saloon. The dark, high-ceilinged burrow is lit splendidly by gaslamps in crystal candelabra. Bottles banked before vast mirrors behind the bar glow like rubies, emeralds, sapphires, topaz. Fastidious bartenders in white jackets attend to one's every need. They'll hold a gentleman's gold and other valuables behind the bar for the evening, ensuring he won't lose his kit and caboodle to pickpockets who rove these streets, thugs, or a sporting gal. The black and white marble floor gleams in a tasteful checkerboard. Polished spittoons stand between each brass and leather bar stool. The air is thick and rich. Among the delightful odors wafts the delicate fragrance of the Reception's speciality, Maryland terrapin.

"He's my man," Daniel says to the bartender, who raises an eyebrow at Zhu. Orders a Sazarac. A four-bit cocktail—a tad dear—but he adores Sazaracs: rye whiskey, dash of bitters, dash of absinthe shaken with ice served in a glass rubbed with anisette. Father would die at the expense. "My just deserts," he says. "I'm celebrating the entertainment of a creative thought this morning."

"What creative thought is that?" Zhu says. Hunched shoulders, voice lowered, delicate hands hid in her sleeves. Very good. Clever creature, after all.

"There's this theory called the persistence of vision."

"Oh, yes." Sly look. "Let me see; that's the principle behind how our perceptual apparatus works. I remember. Led to the technology of movies."

"Movies?"

"Of course, insects and other creatures have evolved other perceptual means. Just goes to show you, that old cosmicist homily is so true. 'What you see is what you are.'"

"What on earth are you jabbering about?" he demands. "How do *you* know about the persistence of vision?"

"Proud of me?" Defiant. "You think I'm some brainless creature, don't you?"

"I never said any such thing."

"Little better than an animal, that's what Muse says. It's not true, as you can plainly see."

Daniel shocked into silence.

"Never mind. Pardon me, Mr. Watkins, I interrupted you. What was your creative thought?"

The director of Pacific Title Insurance Company huddles over bourbon with the president of Bankers Investment Company. Daniel should join them. The very reason he strolls along the Cocktail Route, sir. The biz is the biz, as Miss Malone says. New financing? Just what he needs to refurbish the Stockton Street boardinghouse, perhaps develop those weeds in the Western Addition, too. Can practically hear Father's voice—resonant, stern, scolding, always scolding—"Go *on*, Daniel. He who hesitates is lost, sir."

But Daniel balks. Why can't he linger with his new mistress discussing the persistence of vision? Movies? What kind of word is that? Why can't he do what he wants to do?

Gulps his Sazarac. Ah, finally a sharp feeling against which he can rebel: shirking family duties, carousing with a degenerate woman, guilt. Better and better. Hell with new financing. He'll see about new financing another day.

"I thought about a device," he says, "a machine, a gadget. I envisioned how the seven phases of action of magic lantern shows and Herschel's spinning coin and the painted parrot flapping in a Zoetrope could be made into something brand-new. A device; a device that could make the mermaid swim across a wall as though she were reality itself!"

"I'm sure it's possible," she says. Serious; not laughing at him.

"You are?" At her nod, "I'm sure, too! Trick is to keep the sequence continuous with a mechanical device. Perhaps a miniature steam engine?"

"A steam engine?" *Now* she laughs.

"Why not?"

She shrugs. "Invent this device, then."

"I intend to!" He raises his drink. "To my moving picture machine! I want some lunch. Come help me with my plates, coolie."

She dutifully follows Daniel to the free lunch. The Reception offers free lunch everyday to anyone who buys a drink. Platters crowd the sideboard. A Virginia ham cooked in champagne. A whole goose ringed by quail. Cheddar cheese the size of a wagon wheel. Grilled bear steaks, a side of venison, broiled rattlesnake, stewed rabbit, porcupine cutlets. Composed plates of salami and sausages, sardines and salmon. Prawns the size of a man's thumb. Sweet and sour pickles, celery and gherkins, radishes and water chestnuts, sliced onions and tomatoes, artichoke hearts. Loaves of rye and pumpernickel. Pots of mustards, mayonnaises, ketchups, clarified butter. More cheese: rounds of brie, gorgonzola, mascarpone. Molded domes of liverwurst, pâtés, puddings. Mountains of crackers and crisps. And, of course, in steaming silver chafing dishes, the famed Maryland terrapin.

Daniel heaps plates with delicacies, hands them to his "manservant," and carries a full load himself back to their table. Goes back and heaps more, balancing a dish of terrapin between his thumbs.

"This is obscene, Daniel," Zhu says, staring at the food. "Sorry. But I must say it."

"What is obscene, mistress?" He feels so good after the Sazarac, he starts to take her hand. Stops himself. Wouldn't want to get the fey reputation.

"Well!" Waves her hand at the magnificence before them. "You treat drinking like some sort of . . . hobby."

"And a very fine hobby it is, too, mistress. Followed closely by dining well. Did I tell you I'm planning to start a union for drunks? Can't you just see us in the next Columbus Day parade? We'll wear tuxedos, of course. Put a cask of whiskey in a surrey, give the kids a free taste."

"What about people who don't have enough to eat?"

"What people?"

The Reception fills with more men. Next to the director of the title company and the investment banker crowd politicians, financiers, newspaper men, merchants. Corpulent men clad in striped trousers and fine silk cravats, top hats and brushed bowlers, gaily colored vests, brocaded waistcoats, sable collars and cuffs on cashmere topcoats, fancy canes crooked over arms. Chunks of gold glint at cuffs, on chests, fingers, wrists. Abundant beards and mustaches fur plump-cheeked faces. Though Daniel proudly boasts a thirty-two-inch waist, he would not be unhappy sporting a girth like the ironworks heir, whose waistcoat is fashioned entirely of silvery sealskin.

"What about the coolies in Chinatown?" she says, bending near so he can hear her over the rising din. "Surely you know peasants are tricked or kidnapped, forced aboard clipper ships, and sold into slavery as pernicious as the servitude of black people over which American people were willing to die."

"Not the war again. Mariah was ranting about the war today, too."

"And what about the women? Surely you know that Chinese girls—little girls as young as five—are sold into slavery, then prostitution. They're beaten, stripped of property, starved."

Daniel notices some fellows barge into the Reception's carved mahogany doors. Casually turns to look. Those thugs again. Scruffs in shabby workingmen's clothes. Not the sort of swell welcome on the Cocktail Route, but there's no law against it. Poor devils can eat like kings for the price of a beer.

He doesn't want to hear this talk. Sounds too familiar; like the dreadful lady on the train, Miss Cameron. "My dear mistress," he says curtly, "that is their lot in life."

"They're *people*, Daniel!"

"There's nothing you or I can do about them, even if we wanted to."

Silent, glowering. "Perhaps there's nothing *I* can do. But there is plenty you could do."

"Oh, damn it, Zhu. The coolies and the slave girls, you and Mariah. All women, really. You are where you are due to the forces of evolution."

"That's a theory, Mr. Watkins, about why certain species have bifocal vision or an acute sense of smell or red feathers on their asses."

Startled at her loose language, he shakes his finger at her. "Mr. Darwin's theory explains much about society, too."

"And I suppose," she says, "it's your lot in life to wallow in self-pity over the ruin of your father's business. Punish yourself over your mother's passing. I suppose it's your lot in life to smoke and drink yourself to death."

He orders another Sazarac. "I do not wallow, mistress. It is my lot in life to possess the means to rehabilitate my father's errors. And I shall do so. And prosper."

"And why do you care about rehabilitating your father's business?"

"Family duty. My own means of provision for the future, of course."

"Ah." She leans forward, face flushed, eyes glittering. "Provision for the future. You acknowledge there's a future?"

"Certainly."

"If you care at all about the future, then you must care about the people who don't have enough to eat, Daniel. Don't you see? You must at least care about them because they are a part of the future, too!"

"Not *my* future, Zhu."

"Yes, *your* future. Everyone's future. Everything you do affects everything else. It's all connected. That's the principle behind cosmicism: humanity cocreates reality with the Universal Intelligence. With the Cosmic Mind."

"Don't tell me you're a communist."

"I said *cosmicism*." Flicks her eyes to the side the way she does. Disconcerting habit of hers. Mumbles to herself, "All right, Muse. The tenets. I know." To him, "I suppose I shouldn't talk this way."

"No, you shouldn't."

"But I must say it, Mr. Watkins. The future survives because people care. Live responsibly or die."

He downs his second Sazarac. "Pardon me, Miss Wong, but you've got it all wrong. Eat, drink, and be merry, for tomorrow we surely *do* die."

❘ ❘ ❘

The golden afternoon deepens into shadowy dusk. Men throng the sidewalks and jostle into saloons as Daniel and Zhu stroll along the Cocktail Route. The gentlemen stroll in a leisurely, civilized way, conversing, smoking, chuckling, tossing coins at beggars who beseech the crowd, negotiating with painted ladies who become more frequent at every street corner as night falls.

His mistress's skittishness is contagious. She walks beside him wary, somber. Daniel glances over his shoulder, too. Those thugs again. Sauntering in the crowd, casually turning down Post when he looks. Looks again, and there they are.

He hustles Zhu, quickening their pace, which seems to please her. She moves like a man in her crude sandals. Keeps up with him, *very* good. He likes speed. Speed is the key to the persistence of vision. The telegraph is speed. Modern life is speed. He hurries to each pleasure along the Cocktail Route as though this will be the last time he will ever savor pleasure.

At Haquette's Palace of Art on Post near Kearny, Daniel samples aged Kentucky bourbon, thick and rich and fragrant as exotic oil. Zhu gazes at the profusion of oil paintings—nudes, nudes, nudes. Gaslights glimmer in grand chandeliers, casting a seductive golden glow over the painted breasts and buttocks. Daniel is starving again by the time they stroll into Flood and O'Brien's. He must have the corned beef and cabbage plate washed down with Black Velvets, champagne with a side of stout. Orders a Stone Wall next, takes one sip of Jamaican rum and cider, and cannot go on. Orders a crisp gin cocktail at the Peerless, a Pisco Punch at the Bank Exchange.

He's well lubricated by the time he gets the Pisco Punch. "You must try this," he says to Zhu. "Go on, no one will notice."

"I don't drink, Mr. Watkins," she says.

"You've never tasted anything like it," he insists. Pisco Punch is concocted of a mysterious fiery Peruvian brandy that no one else has ever been able to procure save for the proprietor of the Bank Exchange. "There you go, my dear," he says. Holds the glass to her lips. "Smooth as silk, hot as fire, long as love. Down the hatch."

She is tight-lipped as a temperance worker. Daniel finishes the Pisco Punch himself.

He samples crab stew at the Occidental, nibbles on roast turkey at Lucky Baldwin's saloon in the Baldwin Hotel. Beneath jeweled cornucopia chandeliers, his strange little mistress disclaims over the evils of drink and dining and greed.

"My dear," he says, throwing an arm across her shoulders.

Hell with what other fellows think. "All this talk of the fate of the lower classes. Of the future and my responsibility for the suffering of others. All right, I will grant you it's a shame and a sorrow, but of no consequence. Forget all sorrow! *That* is our highest duty in life: to live. To forget."

"I believe," Zhu says, "our highest duty is to *remember*."

"Don't want to remember. By God, I remember too much."

She rests her hand on his hand beneath the table. "But we *must* remember."

"No. Don't want to."

"What don't you want to remember?"

"Never you mind, mistress."

"Tell me, Daniel."

Remember?

His heart tumbles, spinning him into himself like falling into a whirlpool. Does not want to remember, but he does.

"It was 1881," he says.

Saint Louis languished beneath incipient summer, the fecund heat ripe with fruit and disease. Daniel a lazy boy of seven. Sucked on sugar cubes Mama heaped in silver bowls. Remembered the heat, the rotten smell of mold, of corn whiskey. The heat coaxing sweat off everyone's brow, filming skin beneath clothes, fine silk and crude cotton alike. That smell of mold, mud, mint, Southern Comfort, sickness. Makes him nauseated just to remember it.

Cholera everywhere. Dysentery, too. Father conferring with the priest, city councilmen, merchants, the great landowners, shippers who worked the river. They knew the infection had to do with heat, moisture, rot, perhaps insects, vermin in the water. Powerless—even lazy little Daniel could sense their defeat—before the slippery devilish disease that wrung life so painfully from the gut.

People from respectable families were dying. Funerals with a huge entourage in well-appointed carriages proceeded graveward side by side with the Negroes and white trash who carried their dead in coffins borne upon bare shoulders.

"Seems like she was sick ever since I was born," he tells Zhu, sipping a Bonanza. Some sort of whiskey cocktail.

"That's what she told me. 'Danny, since you were born, I have always been sick.' As if it were my fault."

"How did that make you feel?" Zhu says.

"Guilty, of course." Glares at his mistress. What kind of fool question is that? Does not want to think about his feelings. How did he *feel*, indeed. But she only smiles back at him in the smoky darkness of the bar. "This time she was worse. Much worse. I remember her crying. Crying in the night."

"She contracted cholera?"

"You know"—straining to remember—"I'm not sure what was wrong with her." *Slap of flesh on flesh in the night.* "She would have died of cholera, though, wouldn't she? Like poor Tchaikovsky."

"Well," Zhu says, "she contracted dysentery?"

"I . . . I'm not sure. Oh, but her pain! Our doctor put her on the Montgomery Ward iron tonic. A jigger every two hours."

"Iron tonic?"

"Vile stuff; I tasted it, of course. A concoction of finely ground beef and grains of citrate of iron dissolved in pure sherry wine. I remember the catalog order on her dressing table. The doctor's prescription."

"The doctor prescribed sherry?"

"Certainly. The tonic calmed her, soothed her. Oh, Dr. Dubose often told me demon drink was an evil when taken in excess and without cause. This was *tonic*. Father saw an immediate improvement. I did, too. She calmed down. Her ailment eased. She stopped crying. She grew so ugly when she cried. I wanted her to look beautiful. We all did."

Lights what must be his fifteenth ciggie for the evening, draws the smoke down hard. Welcomes the twitch of pain deep in his lungs. Lets him know he's alive.

Mysterious look from Zhu. "Oh, Daniel. Why are you bound on the same course of self-destruction?"

"Mistress, whatever do you mean?"

"Your drinking. Your smoking." She takes the cigarette in her fingers like a piece of offal, examines it.

"But I love to smoke," he says. "When I haven't had much to eat, smoking settles my stomach. When I've had too much to eat"—pats his waist, for the evening's repast has strained his belt—"smoking settles my stomach, then, too. And one cannot possibly drink properly without a smoke. What's wrong with that?"

"What's wrong? Smoking will kill you. Kill you horribly. Rot your lungs, your throat, induce other cancers."

"Rot. Indeed, mistress, rot."

"You know about cancer in this day," Zhu says.

"In this day. What other day is there?"

"I know you do."

"And when will this horrible death overcome me," he says, "may I ask?"

"One day. Someday. Someday comes sooner than you think."

"Always someday, mistress. I can't think about someday. It is a struggle for me to negotiate this moment now."

She rises angrily, strides out of Lucky Baldwin's.

He runs after her. "Zhu! Zhu!" Gentlemen turn and stare.

Catches up with her, takes her arm. "Mistress. Please. You must behave yourself, this is quite . . ."

She stops, whirls. "I shall not be your mistress if you do not respect yourself. Do not respect your future."

"Very well," he says reasonably. The sudden exertion makes him dizzy. Perhaps he's reached his limit. "Let's walk. Let's talk about the future."

Anxiety sharpens and twists as they stroll along the Cocktail Route, past Montgomery, past Kearny, past Dupont, past Stockton. He starts every time they encounter ragged fellows. Heart pounds as they turn every ill-lit corner. Beneath tobacco smoke and booze and rich food, he can suddenly smell his own fear.

"Daniel, what is it?" Zhu whispers. They reach the end of the Cocktail Route, the Dunne Brothers at Eddy and Market.

"Someone is following us," he whispers back. "Keep seeing them."

"Me, too."

"You have?"

"Yes!"

"Listen, Zhu. I may have enemies."

"What enemies?" She stops, turns, gazes up at him, her strange slanted eyes bright behind her tinted spectacles. In his bleary gaze she is sympathy incarnate. Angel, devil, lady, whore, woman—what? Something turns in him like a knife.

"A fellow defaulted on a boardinghouse my father financed. The note at breakfast; from him, most impolite. Perhaps he's sent a man." Doesn't seem likely, though, even to Daniel. Dotty old Mr. Ekberg? Still, this is San Francisco.

"Perhaps," she says, "I have enemies, too."

"*You?*"

"Chee Song Tong. I went to see a girl today." At his bewildered expression, "The girl who was with me when Miss Malone bought me. The hatchet men took her away. Remember?"

Wasn't sure; nodded anyway. "Why on earth did you go to see her?"

"She's family; friend of the family."

"Really, mistress." Again, her dissemblement. "What is she, then?"

"She's a prostitute now. She's in a brothel. Damn it, Daniel! She's just a kid." Rubs her face with a knuckle. "I've got to get her out of there."

"Does the tong know you want to spring her loose?"

"Not yet. But one of the tong men; he may be interested in *me*."

"You're indentured to Miss Malone," Daniel reminds her.

"Do you think Chee Song Tong cares about that? There are so few Chinese women in San Francisco."

"I get your drift," he says.

The night has become disquiet, stirring with weird shadows. They duck into the Dunne Brothers. The place is gauzy with tobacco smoke.

"I just want a quick shot," Daniel says, "then we'll go home."

"I can't take the smoke," she says. "I'll wait for you by the door."

He greets his fellow tipplers, says hello to dapper Frank Norris, who is drinking deeply at the bar. Daniel pays for and tips back his quick shot, then cuts through the convivial crowd. But Zhu is not waiting by the door.

He senses her distress before he hears her cry, filtering catlike from the alley next to the Dunne Brothers. He pulls the Remington derringer and dashes into the alley.

Not one man, but three. Scrappy thugs in cheap suits and felt hats. They've got her between them, lunging at her as she whirls like a dervish, keeping them at bay.

"She's just a girl," he shouts. "Leave her alone!"

The first thug turns from Zhu and lurches at Daniel. Before Daniel can stagger back, the first thug swiftly kicks, his boot toe connecting with Daniel's wrist. The derringer flies from his hand.

"This a message from Mr. Harvey," the first thug says.

"Who? What?"

"Mr. Harvey says you fuckin' leave his poolroom alone."

Mr. Harvey? The name swims up in Daniel's consciousness like a great ugly catfish, pale whiskers streaming. The shack in Sausalito?

"This isn't worth it, man!" Daniel cries. "It's not worth thrashing us, damn it!"

He backs away. The second thug pounces, punching and thrusting hard fists into his back, his gut, his kidneys.

"So you say!" The first thug seizes him. Knuckledusters pop against his mouth, shooting white-hot sparks through his jaw.

But through his dizziness and pain Daniel sees an amazing sight: Zhu whirls through the alley in some strange purposeful dance. She flies around the third thug, who gapes at her openmouthed.

She assails the second thug beating Daniel. Sickening slap of flesh, grunts of pain and surprise. She worries him away, but the first thug strikes Daniel across the back of the head with the knuckledusters.

The world spins and shatters.

"My dear!" he shouts.

A gay tune pounded out on a piano roars in his ears, filling his head with cacophony.

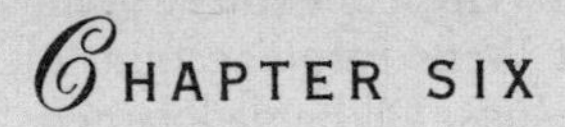

Chapter Six

Absinthe at the Poodle Dog

"Jar me, I'll charge 'em two bits a glass for that bloodred wine," Jessie tells herself as her rockaway and pair trots down Market Street. "Make 'em pay, darlin'. Make 'em pay."

And why not? What is she, after all these years? Still the wee sad orphan, crying herself to sleep. Mum and Pater cold in their graves when she and Betsy, her sweet innocent Betsy, started out on their own. Started out from Lily Lake where they swam like little mermaids so long ago.

Columbus Day turned out to be a very fine day for the eminent judge with a mustache like a walrus and a gut to match—the one who hears tenderloin matters, a long-time railbird—to touch her for twenty gold eagles. Twenty gold eagles! Half her winnings at Ingleside Racetrack. Jessie knows how to pick the nags, there's no more to her luck than that, though naturally every now and then she hears a tip when a nobbler's fixing a race and booze loosens somebody's lip. But how in hell did the judge know she has banked a hundred thousand dollars of her hard-earned cash at Wells Fargo? And what kind of polite conversation is that?

"Good afternoon, Miss Malone, aren't you the lucky one today," his honor, the railbird, said. "Why, I bet you're going to add some pocket change to that Wells Fargo account of yours. Eh, a hundred thousand big 'uns, I'll be dadblamed. That's quite a bundle for a lady like yourself."

"And every penny earned working my fingers to the bone."

"Or on the flat of your back? Oh, beg pardon," his honor said when she sucked in her breath so quickly her liver ached. "Spare twenty eagles for your dear old Sam?"

As if the SOB doesn't get his in the usual way: a brown leather purse on the fifteenth of the month. Gold, of course; a boy from American Messenger Service.

Could she say no? His honor spoke to her discreetly by the refreshment stand. Not a soul in sight to witness the transaction. And she might find herself before his honor's bench—next week, perhaps—if the bulls decide to raid the Parisian Mansion on one trumped-up rap or another. Why, his honor wouldn't know her from Adam then. Or the Serpent.

If that doesn't get her in the neck. Hopping mad, Jessie skillfully navigates the rockaway through jostling evening traffic, reckless hacks, drunk cabbies. The matched geldings—chestnuts the color of rose gold—trot like a dream. She's got an excellent hand with the steeds. Wouldn't let some whiskeyed lunk drive her pair. She's proud to drive her own. The rockaway is a fine vehicle paneled in finest cherry wood, piped and upholstered in chestnut leather. She always wears gloves of chestnut pigskin when she drives. A throw of loomed chestnut cashmere wrapped over her lap. The whole getup costs a fortune to maintain, plus she has to take a cab to and from Harwell's Livery over in Cow Hollow. It's worth it, even if she only goes driving three or four times a month. She holds her head like a duchess as she passes the diamond broker and that wife of his. The wife glares. The hateful look them Snob Hill ladies always give her.

"Pull your eyes back in your sockets," Jessie mutters.

But a tiny corner of her heart always stings when she sees the faces of the wives. Is she forever to be shut out from polite society? Will she never feel respectable?

"If you was more of a slut and less of a shrew, your old man wouldn't come around to me." The sting sharpens. "Would you like to know how he likes it? Two bouncing blonds at the same time, that's how."

Jessie always accommodates the diamond broker. That's why her earrings glitter brighter than the stones on that wife of his. Ha! Soothes the sting a bit. Miss Jessie Malone's diamonds are bigger than the diamond broker's wife's. Miss Malone drives her own rockaway and pair.

But there. A sight catches her eye. Isn't that her Mr. Watkins? On the corner of Market Street and Eddy? She's already had a lousy day! Despite the usual gang of bigwigs and bulls, bruisers and tools promenading along the Cocktail Route—all of them johns some fine night, you can bet your last red cent on that—she could never miss Mr. Watkins's fine cut, his bearing, his refined form into which his spiritual essence has been so purely poured. She always feels a nip of anxious affection at the sight of Daniel, as though he might disappear if she blinks.

And with an awful jolt, she also sees the tangle of thugs. Must be three of them, fists flying. Daniel reels—drunk as usual—while a scrawny, bespectacled coolie kicks and thrusts at the thugs in a peculiar way.

A peculiar way Jessie has seen before. There's a name for it: juju something. Isn't that what Mr. Yakamora called the taut poses and deft moves he once showed her in the parlor of the Parisian Mansion? Mr. Yakamora is a porcelain importer over in the Fillmore. Always asks for robust blonds, though of course he reveres his dark petite wife who waits for him in Tokyo while he scrapes together his fortune in America. The wife has waited eleven years. Or at least eleven years is as long as Jessie has been servicing the needs of her dear friend Yakamora.

Yes, juju something, a form of fighting from the East. Jessie recognizes the movements, despite shadows cast over the fracas. The coolie shrieks and dives, yelling.

A womanly voice. Hasn't Jessie heard that voice before?

Jessie bites the inside of her cheek as Daniel rises, stumbles, swings, and misses. The thugs tear at his fine clothes.

His face is flushed, collar askew, bowler pushed back from his sweating forehead. He throws another punch, staggers. Blood trickles down his face.

Jessie clucks to the pair, cutting through oncoming traffic. Superb, her geldings. A gift from an attaché to the ambassador. Last autumn, it was, a party for some poxy barons who'd invested money in certain municipal bonds and dropped a load at the opera. A swell party, plenty of champagne. Made a bundle that night. And though she'd had the girls douche with mercuric cyanide afterwards, Rosa and Dolores got rotten only too soon. Had to be turned out to Morton Alley. A shame, but the biz is the biz.

Jessie pulls up to the curb, reaches for the glove compartment, finds the silver flask of Jamaican brandy, bites off a nip. Then she takes up her whip, stands unsteadily, and cracks it but good over the thugs' noggins. "Mr. Watkins?" The geldings rear. "Whoa!" she cries, pulling them up, falling back onto the driver's seat. Lands another lashing, this time across their backs.

"That's from Mr. Harvey!" cries the thug in the slouch hat, landing one last punch across Daniel's kidneys. Jessie winces. Can practically feel the blow in her liver. "Keep yer fuckin' mitts off his joint!" Dodging the scrawny coolie, the thugs turn and flee.

The coolie hoists Daniel to his feet, slings his arm across one shoulder, staggers to the rockaway. "Help me, Miss Malone," he says in a ragged voice. Fedora knocked askew. Queue unraveling.

"What the hell?" Jessie leaps down, seizes Daniel's other arm. Together she and the coolie manage to boost him into the back seat of the rockaway where he collapses with a curse and a groan. The coolie takes off his fedora, wipes sweat from his smooth pale forehead.

"Jar me," Jessie whispers, staring. "Missy? Miss Wong? *Zhu?*" For a moment, the person standing before her, breathing heavily, is a puzzle, an enigma. "Is that you?" Angrily, "What in hell do you think you're doing, going about dressed like that?"

Zhu shrugs, smooths her hair, stuffs the fedora back over

her scalp. "Sorry, Miss Malone." Laughs softly at Jessie's astonishment.

"This is *not* funny," Jessie says. "How dare you—*you*, my employee, my *servant*, my trusted . . . How *dare* you gad about in peasant's rags? What would anyone think to see you?"

"It's no reflection on you or the business," the chit says, boarding in back with Daniel.

"It most certainly is!"

"No one saw me, Miss Malone. Can we get out of here? Please?"

Jessie clucks to the pair who canter, magnificently terrified.

All she can do to drive. Traffic is a fiddler's bitch. A stall at Montgomery. Looks like an accident. Beer wagon, beery driver of a cab. Horse screaming in pain, Jessie hates that. Loves the nags. Fisticuffs, the passenger of the hansom disembarking to join in.

Halting the geldings, waiting to get by, Jessie glances back.

It isn't just that Zhu is skinny. The girl is muscular, angular, built like some creature other than a woman. Doesn't slouch her shoulders, doesn't bat her eyes. Has no hips to speak of in those denim trousers. She's so slim Jessie has often feared for her health. She is bold, forthright, almost intimidating in her directness. Holds her head up; doesn't simper or defer. She moves and acts unlike any girl or woman—rich or poor, lady or whore—Jessie has ever met before.

"I'm still waiting for your explanation, missy."

"I got some clothes."

"*Those* are not clothes. You have perfectly fine clothes. I bought you the mauve silk myself."

"Thank you, Miss Malone."

"Then why?"

"So I can go about Chinatown without being noticed."

"Jar me." Ever practical Jessie, though. Zhu actually makes sense. "You could get jugged, missy."

"Jugged?"

"Arrested! Don't expect me to spring you from the cooler."

Zhu peers out the window back to the street corner where the thugs disappeared. "Daniel's got trouble."

"You . . . you were fighting with them thugs."

"You saw?"

Jessie not to be deterred. "How'd you learn to do that?"

"I'm trained in martial arts, Miss Malone," she says matter-of-factly. "Where I came from, I'd been a soldier for years."

"A soldier!" Jessie guffaws. Scrawny little Zhu; a soldier? Jessie owns a painting of the mythical Amazon, her thick loins girded with a leopard skin, her curls bound with leather thongs, her left breast shockingly amputated so that she may more accurately aim her bow and arrow at the enemy horde. The Amazon bends her dreadful weapon in gleaming curvaceous arms. Zhu; an Amazon? "You're no soldier."

"But I am."

"Where? When?"

"In China," Zhu says and gives Jessie such a penetrating look that a chill goes up Jessie's spine and coils at the back of her neck. "In a time far from Now." She bends over Daniel's sprawled form. Pulls out a handkerchief, dabs at a cut on his jaw, a wound on his head.

Then she does something lunatic. Jessie has seen this sort of thing before. The type of rummy who talks to the air. Not a pretty sight. Means drink has softened the brain at last. But Zhu doesn't touch a drop, as Jessie knows well. "Muse," Zhu mutters to no one in particular. "Check our coordinates. Advise regarding evasive action."

A tiny voice—like the whisper of an angel, a spirit from the Summerland—hovers over Zhu. "Assailants are regrouping, Z. Wong," the spirit's voice says.

"Muse," Zhu says warningly, "you will comm in subaud, please."

"Advise immediate evacuation of this sector," the spirit says even louder.

The collision is cleared. Traffic slowly recommences.

"Let's get out of here, Miss Malone," Zhu says.

"Jar me," Jessie moans. Pulse pounds in her throat. Her side throbs. "What was *that*?"

"That's . . . that's just Muse, Miss Malone."

"Your muse?"

"That's right. My guardian angel."

Jessie gasps. "Whoa," she cries to the pair. Whips around and stares at Zhu, who smiles and shrugs. She must consult Madame De Cassin at once! An Amazon with a guardian angel living right under her roof? "Jesus, Mary, and Joseph," Jessie mutters. Crosses herself. A gesture she has neither made nor meant in over thirty years.

Zhu hooks a hand over her shoulder. "Jessie, please! Get off Market Street. Now!"

The Queen of the Underworld knows how to move fast. "Hah!" she cries to the geldings. Turns a sharp left up Montgomery, takes Post. Reaches into the glove compartment, pulls out the vial of smelling salts. Tosses the salts over her shoulder to Zhu. "Give him a whiff. That'll bring him around."

Daniel mutters, "Father." Voice slurred and furious. "Cared more about your gold than her, damn you. *Damn you!*"

"Ssh," Zhu murmurs. "We'll talk about it later. You've got to sober up, Daniel. Pull yourself together." Voice of a sweetheart, pleading.

Jessie arches her brow. There is no mistaking that throb, that trill of passion, of unreasonable devotion. A sweetheart! Have they been carrying on right under her nose? Not sure she likes that notion. Zhu is her servant, bought and paid for. She has no right to be fraternizing with boarders. She has no right to do anything save what Jessie permits or directs her to do. What if they argue and Daniel, a paying guest, ends up leaving? No, she'll have to speak to Zhu.

Besides, an affair between them rubs Jessie the wrong way. If it's not true courtship leading to marriage, a man should pay for it. That's Jessie's rule. She is not at all pleased that Daniel has not availed himself of her girls' charms. His aloofness is an insult. No, he prefers to play with hearts, take advantage of waifs and strays the likes of Zhu Wong, who was ruined by love before. It's a shame. Daniel is less moral than her johns, that's what Jessie thinks. Family or sport, that's the choice men have. And if it's sport, they must pay, darlin'. They must pay.

Zhu hands back the smelling salts. "He's too far gone for that. You would not believe the booze he's poured down his throat in the past few hours."

"Oh, indeed I would, missy," Jessie says, pulling the rockaway over to a curb and reining in the pair. "He's the adventurous type. Likes to try every hooch in every joint, that's his problem. He should stick to champagne. Champagne is good for the blood. Look at me. Solid as a rock. Steady diet of champagne."

"No goddamn champagne," Daniel mutters.

"Come on, then. Haul him out, missy," Jessie says. She has got more drunken men up on their feet than she could shake a stick at. "Let's walk him around. Maybe he'll chuck it up. Feel much better then."

"Wait, I've got something," Zhu says. Searches her pockets.

Jessie watches curiously. Like a little man she is, though in fact Zhu is taller than most. Why does she seem mannish? Perhaps her wiry strength, yet with quick feminine grace like a cat. Feminine? What does feminine mean? Odd as Zhu is, Jessie finds her intriguing in a way that her own girls with their lace and lushness and simpering ways cannot match. Jessie isn't sure *what* Zhu is. Like something out of that nutty novel, H. G. Wells's *The Time Machine*. Some fantastic person out of a fantastic world, familiar yet vastly strange.

Zhu takes out a vial of liver pills. Taps one out, breaks the pill over Daniel's face. A mist spreads, like stepping on an old puffball mushroom in the woods, dispersing fairy powder with your toe. The mist floats gently over Daniel's eyes, his nose, his cheekbones, his slack mouth.

He bolts up like a man dosed with strychnine, cheeks blazing. Dark eyes gleaming like a wild creature while the snarl of drunkenness lingers. A spasm twists his face, a face that Jessie has grown too fond of. Why is she so proprietary toward Mr. Daniel J. Watkins? Why did she take him in so readily when he couldn't pay her a red cent? Hardly a policy of the Queen of the Underworld! Oh, he gave her the painting of the mermaid. But bills don't get paid out of Art. No, some deep, nameless anxiety wells in her as she watches him struggle into wakefulness. Why?

Strange disquiet, too, as she watches Zhu with him. The sight of them together, knowing that Zhu loves him before she herself seems to know, fills Jessie with fear. Can smell it beneath her patchouli, the sharp stink of fear. This woman and man plunge toward a catastrophe they don't even see. But why? How? What?

"What in hell are you doing to me?" Daniel struggles to sit up, flings Zhu's hands away as she tries to help him. "Bitches, that's what you are. Both of you. The madam and the mistress, what a pair."

"Watch your trap, Mr. Watkins," Jessie says.

"You're all the same. Whores. You want me for your slave, your lapdog, your pet pony. I'll have none of it. None of it, you hear me? Prince Albert is right. The procreative process is merely a necessary evil for the civilized man. An unfortunate waste of precious bodily fluids. What you do, Miss Malone, is pander to the lowest animal activity of which man is capable. It is beneath me, madam."

Zhu studies him. The missy has a strange way that she looks at things, as though her very eyes are taking photographs.

"Oh, you'll come around one day, Mr. Watkins," Jessie says. "Your little gentleman friend won't respect your tired old morality. He'll want his due."

"You know nothing, madam, of morality or my cock," Daniel says. "That's the one decent thing Rochelle did for me, besides dancing the cancan and not dosing me with the pox. She made my destiny clear for me. What *you* do"—he says to Zhu, face flushed, sweat trickling down his cheek—"is crawl at my feet. Go on, mistress," he shoves her off the seat. "On your knees."

Jessie is sure Zhu will hop out of the rockaway and flee as nimbly as she hopped in, but she does no such thing. Face glazed, she kneels before him. Shudders as though possessed.

"Crawl, I command you," he whispers.

"Damn it, he's jagged, missy," Jessie says. Reaches for the

whip. Can she use it on Daniel? Is he even capable of being threatened? She's never seen a man in such a state! Pie-eyed, wobbly, yet dangerously alert. White-knuckled with the violence booze unleashes, quick with the capability of sobriety. "What in hell *did* you do to him, Zhu? What was that mist?"

"Just a neurobic. Doesn't seem to help much, does it?" she murmurs, gazing up at him. As though she would move him by her will alone.

You cannot move men by your will! Jessie wants to shout. Suddenly recalls he packs a pistol. And a knife.

"What can I do for you, Daniel? What would you have me do? What do you want?" Zhu lays her cheek on his knee.

He starts as though she has slapped him. The ugly spell is broken, his eyes slicked with contrition though his mouth is still hard. Rubs his forehead, squeezes his eyes shut. Growls to Jessie, "Give me your flask, madam."

"He's had enough," Zhu protests, but Jessie gladly hands over the rum. Better to have the man dead drunk than to encourage this dreadful mood.

He gulps the liquor, grimaces.

Jessie is aware of trembling. As though the three of them have leapt a hurdle, barely clearing some invisible edge.

"I want sport." Petulant; bad boy. "I want to see some sport fitting for a man."

"Let's go home," Zhu says.

"What about the jousting tourney, madam?" he says to Jessie. "I've heard of it, but not seen it."

"Can't we go home?" Zhu says. "Haven't we seen enough violence for one night?"

"Perhaps that's it," Jessie says. "Perhaps our Mr. Watkins is still excited after your encounter on Eddy Street. He wants more."

He tips the flask again. Rum restores his smile. "You're completely right, Miss Malone. I want more." Helps Zhu back onto the seat beside him, smooths her tunic. "I'm not tired, mistress. Indeed, I'm bored with this evening. Take me to the jousting tourney, Miss Malone. Is it far?"

"They joust," Jessie says, "at the top of Telegraph Hill."

Daniel grins. "By God, let's really see some blood tonight."

❙ ❙ ❙

They clatter north up Kearny, the uneasy street where Chinatown meets the Barbary Coast. Past the shooting galleries and fan-tan parlors, opium dens in basements below laundries and produce markets, the Chinese brothels catering to white men, the cribs where the Chinese men go. Past the bustling intersection of Broadway and Dupont.

Jessie turns into the Latin Quarter where Italian and French, Portuguese and Spanish, Mexican and Peruvian crowd chaotically together. The rich in row houses or pink stucco villas angling up the steep slopes of Telegraph Hill, the poor in shacks along the waterfront where the bagnios offer Mexican girls who net the fishermen's trade.

Tonight the quarter spills onto the streets and alleys in celebration of Columbus Day. Wine and oregano scent the air. Lovers linger at street corners. Everything is open late, the markets and shops, fish and vegetable stalls, pasta and sausage factories, cheese makers and wine presses, bakeries and pensions.

In the back seat of the rockaway, Daniel sits bolt upright, silent now. Smoking cigarette after cigarette, flicking half-smoked butts into the street. Zhu perches on the far side, away from him. Carefully tucks strands of hair into her queue or under her fedora, straightens her trousers. The tinted spectacles hide her eyes. What a masquerade! Jessie clucks her tongue. Zhu composes her face, transforming herself into a pale, shadowy person of indeterminate gender.

"Hey, Rosita!" Jessie waves to the pasta maker she knows, a nice widow whose husband—known for his appetite and cruelty—dropped dead in Jessie's parlor one night. Ticker up and went, butter still on his chin, one hell of a bruise on Li'l Lucy's rump. "Well, he won't trouble none of us no more," Rosita had said when she came to collect his corpse. "What does he owe you?"

"*Ciao, bella*." Rosita leads the geldings into the narrow courtyard behind her warehouse.

"Two hours, tops," Jessie promises.

"Sure, sure."

Then she, Zhu, and Daniel stroll through the festive crowd to Greenwich Street. Tracks of the Telegraph Hill Company Railroad go straight up to a golden half-moon rising in the east. A cable car rumbles up the track, stops for the load of passengers. They board. The cable car groans and clanks and sways up the torturous grade. Zigzags slowly up, taking all and sundry to the jousting tourneys where Mr. Duncan C. Ross presides as king of the broadsword contest.

The cable car reaches the crest like a whale breaching and lumbers onto level ground. They disembark at the tiny shingled station perched at the very edge of the precipice and walk across dusty brown grass. Daniel is green, Jessie is feeling none too frisky herself, but Zhu's gaze is riveted on the spectacle at the crown of the hill.

"So different," she murmurs.

They call it the German Castle, this hulking medieval turreted monstrosity at the top of Telegraph Hill. The hulk has been rebuilt twice. The new developers have rechristened this latest attraction the Telegraph Hill Observatory.

"Oh, it ain't all that different, missy," Jessie says. A snort for a nickel from a vendor's jug considerably improves her constitution. Daniel follows suit. "Still the good old German Castle to me."

The Bear flag flaps from the western turret. Four American flags decorate the eastern tower. Daniel purchases his second shot. Feeble gaslight obscures men milling about the grounds. Deep drunkenness, whooping, tipping of flasks, jostling of one another with anticipation.

A short, slender woman in a beribboned, tightly corseted dress and a wide hat with a veil drawn over her face wanders about the crowd. Gloved hand poised demurely at her throat. Helpless little thing. She approaches a man in the rough, ill-fitting suit of a laborer, his collar ripped open for air, straw boater pushed back on a sweat-plastered forehead.

She engages him in conversation. Pleading for something, touching him hesitantly on elbow and wrist. The rough man sways on his feet, fascinated, charmed. Mouth hanging open, eyes goggled. The woman suddenly collapses into his arms. He catches her. Clears a space for her in the crowd. She awakens, clutching him. Does her hand dart down beneath his belt? The rough man blushes, glances guiltily around. She unsteadily rises and swiftly escapes. Pushes on through the crowd, which grows larger and more vociferous as contestants mount horses in a paddock on the eastern slope of the hill.

"There's your pal," Jessie says to Daniel, unable to conceal her grin.

"Who?" Daniel peers.

"Fanny Spiggott," Jessie says.

"Fanny Spiggott?" Zhu asks.

"The fainting pickpocket," Jessie says. "Mr. Watkins has made the lady's acquaintance. Ah, well, the biz is the biz, and this is a fine night for it. Miss Spiggott probably started out a poor girl with no family or husband. Like me." Jessie toasts the dip. "Get what you can, missy."

"*Lady?*" Daniel sputters. "I'll have a word with her! Where is she?"

"Gone," Jessie says. Pushes impatiently toward the field of combat illuminated by bright gaslamps. "Look, they're starting!"

A huge, muscular man canters into the field on a husky dapple-gray stallion. He wears a Prussian helmet crowned by a gleaming spike, blue military jacket hung with a vest of chain mail, breeches, black leather boots. His face is obscured by a fencing mask, but Jessie spies his bushy black mustache and brows, his bared teeth. To thunderous applause and cheers, he circles the field, brandishing a cavalry saber.

"Ross, Ross, Ross!" roars the crowd.

Mr. Duncan C. Ross promenades, cutting the air with his saber. Jessie can hear the weapon whistle as he canters past. Once enlisted in the Royal Scots Greys, Ross makes a living as a professional wrestler and an instructor of swordsmanship. Every week in summer and the balmy days of autumn, he takes on challengers at the German Castle.

"Twenty on Duncan bloody Ross!"

"Fifty on Ross by ten!"

Fists full of silver and gold, gamblers furiously place bets with the croupier below the western tower. The croupier sits at a rickety table, quill pen savagely scribbling odds and point spreads on a ledger, surrounded by four men bearing pistols.

Another tremendous rider charges into the field on a lithe black horse. Slighter in build, but no less charismatic and finely wrought, he wheels and rears his horse. His fencing mask cannot conceal his bright gold beard. Gold hair protrudes from the rim of the helmet fitting over his ears to his jawbone like the armor of an ancient gladiator. A vest of solid armor is strapped over his gray padded jacket festooned with burgundy braid and gold epaulets.

"Walsh, Walsh, Walsh!" shout the contender's partisans.

Jessie feels her own blood boil. Still, it's awfully barbaric. Better that men spent their hard-earned bucks on the gentle sport of love. But she can't help it. The mood infects her, too. Cheap whiskey and blood lust course through her veins.

"Oh, he's my favorite!" Jessie shouts in Zhu's ear. "That's Charlie Walsh, ain't he a daisy? He's a sergeant. Rode with General Sherman in Atlanta. They say he won a dozen duels by sword in Mexico!"

"This is *terrible*!" Zhu shouts back.

"Aw, you betting on Duncan?" Jessie says.

Walsh whips out his saber. He and Ross rein in their horses at the opposite ends of the field.

"The points are dull, that's what I've heard," Jessie shouts to Zhu. "But the edges are razor-sharp."

A referee clad in a scarlet vest and top hat steps into the center of the field. "Gentlemen!" he shouts above the din of the crowd. "The rules are these! Each contestant will approach the other at full gallop and endeavor to strike his opponent's armor! A proper blow to the armor scores one point! A blow to the helmet is disregarded! Striking a man below his armor or striking his horse is penalized by minus one point! He who scores one and twenty points is the victor!" The referee places a whistle to his lips. "Ready! Steady! Go!"

They charge! The horses wheel, hooves thunder across the grass. The contestants raise their swords. In less than an instant, they cross paths in a whirlwind of dust. A tremendous clang, metal meets metal, and the horses gallop to opposite ends, where boys leap up and seize their lathered bridles. The crowd cries out, backs away from the field as Ross's stallion lashes out with a hind hoof.

"Zero up!" shouts the referee.

The crowd groans. Gamblers scramble to the croupier, placing new bets.

The contestants turn.

"Ready! Steady! Go!"

Again they thunder across the turf, spewing clods of dirt. Walsh does not raise his saber, but holds it down to his thigh. A lump rises in Jessie's throat. What is he doing? As he passes Ross, he ducks away from Ross's flashing saber, which Ross, taken aback at the lack of resistance, aims poorly. Walsh spins at the waist as Ross passes and clips him smartly across his shoulder blades.

Tumult of cheers and boos. When Walsh wheels at the opposite end of the field, Jessie sees blood leaking through his breeches in a bright line.

"One point for Sergeant Walsh! One penalty for Mr. Ross!" shouts the referee.

The tumult gets louder. A fracas breaks out at the croupier's table. "Cheating! That's cheating, he can't friggin' hit 'im from behind!" The armed guards hustle the protesting gambler away, toss him out into the crowd.

The contestants rein in their horses, whirl, and pause. A boy offers Sergeant Walsh a rag, but Walsh waves the rag away. Golden sneer beneath the fencing mask. Ah, darlin', Jessie thinks, heart pounding in her breast. Careful.

"Ready, steady, go!"

Jessie finds herself shrieking as they charge again. "Get him! Get him! Get him, Walsh!"

Ross brandishes his saber at shoulder level, yelling, "Face me, you bastard!" He whacks Walsh as he gallops past, striking him full across the chest.

In the instant of passing, an enraged Walsh whips his saber up and heavily down again.

Ross roars in agony, plummets off his stallion. When the dust clears, Jessie can see that his helmet—his Prussian helmet!—is split in two. A mob descends on his fallen form.

"Did you see that?" Zhu shouts. "Did you see what he did to his helmet? His skull must be shattered!"

Jessie seizes her hand and the two women push toward the wounded contestant. "See here!" Jessie shouts. "Look out! I know a thing or two about injuries! Clear the way! Stand aside!"

"Die, die, die!" chants a contingency of the crowd, guffawing, spitting, slapping shoulders. Certain gamblers will win a premium should Ross go to his ultimate defeat.

Another contingency, red-faced and enraged, throws off topcoats, fumbles with cuff links and buttons, rolls up sleeves. "We'll not hear your crap about Mr. Ross!" the gang yells, advancing through the shadows.

"Stand aside, I say!" Jessie says. Indeed, she does know a thing or two about the healing arts, as any madam must if she's to stay in the biz. She dressed Mr. Mattinger's wound when he tumbled down two stairways at the Parisian Mansion and struck his forehead on a brass spittoon. She's seen plenty of drunk and disorderly fellows, enough fisticuffs and goings-on to fill a book, not to mention what Jeremiah Duff did one night to Li'l Lucy.

The crowd reluctantly lets Jessie and Zhu through. Jessie kneels before Duncan Ross. A skin-and-bones fellow with tobacco-stained hands weeps as he cradles Ross's head.

" 'Ere, it's that scarlet woman," says another fellow standing over them both. A rat of a man, pink eyes and pointed face beneath his cheap bowler. A crib customer, Jessie would never let a creep like this into the mansion. "Don't let 'er touch 'im. She might give 'im the pox."

"And who in hell are you?" Jessie says, restraining herself from spitting in the rat's eye.

"We're 'is trainers, madam," the rat says, "and you'll do well enough to leave 'im alone."

"Take your hands away, you lunk, and let me have a look," Jessie commands. Zhu kneels beside her.

Duncan Ross's proud head is drenched in blood, which pools and coagulates, nearly making Jessie retch from the irony stink of life leaving the body. She smooths back the black hair, smooths away the blood, working her fingers down into the tear in his scalp until she feels the cracked wound itself. A jagged edge etched across his very skull, each portion of bone canting away from the other.

"Jar me," she whispers. "It's hopeless."

But Zhu gently places her hand over Jessie's, works her fingers down, feels. Suddenly she's got a knife in her other hand. She bears the blade down on poor Mr. Duncan Ross.

"What are you *doing?*" Jessie whispers. What will this mob do to them both if it finds a strange Chinese woman, dressed as a coolie, hastening the end of their champion?

"Ssh," Zhu says with a slight smile. Clicking a little knob on the hilt of the knife, she firmly and swiftly presses the blade across the wound on Ross's skull as though slicing a melon.

Jessie's stomach clenches.

But Mr. Ross's skull does not split open. Zhu withdraws the knife, runs her fingers through his scalp. "Feel now."

Jessie runs her fingers through the black hair again, searching for that awful edge of ragged bone. But there's nothing. His skull is smooth and whole again. The blood comes from the scalp wound, which should heal all right if it doesn't get rotten first.

Jessie turns to Zhu, openmouthed. Her heartbeat throbs in her stomach beneath the stays of her corset. "What?" she whispers. "How?"

Zhu tucks the knife into a pocket. "Just my mollie knife."

"Go on," Jessie says. "That's a miracle! Let me see. A mollie knife? Where'd you get it?"

But Zhu stands and helps Jessie to her feet. Daniel sways over them, barely keeping his balance. Still, Jessie can see from the puzzled look that he saw it all. He frowns. The crowd begins to twitter and honk, inarticulate beasts on the verge of panic. A weird sound unlike any Jessie has heard before. The start of a melee, the start of a riot. She's read about the union strikes in Philadelphia and Chicago, how when violence starts the crowd changes into some great ravening monster, without reason or sensibility.

"The bulls are here," Daniel says, oddly calm and composed. "Ladies, let's go."

A squad of blue-suited, red-faced, cursing police scramble over the ridge by the cable car, wiping dirt off their hands as they gain the summit. Hoisting out billy clubs.

Daniel seizes Jessie in one hand, Zhu in the other, steers them toward the opposite side of the jousting field, beyond the grounds of the German Castle to the far perimeter of Telegraph Hill where the slope angles down into velvety darkness and rude shacks cling to the cliff. Contractors have ruthlessly quarried the hill, blasting granite and shale from beneath the very feet of settlers perched on their fine precipice, carting rock away to pave city streets. Other spectators from the jousting tourney scramble and careen down the rugged hillside, too. No one wants to get pinched. In the dim lamplight, Jessie spies Fanny Spiggott on the arm of a solicitous gentleman. How many treasures will Miss Spiggott's nimble fingers free from the topcoat and vest of her gallant before they reach the bottom of the hill?

"But I'm wearing fine shoes!" Jessie protests as Daniel guides her down the rocky slope. Zhu deftly takes the slope in her flat coolie's sandals, loping from grade to grade like a goat. She offers a hand. Jessie declines.

"I'll take the low road myself, thank you, missy." A blue funk settles over her soul.

For Zhu Wong is a Chinese girl, a chit, a wench. With unusual qualifications and bizarre predilections, yes. A smart kid, perhaps even a trusted cohort. But she's Jessie's servant, for God's sake. Jessie's possession, purchased by gold and a contract of indenture under which the creature must serve without question. In short, not a *person*. Not a person the way Mr. Daniel J. Watkins is a person, a citizen, and a gentleman. Certainly not a person with a station.

Yet this person—this Zhu Wong—has done something Miss Jessie Malone has never been able to do.

Save a man's life.

❜ ❜ ❜

"Absinthe! I must have absinthe," Daniel says. "Nothing else will do."

They climb down Telegraph Hill to Green Street, leaving the cries of coppers and the melee behind. Trudge back to the pasta factory, collect Jessie's rockaway and pair from Rosita.

"Please, Daniel," Zhu says. "Please."

"Don't go temperance on me, mistress. I warn you."

"Try another neurobic. Let's go home." Zhu tries out an amorous look, but she's better at slugging thugs and working miracles than she is at flirting. Jessie will have to coach her. The coolie clothes don't help.

"'Neurobic'; by God, what is a 'neurobic'? Absinthe, I say. Nothing else will do!"

"Let me tell you something, missy." Jessie climbs into the driver's seat, Zhu and Daniel climb in back. Jessie clucks to the geldings. They plunge into the night. "Can't tell a man like Mr. Watkins what he can't do. Ain't that so, sir?"

"That's so, madam." He laughs, cheered by the jousting tourney. "By God, Queen of the Underworld." Hooks his hand over her shoulder. "Where can I get absinthe in this burg? And not some damn cocktail. A proper bottle of Pernod Fils."

"Sure and I'll try a taste meself," Jessie says.

"Jessie," Zhu says. "Know that pain in your side? Your kidneys could be quitting. Absinthe is the last thing you need."

"Missy, my kidneys have been quitting for the past twenty years."

"Between the absinthol, thujone, and ethanol, you'll wind up with lesions on your brain. Wormwood oil is highly toxic. It could kill you."

"Jar me, missy," Jessie says, turning to glance at her, "what won't you come up with next?"

"Eat, drink, and be merry," Daniel says, "for tomorrow we

die." Jessie smells the good strong scent of his cigarette. "Miss Malone, my mistress has been lecturing me all night long about responsibility. Responsibility and the future. Why, I do believe," he says, "our Zhu is a preacher, a chemist, a physician, *and* a prestidigitator." To Zhu, voice tight, "Where'd you learn that trick with Duncan's skull?"

"It's just my molecular knife," Zhu says. "The mollie knife induces molecular recombination, that's all."

"Molecular recombination," Daniel says, "that's all. Miss Malone, what about that bottle of Pernod Fils?"

"We'll cut and run to the Poodle Dog," Jessie says. "Good old Pierre is sure to stock the Green Fairy."

Sweat slicks Jessie's skin. Feels all done out. She knows of a bathhouse on Turk Street that services ladies of the evening with or without their johns. A bath would be lovely. But after all this exercise she is hungry enough to eat a grizzly bear and thirsty as a fish. The rockaway passes a messenger boy idling on the corner. "Whoa!" she calls to her geldings. Calls to the boy, "You!" Scrawls a note to Daphne:

SERVE RED WINE AT MIDNIGHT,
FOUR BITS A GLASS.
MISS MALONE.

The door maid will stick around the Parisian Mansion till one, if she knows what's good for her. Jessie turns the rockaway downtown, back to the glittering boom and bluster of the Cocktail Route. Beneath golden gaslight, the nighttime crowd celebrates Columbus Day with increasing glee. A quartet of aspiring young tenors and baritones offers ballads for coins to be tossed in a neat row of upturned top hats. "They ain't bad," Jessie calls over her shoulder to Zhu and Daniel and tosses her contribution across the macadam. "Make the Tivoli Opera House sure if they don't die first."

"Tomorrow we die," Daniel says.

"Tomorrow we *live*," Zhu says. "We've *got* to."

Down they go to the hubbub of the city. A kinetoscope booth attracts Daniel's glance. Zhu leans out and stares at a couple of bespectacled communists shouting the philosophy of Karl Marx at an uneasy crowd of roughnecks. The Salvation Army bangs a bass drum next to a pitch man selling Kickapoo tonics beneath a showy flare.

Jessie turns into Bush at Kearny, finds the little turnabout alley, hitches her geldings at the back door of the Poodle Dog. Several drivers and their hacks linger on the pavement, watching the crowd, smoking, joking. Two soiled doves dally with them. The doves tilt straw boaters over their spit curls and titter like lunatic schoolgirls. Even in the golden light Jessie can see the ravage of smallpox on their faces. *There but for the grace of . . . Somebody.* Has Jessie seen them before? So many scarred women flock to the Parisian Mansion looking for work. So many are turned away. Can't remember all the ravaged faces.

"Evening, Miss Malone," calls Finney.

"Hey, Jess," calls a bold new boy.

"Old Pierre don't want no Chinks," says another driver when they disembark.

Jessie at a loss because of course the Poodle Dog is a class joint but Daniel says at once, "He's my man," and they all slip into the back door.

Ah, the Dog, how well Jessie knows this place. The scarlet and gilt, shimmering crystal and silver. Another home, another warm parlor. How the Dog once used her. How she's used the Dog herself over these many long years.

Through the furtive back door and up the stairwell. But Jessie cannot resist. She peeks out through scarlet curtains at the first floor of the Poodle Dog. Wink of diamond dog-collars on cashmere-clogged throats, closely covered wrists, chastely laced hands. The Parrot sisters, those Flood girls, parties of ladies from Rincon Hill and the Smart Set from South Park dining with doddering great-uncles and creaky grandfathers. That's who dines here now on world-class French cuisine. On the first floor, anyway.

Zhu peers over her shoulder. "They eat well, don't they?"

Jessie laughs. Lovely scent of lobster steamed in sweet cream infuses the room. Solicitous waiters glide across the floor, inquiring what the ladies want. The Smart Set is a well-larded crowd. Jessie touches her corseted waist. Even with her joie de vivre, she can be proud of her figure. Has her stuffing in all the right places. She'll fit into Mr. Worth's new Parisian dresses if it kills her. Plenty of the Smart Set are daughters of those who plied Jessie's trade in the good old days in this very same fine establishment. The gold rush days, before Mr. Ned Greenway—the scum—started keeping track of who came from where and how and why.

"Let's go upstairs," Jessie whispers to Zhu.

Jessie, Zhu, and Daniel climb the stairwell to the second floor of the Poodle Dog. They peer through another lush fringe hanging over the doorway.

"By God, isn't that your Mr. Heald?" Daniel says.

The second floor of the Poodle Dog is well attended by Snob Hill residents and other renowned gentlemen of impeccable credentials. Well attended also by beauties of the city, the ones known as homewreckers. Jessie glances curiously at Zhu, who in her coolie's rags is a far cry from these jeweled ladies. Yet this is the set Zhu should belong to: the mistresses. In the mauve silk, which sets off her golden complexion and remarkable eyes, Zhu would look fine here, even without jewels. Some are actresses, singers, or dancers. Some are beautiful, some beautiful and smart, some smart enough to make themselves beautiful. A mistress makes her way in life as the devoted companion of a wealthy gentleman, one gentleman at a time. Which does not mean, of course, that these same gentlemen do not take their ease in Jessie's parlor. Jessie has fended off more jealous mistresses than wives at the front door of the Parisian Mansion, though only a wife had the gumption to show up with a horsewhip and demonstrate its use when her husband stumbled outside.

Jessie scrutinizes Mr. Heald and his dining companion, a petite French woman. Sure and her red hair is dyed and her dress two seasons old. "My diamonds is bigger," Jessie sniffs.

"Sorry, Miss Malone," Zhu says, catching everything with those eyes of hers.

"Missy, I could *never* live at the beck and call of the likes of Mr. Heald, and that's what a mistress must do." Significant look at her and Mr. Watkins. "Mr. Heald is merely my dear old friend. *I* am my own mistress."

"Good evening, Miss Malone," says a woman.

Jessie turns. His honor the railbird attempts to hurry past them as he climbs the stairwell, arm in arm with Daisy, one of Jessie's Parisian Mansion blonds. Daisy giggles and waves.

"Why, good evening, Your Honor," Jessie says. "Looks like my twenty double eagles will be a-flyin' back to my own little hand, won't they, darlin'?"

His honor's mouth drops open. Wasn't expecting to pay *that* much for his evening's pleasure. Wasn't expecting to see Miss Malone en route to the third floor of the Poodle Dog. Well, he knows now, doesn't he?

Jessie climbs the stairs after the couple, mightily pleased. The unctuous old doorman greets them at the top of the stairs, ushers them down a hushed hallway past a score of closed doors, to the next available private suite.

"Is this satisfactory, Miss Malone?" says the doorman with an arch look. Uncertain what to make of Jessie's latest ménage à trois. She has met the old fart at the top of the stairs for all the many long years she's been taking guests to the Dog. The arch look annoys her.

Jessie surveys the suite—red velvet carpet, plush chairs, a divan, gilt dining table, a silver bucket with champagne on ice. The paintings have gotten dull over the years. Seascapes and mountains.

"It'll have to do," she says, handing the old doorman a measly tip. "Bring us Pierre's frog's legs *sauté sec*, cracked crab, and a bottle of Pernod Fils."

She plumps down on the divan, pats the cushion next to her. Smiles up at Daniel. Daniel's eyes glitter. Jessie sighs. He cares nothing for their midnight tryst. Cares nothing for his mistress, if that's what Zhu has become. He only wants his Pernod Fils. Zhu roams about the suite, examining the furnishings and paintings.

"If your mother could see you, Mr. Watkins," Jessie says.

Daniel regards her coolly. "Absinthe is my mother, Miss

Malone. The mother of my happiness. She is the Green Fairy. She is holy water, the sacred herb."

"The brain lesions will make you mad," Zhu says, "if you don't keel over from a stroke first."

"She has green eyes, the cloak of a forest queen, and opalescent skin. She is *ma mere*." Daniel seizes Zhu's wrist, makes her sit in the chair next to him. "She is the mistress I love best. Her eyes are greener than yours. Jealous, Zhu?"

The doorman knocks. Zhu leaps up, opens the door. A waiter enters with the dark green bottle, neck wrapped in silver foil, a carafe of sparkling water, a dish of sugar cubes, three bell-shaped glasses. And three absinthe spoons, polished silver, the flat bowls of which are punched out in lovely elaborate filigrees.

Daniel seizes the waiter's tray. Hands shake with excitement as he sets the bottle, carafe, and sugar cubes just so. Distributes the glasses, places the absinthe spoons over the mouth of each glass. A dark look. "Let's see that knife of yours, mistress."

"Yes, the mollie knife," Jessie says. "Let's see it." Tosses coins onto the tray. The waiter vanishes.

"No, no," Zhu murmurs.

Daniel reaches into her pocket, finds the knife.

Zhu protests, flails at him, but he finds what he's looking for. Pushing Zhu away, he and Jessie bend over it. The knife is the same size and shape as Daniel's Congress knife, except for the sapphire knob protruding from the hilt. Daniel takes a sugar cube, takes the mollie knife, cuts the cube in half. Then pushes in the knob on the hilt. Imitating Zhu's work on Duncan Ross's skull, he guides the blade back over the cut. The sugar cube mends itself whole.

"Jar me," Jessie says. "It's a goddamn miracle!"

She and Daniel trade astonished glances. She turns to Zhu. The missy sits, shaking her head.

"Don't look so sour," Jessie says. "Mr. Edison would give his right arm for that."

"By God, how true," Daniel says.

"How is it done?" Jessie says.

"I told you." Zhu sulky. "It's a mollie knife, like I said."

Takes the knife back from Daniel, tucks it into her pocket. "A molecular knife, of course."

"Of course," Daniel says. "Induces molecular recombination, whatever that means. See, I wasn't that pickled." He uncorks the absinthe, pours three rounds.

"Pretty," Jessie says. The liquor is the color of a peridot.

Daniel balances a sugar cube in the bowl of each absinthe spoon, drizzles water over the cube. The cube dissolves. Sugar water drips, turning the liquor murky. "After the first glass you see things as you wish they were. After the second, you see things as they are not. After the third, you see things as they really are, which is the most horrible thing in the world." Daniel sips. His eyes turn murky the way the liquor did. "Mr. Oscar Wilde said that. Something like that, anyway. Cheers."

Jessie pours water over her own sugar cube and glass, baptizes Zhu's cube, too. Whispers as she leans over Zhu, "We'll not stock absinthe at the mansion, missy. The gentlemen will never get around to fucking." Aloud, "To your health, Miss Wong."

"I'll pass." Zhu pushes the glass away.

Daniel pushes it in front of her again. "How is it your mollie knife rejoins that which has been cut asunder, mistress?"

Zhu watches her sugar cube deliquesce, the liquor cloud like an alchemist's secret formula. Shrugs. "Matter is made up of molecules. Molecules are made up of atoms connected together by bonds. When you cut something, you break the bonds. The mollie knife merely rearranges the electrons, forming ions. The ions are attracted to each other and reform the bonds. Molecular recombination. It's not so hard, really."

Jessie sips. What a taste! Like chewing on forbidden herbs in one of those paintings of a celestial mountaintop, goat-footed satyrs taking liberties with winged nymphs. An ancient green, evil and pungent. They say mad monks brew the stuff. Absinthe careens into her blood. The gaslight glows more golden. The eyes of her companions deepen into pools. Their faces take on a strange nobility.

"Re-form the bonds," Jessie says. "That's downright romantic, Miss Wong. Isn't that romantic, Mr. Watkins?"

But Daniel glares at Zhu over his glass. "You're lying, mistress. You're making up stories. Like the *Wandering Jew.* Like Mr. Wells and his time machine."

"I don't lie," Zhu says. "My dear Mr. Watkins, that's one thing I never do."

"Yes, you do." The angry god scowling at his impudent mortal. "Every chance you get."

Jessie makes a quick gesture to Zhu, *easy does it*.

The waiter knocks, brings in another tray with covered dishes, shell crackers, long-stemmed forks, bowls of melted butter. Relieves the dishes of their covers, revealing steaming scarlet crabs, lovely slender frog's legs drowning in a pool of white sauce.

"She's a goddamn liar, Miss Malone," Daniel says.

Jessie tips the waiter, who scurries out. "Now, Mr. Watkins." Appeasing. Sometimes appeasement doesn't work with an irate gentleman. She's seen plenty. Daniel so edgy tonight; Jessie doesn't like it. Drink ought to cheer a man, not make him violent and mean. She breaks off two fat crab claws, spoons frog's legs, serves Daniel a fragrant dish. "Our Miss Wong did a wonderful thing tonight, Mr. Watkins. She saved a man."

Serves Zhu a dish, too, which she waves away. "It's midnight, Miss Malone."

"Sure and what does the time of day have to do with cracked crab?" Jessie says.

"Pah," Daniel says. Knocks the absinthe spoon from Zhu's glass. Clatter of silver on the tabletop. Picks up Zhu's glass, bidding her to drink. "We don't know what my mistress did. Perhaps Duncan Ross will wind up a lunatic with blood on his brain." Pours himself another round. "If the mollie knife is real, where can I get one?"

"You can't," Zhu says. Wistful smile; sardonic tone.

Jessie sips more absinthe. "Jar me, what an odd chit you are, Zhu." The walls of the suite soften into lovely pink clouds. Suddenly notices a moth swirling and circling in the glow of the gaslight. Like a little angel, yes, a tiny woman with golden wings. . . Jolt of alarm. Champagne never makes her *see* things like this! Another sip, and the alarm melts into a peculiar numb bliss, melts away like the sugar cube. Jessie plucks another sugar cube from the dish, sets up her glass. "What about the Montgomery Ward catalog?" she says. "They've got everything."

"I've never seen a mollie knife in Montgomery Ward," Daniel says. "Or in Sears, Roebuck."

"Not even Sears, Roebuck stocks a mollie knife." Zhu laughs. Takes a tiny sip of her absinthe. "Gah, that's vile." She clutches her stomach. "It burns!"

"Then where did you steal yours?" Daniel demands.

"See here, Mr. Watkins," Zhu says, flushing. "I don't lie and I don't steal. My mollie knife was given to me for the Golden Nineties Project. I am a Daughter of Compassion, and I've had just about enough of both of you today. Columbus Day, red wine; man's conquest." Meaningful glance at Daniel. "You should all be grateful I even agreed to t-port to this spacetime."

"Spacetime," Daniel says. "You said that before. She said that before, Miss Malone. Keeps talking about 'your day,' and 'her day.' "

"That's right," Jessie says. "She's mentioned 'her day' to me, too."

"What on earth do you mean by 'spacetime,' mistress?" Daniel says to Zhu.

"Why, all of space and all of time, which are a whole," Zhu says. "One does not exist without the other."

"No, no," Daniel says. "You see, Miss Malone? You women are confused. There is space. There is time. The one has nothing to do with the other."

"Each *is* the other, Mr. Watkins," Zhu says. "There is no distinction. There is only One Day, existing Now. Existing always."

"All right, missy," Jessie says. Loves a good spoof, but the sip of absinthe and this talk make her head spin. Still, she saw the mollie knife work with her own eyes. And what about the little voice? The spirit. "Why did you agree to . . . t-port to this time? To this space?" Guffaws. Often picks up the trade talk of her johns, but she can't quite get the missy's talk right. "To this . . . spacetime?"

Zhu sighs. "I'm not even sure myself anymore."

"Oh, come now, mistress," Daniel says. "You were doing so well. Surely you can dream up something."

"The girl is in jeopardy. More jeopardy than anyone knew." Zhu sips absinthe again. "I will get her to the home. I will." Takes off her fedora, the spectacles. "Look. I'm not supposed to reveal my true identity under Tenet Five of the Grandfather Principle."

"Oh, my. And who are you truly?" Jessie says. Wink at Daniel.

"Why, I'm from 2495," she says quite somberly.

"Are you sure?" Jessie says.

"Quite sure."

"You're not from, say, a million years in the future?"

"Certainly not."

Jessie whispers to Daniel, "I guess our Miss Wong didn't read Mr. Wells's novel."

"Mr. Wells's novel?" Zhu says.

"*The Time Machine*."

"Hot off the press in England," Daniel says. "*The New Review* ran the series. Good stuff." To Jessie, "You're right. She's got the dates all wrong."

"Mr. Watkins lent me his copy," Jessie says while Zhu stares at them both, bemused. "It's a very nice story. Better than yours, missy. You should make it a million years in the future. Much more exciting."

"Make it . . . Miss Malone," Zhu says. "I'm not making this up. I'm really from six hundred years in your future. So is the mollie knife, if you must know."

"Well, that's settled," Jessie says, digging at her crab claw. "You'll have to wait a bit to get your knife, Mr. Watkins."

"Pah," he says, but tucks into his crab, cheered by melted butter. "I bet I'll find a mollie knife in the Montgomery Ward catalog after all."

"I thought *you* thought my mollie knife was a miracle." The missy watching them again, clearly disappointed.

"Mr. Edison's lightbulb—*that's* a miracle," Jessie says. "And the cable cars? The transcontinental train?"

"Scotch Oats Essence," Daniel says. "Now *there's* a miracle." Raspy whisper to Zhu, "I hear they'll have a cure for cancer by the turn of the century."

"I don't believe it," she says quietly. "I don't believe *you*."

"Missy," Jessie says, wrinkling her brow, "how can you really be from six hundred years in the future? The future doesn't exist yet."

"But it does," she says. "Look, I'm no expert on this, either. But spacetime isn't a line, it's a whole. For every moment in the past, there is a future. The future always *is*, just like the past always is. All reality is One Day that exists Now; exists forever." Dares a third sip of her absinthe. "What cosmicist theory has always suggested, and what the practice of tachyportation shows, is that reality doesn't always exist the *same*. That the probable nature of reality on the quantum level applies to everything. Applies to us, too. We're living in a multiverse."

"Multiverse?" Jessie says.

"The fact that I'm here, and that I'm conscious I'm here, is constantly affecting what happens." Zhu considers her own words. "What happens in the past affects the future." Looks up, flicks her eyes to the side in the peculiar way she does. "I guess with tachyportation, the future also affects the past."

"Tall tales," Daniel says mildly. Absinthe flattens him like a stone rolling over his soul.

"No, I think I see, missy," Jessie says. "I think I get you. It's like when you remember something, and then you learn something new about what happened or you feel something new, understand something new. And suddenly the memory isn't the same anymore. And it's as if the whole world, the whole past, has changed!"

Zhu gazes at her. "I'll remember you said that, Miss Malone."

"Like me and Betsy," Jessie says. "My sweet innocent Betsy, long gone to the Summerland." Nearly starts to cry. Dabs at her eyes. "I thought she was wicked, but now I know she was just young. Young and innocent." No more Green Fairy for the Queen of the Underworld. "If only I could see things as I wish they were."

"I think I'm starting to see things as they are not," Daniel says.

Zhu frowns. "Me, too."

NOVEMBER 2, 1895 ▼ ▼ ▼

El Día de los Muertos

Nine Twenty Sacramento Street

Death struts the streets with a grin and a swagger, a striped serape thrown rakishly over his shoulder. Death tips his sombrero. Zhu wends through the crowd at the corner of Montgomery and Market, a leather-bound Bible tucked under her arm. A gift for Miss Donaldina Cameron. Better have something in hand for her first appointment with the director of Nine Twenty Sacramento. Death hands little skulls made of crystallized sugar to squealing children who jostle for a view of the parade.

"El Dia de los Muertos, Day of the Dead," Muse whispers. "The Roman Catholic Church calls it All Souls' Day. In America, we observe Halloween. Before the Spanish came to Mexico, the aboriginal people viewed death as the germ of life. Death and life intertwined in their cosmology. Death was neither revered nor feared; not completely understood, perhaps, but experienced. Celebrated."

"And your cosmology?" Zhu says. "Have cosmicists attained this peace of mind?"

"Peace of mind is within the individual," Muse says. "No

philosophy will confer peace of mind if you won't have it, Z. Wong."

Death laughs, robust and antic.

"What's the value of life, then?" she says. Anxiety closes cold fingers over her heart. Will Miss Cameron cooperate with her plan? "Cosmicists speak of the Great Good, equalizing humanity with all creatures and things. Does a cosmicist accept the death of a child as the same as—say—the destruction of a butterfly? Suppose it's a rare butterfly and the child is one of twelve billion. Is the aurelia's destruction more important?"

Catches herself. The *aurelia*?

"All this talk of death and destruction, Z. Wong," Muse says. "Are you melancholy again? You must try to fight this depression."

Muse solicitous, cajoling. When has Muse cajoled her? Capricious artificial intelligence; an oxymoron? Even with ambiguity tolerance, AI is not capricious. Not supposed to be, anyway. Muse has been informative, goading, astringent, rebellious, even cruel. But Muse solicitous? Has Zhu really been melancholy?

When? She's lost all track of time.

"Get on with the Golden Nineties Project." That's more like Muse.

"I'm getting on with the project." Zhu quells her annoyance, together with a sneeze. After four months of Zhu's agony unabated by the antihistamine in her pharmaceutical supplies, Muse has formulated a decongestant, plus antiallergen, that she can mix out of her own pharmaceuticals plus a touch of fresh nettle. Zhu went out and bought a mortar and pestle at the Snake Pharmacy at once. The decongestant still doesn't work one hundred percent. Browsing through Jessie's Montgomery Ward catalog for a Polyopticon Wonder Camera for Daniel, she happened upon the Patent Dust Protector—a little nickel-plated gas mask. Cost ninety cents, "ounce of prevention worth a pound of cure," guaranteed, lasted a lifetime. She ordered one, posthaste; five cents delivery charge. "I'm going to see Donaldina Cameron today. Who do you think the Bible is for?"

Since the Archivists' plan for Zhu to seek employment in the Presbyterian home got derailed by her rescue from the hatchet men by Jessie Malone, Zhu's efforts to contact Cameron have met with resistance. The mission put her off for weeks. Her respectful requests for an audience with Cameron were returned less respectfully. Cautious people, these Presbyterians. Muse consulted the Archives and discovered that the old warhorse of the home—one Miss Margaret Culbertson—suffers from ill health. Miss Cameron has assumed new responsibilities of temporary director.

Muse excited. This is a breakthrough for the Golden Nineties Project. "You must convince Cameron to rescue the girl."

"Now that I know where Wing Sing is, I will." But Zhu is troubled. "You still cannot find any trace of me in the files on Cameron?"

"Don't concern yourself," Muse says. "Cameron dealt with scores of Chinese women, many of whom remained anonymous."

"Anonymous," Zhu says. "That's what I am, all right." Swallows her resentment. Chiron made it clear right from the start: Chinese women of this day are anonymous.

Zhu slogs through the crowd. The Mexican community of San Francisco—from the Latin Quarter, from south o' the slot, from the valley—has turned out for the parade. Horsemen rear and wheel with ringing spurs, bands blare with their own unique sound of brass, guitars strum, maracas clatter. *Olé!* People promenade in costumes and papier-mâché masks depicting skulls. Some costumes are sly caricatures: a rich lady in a stole of chicken feathers and tiara of cardboard, skull made up with salacious lipstick and eye paint; a priest piously bearing enormous candelabra comprised of skulls, gaudy flowers hung from grinning teeth; a rowdy soldier in full dress uniform dangling green and red skulls from the brim of his cap, his bandoliers, his jacket sleeves, a carved wooden rifle; a morose barefooted peasant, a patch slung over the hollow eye socket of his skull mask, braided mustache swooping over his bare jawbone. A hound trots with the peasant, its clipped black fur painted with an elaborate canine skeleton in bright white and green.

No one escapes Death.

People guffaw, point at each new mockery. But Zhu cannot laugh. "What does it mean?" she asks a boy on the sidelines. Whooping at the parade, popping candy skulls into his mouth. A gangling teenager, all long hands and feet, narrow swarthy face, eyes like beads.

"To me, *senorita?*" he says. Face sunny and open. Not at all afraid of her the way children—and adults—of her day cringe from strangers, from anyone unknown. "Well, you're going to die sooner than you want, so why cry about it, eh?"

Death insists on presenting Zhu with a bouquet of pink paper flowers theatrically extracted from an embroidered shirtsleeve. *Why cry?* How sensible: this parade and its celebrants mocking death are psychologically healthy. She hands the flowers to the boy and tries to smile, but her mouth is numb. *Sooner than you want.* As soon as you are born, you know you will die. And the other way around? As soon as you die, you know you will be born? But that's reincarnation: an antiquated superstition strangely persistent in Zhu's day, though modern science has never proven its truth. One of those primitive peasant beliefs, stubborn and irrational.

Then why is her heart filled with a chill? The boy gives the flowers to a girl, darts away with his friends. These people will not witness the massive death that modern people face. World wars, holocausts, cancer epidemics, plagues like AIDS and herpes complex three and nuevo tuberculosis, ecopoisonings, the dreadful radiation syndrome. So many new forms of massive death.

"They know nothing of death," Zhu whispers, watching the boy go.

"Of course they do." Muse sardonic. "People die in their twenties of tuberculosis; there's no cure. They die of dysentery, plague, cancer, yellow fever, cholera, typhoid fever, syphilis, childbirth. This time knows as much about death as yours."

"Fair enough," Zhu says. "But they still revere *life*, despite el Dia de los Muertos. They assume that life—the creation of life, the preservation of life—is humanity's highest value. Can we say the same, Muse?"

Muse silent.

▼ ▼ ▼

Zhu did not know if she could say the same about 2495 when spring came to Changchi, and the Daughters of Compassion geared up for another campaign. The World Birth Control Organization had conducted a new lottery under the Generation-Skipping Law. The lottery was random, of course, but critics claimed a disproportionate number of couples in Chihli Province had been chosen to skip. Protestors staged demonstrations, filed complaints in World Court. The local office of the WBCO was firebombed. The ranks of the Society for the Rights of Parents swelled.

Zhu had always loved spring. A time to take off the sour padded winter jacket, get out of the domes, bask beneath a restored sky in the sun. Cool breezes rippled feathery leaves of new wheat sprouting in the undomed plots. Agriworkers bowed over the land, spreading manure, planting millet and peas by hand. Of all the wonders of the world, no machine or robot had yet been invented that could take a delicate seedling and coax soil around it just so.

Had always loved spring; but not that spring. That spring started out with omens. With the first thaw, wild dogs slunk out of the mountains and harried field workers. The dogs attacked a seven-year-old girl walking alone at dusk from school to her family's apartment, half devoured her. She died the next day. Then a hailstorm whipped through the province, damaging four of the big public domes, thousands of residential units and vehicles. When the hailstones melted, they released methane. The air smelled like an open sewer. Undomed fields faced ruin.

The Daughters of Compassion faced ruin, too. Someone dumped excrement in the compound's water recycler, and, before anyone realized their water was contaminated, nearly everyone had contracted dysentery. Always thin, Zhu dropped twelve pounds. She was still weak, wobbly, and running a fever when she, Sally Chou, Hsien-e, and Pat Greenberg trudged through the square of mud and cracked concrete that was Changchi's civic center.

"Door to door," Sally was saying. "That's how we've got to contact them. WBCO will supply names and addresses of the skipcouples. We'll drop off literature, schedule an appointment after."

"I think we should meet with the husbands, too, not just the women," said Hsien-e.

"Sure, if they'll agree," Sally said. "In my experience, it won't happen."

"Don't you think we need to forge a new experience?" said Pat. "You're just reinforcing retrograde attitudes if you make only the women responsible for observing the law." Pat was another American expatriate who'd come to Changchi looking for her daughter, an exchange student who had fallen for a local and never gone back to New York. She argued with Sally night and day, but then everyone had been puking their guts out for weeks. They all felt like hell.

"I say stick with the plan," Sally said. "We're the Daughters of Compassion."

"No, I think you're alienating—" Pat said.

Zhu couldn't take it. Her head was throbbing, a metallic taste rose in her throat, her gut was gurgling. "Could you please just both shut *up*?" she said. She looked up from the mud, her vision preternaturally clear. "Oh, shit," she added, some instinct kicking her in the butt.

A surly crowd had gathered in the square. The Society for the Rights of Parents had set up a stage and podium, a sound system patched to a utility pole. A speaker in a suit and tie paced back and forth across the tiny stage.

"The Generation-Skipping Law flies in the face of values held dear by humanity for all time!" said the speaker. "The law robs us of our heritage, robs us of our tradition, robs us of our future!"

"If we don't have the law, we won't *have* a future," Sally yelled. "We won't have enough food, enough living space, enough water. You think that shit-smelling hail was bad?

How'd you like the air to smell like that all the time? How'd you like the water to taste like that all the time?"

"Damn it, Sally," Zhu muttered but Pat was clapping Sally on the back for once.

The crowd began to boo and grumble. Heads snapped around, hard eyes stared. A gang in Parents' armbands drifted from the stage to the edge of the square.

"Here we go," Zhu said, wrapping her arms around her ribs. Her teeth chattered like the clatter of hailstones.

"You believe that overpopulation propaganda?" the speaker said. "It's disinformation, people. A hoax! A sham! When we have more people, we have more brainpower, more musclepower. We can overcome problems of supply, overcome pollution! We always have, and we always will."

"The only reason you had something to eat today, brother," Sally shouted, "is because we imposed the law! We have restored the atmosphere, maintained production, maintained zero population growth because of the law! You would not have shoes on your feet, brother, if we had not enforced the law!"

"Let's get out of here, Sal," Zhu said.

"The law!" Pat shouted, then faltered. Glanced at Zhu, fear in her eyes. Understood suddenly their precarious situation. Pat and Zhu started backing away from the crowd advancing on them.

Hsien-e slipped through the crowd and was gone. Zhu remembered the back of Hsien-e's head, her ragged crew cut. Thought, ridiculously, *cowardice is the better part of sanity.*

But Sally Chou was never one to back down from anything. "We've always had famine in China!" she shouted as Pat tugged at her elbow. "We've always had disease! We've had bad air, bad food, bad water for three hundred years! We've never had enough! In the old days, communism redistributed wealth, but that was a sham. A sham, people! Communism redistributed wealth from the rulers of the empire to the bureaucrats of another empire. That's all! Don't you get it? We can *never* have a decent quality of life for all of us under any form of empire till we the people control ourselves, control our families. Educate ourselves. Till we bring our population *down*."

"Fascist!" the speaker shouted back. "Traitor to the people!"

"Fucking Daughters of Compassion!" yelled someone in the crowd.

Pushing, shoving, suddenly fists were pummeling Zhu's sore guts, and she was flailing with her own fists, the karate only as good as her own strength, which was next to nothing. Sally and Pat screaming, whistles shrieking, the speaker's voice fuzzy with feedback.

She was down on the ground in no time, curled in a fetal position, hands protecting her head, the back of her neck. Someone ripped her jeans down; she felt a man's hard body against her butt. Unmistakable sting of a knife whipped across the backs of her hands before she vomited in the cold mud and passed out.

They beat Sally pretty bad. Cut up Zhu a bit, bruised her ribs. Didn't rape her, after all. She only fully appreciated her good fortune when she thought about the incident later, nearly vomited again at the memory of that hard body behind her. Pat was stabbed a half dozen times. The WBCO transferred emergency funding and the Changchi medcenter sent her down to Beijing on a whirligig. Zhu heard she died. Later that she was critical, but pulling through.

The mood at the compound became nearly unbearable, a volatile mix of acute fear and red-hot outrage. Several comrades quietly moved out at once. But for those who remained, a new fervor infected everyone.

Sally was up at the front of the mess hall the very next day, fiercely proud with her face swollen and discolored, bandages swathing her head and shoulders. Arm in a sling, she held her cigarette in the slinged hand, insisted on twisting her head down and the arm up to suck herbal smoke in a torturous mime of self-sacrifice. Contaminated the air in the whole dome with her smoke. No one had smoked a combustible inside the main dome for nearly a century. No one seemed to care.

"We will not be intimidated!" she shouted.

"We will not be intimidated!" everyone shouted.

They posted guards around the compound twenty-four hours a day. Sally managed to come up with fifty assault rifles, no one knew from where. And in her feverish struggle to keep the Daughters alive, Sally also managed to come up with the patches. Black patches. This was the point in the campaign when the Daughters of Compassion first started using black patches. They told no one, of course, especially not the WBCO.

Zhu was in the dorm, resting. Sally wouldn't let her stay at the medcenter. She wanted her in the compound, under the Daughters' guard. The medic used a mollie knife on Zhu's cuts, which knit the skin just fine. But trauma purpled the wound sites. The swelling was ugly. There wasn't much the medic could do for her ribs, either. Zhu lay on her cot, bruises throbbing, gut gurgling, despair clogging her heart when Sally came in and sat beside her.

"Give me your leg, kiddo." Sally pulled the sheets down.

A little sting behind her knee next to the contraceptive patch. Slowly—was it possible?—the throbbing eased, then subsided. Even her gut settled down. She actually sat up. Twisted her leg and looked. There, a patch of silky black next to the bright red square of the contraceptive patch. "What is it?"

"Feel better?" Sally grinned, a cigarette dangling from her lip.

"What is it?" she said again. Better and better.

"Take it easy. You don't know your own weakness. The patch masks it."

"The patch?"

"It's an opiate synthy with some kind of upper. What they call a speedball. Black patch."

"Damn you, Sally." Zhu had endured her teen years without so much as tasting beer, let alone experimenting with the drugs that floated through even a jerkwater burg like Changchi. She must have looked horrified because Sally guffawed until she choked and fanned her face with her hand.

"Don't worry about it, I can get more."

"But do you think this is a good . . . ?"

"I think it's a *great* idea. Kiddo, they use the black patch for medical treatment. It's okay. Releases the stuff over time, know what I mean? Just drizzles that sweet dope right in. No problem. Listen, Zhu," she said, growing serious, "between the bug in your gut and our pals in the square, you're halfway to nowhere. And I need you up and running." She pulled out hardcopy. "We got information that the Parents are hacking our d-base for stats on skipcouples, skipkids. The lousy so-and-sos. Anyway. We gotta get to those folks before they do."

"All right." Zhu remembered swinging her legs down from the cot and thinking that a nutribar might actually taste good.

"Plus, we gotta go down to the schools, talk to the teens, the twennies." Sally yammered on, stabbing at data on the hardcopy with her forefinger. "Plus, we heard they're aiding and abetting illegal pregnancies, setting up birth clinics, shit like that."

"Okay. All right. I get it."

But Zhu had not gotten it. She had no inkling then, no premonition at all, that this was another step down the road to chaos.

No; she smiled. Felt *much* better. Could hardly feel the pain anymore.

▼ ▼ ▼

Zhu strides toward the invisible walls of Tangrenbu. Her anxiety deepens. The probabilities do not favor this meeting. The Archives do not support her presence here at all: at another compound, another refuge for women, so far away from Changchi and the Daughters of Compassion.

Nine Twenty Sacramento is an imposing brick building with a domed roof poised at the crest of a hill steeply angling up to Nob Hill to the west, down to Tangrenbu to the east. Iron grilles are bolted over the windows. The place looks like a fortress or a prison.

The stench of Tangrenbu permeates the autumn air. Chinese men in their denim *sahms* trek silently by, but Zhu can feel the pressure of their eyes, their muted anger at her presence before the controversial Presbyterian mission. Dressed in the proper clothes of a white woman, veil drawn over her face, hair pinned up beneath her Newport hat, she conceals her race from the bachelors. Someone throws a pebble, striking her shoulder blade. She does not turn. She lifts the door knocker, sending a resounding *boom* into the rooms behind the massive walnut door.

A worried young Chinese woman cracks the door open, peeks out over a chain lock. Whispers, "Who?"

"My name is Zhu Wong. I have an appointment with Miss Cameron. She's expecting me."

The door bangs shut, locks click. The door reopens. She is quickly ushered inside by the young woman and shown to a straight-backed chair. She waits, sniffing astringent air. Scents of polish, lemon soap. So different from the smell of Tangrenbu outside. She runs her finger down the arm of the chair. Not a speck of dust.

At last a plump white woman appears. Indeterminate age, graying hair, pince-nez perched on her nose. She looks worried, too. "Good day, Miss Wong. I am Eleanor Olney."

"Good day. Excuse me, Miss Olney, but I'm not the bill collector."

"Yes?" Miss Olney says.

"Well . . . Why does everyone look so frightened?"

Penetrating look through the pince-nez. "We had to dispose of a stick of dynamite today."

"A stick of dynamite?"

"On our stoop, Miss Wong."

"Who would put dynamite on your stoop?" Dynamite? For a couple of women and their collection of children huddled in this barred refuge?

"The highbinders, Miss Wong," she says dramatically, but Zhu knows the *boo how doy* are worthy of her sentiment. "The tongs are displeased with our new associate director. She's thrown the slavers into quite a whirl."

"I see." Zhu looks warily around. A shadow ripples at the far end of the dark hall. Muse posts a string of statistics on the tongs in her peripheral vision. When she looks back, Miss Olney has tucked her pince-nez in a pocket. Or has she? Zhu stares. No marks on her nose and face like you'd usually see when a habitual wearer takes her glasses off.

Watery pale eyes above pouched cheeks regard her doubtfully. "This way, Miss Wong. Lo Mo will see you now."

"Lo Mo?"

"The Mother; with Mrs. Culbertson on leave, that's what the girls have started calling her, though her family calls her Dolly and some of her friends call her Donald. You," she says sternly, "may call her Miss Cameron."

Zhu walks through hushed halls, button boots clattering on immaculate wood floors. After Jessie's excesses, these rooms are almost too austere, set with a few sticks of furniture, and scrupulously clean. Whitewashed walls are relieved by a couple of tiny paintings that have been parsimoniously doled out: a blond Jesus, his blue eyes cast to heaven, surrounded by blond children; an unsmiling Mary in a hooded robe, coddling lambs and doves. From a distant room children's voices dutifully recite the English alphabet.

Two little girls, their black hair tied up on their heads, kneel on the floor with brushes and pails of soapy water and meticulously scrub the floor. An open door reveals a group of girls seated at tables busily sewing dresses and shirts, fabric heaped before them. Steam and the scent of starch stream from another door where older girls bend over washtubs and piles of laundry. At the end of the hall, three girls sit at a table with silverware, a tea set and silver tray, jars of polish, rags stained with streaks of black. Their low conversation falls silent as Zhu walks by. Glancing black eyes; Zhu cannot tell if the girls are fearful or curious, but a peculiar tension grips them.

The girls are all Chinese, of course. Wards of the home.

Miss Olney shows Zhu to an office. Donaldina Cameron sits behind a large rosewood desk, implements of business precisely arranged upon it. She is only twenty-five, but her chestnut hair caught in a pompadour is broadly streaked with white, making her appear much older. Her fair complexion is ashen, her expression harried. A lovely woman, Scotch, with broad bold brows, large eyes, prominent cheekbones, an almost sensuous mouth. She wears a billowing black voile skirt, a plum shirtwaist with leg-o'-mutton sleeves hand-folded in tiny pleats. At her throat, an Art Nouveau brooch. With a start, Zhu looks closely, but the curves of gold are the wings of a dove. Expensive; the sort of clothes and jewelry a fine lady would wear. Out of place, unexpected, in this spartan fortress. A Chinese girl brings in a freshly polished silver tray, serves tea with wedges of lemon in celadon glazed porcelain.

"A gift for you, Miss Cameron," Zhu says deferentially and hands her the Bible.

Miss Cameron looks Zhu up and down coldly. "Miss Wong. You look like a proper young woman. Is it true you are employed by that scourge, Jessie Malone?"

Zhu hesitates. Anger quickens at this fine pampered lady. Muse flashes a warning in her peripheral vision. She bites her tongue; of course, she needs Cameron's help. How else will she get Wing Sing into the home? "I am just the bookkeeper." At Cameron's contemptuous glance, "Miss Malone isn't so bad. She's fair."

Cameron takes the Bible, runs her finger down the leather binding. "That's the first time I've heard someone call a purveyor of human flesh fair." She looks exhausted. "What can I do for you, Miss Wong?"

"I know of a girl." Zhu tells Cameron about Wing Sing, Madam Selena's on Pacific Street.

"I know Selena," Cameron says, suddenly freed of her foul mood. Her eyes come alive. "Selena is despicable. Mrs. Culbertson rescued a five-year-old from that place last spring. The child had been smuggled in and sold as a *mooie-jai*; a household slave, Miss Wong. Selena poured boiling water on the child's hands when she didn't serve tea properly. Let's see." Cameron seizes a ledger on her desk, leafs through the pages. "Selena's got a trapdoor on the roof leading up from the southeast bedroom. There's a butcher shop in back with an adjoining roof and a fire escape. They'll have to be watched." She slaps the ledger shut. Eyes narrow. "Why do you want to rescue this girl?"

"Because. . ." Zhu feels uncomfortable lying to Cameron. "She is a distant relation of mine; a cousin. I don't want to see her live like that."

"I see. You wouldn't by any chance intend to recruit your distant cousin for Jessie Malone's Morton Alley cribs?"

"No, no! Nothing like that!"

"Well, Miss Wong," Cameron says. "Your employment hardly recommends you. We've been deceived many times by the likes of you."

Zhu steadies herself. The force of Cameron's self-righteousness makes her feel every inch an accused woman. "I want her to live here," she says with genuine passion. "She *must* live here. She's *supposed* to live here. Please, I implore you, Miss Cameron. Take Wing Sing into your home. Make her safe."

Cameron scrutinizes Zhu. The gleam in her eye returns, a slow smile. She rubs her hands with glee. "Very well! Let's go rescue her."

Cameron sends a messenger to the callbox on Kearny Street and an officer with the patrol wagon there takes her message to the Chinatown station. Before Zhu has finished her tea, a quintet of local bulls shows up at the door bearing hatchets, sledgehammers, crowbars, ropes, wedges, and determined scowls.

"Hallo there, Mr. Cooke, Mr. Andrews, gentlemen," Cameron greets them briskly. The policemen are dapper in bowler hats, high starched collars, cravats, tweed jackets neatly buttoned. "This," she says to Zhu, "is our raiding squad." She tells the bulls Zhu is her informant and mentions Madam Selena, whose name excites chatter, flexing of manly muscles, twitching of mustaches. Off they go, crammed in a brougham, bound for Pacific Street.

The plug-ugly Stick Victorian has got a red light burning in the window, despite the ordinance. Cameron confers with the police. Two bulls scurry around back to stand guard over the fire escape leading down from the roof of the butcher shop. The rest of their party strides to the front door of Madam Selena's. To Zhu's amazement, Cameron hoists her skirt and petticoats and bounds up the front stairs, leading the way. Zhu follows.

"Even the highbinders don't dare harm me," Cameron declares. "Stay close. You'll need to identify her."

They climb to the porch, smartly rap on the front door, which—Zhu notices for the first time—is equipped with an outer door made of iron bars that at the moment is firmly shut and locked. Cameron vigorously seizes the door knocker shaped like a rooster. Nothing. Curtains shiver in an upstairs window.

"Mr. Andrews?" Cameron says.

Andrews steps forward and wields his ax. In a moment, he's completely smashed the wood all round the door frame. Cooke applies the crowbar, plucking bolts right out, and flings the door open. Andrews smashes the ax against the second front door, splintering the wood. The third bull kicks the door in.

Cameron storms in, black skirts billowing. Zhu steps into the parlor. Andrews whirls, smashing rosewood chairs, tables, statuary, the lewd paintings on the wall. Cooke kicks at spittoons, vases, sends porcelain shattering against the baseboards. The third bull heaves the lamp with its red light through the front window. Selena's women fly out of rooms, shrieking, scrambling here and there, to the back of the house, upstairs.

Zhu and Cameron charge up the stairs, Zhu leading now, recalling the bedroom where she last saw Wing Sing. Madam Selena, in a black silk nightgown and robe, steps out of Wing Sing's bedroom. She slams and locks the door, stands defiantly, barricading the room with her body.

"That's it, at the end of the hall!" Zhu cries. Stares: was that a figure darting behind Selena into the room? No, it can't be. Selena just closed and locked it. Her breath rasps in her throat. Dizzy, disoriented.

Madam Selena heaves herself at Zhu, cursing and punching. "You go now! No one here!"

Andrews swings the ax, Cook wedges his crowbar in the lip of the door. They pop the bedroom right open. Cameron and Zhu rush in.

"No one here!" Selena cries. "*Fahn quai.*" She spits.

And there is no one. The bedroom is empty. Cameron throws open the closet, throws back the bedclothes, kicks at the flimsy wire frame of the bed.

"She not here, *fahn quai*!" Madame Selena says. "You devils!"

"Wait," Cameron says, cocking her head. Puts her finger to her lips.

Zhu strains, listening. There; a tiny scratching sound?

"You turn into a turtle!" Selena yells. "All your children turn into toads!"

Cameron seizes the bed, struggles to push it away from the corner. Andrews and Cook join in, shoving the bed frame across the room. Andrews breaks the washstand with one stroke of the ax, sending water and basin flying. Cameron hugs the walls, tapping, listening. "Listen for a hollow sound," she says. "There's a secret compartment in here, I know it."

Zhu follows suit; hears nothing unusual. Cameron wipes her forehead, flushed and sweating.

Again, a tiny scratching.

Cameron drops to her knees with a cry of triumph, scratches at the floor with her fingernails. Zhu pushes her aside, runs the mollie knife down the crack between the floorboards. Cooke applies the crowbar. A loose nail flies up out of its hole, two boards easily pop up.

And there, in a narrow space under the floor, curled up in a silk robe: Wing Sing wide-eyed, trembling.

"Ai!" screams Madame Selena. "All go to hell!"

The house cook and a tong enforcer stand watching at the door, but they make no move. The enforcer smiles a little, stares boldly at Zhu. She has never seen him before.

"Wing Sing," Zhu says gently. The girl is glassy-eyed, crudely smeared with face paint. Drugged? Her mouth hangs open, limbs limp. Her coiffure is disheveled. She wears the same apple green silk pajamas, now soiled and wrinkled. Foreboding rises in Zhu's throat. She glances at the girl's feet. Still the same straw sandals threaded with green silk. But her feet are sheathed in thick white cotton stockings. Bound? Unbound? Zhu cannot tell. "We're going to go now, okay?"

Wing Sing stares at her. "Jade Eyes?"

"Yes, it's me. We're going to take you home." Hates lying! "To the home," she says, as if that makes a difference.

"My jade, my gold," Wing Sing says. "My dowry. I take my dowry!"

"Where's her jewelry?" Zhu says to Madam Selena. "I know she's got some jewelry."

The madam shrugs. Zhu turns to Cameron. Cameron tears around the room again, tapping, prying. Finds another secret compartment in the floor of the closet. Cooke breaks it open. There, the rosewood box! Zhu eagerly seizes the box, catches Cameron's quizzical look.

"I told you, she's my cousin," Zhu says. "I know this girl brought a dowry from China. Let's see if Selena has stolen the only wealth this girl has, together with her girlhood."

"Indeed, yes, let's see." Cameron won over. Eagerly flings back the lid herself.

She will have it.

Glitter of gold, bracelets of jade, earrings and rings. Zhu peers breathlessly. There are several new pieces she does not recognize, amber, lapis lazuli, a trifle made of freshwater pearls. Please. Zhu doesn't care how or where the girl got the aurelia, if a john gave it to her, if she bought it herself at Colonel Andrews's Diamond Palace. If it materialized out of thin air. Please make this right; Wing Sing is supposed to possess the aurelia. Please, she's got to be the one.

The aurelia isn't there.

Cameron beams. "Praise Jesus Christ!"

Andrews hands his ax to Cooke. With a gentleness Zhu did not think possible, the policeman lifts Wing Sing in his arms.

❙ ❙ ❙

"Hello, dear," Miss Eleanor Olney says to Wing Sing, waiting in a tiny dormitory with several beds. Zhu and Cameron lead the trembling girl inside. Olney has got a basin of steaming water ready, soap, a wash cloth, and towels. White towels, a little threadbare, but crisp. "Let's get you clean, dear."

Her tone implies more than physical dirt.

Wing Sing looks at the homely walls of Nine Twenty

Sacramento. The sticks of furniture, the bare wood floors. The other girls peek at her with their scrubbed faces, disciplined hair, rough cotton clothes. Wing Sing backs away from Olney, hugging her silk around her. Despite the wrinkles, her apple green pajamas, the black and yellow embroidery, intricate pattern of willow leaves, gold satin frogs, stand out in this plain place like some glorious pennant of sin.

Olney advances, bearing a dripping bar of soap. "Now, dear. Take off those rags and let me wash you."

"You not touch me, *fahn quai*." Wing Sing spits at her.

"Come on, Wing Sing," Zhu says.

"The girl may have a little trouble adjusting," Cameron says. Somber, reasonable; triumphant, too. "They often do."

Olney seizes a green silk sleeve. "I can't get you clean if you won't take off your clothes."

"Oh, ho!" Wing Sing says. "You not pay, I not take off clothes."

"Really!" Olney says. Glares at Zhu.

"You know where she's been," Zhu says, glaring back.

Wing Sing seizes Zhu's sleeve. Pleading. "Jade Eyes, I go home, okay?"

"You are home, dear child," Cameron says, taking Wing Sing's hand. Wing Sing flings her hand away. "We'll get her busy soon enough, Eleanor. Sewing; she seems to like clothes." To Zhu, "Do you know if she can sew?"

Zhu shakes her head. Worried now. The kid has got to stay in this place. She's supposed to live here. Harshly, "Wing Sing, take off the dirty clothes and wash that crap off your face," she says. "You won't need it here."

The two Presbyterian women throw a startled glance her way. Zhu doesn't care. Maybe brusqueness works where kindness fails. The madams and johns push these young women around. The girl isn't used to kindness. *Retrograde attitude*, Pat Greenberg's voice echoes; *forge a new experience*. Zhu shifts uncomfortably.

"I not sew. I not sew!" Wing Sing wails. "I have maid; *she* sew!"

"Get the jewelry box," Cameron murmurs to Olney. Olney makes a motion to take the box, but Wing Sing clutches the box to her chest and backs up all the way into a corner, rolling her eyes.

"I don't think you should take her jewelry," Zhu says. "That *is* her dowry. All she has from her family."

"Miss Wong, do you really suppose it's hers?" Cameron snaps.

"Wing Sing, is the jade and gold really yours?" Zhu says.

Wing Sing weeps. Tears course through her white makeup, streaking her cheeks with eye paint. "Jade Eyes, you know my mama give me dowry. My mama not know how the man to be my husband take me to Shanghai and sell me. You say I to marry! You say I have my own home, my own daughter."

Zhu turns on Cameron, matching, for once, the director's self-righteousness. "This girl was tricked by a would-be husband, Miss Cameron," Zhu says. "She's not a thief, and she's not a whore. She says her mother gave her this dowry. She says she was supposed to marry. Isn't that right, Wing Sing?"

The girl nods. Cameron exchanges a long look with Zhu, and Zhu can see in Cameron's eyes that her soul flies out to Wing Sing.

Muse posts a file in Zhu's peripheral vision. The Archives may not substantiate Zhu's presence here, but they amply support Wing Sing's. Someone like Wing Sing.

Zhu softly to Muse, "Yes!"

"All right," Cameron says. "Let her keep the jewelry." The director with her rules. "Clean her up, Eleanor."

Zhu and Cameron close the door to the dormitory, leaving Miss Olney to her task.

Wing Sing yells, "I go home, now, okay? I go home!"

❙ ❙ ❙

"My apologies for any misunderstanding we may have had earlier," Cameron says over cocoa. Aromatic chocolate in a rose-glazed cup. Another exquisite tea set brought in by a girl. Cameron takes up a rose silk fan, manufacturing a breeze over her face. A spirit of camaraderie graces them after retiring to Cameron's office and comparing notes of Wing Sing's successful rescue. "You're good at this."

"You're good, too, Miss Cameron," Zhu says, sipping cocoa.

"You're a strong young woman," Cameron says. "You understand them. I confess I'm impressed. I could use you here."

"I confess I wanted to seek a position here."

Surprise in Cameron's eyes. "Why didn't you?"

"Something . . . happened. Something unexpected." Zhu's words ring strangely in Cameron's quiet office. Unexpected; what? Jessie Malone? Daniel J. Watkins? Zhu herself?

"Ask for a position," Muse whispers in her ear, subaud mode.

But Zhu sips cocoa silently. The home is very nice. Yes, it does remind her of the compound at Changchi. But how can she leave Jessie? How can she possibly leave Daniel?

Cameron ruefully examines her ravaged fingernails. Perspiration stains bloom in the underarms of her plum shirtwaist. Her pompadour is wispy, her skirt less crisp. She unpins the brooch at her throat, tosses the gold dove on her desk. Yet she is restored as the gracious hostess of her spanking-clean brick house. She takes up her ledger, dips a pen, commences writing an account of their afternoon's activity in precise curling script. Softly, "I feel so grateful to Our Father every time we undertake a successful rescue."

"Everyone is so grateful to *you*, Miss Cameron." Zhu cannot resist adding, "You enjoy the excitement, don't you?"

Cameron smiles a little. "Perhaps you're right. I only hope our Wing Sing will find happiness here. I cannot guarantee her that."

A prickle of alarm climbs up Zhu's spine. Cameron is nothing like she expected; now the unexpected rears again. *I cannot guarantee;* but of course she can. She must. "How is Miss Culbertson getting on?"

Cameron rubs her forehead with her thumb, smooths back her pompadour. That skeptical look. "Forgive me, Miss Wong, but how do you know about Margaret?"

"Everyone knows about Miss Culbertson. She's . . ." Muse posts a phrase in her peripheral vision. "Miss Culbertson has been doing her good works in the city for years."

"Of course," Cameron says. As though peeling off a mask, she suddenly looks gaunt, haggard, fatigued. Sets down the ledger, her pen. "The director is ill, as you know. I am swiftly finding myself in her place. I'm sorry there's so little time to train someone permanent. I'm not getting many responses to the advertisement I placed with our congregation."

"Advertisement?"

"For a new director. A permanent director."

Zhu sits up. Donaldina Cameron is the new director. The permanent director; she will manage this mission just about till the day she dies. The Archives are unequivocal about that.

Or are they? The probabilities don't support Zhu here, either. There is no record of her relationship with Cameron. The spartan room suddenly seems gossamer. Zhu rubs her eyes; what can she do?

"Miss Cameron," she says, "could you conceal my identity as your informant in your account of this afternoon?"

"Well. . ."

"I also have cousins in Chee Song Tong. It could be awkward for me. Please understand."

"Very well," Cameron says. With sympathy, "I do understand."

"And I thought . . . well, it's my understanding that you are to be the new director."

"Heavens, no, Miss Wong. I intend only to stay till the Chinese New Year next February. I have a fiancé."

Chinese New Year? That's Zhu's departure date, as well. "Fiancé?"

"Oh, yes." Cameron blushes. "We intend to marry in the spring. Charlie is a wonderful man, God bless him." Troubled smile. "Well, you know, he's a man. But I'm so looking forward to marrying and having my own home. My own children."

"But," Zhu says, "you're superb in this position."

"I'm sorry, Miss Wong. No, I can't possibly stay."

"But you have to stay."

"May I ask why?"

"Because the girls need you."

And Zhu wants to say: because you *do* stay; because it

is your destiny. The Archivists know all about Donaldina Cameron. Her life is thickly documented, a tribute to her single-mindedness, her faith. Her devotion to this Cause.

"Sacrifice," Muse whispers. The monitor's voice seems to hover in the air above Zhu. Spontaneous projection mode again.

"Damn it, Muse," Zhu whispers. "*Quiet*."

Cameron looks up from her cocoa curiously.

A chill runs down Zhu's spine. What is destiny for any human being? What becomes of probabilities that collapse out of the timeline? Does destiny depend on who witnesses?

Zhu's stomach clenches. Will she violate Tenet Three if she could influence Cameron now? In the sweep of history, no one will ever know she was here. She is anonymous.

"Surely," Zhu says, voice rasping in her throat, "you know how they need you."

"They need someone, yes, but they don't need *me*," Cameron says. She rises and shuts the door to her office. She sits again, slumping behind the rosewood desk, and bows her face into her hands. Her shoulders begin to shake.

"I have a *life*, Miss Wong," Cameron says. "I have a life with books and music and flowers. Pretty clothes, jewelry. I want my life back again. I want my own house, not this place. Charlie loves me. We're going to marry in the spring, like I told you. That's our plan." Raises her face; her eyes are anguished. "I *hate* the brothels. I *hate* the cribs. I *hate* what the highbinders are doing to these girls. It is more loathsome to me than I can possibly say. My soul shrinks from it. It's horrible. Horrible!"

"Then you *must* stay," Zhu says.

"No! I cannot stand it!"

"But Lo Mo, you understand so well. . ."

"Lo Mo. Lo Mo. I am *not* their mother. Don't you understand? I can barely sleep. Food is ashes in my mouth."

"You'll endure, Lo Mo," Zhu says.

"Why?" Cameron demands. "Why should I give up my life?"

And then something outrageous happens.

"Because this is your Cause, Donaldina," Muse says in a

high, clear voice. Muse projects its voice into a far corner of Cameron's office.

Cameron gapes. Slowly sputters and gasps. Stares at Zhu with a mix of awe, suspicion, a good dose of fear. "What is this deviltry that clings to you, Miss Wong?" she whispers.

"Oh, my," Zhu murmurs sarcastically to Muse.

"I am the Chinese woman's own sweet guardian angel," Muse says. "Not that she deserves me."

"Please," Zhu mutters.

"Fear not, beloved sister." Muse shameless. "Gird up thy strength and plunge onward, oh sister of mercy. Your blessed path lies before you. Do not shirk from it."

"My blessed path is with husband and family," Cameron says. "As you should surely know, angel, since God knows all and everything that is to be."

Zhu blinks. Her left eye begins to throb. Muse swiftly downloads a file from the Archives into her optic nerve.

"Please open your eyes, Z. Wong." Muse perfunctory.

Zhu opens her eyes, and Muse projects a holoid field into the center of Cameron's office like a luminous blue wall hovering a foot off the polished wood floor.

Cameron's cup of cocoa crashes.

"Easy does it," Zhu whispers. "Don't give her cardiac arrest, all right?"

"This is what is to be," Muse says, voice ringing like a little silver bell.

Zhu sits bolt upright. *What is to be?*

A pastoral scene as big as the whole wall springs into the holoid field. People saunter across a grassy field past a carousel, a gothic stone mansion.

"Why, that's Golden Gate Park," Cameron says. "The carousel. And the Sharon building. We took an outing in the park only last week."

A young fellow strolls by in a Prince Albert cutaway, a shabby top hat, his hair straggling over his collar. Peculiarly, he wears the blue denim trousers of a coolie. He turns; Zhu and Cameron gasp at the same time. His shaggy mustache and round spectacles are all right, but his face. . . His face is painted bright pink, blue, and green, the garish colors wrought in paisley shapes familiar in fabrics loomed in the golden nineties. But those colors! On his face!

"What has he done to his face?" Cameron whispers.

A young woman runs up to him. Again Zhu and Cameron gasp. She wears a thin cotton T-shirt through which her uncorseted, unbodysuited breasts bob alarmingly, a long paisley skirt, no shoes. Her feet are muddy. Zhu meets Cameron's look; *no shoes?*

More young people—men and women—stroll around the carousel, the Sharon building, both of which are new attractions in Golden Gate Park in the golden nineties. Some appear more disheveled than new immigrants after a transcontinental journey. Shaggy matted hair spills down skinny backs. Laughing blithely, they wear clothing with holes and patches, clothing only the most degraded beggars wear in the golden nineties. Yet there: a woman all in scarlet velvet with a feathered hat; a man in muttonchops and a straw boater.

"Look," Muse whispers.

An old Chinese woman in her sixties or seventies pushes a wheelchair across the grass. The Chinese woman is robust, gray hair threaded with black, in a padded jacket just like a thousand other Chinese women in San Francisco. Another woman reclines in thc wheelchair. Her white hair is neatly tucked into a pompadour. Slim and fragile with advanced age, she smiles at the sun, at the carousel, at the young people in the park.

"Dear God," Cameron says, "it's me."

Zhu leans forward, astounded. "Are you sure?"

Sharp look. "Wouldn't you be?"

Zhu doesn't know, but the strong Scotch face, the eyes, the hands, the mouth, even the hairstyle, her bearing. Donaldina Cameron, all right. But when?

The images in the holoid blur and then a tall, slim man in jeans and a leather jacket, his bright red hair tumbling down his back, steps into view.

"Chiron Cat's Eye in Draco!" Zhu's turn to shout.

"You know that young man?" Cameron says.

"It's 1967!"

With Chi walks a pretty young woman with long, light

brown hair. The lovely couple strolls past the Chinese woman, the elderly Cameron in her wheelchair.

And something happens:

The elderly Cameron nods and smiles at Chi, exchanges a few words. The old Chinese woman turns to stare at him. Gleam of green in her eyes. Her mouth gapes slightly. She reaches into her padded jacket and pulls out something shiny, something gold, winking with diamonds and bits of multicolored glass.

The aurelia.

The old Chinese woman hands the aurelia to Chiron. He slips it into an inside pocket of his jacket.

The holoid winks off, leaving the luminous blue field. The field shrinks into a pinpoint and disappears.

Cameron's office is silent but for the ticking of her clock. Cameron stunned, slack in her chair. Cocoa pools at her feet.

"The truth is, Miss Cameron," Zhu says, clearing her throat, "you have no choice but to go on at Nine Twenty."

"Truth!" she finally manages to say. Cameron's face is the color of soap, the harsh soap of this time made with tallow and lye. "The truth is, Miss Wong, I have plans."

"Abandon your plans. You will never marry. You will never have a house of your own or children of your own. You will have this: this is your Cause." Just as Zhu had her Cause. And will have her Cause when she returns from the golden nineties to the nineties she knows, nineties she wishes she could forget. "Will you dispute with an angel? Dispute this vision?"

Cameron goes to the door, calls in the serving girl who stoops, sweeps up the shattered cup, and swabs cocoa, drenching a white rag in dirty brown. Cameron's lips are tight. "Your vision proves nothing but my longevity, for which I am duly grateful, Miss Wong."

"But don't you see? Your companion, the Chinese woman. The vision proves . . ."

"Your vision proves nothing." Says to the girl, "You may go." Whirls on Zhu, eyes blazing. "I have Chinese servants now. I shall have Chinese servants in the future."

"How cruel, Miss Cameron."

"Nothing can compare to your cruelty today, Miss Wong." Cameron opens the door. "I appreciate the fair sex of the Oriental race. I shall always be kind to them. I shall always recognize my Christian obligations. What more, what more can you demand of me?"

Zhu sets down her cocoa. With only the slightest trace of irony says, "Then I'll leave you, Miss Cameron, to your obligations."

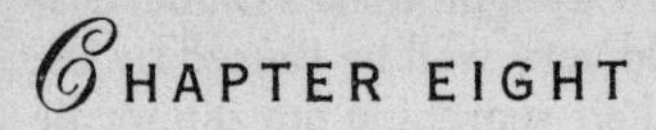

CHAPTER EIGHT

A Miraculous Cure at Dr. Mortimer's Clinic

"To Death," Daniel toasts Mr. Schultz, "in marvelous Californ'."

"*Mira muerta, no seas inhumana, no vuelvas mañana dejame vivir*," croons the singer through his happy skull. Ricardo, the one-eyed waiter, grins.

"To el Dia de los Muertos," Schultz says. "*Sehr gut, nicht wahr?* Speaking of which, Danny, got myself in a bit of a fix."

"Life and death?" Daniel says.

"You might say," Schultz says.

Daniel pours two more shots from a dust-furred bottle of mescal. Drowned worm at the bottom. Splendid rotgut with the disconcerting effect of making everything seem as ominous and strange as a nightmare. A more decadent drink than the Green Fairy, though the taste is vile. He and Schultz lounge about a table in Luna's finishing the last of their fifty-cent Suppers Mexican. Frank Norris's recommendation amply deserved. Quaint place: bright peasant pottery, dried gourds, silver trinkets, red-and-white checked tablecloths.

The singer in native costume and a papier-mâché skull mask plays a fair guitar. Skull mask quite a fright. Makes Daniel dyspeptic, though his distress could very well be caused by the Supper Mexican. Remains of their scorching hot dinner lie scattered in colorful crockery. Spicy pork sausages, pickled vegetables, guacamole, enchiladas, chile con carne, tortillas, chiles rellenos, frijoles fritas, salsa, sweet tamales.

Schultz sighs and knocks the shot back, licking salt off the rim of his glass. "Been given the boot."

"Things crummy in Far East shipping?"

"Things are bang-up in Far East shipping. Not so bang-up for me." Schultz pours yet another shot. Just a tiny one.

Daniel's tongue quite numb. "Why so, old man? You seem to have been doing well enough. Plum position and all."

"Can't control the drink," Schultz says. "God knows I've tried. Hit the brandy right at breakfast."

"Don't I know, sir," Daniel says. "Not to mention Miss Malone and her bloody champagne."

"She's forever pouring me a round and adding it to my bill," Schultz says.

"Brushes her teeth with the bubbly," Daniel says.

"At any rate. Showed up corned at the office one time too many," Schultz says. Gloomy. "Not that the old man doesn't. He just manages to hold his liquor better, is all."

"Plus he's the old man," Daniel says.

"Guess we've all got an old man somewhere," Schultz says.

"By blood or bad luck," Daniel says.

They laugh unhappily.

"Lousy bit, Schultz."

"At any rate." Schultz's huge mustache stiffens. "Don't suppose you've got any paying work, do you, Danny? Help out a pal? Not asking for a handout, you know. I'm no bum."

"Wish I did," Daniel says.

"Just sold that property of your *vater*, though, didn't you?"

"Patch of worthless weeds way out on Geary Street," Daniel says. "Nothing much doing out there in the Western Addition. The rest of the deadbeats are giving me grief, I can tell you that. That old fool Ekberg on Stockton Street has stalled for weeks. The other lot has got no takers. As for Mr. Harvey in Sausalito, the good gentleman sent thugs as his answer. Thugs, sir! Followed me, Schultz, while I was taking my stroll along the Cocktail Route. Worried me a bit."

Would rather not confess that Harvey's thugs gave him a goose egg on the noggin, sore kidneys, and a bad scare. Not to mention he's seen suspicious characters skulking about Dupont Street. Finds himself coming and going through the tradesmen's door. An unhappy way to live. Been screwing up his courage for weeks, go confront the son of a bitch himself.

"Perhaps you need a manager, Danny."

"Can barely find enough to manage myself, Schultz. Some real estate empire, eh?"

"Still you've got something, anyway," Schultz says, an unattractive look of envy spilling over his large, puglike features. Downs the shot, decides against another. Toys with the bottle, though. "I haven't got one thin dime. And I still can't quit the drink. I tell you, Danny, I'm sick and tired of it. What I need is a cure."

A cure.

They both meditate over their mescal as the singer launches into another melancholy ballad, "*Esta alegre calavera hoy invita a los mortales para ir a visitar las regiones infernales.*"

Daniel knows no Spanish, but the meaning leaps right out at him: we invite you mortals to visit hell. Mescal, by God. Does not know Schultz quite well enough to confide his darkest secrets, but Daniel is no fool. He knows exactly what Schultz is talking about. Knows he behaves like an ass when he's stinking. Look how he treats his mistress. Indeed, he suddenly realizes—ah, mescal—he does not notice Zhu at all till he's stinking. A precondition of sorts, that he's stinking before he goes to her. And then what he does to her; what he does.

Isn't sure where the cruelty comes from. Even less sure why she takes him on when she has amply demonstrated she's no whore or dimwit. Smarter than ten gentlemen strolling the

Cocktail Route. Claims she's from the far future like a creature out of Mr. Wells's novel, which only makes him angrier with her when he's stinking. She goes temperance on him. Drinking's going to kill you, she says, tears lingering on her lashes. Lunatic, he says, off to the loony bin with you, mistress.

Wakes up after a binge feeling soiled, stupid, contrite.

Binging every day. Brandy with breakfast, sir, to start.

But that's just his scruples. What about his physical constitution? His health, which he's always taken for granted. Nosebleeds; sore throat. Paunch thickening the stomach; guts on the blink. Trembling hands. Perpetual headache till he tips another and yet another headache when he comes round again. Not to mention the melancholy, the guilt, the way strange memories of his father and mother intrude on his peace of mind. And so on and et cetera, and he cannot abide this anymore. Sick and tired, indeed. Must be something he can do.

"Know of a cure, then?" Daniel says cautiously.

"Mm," Schultz says, giving into the mescal after a short struggle. "Heard a fellow talking about it at the Bank Exchange. Dr. Mortimer's miraculous cure for dipsomania. Guaranteed, money back. There's the trick for me: money. Costs a bit, but worth it, the fellow said."

"This Mortimer; he's in San Francisco?" Daniel says, cautiously apportioning the last finger in the bottle between himself and the worm. "To the handmaiden of Death," he says toasting the worm.

"*Ja*. Dr. Mortimer's got a clinic in the Monkey Block," Schultz says and empties the bottle's remnants, worm and all, into his glass. Suddenly looks green. Dashes out Luna's front door to the gutter where he noisily airs his paunch. The maître d' and a scullery maid come running with buckets of hot salt water. Scowling, vituperative, they vigorously splash the pavement. Poor reflection on their fine establishment, Mr. Schultz.

Daniel picks up the tab. A dollar for two Suppers Mexican. Dollar fifty for the mescal, terrific rotgut. Reluctantly counts out coins. Not exactly flush himself. Sees Schultz outside on his hands and knees, scorned, spattered, and heaving. What won't a drunk do, Daniel wonders, to stiff his pals for the bill?

❜ ❜ ❜

By God, sir, a word to the wise has saved many a poor soul. Daniel hurries down Columbus to where the avenue meets Montgomery Street and veers south into the financial district. Two men in fishermen's togs, caps pulled low over coarse faces, fall in step behind him. He sprints like a schoolboy for half a block till he reaches his destination. Ducks inside the four-story monstrosity: the Montgomery Block, fondly Monkey.

Stands hidden by the door, watching. The men pass by, disappointment tugging at their faces, sniffing like bloodhounds. Ha. From Mr. Harvey again? This has gone too far. He fingers his Remington. Perhaps he could employ old Schultz after all. Does Schultz carry a gun?

Takes a deep breath, aware that the dose of fear has cleared his head. Dizzy, slightly ill. He could use a drink, sir. Slight hint of mold. The Monkey Block, Halleck's Folly, was once the largest commercial building on the West Coast and a prestige address, too, though no one knew if the hundred cavernous rooms would ever be fully let. Daniel has heard plenty of tales sipping Pisco Punch at the Bank Exchange or dining on chicken Portola at Coppa's Restaurant, two of the congenial establishments on the ground floor. Up and down went the fortunes of the Monkey Block as fashion and commerce went their fickle ways. Quite cheering, the contemplation of history. To know that other men of means, wit, and dynamism had lost their fortunes to the whim of chance and economics makes Daniel feel less of a dunce. Perhaps bankruptcy wasn't a sin, after all.

The law firms, stockbrokers, and mining companies that once filled the spacious suites have all departed for fancy new skyscrapers on Market Street. Now the Monkey Block is a hotbed of bohemians. In a massive effort of will, Daniel declines a visit to the Bank Exchange for a quick one and climbs the white marble stairs. His footsteps echo off high ceilings. Sunlight cascades through enormous windows at the end of each hall. He peers in an open door. A man poses a woman draped in white muslin before another sun-drenched window. Daniel gawks. Is she in her birthday suit? Painters, musicians, and writers appreciate the spaciousness and light of these old rooms. Good history, here, too. The great Robert Louis Stevenson visited the place in '88 before setting off for the South Seas. The model laughs. "Come in," calls the painter. "Do you collect art?"

"Another time," Daniel calls back.

He walks by a series of billboards depicting palms, staring eyes, mystic triangles, astrological signs. A hall of fortune-tellers. Then calligraphy, gilt and red signs showing the weird little legs of the ginseng root. He glances in the door: Chinese herbalist. Huge straw baskets laden with roots and barks and sticks and God knows what. Bizarre things—he would rather not guess, they look rather gruesome—float in jars of murky fluid. A tray of lizards, serpents, other unidentifiable creatures split and dried like beef jerky. Down the hall, a billboard set outside the suite: poster of a man's body with his internal organs and nerves and blood vessels showing. Poor fellow an Oriental; lines and arrows drawn all over showing currents of energy, Daniel guesses. Myriad needles poised at certain points. Acupuncture, that's what they call it. Brr, needles. Not for him.

Then a slew of tailors with their bolts of cloth and dead-faced mannequins, and dealers in goods too old to be new, too new to be antiques. Rents must be affordable at the Monkey Block these days. On the second floor, Daniel finds another open door, yielding to a spectacular room. The floor of the room on the next story has been torn out; a winding cast-iron staircase leads precariously to a mezzanine. Altogether the ceiling must be thirty or forty feet high. The room is entirely lined, floor to ceiling, with shelves amply stocked with books. Books, books, and more books—some crumbling and dirty-looking, but many finely bound in leather with gold and silver leaf glinting on their spines. Daniel has never seen so many books.

"What is this place?" he whispers to a clerk who passes by,

arms laden, eyes misty—evidently—from hours of concentrated reading.

"Why, this is Mayor Sutro's private library," the clerk whispers back, startled from his reverie. "He'll have a million books before long." Shoos Daniel out and shuts the door.

Third floor, fourth floor. Huffing and puffing up the stairs. Zhu claims chain-smoking is what causes his shortness of breath. What nonsense. He taps out a ciggie. It's this indolent life he's assumed in San Francisco, lazier and boozier than his time in Paris. *That's* what has stolen his breath. Dust has gathered along the baseboards. Quite a few vacant suites on the fourth floor. Apparently other gentlemen are not eager to hike up four flights of marble stairs. Lovely view, though. Perhaps he could establish an office when business picks up. Happy thought: Daniel J. Watkins, Esquire, etched on glass. But what is he? Real estate broker, spinner of pictures, dreamer, drunk?

No, not a drunk. Not anymore.

There, a sign at the end of the hall: Dr. Mortimer, Physician.

Daniel hesitates. He could simply cut down. Skip brandy for breakfast. Hell, don't breakfast with Jessie Malone at all. Shamelessly swilling champagne, the Queen of the Underworld is a terrible influence. Stay away from the Cocktail Route, lay off the Green Fairy, not to mention mescal and Pisco Punch. Buy a bicycle. Bicycle riding, there's the ticket. Fabulous for the health, they say. Put him right in no time. A nice two-wheeler with one of those silver bells, a horn, a silver flask . . . Licks his lips. By God, he's dry.

As though sensing his presence through the smoked glass, the physician bounds out into the hall. "Hello, there!"

" 'Lo." Suddenly ashamed.

The physician makes a show of sniffing Daniel's breath. Unpardonable rudeness from a total stranger. Would warrant a good pop in the trap.

"You're here for the cure?" Mortimer says, undaunted by whether Daniel will take offense. After all, Daniel is stinking. Doesn't wait for Daniel's nod. Promptly seizes him, shepherds him inside, practically flings him into a large burgundy leather chair.

A full skeleton dangles from an iron rod in the corner. Hand-colored lithographs of bodily organs line the walls behind Mortimer's spartan walnut desk. The opposite wall is less comforting: stoppered jars containing decomposing organic matter in formaldehyde. Daniel compares the preserved rot to the lithographs, spies a brain, a kidney, a curl of intestine. Can't identify the rest. Doesn't want to try.

"Now then, young sir," Mortimer says. Absolutely blazing with energy. In his early thirties, perhaps, with a receding hairline, a neat French mustache. Penetrating brown eyes sparkling with deep sympathy. Excellent physique, Daniel can't help but notice. Trim and wiry beneath his well-cut brown serge suit. In his shirtsleeves and vest, at the moment, slim waist nicely cinched. Daniel rubs his own gut. Mortimer bustles about, offers him water in a cut-crystal glass. Makes a show of whipping out a clean new file, snapping it open to a questionnaire. Dips his pen into an ink bottle and sits, poised, rosy-cheeked and bright-eyed, observing Daniel with keen warmth.

Daniel tips the water to his lips. Last thing in the world he wants. Poor Tchaikovsky. Sips nonetheless, encouraged by the physician's energy and kindly purpose.

"You *are* here for the cure?"

"Indeed, yes."

"Splendid." Scratch scratch of the pen. Takes Daniel's vital statistics. "Mhm, twenty-one. Mhm, Saint Louis; real estate, you don't say. Splendid." The lively eyes flip up. "Now then, young sir. Drinking every day, are you?"

"Afraid so."

"When do you start?"

"At breakfast, of course."

"And continue till night?"

"Yes. Well into the night." Kneads his forehead. Mescal is leaving a nasty ache behind his eyes. Licks his lips. So dry. Just a shot, a little shot, of something.

"Hung over now, are you?"

"What do you think?" Getting annoyed.

"Splendid. Got the shakes? Mhm." Scratch scratch. "Bowels loose? Nosebleeds? Dyspepsia? Aches and pains? Mood swings? Melancholy? Seeing things?"

"Seeing what?" Daniel asks.

"Dunno. Things crawling in the corner of your eye, you know. People out to get you."

"Nothing like that." Were the men in the fishermen's togs just his imagination? No, Harvey's thugs were hardly imaginary. The goose egg on his noggin is still tender.

"Splendid. Beat the wife?"

"Not married."

"Beat the mistress?"

Daniel is silent. His mistress says she's from six hundred years in the future. She's insane, quite insane, slipping her eyes to the side when she thinks he's not looking, muttering to herself. Talking in voices. He remembers the first time he heard one of her lunatic voices, which she managed to project with the facility of a professional ventriloquist. Made the hair stand up on the back of his neck. What he sees in her he can't possibly say—when he's sober. She's Chinese, a servant, a convenient piece of tail. Yet he saw her heal the crack in a man's skull. Sees her add and subtract columns of numbers that would make his head swim. And when he's stinking, the mere sight of her excites the snake of lust. When he's stinking, she robs him of his sense and good graces. Green-eyed mermaid, tempting him deeper and deeper into depravity. Yet her gentle strength, her tender entreaties not to harm himself, while he harms her so much with his cold fury and his sudden assaults on her womanhood. In some ways she's been better to him than his own . . .

He hardly knows this man, physician or not. How can he possibly say any of this aloud? *You see?* he berates himself. He thinks too much when drink is in him. Thinks and thinks till he's half-mad himself.

Says at last, "Can you help me, Dr. Mortimer?"

"Can I help you?" Mortimer flings his pen down, caps the ink. Stands, paces. "Do you know the deleterious effects of alcohol on your health, young sir? Have you any idea?"

"Hard on the liver," Daniel says. "I know that."

"The liver, yes. Splendid." Mortimer sprints over to the wall of jars, taps on one specimen. Wears a thick gold ring, which he employs to produce a resounding ting on the glass. "When your liver goes, you will die, young sir, for the liver extracts all poisons from the body, and you are poisoning that stalwart organ every day that you drink! But that's not all. Your kidneys, young sir"—another tap on a jar—"are also being poisoned. Once the kidneys go, *sppt*!" Penetrating look. "Then there's your bowels. Your bowels will loosen and loosen till you can no longer hold your waste. Your stomach lining will be eaten away as though acid has been poured upon it." More taps, more jars. "Same for your appendix, your colon, your heart, your esophagus." Mortimer sprints back and leans over the desk, eyes burning. "And what about your brain?" he says ominously. Merely points at the jar filled with a clot of cottage cheese bobbing in the preservative.

"What about my brain?" Daniel says, shrinking back in the chair.

"Your brain is riddled with hemorrhage, young sir!"

"By God." Daniel loosens his collar.

"Young sir," Mortimer says, sprinting over to the chair. Pulls up a stool, leans intently into Daniel's face. "I am not a moralist. I am not a temperance worker. I am a physician. And well I know how the cares of our modern daily life weigh heavily upon us all." Mortimer sighs deeply, cups his chin in his palm. "Do you know how man used to live? Man did not live in these accursed cities, filled with bad air and noise and poxy women. Man did not live subjected to the factory boss or the capitalist. Did not live, I say, chasing after the filthy lucre just to survive. No, man lived in the country, in the field, in the forest, in the jungle. In paradise, young sir. Man was free. He worked as he pleased, took his ease when he would, ate and drank healthfully and abundantly. And man in these blissful times had another healthful amusement besides the hunt, the games, the songs, the virgins."

"What other amusement was that?" Daniel says. Sitting up now.

Mortimer moves closer. Lavender cologne over the athletic smell of sweat. "In our very own New World, south of the border, is a marvelous plant known to the glorious gold-drenched civilization of the Incas. The divine plant of the Incas, young sir. Plant of the heathen goddess, a sacrament used extensively in the arcane ancient rituals."

Daniel sips his water, still thirsting for a drink. Perhaps less so now.

"Mere Indians were not the only ones to know of the divine plant, however," Mortimer says. "No, the heathens could scarcely understand the great gift they took so readily from their jungle paradise. It was the conquistadors, those stern men of swordsmanship and domination, who discovered the divine plant for the rest of the civilized world. For they knew it as a healthful boon. The sacrament of the heathen gods was thus laid at the feet of modern civilization."

"This is a cure from the Spaniards, then?" Daniel says doubtfully. He has no great love of Spaniards. Indeed, el Dia de los Muertos, custom of the Indians of whom Mortimer speaks and the morbid Spaniards, has left him so distressed that he finds himself here, on the fourth floor of the Monkey Block.

"Young sir, the divine plant has found its way into our American cities in manifold ways," Mortimer says, leaning closer still. "We are not dependent upon the Spaniards, not at all. Now it's quite true that the divine plant had found its way into the hands of the Negro dockworkers in New Orleans. But these humble persons—who engage in physical labor the like of which I'm quite sure neither you nor I have ever experienced—have only proven the multitudinous benefits of the divine plant. An observer I know personally witnessed the increased endurance, the remarkable persistence, the stamina, the building up of sheer strength, the suppression of appetite, not to mention the cheerful disposition—without drink, mind you—among these hard-working men."

"Without drink?" Daniel says.

"Without drink, young sir, and laughing in the sun. Mind

you, scientific experiments have been conducted by myself and other eminent physicians throughout the country. Some have conducted trials with dogs. Others have plunged ahead with human patients. The results are most encouraging!"

Mortimer stands, sprints around behind his desk, and produces charts, diagrams, ink drawings, more lithographs in full color. "The divine plant is a stimulant, understand that first of all, young sir. And as a stimulant not only does it produce all the salubrious effects I just mentioned, but works a cure for anemia, bronchitis, debility, la grippe, sore throat, angina pectoris, lung troubles. Gastric carcinoma, pneumonia, typhoid fever, not to mention shock and sexual exhaustion." Leans over the desk, directs his blazing brown eyes into Daniel's dazed gaze. "Melancholia, of course. Need I add the cure for dipsomania?"

"I'll try it!" Daniel says.

"The cure is guaranteed," Mortimer says, sitting and folding his hands. "But of course, it's up to you, young sir. Dipsomania of your sort is a powerful disease. Need I remind you, I am not a moralist. I am not a temperance worker. I am a physician. If you must go back on the bottle—after the divine plant of the goddess!—there is not much more I can do for you."

"Please, please let me try it!"

Mortimer gestures, leads him to a side table. A wide flat mirror is set into the sort of silver tray a wealthy woman might use to display her perfume bottles or liquor decanters. The physician reaches into a drawer, takes out a vial of fine white powder and a straight-edge razor blade. Spills mounds of powder on the mirror, chops at them like a Chinese cook preparing suey. Rearranges the powder in long fine lines. Takes out a straw wrought in silver with little cunning designs of snakes entwined about the shaft.

"You take it like this," Mortimer says and, with a vigorous inhalation, promptly sniffs two lines of the powder through the straw into his nose. "You try now." Coaching, "Take one nostril, then the other."

Daniel does.

A short blast of pain, the new discomfort of an astringent

powder up his nostrils. A bitter taste in the back of his throat. His eyes pool.

Medicine; why must medicine always be so dreadful?

And then an infusion of sheer energy careens into his brain. A short blinding moment, a dizziness, like when he imbibed puma piss on the Overland train. The whole world reels and spins.

The divine plant does battle with the last of the mescal, with whatever hemorrhage booze may have inflicted on Daniel's poor brain. Does battle and emerges victorious. The moment of reeling blindness passes instantly into a sheer wash of pleasure, good health, and stimulation. Bliss, vigor itself, a gift from the heathen gods!

Daniel straightens up, laughing, powder spilling down his mustache and mouth. Licks the bitterness. It's delicious! Can feel blood tumbling through his heart, his brain, his liver, cleansing and strengthening.

"Dr. Mortimer, I'm cured!"

"Well now, well now," the physician murmurs. Reek of sweat a little stronger. Lavender can't mask it, but that's all right. Mortimer goes to his desk, flips open the folder. Scratch scratch of the pen. "It's up to you, young sir, as I've said. Would you like a prescription?"

"Of course! How much?"

"Five dollars, please."

Only takes money, that's what poor old Schultz said. Daniel counts out coins. Proceeds from the sale of the lot in the Western Addition seem to be flying out of his boodle book like pigeons startled from a roost. No more dinners out for a while. His rent at the boardinghouse is supposed to include board; Mariah's cooking is good enough. Will have to do, anyway, without congenial company. He's cured of the Cocktail Route.

"What is this divine plant of the Incas called?" Daniel says, handing over the money.

"Young sir, to the ancients the sacrament was called coca. The heathens plucked leaves right off the miraculous tree and chewed them as a cow chews her cud." Dr. Mortimer hands over a receipt, a tiny silver spoon, three vials of white powder. "We modern physicians have a scientific name." Chuckling. Pleased to have successfully dispensed the cure to another worthy young man. "The sacrament is refined now, of course, as you can plainly see." Sniffing, whiffling like a winded steed. "We call it cocaine."

❙ ❙ ❙

Cured! Daniel has reclaimed his soul, restored his health. He is back from the Dead!

Invincible! This must be how a Titan feels, thundering across the primordial world, fearing no one, shrinking from nothing. Daniel's blood soars. The pathetic stupor of mescal long gone. A god of the ancients, he is. Mythological muscles, brain swooping like a hawk, eyes taking in the full splendor and squalor of Montgomery Street in one omniscient glance as he steps out onto the sidewalk.

And what a sight it is: the painted chippies decrepit in their shame. The proper ladies bound up in their corsets and sweating in heavy dark dresses. The bloated men of all classes leering, filled with their self-importance and stupidity. Drunk, of course. And el Dia de los Muertos, lunatics cavorting all over the city in death's-head masks, making mockery of the final solution to all man's ills.

He is restored from the Dead!

Daniel hesitates on the corner of Columbus and Montgomery. The weird angle of the streets is like a fork in the road designed by the Devil. His destiny is clear: settle Father's paltry real estate dealings. Make the deadbeats pay, chuck them out in the street, if necessary. And then?

Then he *must* figure out how to make photographs project on a wall in a sequence so that the persistence of vision makes each image a whole. Designs leap through his mind. Flip the images like a deck of cards? Spin them round like a Zoetrope? Wrap a roll of photographic paper on a spool? And then? Why, the story of civilization could be told. The empires of the East, of Europe, of England. Finding the New World, every sacrifice and adventure. America's story, the Pilgrims at Plymouth Rock, the great war, the conquest of the West. The story of San Francisco herself, the gold rush, the building of this marvelous city. How many thrilling stories if only one could figure out how to spin static images till they come alive.

Dr. Mortimer's cure is a rousing success. Divine plant of the Incas. Daniel can think more clearly than he has in years.

His heart throbs with a glowing pleasure. Thoughts of sin swell in his mind. A happy side effect, apparently, encouraged by healthful radiance. He could take care of his vile need at once. Can see a red light glowing in a little window on the third story of a commercial building two doors down. But Daniel J. Watkins does not pay for it. Daniel J. Watkins does not go to whores.

No. Where is his mistress?

He flies downtown to Sutter Street, barges into the Parisian Mansion. Finds Zhu and Jessie Malone conferring in the parlor, Li'l Lucy weeping. Several other whores stand about with troubled faces. The ugly little Peruvian maid watches from the sidelines with a look of smug triumph.

"Please, Miss Malone," Li'l Lucy says. "Just one more chance."

"The last time," Jessie says. "Don't say I didn't warn you, Li'l Lucy, because I have. I have warned you over and over. I'll not have a poxy girl at the Parisian Mansion."

"We can try to get her symptoms treated," Zhu says. "The disease goes into remission. It's not her fault."

"It is her fault!" Jessie pours champagne.

"I was just saying earlier today that you're fair, Miss Malone," Zhu says. "Don't make me regret those words."

"She's got to douche," Jessie says, "and she doesn't. She gets drunk, she passes out. . . ."

"She gets beat up," Zhu says.

"Please, Miss Malone," Li'l Lucy whimpers. "Please."

"Have you heard about this method of birth control called condoms?" Zhu says. "The girls should use them. You could practically eliminate your problems with disease, not to mention pregnancy."

"Condoms?" Jessie says. "Missy, if this is one of your gadgets from six hundred years in the future, I'm sure we can't just go down to Mr. Kepler's Sundries and pick up a few."

"But you can," Zhu says. "I saw an article in *The Argonaut* the other day. I thought you loved new things, Miss Malone. This is the newest thing in French brothels. Really, I don't know why you don't use them as a regular practice in your business. I understand that condoms have been around since the 1700s."

"Sure, and I daresay every sporting gal in town would use them if we could get them. What did you say this condom thing is made of?"

"Well, in this day, they're made of sheep intestine."

"Sheep intestine!" Jessie roars and sputters. "You think any one of my gentlemen is gonna put a sheep intestine over his jockey, you're nutty, missy." She gulps her champagne, pours another. "Sheep intestine!"

"Mistress," Daniel says. "I want to see you." To Jessie, "Is there a room we can use?"

"Take Li'l Lucy's room," Jessie says. "She won't be needing it anymore."

"Please, Miss Malone," Li'l Lucy wails and slides off the couch, falling to her knees. Clasps her hands. "Please, please."

Daniel takes Zhu's elbow and leads her upstairs. She points out Li'l Lucy's room. Frilly and cheap, the place reeks of lilac cologne, cigarette smoke, spilt whiskey. He locks the door.

"What is it?" she says angrily. "I was in the middle of business."

"You were in the middle of whores' business, mistress. I want you now."

She stares at him, astonished. "Want me for *what?*"

He shucks off his jacket and vest, drops his trousers. His manly virtue is tumescent. By God, he'll spill his precious bodily fluids any moment.

Still she makes no move. "You never ask," she says. "In all this time, it's always the same. I don't know why I let you. You wait till you're drunk, and then you launch your attack. You never ask."

"I'm not drunk now," he says imperiously.

She regards him curiously.

"Nor am I asking." Those slanting eyes of hers, bright green irises. Not like Mama's deep sea eyes at all. Quite alien. Which suddenly excites him more than he's ever felt toward her before. "I *need* you, mistress." *Ask*. Well, he is turning over a new leaf. "Please. You know how I adore you."

She shakes her head, sidles toward the door. "I don't know why I let you. . . . something comes over me. . . . it's like I'm possessed. . . ."

Cannot stand it! He has been a gentleman, and he is not drunk. He seizes her, relieves her of her jacket, shirtwaist. Rip of silk. She silently struggles, but he is invincible, he is a god. She is a tiny writhing thing in his hands. He spins her around, seizes the laces of her corset, rips apart the knot, pulls and pulls as tightly as he can. She gasps.

"You really are too fat, mistress," he says, reknotting the laces. "You should have some ribs taken out." Indeed, this is very nice. He can circle her entire waist with his two hands. He whirls her around, presses her down on Li'l Lucy's bed. Her face, wide-eyed, distraught with lust, in a trance of sinful ecstasy. "Please, mistress," he whispers.

She takes down her bloomers.

"I know you hate it," he says, smiling at her cooperation, "but you must help me now."

And he takes her, feeling every sensation like he's never felt sensations of the carnal act before. Divine plant of the Incas! Sacrament! He plunges, he rocks, strange-smelling sweat films his skin. He hears her gasping, feels her movement. The dreadful moment of sexual transport overcomes him like a seizure, an epilepsy of sensuality, a small death.

He rises off her, falls back on the bed, spent for the moment. She leaps up, reaches behind her with urgency, unlaces the corset. Gasps. No matter; no matter. She is a woman, she isn't supposed to like it. His breath slows. The fingers of a headache squeeze the backs of his eyes. The supreme brilliance of the cure begins to fade.

Fade! He could weep with disappointment. He never wants this exultation to end. He sits up, hands shaking, and retrieves his jacket. Ah, the vials, the silver spoon. Trembling, weak, he uncaps a vial, dips the spoon. Unsure of his technique, he awkwardly inserts the spoon into his nostril, and inhales as vigorously as he can.

She watches him, openmouthed.

The bitter sting in his nose, on his tongue. Fluid gathers in the back of his throat. And then the sweet bloom of power, the radiance of health.

"Daniel," she says, "what in hell are you doing?"

He doesn't like the prudish expression on her face, doesn't like it at all. "I went to Dr. Mortimer for the cure, mistress."

"The cure?"

"For dipsomania. I'll not be a slave to drink anymore."

Li'l Lucy has got a carafe on the bed table. He takes out the stopper, sniffs. Dreadful whiskey the whore swills, but he tips the bottle, floats a taste on his tongue. Just enough to wet his whistle, which is suddenly quite dry. Not bad; doesn't even make him drunk. The divine plant of the Incas is too strong for that. Still, the effect is very nice, soothing his jumpy nerves. He puts the carafe down. That's right. He can put the bottle down any time he wants. He is cured.

"Daniel," Zhu says, "what cure?"

"Dr. Mortimer says it's called cocaine."

"Oh," she cries. "Oh, Daniel. You must not . . . you must give it to me."

"I should say not!"

"You don't know what it is."

"It's the divine plant of the Incas, mistress. I am restored from the Dead."

He splashes water on his face, dresses, and heads out the door. The spoonful of powder produces somewhat less effect than his first taste at Dr. Mortimer's clinic. Not as high a dose perhaps. Encouraged though faintly disappointed, he strides through the parlor, past the little drama he witnessed on his way in, still unconcluded. By God, weeping whores.

Daniel J. Watkins will not linger in a sordid place like the Parisian Mansion. This is a place for the weak among men, the ones who exhaust their essence on degraded creatures like Li'l Lucy. He will do no such thing. He heads down Market Street, bound for the ferry. Invincible once more, clear-headed and powerful, he knows what he must do. He must confront that bastard Harvey, once and for all.

"Daniel! Daniel!"

Zhu hurries behind him, following like a spaniel. Her face is flushed, the ribbons from her Newport hat stream behind her. She wears her mauve silk. Most becoming with her golden skin, black hair, those emerald eyes. With a sudden pang, he realizes he *does* adore her, but the realization does not overwhelm him in a maudlin way like when he's stinking. Indeed, in some peculiar fashion, Miss Zhu Wong has changed his life. He can admit that privately in his own thoughts. Perhaps her entreaties *are* what inspired him to seek the cure. And his fate—the great fate he felt so clearly on the Overland train—has subtly altered.

That she clings to this lunacy about being from the distant future has a certain charm, really. An insouciance, especially in one who comes from an inferior race, one who would in any other circumstance be advised to keep her mouth shut. Her lunacy is not the raving of the ill, whom he has seen, but rather is supported by a quick intelligence, an extraordinary knowledge of things a woman should not rightly know, and, of course, her clever accoutrements.

He pauses, permitting her to catch up.

"Where are you going in this state?" she demands, panting as he resumes his steady pace.

"I think it's time Mr. Harvey squared his account with me."

"Ah." Her concern touching. She was there when the thugs attacked him on the Cocktail Route, after all. "Don't go while you're intoxicated."

"I am *not* intoxicated. I'm cured!"

"You are intoxicated with cocaine."

He stops, whirls. "I am *cured*, don't you understand?"

"All right," she says, "all right. Don't go alone, then." His little stoic. "Let me come too."

At an earlier time, he would have scoffed. Says now, "Have you got your mollie knife?"

"I do."

He regards her. The slim, muscular form somehow out of place in her clothes. It's as though he never really looked at her before. Senses her essence, the force of her personality. For she is forceful, his little lunatic. Remembers her—vaguely, he was stinking, of course—in coolie's rags, whirling, striking out, hands poised. Perhaps if he can swallow his pride, he'll ask her about her martial technique one day.

"Can you cut materials sturdier than a sugar cube with the mollie knife?"

"I can."

"Very well. In truth, I could use an ally. We've met Harvey's thugs before, haven't we, mistress? But don't interfere in my business, you understand that?"

"I'm forbidden to interfere," she says. Sudden sadness. "Under Tenet Three of the Grandfather Principle."

"Grandfather Principle?" Proud to show off now. See how the cure even makes him smarter? "And all your talk, Miss Zhu Wong, of social reform and caring about others who haven't enough to eat."

Puzzled look. "What on earth do you mean?"

"I am," he says pointedly, not stinking now, not stupid with drink, "occasionally a scholar. I've heard the talk from politicians in the old Dixie states. The old masters just can't give up the ghost. Want to use what they call grandfathering to deny the vote to the progeny of former slaves and pack in the uneducated Caucasian vote. Quite a movement. They say they'll have themselves amendments to several state constitutions by the turn of the century."

His mistress looks at him askance, rolls her eyes to the side, then laughs. "Oh, my! Not a grandfather *clause*. The Grandfather *Principle*. A fundamental of tachyportation, my dear Daniel. Under rules set by masters you cannot possibly know."

Prickle of proprietary fervor. Daniel doesn't like the notion she could have other masters besides himself. Who, for instance? Jessie Malone? Very well; once he secures more capital, he'll buy whatever remains on his mistress's contract from the Queen of the Underworld. Perhaps they'll leave 263 Dupont Street behind, find a proper house of their own. Wouldn't Father split his gut over that? His only son, living in sin with a Chinese woman. But clearly Zhu doesn't mean Miss Malone. Masters he cannot possibly know? Doesn't like that at all. *He* is her master.

"*I* am your master," he says.

"I *knew* you were going to say that," she says, "but you're wrong."

"Indeed?"

"I belong to no one. Perhaps not even to myself."

Her pale little face is so distraught that he takes her hand. "Poor mistress. I'm such a beast to you, aren't I?"

She looks down at their clasped hands as though at a bottled freak in a dime museum. "No," she murmurs. "I could resist you if I wanted to. Somehow I never do."

A dreaminess infuses her distress. She looks like one of Charles Chaplin's painted nymphs tossing in a brutal sea, her back broken, her expression one of tortured ecstasy.

"You know how I adore you." Stock expression, but he's stricken by her melancholy look. Perhaps he should induce her to try Dr. Mortimer's cure?

"I know," she says. "That's what's so strange. I *do* know. *Never* supposed to happen this way. Yet here we are."

He pats her palm. "My poor little lunatic. Let's go before I lose my nerve."

Hand in hand they stride past another parade for el Dia de los Muertos. Roughnecks on horseback, wearing skull masks, passing bottles of tequila, mescal, and beer, hooting and hollering like maniacs. Daniel takes Zhu down to the ferry building. The *San Rafael* bobs at the dock, a black and white steamer more modest in size than the *Chrysapolis* but with more elegant lines.

They board, bound for Sausalito and Mr. Harvey's nefarious establishment. Two dozen bruisers in tawdry togs crowd the decks, feisty with booze, puffing hand-rolled ciggies stinking of cheap tobacco.

He heads for a deserted, wave-spattered spot on the prow, towing Zhu after him. The cold salt air whips his face. Scent of the deep ripe sea, of mysteries and distant destinations. *Never supposed to happen this way, yet here we are.* "All right," he says, feeling fit from the spoonful, downright indulgent toward his mistress, and piqued by her strange mood. "Tell me what you mean by 'the Grandfather Principle.' "

"As I told you and Miss Malone, I'm from the future."

"Six hundred years in the future," he says, still indulgent.

"Yes," she says. "We have a new technology like you have electricity and telegraph and telephones. In some ways, tachyportation is no more amazing than those technologies. And a good deal less practical, as it turns out. It's not something that benefits the people, really. More like early space travel. A huge financial investment with no immediate return for society at large. The propaganda made people think everyone had a direct stake, but, really, the technopolistic plutocracy was the main benefactor. Not that the Luxon Institute for Superluminal Applications is a part of the plutocracy. The technopolistic plutocracy is long dead. Or perhaps the LISA techs deceive themselves."

"Zhu," Daniel says. "If you want me to concede that a woman like you actually has a brain, I will. But I cannot understand a word you're saying."

She smiles. "The LISA techs shut the shuttles down a few years after I was born. T-porting released dangerous pollutants into the timeline. That's what Chi said."

"All right," he says. That peculiar ache scrapes behind his eyes again. So soon? He finds himself reaching for his vial and spoon the way he reaches for his ciggies. At her sharp glance, he refrains. Finds the ciggies instead and lights up, cupping the match against the wind. She actually helps him, despite her protestations against his smoking. "Pollutants; like bad water?"

"Exactly," she says, "like bad water." Gazes here and there, searching the bay as though she's looking for something that's supposed to be there. "Anyway, the Grandfather Principle states that a tachyporter cannot t-port to the past and murder his or her own lineal ancestor. Her grandfather, if you will. Because if the t-porter could do that, she would not exist in the first place to go back and do the deed."

"I see," he says, not sure if he does.

"It's what we call a paradox," she says, nodding sympathetically. "Well, the tenets go on from there. All the way down to whether a t-porter like me gets herself killed in the past and winds up trapped in a CTL."

"A CTL?"

"A Closed Time Loop. If I should die here and now, I would always have to be born in my time, make the t-port, and come back again. Like a revolving door."

"Revolving door?"

"Never mind." She frowns. "Except no one knows what it could be like. I mean, being *in* a CTL. Chi suggested they thought Betty became conscious of it. But how would you know? Theoretically, a CTL has no beginning and no end. It just *is*. Then where does consciousness begin?" Shakes her head, her ribbons flying. "Anyway. Tenet Three of the Grandfather Principle says I cannot get involved with you, Mr. Watkins."

"Ho," Daniel says. "Sounds more like your grandfather than your Grandfather Principle, mistress."

But she will not acknowledge his jest. "Cannot harm you, cannot help you. Daniel, the booze is one thing. That cocaine you're snorting is many times more addictive! And just as bad, if not worse, for your liver, your heart, your blood pressure. Wait till you see what it does to your sinuses."

"By God!" He hits his forehead with the heel of his hand. Still jesting; she really is too serious. "There is just no pleasing you."

"Pleasing me has nothing to do with it."

"Mistress," he says, "you'll be the death of me."

The *San Rafael* pitches. Zhu stumbles to the railing, stares out at the shifting bay as though the natural beauty is an abhorrent thing. "That's just it, Daniel," she says. "You're killing yourself and there's nothing I can do."

"Now, Zhu," he says, coming to comfort her. "Eat, drink, and be merry, for tomorrow we die!"

But his tenderness and generosity—a rare thing for him, he admits—cannot assuage her.

"Oh, Daniel," she says, "you're not the object of the Golden Nineties Project. That's why I cannot understand what's happening. Muse can't or won't explain. I'm afraid Muse is defective or malfunctioning. Or worse."

"Mistress, please," Daniel says, catching her hands. "Really . . . this is too much. Only men possess the muse. The muse is for the great artist. Women have not the capacity."

She listens carefully for a moment, straining to catch his words above the wind and waves, then rips her hands away. "Don't be stupid, Daniel," she says. "Women have every capacity men have. And then some. Wait till you see the twenty-second century. Ha! The greatest artists and writers and holoid makers of all *time* lived then. Magda Mira, the death cult writer, and Kiku Tatsumi, the telespace artist. You ought to be *ashamed*, Daniel J. Watkins."

He is taken aback by her outburst. Muse, indeed. "You behave, lunatic."

The *San Rafael* unceremoniously knocks against the dock, throwing them both off their feet.

❜ ❜ ❜

He guides her off the boat onto the dusty shore of Sausalito. A homely port: raw streets pocked with potholes, railroad tracks laid in unsightly grooves right up to the terminus, a stinking slough thick with bilge. Apples and lumber from the north come through here. A spectacular Queen Anne mansion perches on the brink of a hill, a French provincial further up, something huge and Georgian further still. Playground for the rich, as well. The prestigious Pacific Yacht Club is down the shore. Several lovely large hotels with lyrical names like Casa Madrona and Alta Mira are stationed well away from the riffraff. The waterfront teems with saloons, the reek of beer, guffaws, shouts of brawlers. The two dozen bruisers reel off the steamer, heading straight for the rowdy district. Painted chits promenade. Daniel can see their scabby facepaint from here.

His gorge rises in his throat. Recalls another debarkation months ago. Fanny Spiggott, the fainting pickpocket. Nearly ruined his debut in marvelous Californ'. Had to beg Jessie Malone for his room and board. Traded a painting worth seven thousand dollars for four months' rent. The thieving whore! Daniel had gone to the police after seeing Miss Spiggott again at the German Castle, plying her filthy trade. But there was nothing the bulls could do. Every now and then, one of Miss Spiggott's victims manages to catch her red-handed, they told him, and off she'll go to the cooler for an overnight stay. Probably cons the night watch out of tea and pastries. Probably paying off the bulls, who had smiled at the mention of her despicable name.

He glances down at Zhu, suddenly sour. An ugly suspicion warps his heart. Anger quickens his blood.

She catches his glance. "What is it, Daniel?"

"You women," he says. "You're all whores in your hearts, every one of you."

"What have I done?" she says, startled.

"I need a line and a drink," he says and promptly steps into Pete Fagan's Saloon.

"What have I done?" she says, following. "Daniel?"

He throws a shot of whiskey into the back of his throat and sits at a table. Takes out the vial, the spoon.

She sits before him, ignoring stares. Eyes moist. Mama's old trick. Neither Zhu nor any other woman will *ever* sway him that way. *I've always been good to you, Danny, haven't I?* How he tried to please her, always to please her, no matter what.

"You change so quickly," she says, peering at him. "I hardly know you from one minute to the next."

He sniffs a spoonful. Improving the technique. "Out to ruin me, all of you."

"*That's* going to ruin you," she says.

"See what I mean?" he says. "I tell you, this is my cure."

"Cocaine is a powerful, addictive narcotic. I notice you had a drink, anyway."

"Calms my nerves, mistress," he says, "that's all." Permits a warning tone in his reply.

"I thought you've been cured."

"Whores in your hearts," he says, ordering another whiskey. Savors the turn of phrase, along with the booze. "Out to ruin me, every last one of you."

"What about your mother?" she says. Permits a goading, insolent tone into her question.

"She's a fine example," he says. "Yes, Mama would have ruined me, too. She was always stinking. Probably why she allowed herself to be beguiled by such common men. No wonder Father beat her. Now I can understand. She *was* just a whore, after all." Smiles at her. "Don't look so stunned, mistress. She even got herself in the family way with another man. Carried a bastard."

"You mean you've got a sibling?" she asks, eyes sparkling with greedy interest. Women always have such avidity for family matters. "Brother or sister?"

"*Carried*, I said." He stands. "Time to find Mr. Harvey."

Strides to the door, staggering a little as he descends the stairs outside. Second stair poorly installed. Not his fault. Mr. Pete Fagan, bucking for a lawsuit. Between the spoonful and the shots, he is ready to face the Devil himself. Puts his hand on the Remington, blood simmering as he strides down Water Street. Where is the lousy son of a bitch?

And there, a commercial building in a row of them: Harvey's. Pioneer architecture, all straight lines and weathered wood, the plainness relieved only by a row of craftsman's gingerbread along the eaves with several scrolls knocked out like rotten teeth. Why on earth did Father ever extend credit on this piece of excrement? Blood pounds in his ears as he steps inside. Thick haze of tobacco smoke, stink of booze, and pandemonium.

A boy bounds past him and brushes him aside, nearly knocking Zhu off her feet. "Say, now!" Daniel cries, but the boy clatters down the stairs and is gone. Men are yelling, flushed and gesticulating, striding back and forth across the barroom, gathered around a long table at which croupiers sit in shirtsleeves and vests, taking coins, making notations in their green leather ledgers. A wizened little operator sits at the end of the table, bending over a telegraph set. Next to him, a burly red-haired fellow, his muttonchops like great flaming wings, announces the latest news from the operator in a voice that manages to soar above the din.

"Aaaand this just in: at Saratoga in the sixth, Saratoga in the sixth, it's Diamond Jim Boy, Diamond Jim Boy wins, gentlemen! Just a moment; Her Majesty's Aristo to show, aaand Baggage Smasher to place!"

Men cheer and scramble to the croupiers' table. Others groan and punch their neighbors, seize their own beards, or stare stoically into their whiskeys.

"Say, mister, what's a gentleman like you doing in a joint like this?" says a sardonic voice. "Pretty game." Daniel turns. Handsome, rough-looking kid, big hands, dark hair curling over his collar. No stained fisherman's togs for Jack London this time. He wears the rumpled tweedy jacket and trousers, disheveled collar and tie of a college man. Spies Zhu; his eyes widen. Tips the shot in his hand. "You're game, too, sister."

"Mr. Jack London," Daniel says, "may I present Miss Zhu Wong."

"Awfully game, Miss Wong," Jack London says. His smirk hints at the crude thoughts he surely entertains. To Daniel, "Never figured you for the broad-minded type, mister. My congratulations."

"Miss Wong is an employee," Daniel says.

"Of Miss Jessie Malone," Zhu finishes for him.

"A working girl?" Jack London says.

"I'm the bookkeeper."

"No foolin.' When the revolution comes, all us wage slaves will cast off our chains of bondage. And the revolution will come to America, Miss Wong, I guarantee it."

"What revolution is that?" she says.

"Come on, Zhu," Daniel says. "We have other business here."

"Why, the socialist revolution, Miss Wong," Jack London says, "though I don't suppose you know a thing about it."

"You mean the seizure of private property for distribution to the masses?" she says tartly. "The Chinese people will engage in such a revolution with blood and guns. Your United States of America never will. But your government bureaucracy and its ally, the police state, will grow. Grow inexorably, shielded by an ever-shifting rhetoric of crisis and the entrenchment of power so that your people will not recognize what their society has become till it's too late."

"You don't say?" Jack London says.

Daniel snorts. "You must forgive my little lunatic."

Jack London waves him away. Orders another shot of whiskey, downs it. "Where are you from, Miss Wong?"

"China," she says. "Sadly, my people will exchange their revolutionary fervor for pervasive reinstitution of private property, vested interests, traditionalism, and favoritism as surely as your people will exchange their personal freedom, enterprise, economic mobility, independence for a semblance of security. In the end, both wind up with the rich and the poor stratified anew. The powerful and the powerless. A world wracked by pollution, overpopulation, and violence. Only refinements of rhetoric will separate our societies. Perhaps that was all that really separated them in the first place."

"She's a genius," Jack London says to Daniel. "She's too good for you, mister. Let me have her."

To Daniel's surprise, Zhu smiles at Jack London. "What is this place, Mr. London?"

"Miss Wong, this is a poolroom," Jack London says. "No, there's no pool table. The technical definition is an establishment for organizing a betting pool; hence, a poolroom." That smirk; he takes Zhu's arm. "Can I buy you a drink? No?" More amazing, she takes his. "See that guy over there working the telegraph? Picks up race results from tracks all over the country. And those guys?"—pointing at the rows of tables, the money changing hands—"Make book. And those guys"—jerking his thumb at the bar—"make sure everybody stays loaded. San Francisco and Oakland outlawed poolrooms in '94. Too corrupt, they said. Fleeced the working stiffs out of their hard-earned dough while the poolroom operators cleaned up. But the board of trustees of this fair burg were persuaded—persuaded generously—by various gambling entrepreneurs that the sport of kings, a shot of rye, and a marvelous view of the bay go hand in hand." Winks at Daniel, juts his chin at something over Daniel's shoulder. "Why, here's the esteemed proprietor of this establishment now.

Say, Mr. Harvey, I'm putting ten dollars on Argle-Bargle to win in the fourth at Pimlico. What do you think?"

Daniel whirls and confronts the man.

Of medium height, slight build. Little hands, pared fingernails. Pleasant nose and mouth, well-shaped cheeks and forehead. All right; but then: dead white skin of the habitué of the night, late mornings, and cloistered afternoons. Harvey's black hair curves in a great, greasy roll cascading back from the pale forehead and falling down his neck. A black beard spreads over his concave chest like a fur bib. Worst of all are his eyes. Huge pop-eyed things, mismatched and strangely shaped, dark bags of flesh beneath them, glassy staring pupils within them, the right slightly wandering toward the left. His hands twitch.

"So you're the fuckin' son," Harvey says. Two thugs appear instantly at his side.

Zhu drops Jack London's arm and goes to Daniel's side.

"Say, Mr. Harvey," Jack London says. "This guy's okay by me."

But Harvey hears nothing, not even that Argle-Bargle has won at Pimlico. "Heard about your pretty face," Harvey says, pushing Zhu aside, shoving his hideous face up to Daniel's. In his little right hand, a gleaming curve. Bowie knife, a long evil thing for killing and skinning. "This poolroom is mine, Watkins. Your rich daddy ain't got a thing to do with it. Fuckin' go back to Saint Louis. We don't want your kind here."

Jack London's hand closes over the little right hand. A gang of hard-faced men steps up behind Jack London. Got their own fists clenched.

"Say, Mr. Harvey," Jack London says. Congenial. The tension lessens a bit, but not much. "This guy's a friend of mine. What's your gripe?"

"He means to take my property away from me, that's my gripe," says Harvey. He's got a hissing voice that somehow cuts through the din just as surely as the announcer's bray.

"Now why would he do that?" Jack London says. Hand still over the grip of the Bowie knife. Daniel stands very quietly. Zhu's hand on his arm a steadying influence.

"His daddy loaned me money to buy my land and my building, only I ain't sending no gold back to Saint Louis," Harvey says.

"Is this a legal debt?" Jack London says.

"Did I sign fuckin' papers, you mean?" Harvey says.

"That's what I mean," Jack London says.

"Hellya." Chortles at his thugs. "How else you think I got the dough?"

"Has Mr. Watkins cheated you?" Jack London says.

"No rube from Saint Louis gonna cheat me," Harvey says.

"Then why won't you repay the debt like you're supposed to?" Jack London says.

Everyone in the poolroom stops and stares.

"What if the gold don't get there? What if his daddy don't credit me?" Harvey gives a show of being reasonable. Doesn't work. The deranged gleam returns to his popping strange eyes. "Anyhow, it's *my* establishment. Ain't his. *I* puts in the sweat every goddamn day. *I* takes the losses. And *I* takes the gains."

"Mr. Harvey," Jack London says, "I'm afraid you're going to have to repay Mr. Watkins his legal debt."

"Aw," Harvey says, pressing the knife.

"At least till the revolution comes," Jack London says, pressing back. Daniel is relieved to see that London is superbly strong. As strong as Daniel was before drink debilitated him.

"Aw, shit," Harvey says. Yanks his hand, the knife, and himself away. Stalks back to the bar. The shouting crowd closes in around him. He turns. "I'm going to kill you, Mr. Watkins." Harvey smiles, an awful sight, like the gingerbread on the eaves. "Mark my words. I'm going to fuckin' kill you."

Jack London shakes his head. But his smirk, so sardonic before, is cold. "A capitalist. I knew it." Jack London turns and stalks out of Harvey's poolroom.

DECEMBER 5, 1895 ▼ ▼ ▼

The Artists' Ball

CHAPTER NINE

Prayers in the Joss House

"Betsy?" Jessie murmurs in the dawn. "My sweet innocent angel, is that you?" Tosses and turns, unable to find comfort in her cashmere bedclothes. Her side aches. Head, too, which never did before. Everything has become strange.

Why can't she see things as she wishes they were? Gift of a second glass of absinthe. Toss, turn, toss, turn. Everything tossing and turning. Why can't she see what she wants to see anymore?

It's no use. Gets up, goes to her window, throws open the watery glass. The city wakes, milk wagons and vegetable vendors rattling on their rounds. Neigh of horses, honk of a donkey. *Ssh-ssh* of street sweepers' sprinklers. Fishermen long gone, the last straggling trawlers cutting through shifting darkness between the graceful shoulders of the Golden Gate. To the east, the bay shimmers. First glimmer of sun illuminates the world behind the Oakland hills, soon to grace them all. Air fresh as crushed eucalyptus leaves. Winter chill, the night's stink blown clear.

Why so dark a heart in the dawn?

And up at dawn the previous day and still she can't sleep. Another lively night at the Parisian Mansion. Couple of local bulls stopped in for midnight supper. Stayed on for drinks and smokes, a ride in the saddle. Ah Chong beaming. His terrapin makes men randy. "Is my spice," he claims. Got a new girl. Lovely thing with flaming red-gold hair and such bad teeth she never smiles. Good racket. Who ever knows what'll boost the charm of a fallen angel? Says she's seventeen. Sure and without her paint, she looks like a schoolgirl barely out of diapers.

Schoolgirl. "Betsy?" Jessie's gorge rises.

The bulls got it all free, of course. The law has been leaning on her more and more these days, not to mention the bench. His honor the railbird's touch for twenty eagles at Ingleside was just the beginning. Mr. Heald regretfully informed her that her monthly civic contribution had increased by as much, and he still had the nerve to ask her to play the skin flute.

These days.

Bad luck coming, Jessie knows it, as surely as she knows winter's coming. Presses fingers lightly to her liver pulsing beneath her skin. Needs a dose of Scotch Oats Essence just to lace up the corset, and lacing tighter than ever. Wasp waists the rage in Paris.

Says out loud to no one, "Jar me, what diamonds shall I wear tonight?"

Sure and that's all; excitement over the annual Artists' Ball. The bohemians call it their Mardi Gras, winter cheer instead of spring like in New Orleans. Tonight at the San Francisco Art Association, beneficiary of the mansion old man Hopkins abandoned high atop Nob Hill. First bash of the season after which the holidays begin, Mr. Ned Greenway separating everyone into preferred lists and other lists, upon none of which Miss Jessie Malone ever appears. Mr. Greenway; fat little snob. How do these bores manage to promote themselves as arbiters of taste? He's just a champagne importer. Swills his own wares. Never been civil to her since she procured her own supplier of California champagne in Napa, declining Greenway's outrageous markup on the imported French. Sit down with a blindfold on and taste for yourself. Is French champagne really better than Californian? Not to Jessie.

Nob Hill, Snob Hill. That's what the maids and butlers and tradesfolk call it when they take their ease south o' the slot. A jest among sporting gals, too. Snob Hill; a rat's nest of mansions perched cheek by jowl on a hill too small for them all. City seat of the Social Set, though the Silver Kings, Sugar Kings, Railroad Kings, Sundries & Dry Goods Kings, not to mention their scions, think nothing of descending from their gilded perch for an evening's frolic at a congenial locale like Miss Jessie Malone's Parisian Mansion.

Make them pay, darlin'. Some of them kings of industry and their families are worth tens of millions of dollars. Just imagine! Factory wages five to eight dollars a week. And Jessie's boardinghouse for gentlemen, of which she is very proud, with a custom paint job, good roof, no leaks in all these years, her own private suite plus four luxury rentals, and architecture that Zhu has proclaimed a vintage specimen of Stick-Eastlake cost Jessie seven thousand dollars, cash. And she thought *that* was expensive.

The biggest, fanciest rocks she's got. Sure and that's what Jessie will wear to the Artists' Ball. Her jet beaded dress with the décolleté that'll make the roving eyes of them Snob Hill gentlemen pop out. A lucky break, the Artists' Ball. Common folk like her with better diamonds than the diamond dealer's wife can mix with the Social Set. In front of everyone, not skulking about after midnight. Open invitation; now that's what she likes about artists. No one is turned away from artists' parties.

Hears a sigh behind her, an unearthly whisper. Whips around, knocking her elbow on the window pane. "Betsy? Is that you?"

Bedroom sunk in shadows. No one there.

But she feels it, her long lost angel's presence. Schoolgirl. And there! A slim little shape, a beckoning shade. "Betsy? Mother of God!"

The whole damn boardinghouse has been haunted since Madame De Cassin's séance. The awful time when the sitting room went black and white and strange, everything strange, and a demonic presence descended upon them all. The eminent spiritualist's cleansing rituals have done nothing to dispel the evil influence.

Nothing has been the same since. When was that, the Fourth of July? A half year ago, then?

No, nothing is the same, she can't see anything the way she used to. Mariah sneaking off to her meetings, a meeting every other week now, it seems. Poor Mr. Schultz, who was such a good egg. Down on his luck, now gone. Drank rotgut one night, got the cramp, blood on the stomach, and gone in three days. Zhu had a name for it. Pair o' something, she called it. Pair o' what? Jessie asked. Fatal ulcers, Zhu said in that voice of hers, aggravated by drink. Like Jessie is ignorant, which she most certainly is not.

Haunted, strange; nothing as Jessie wants it to be. Zhu herself, such a levelheaded girl despite her talk about being from six hundred years in the future and proceeding to heal a crack in a man's skull. Sure and Jessie believes her. Why not? Where else would you get a mollie knife? If Mr. Wells says people can travel back and forth in time, then one day they probably will. We're modern now, miracles happen all the time. The news from Europe is they think they'll cure consumption. They'll invent a horseless carriage that everyone can buy. They'll fly to the moon. And serious Zhu, the little Amazon, put on her coolie's rags and showed Jessie how she could toss a man over her shoulder with her bare hands. Smart wise Zhu, lecturing Jessie about her diet and her drinking. About using condoms, of all things, to keep off the pox.

In this strange half year, Jessie has come to care for Zhu. Hasn't cared this way for anyone in many long years. So many strange stories the missy has told her on many dawns. Zhu has talked endlessly about a red-haired man. Claims he lives six hundred years in the future, that he sent her here, that he didn't tell her the whole truth. Jessie can read between the lines. A family sort of way is how Jessie feels toward Zhu.

So it makes no sense, Zhu going nutty over Mr. Watkins. But it's true. Jessie's got eyes in her head. Oh, he's a handsome kid, no doubt about that. Charm the bloomers off any dimwitted chit. But Zhu? He probably doesn't tell her the truth, either. And it's worse than that. He doesn't just take her for a roll in the hay. Sometimes he lays his hands on her. Jessie glimpses bruises through Zhu's lace cuffs. What doesn't Jessie see? Worst of all is how he badgers Zhu. Gets in his moods. Then sweetness and light after, he's so sorry. They always are.

Hard to watch. Jessie herself danced many a cruel waltz like that, years ago.

Not to mention Zhu thickening in the breasts and waist, despite her disdain of food and ever tighter corsets. Does she know she's been in the family way for several months? Miss smart aleck. Wits don't help when it comes to her own well-being. These book-learned kids can be pretty dense about the facts of life. Jessie has kept her trap shut. Waiting for the right moment to mention the unmentionable.

And Mr. Watkins? Now there's another story. How he's changed since he first charged through her door, all bright-eyed and reeking of booze in his dusty suit and bowler. His drinking was bad enough. Now he's got the cocaine habit, gone gaunt and strange. Jessie liked him better drunk. Now laughing one minute, the Devil the next. In a blue funk after that. Bloodstained handkerchiefs. Thinking someone is following him, which in fact someone is. Jessie has not only seen the thugs waiting on the corner, she's heard plenty of rumors. Bad business; a bum deal of his father's.

Sure and he doesn't need to be hopped up. Jessie knows about cocaine. She uses the stuff as a remedy, soaked in lint and topically applied, for excessive female masturbation. A nonproductive activity in her establishments, whether on Sutter Street or Morton Alley. Makes tender flesh numb. Dentist used it on her gum when he pulled her back chopper. She declines the spoonful of powder Daniel offers. Why make yourself numb and half-mad to boot? Mr. Watkins a zealot, says it's curing his dipsomania, though he drinks just as much as before.

Nothing like Jessie wants it to be.

Foreboding so intense, she just can't sleep. She stumbles

across the shadowy bedroom and dresses in the dark. Laces the corset, a little loose. Still pain. Hurries down to the smoking parlor. Where in hell is her Scotch Oats Essence? Bottle nearly empty. Mr. Watkins has a fondness for the medicine, too. She tips it to her lips, but the foreboding won't flee before the soothing syrup.

Strangest of all is Betsy. Betsy haunting her, haunting her thoughts more and more. Not that a day ever went by since Betsy's death when Jessie didn't think of her sweet innocent angel or pray for her. But her thoughts of Betsy have always been of Betsy's present happiness. Is she content in the Summerland? Does she have friends, sweethearts? Things going well for her? God knows, but for her beauty and buoyant nature, things seldom went well for Betsy in this life.

Now all Jessie can think about is this life. The life Betsy had. The life Jessie has. Why Betsy died the way she did.

Why, why, why?

Harsh jangle of bells bursts into her ear. Damn near jumps out of her skin. The new telephone in her parlor rings again. Pacific Bell, that's what they call the new switchboard, though who in town is connected? She's got lines from the Parisian Mansion and Morton Alley to the boardinghouse, the fire stations, Gump's, and the lower Dupont callbox. Not much else. The Queen of the Underworld and the chief of police have the best connected telephone lines. Even wealthy men like Mr. Heald, his honor the railbird, and the diamond broker resist installing telephones in their private residences up on Snob Hill. No, they'd rather communicate the good old-fashioned way. Send a handwritten note by messenger boy saying they won't be home tonight. Who wants to speak with the missus? Who wants to explain, fend off her remonstrations?

Jessie claps the set to her ear, the handpiece to her mouth. Awkward contraption, no matter how convenient. "Yeah?"

Garble, garble, garble. ". . . 's Bertha, Miss Malone." Door maid at the Red Rooster, Jessie's Morton Alley cribs. "New girl showed . . ." Garble.

"A new girl showed up?" Shouting, wake up the house.

"Yeah," Bertha shouts, "she says . . ."

"I'll come down and look her over—*later*." Suddenly tired at the prospect of going down to Morton Alley.

"Tong men . . . says she's gotta get off the street."

"*Tong* men. She a Chink?"

"Yeah, I *told* you. On the lam, she says . . ."

"All right, all right." Claps the handpiece onto the set.

Suddenly *awake*, not pleasantly; sick kick-in-the-gut awake. Even the Queen of the Underworld would rather not tangle with tong men. But the biz is the biz and you may find yourself purchasing their merchandise now and then. Too little Chinese tail in this town, and Morton Alley so popular with the bachelors and the sailors. A crib like the Red Rooster can always use a bit more.

Sets the telephone down. Shaky. "Mother of God, Betsy," she whispers, "I don't know if I can tolerate the biz anymore."

Jessie goes upstairs to find Zhu.

❙ ❙ ❙

Jessie lets herself in without knocking to the suite Zhu and Mariah share. Hears Mariah banging a coffee pot in their little kitchen, humming, sometimes talking to herself. Jessie tiptoes across the dark parlor. Knocks softly on the door to Zhu's bedroom.

Sleepy voice within, "Yes?"

Jessie hesitates. What if he's there? Never caught them in bed together all these months. Of all the things she's seen in her time, lewd things, lascivious things, sometimes depraved things, suddenly Jessie doesn't want to see her Zhu in bed with Mr. Watkins.

"Yes?"

What choice has she got? Who else she can rely on at a quarter to five in the morning? Jessie pushes the bedroom door open.

And there he is, stretched long and lean in the dim golden light of the lamp next to Zhu's bed, his dark hair tumbling across the pillow next to her. She rises, one of her pretty eyes nearly swollen shut. Dark bruise over the eye and half her cheek. Lip swollen, too, split and bloody.

"Oh, Betsy," Jessie murmurs, blinking back tears.

Zhu sits, turns up the lamp. "Jessie? Jessie? What's wrong?"

It's Zhu, of course, not Betsy, and there is no man beside her. Just the long crumpled roll of sheets and blankets she kicked off in the fitful night. She leans into the light, dispelling the shadow across one side of her face. Tilted green eyes, sharp cheekbones, the sleepy curve of her smile.

"Jessie?"

Faint, she must be faint, everything whirling. No sleep. Hasn't slept since the day before yesterday. "Ah, Zhu," Jessie murmurs. "That was one hell of a premonition. I don't want to repeat it anytime soon."

Zhu bounces out of the bed and comes to her. Strong little arms, can toss a man over her shoulder. So serious, her serious Zhu. Never met anyone like her girl from the future. If only it were true. Serious now, face taut. "A premonition? What do you mean?"

"I get feelings. I see things. Never mind. You gotta come with me now. I've never taken you there before. You're too good, missy, and that's a fact. But I gotta take you now. A Chink showed up."

"A Chink?"

"Jabbering about tong men. She's probably worth it." Jessie seizes Zhu by the collar of her nightgown, frail fabric like a butterfly's wing. "Get dressed."

"A Chinese girl?" she repeats, still stupid with sleep.

"Who else can help me handle this, Pearls Before Swine?"

"I'll go." Then angrily, "Don't you call her a Chink."

"All *right*," Jessie says. "Hurry up." That's her Zhu, throwing off the nightgown without a care. Jessie watches. Lean muscles, long bones, pale golden skin, so unlike any woman Jessie has ever seen, and she's seen plenty. Swift and sure in the wardrobe, finding her stockings, garters, corset, slip, underskirt, bodice, dress, jacket, gloves, hat, veil. All in cerulean blue.

"Where are we going?" Zhu says.

Jessie laces her up, tight and tighter. Sees bruises dappled across her back. Or is it only the dawn light angling across the architecture of her back?

"We're going to Morton Alley."

❙ ❙ ❙

Another strange night with Daniel, and though he left as he always does—he never spends the night with her—Zhu is uneasy. He is deeply into cocaine and drink, yet under Tenet Three of the Grandfather Principle, she cannot help him. What he does is what he has always done. Always will do. There is nothing she can do or say. She cannot interfere with his destiny.

A Chinese girl showing up at Jessie's cribs in Morton Alley? Now that is something she's supposed to do something about.

Zhu fastens her button boots and then she's off with Jessie Malone. Jessie's rockaway and pair are stabled far away in Cow Hollow. No cabs in sight at this hour. They stand, irresolute, at the stoop of 263 Dupont Avenue in the burgeoning morning while saloons, bathhouses, and gambling joints across the street eject the last of the deadbeats and admit fresh customers.

"It's getting light, let's just walk," Zhu says.

"Oh, missy," Jessie says, grimacing, holding her side. "I don't know if I can."

Zhu grimaces, too, to see her. Jessie's got a serious medical problem, that's what Muse says. Kidney disease, cirrhosis of the liver, possibly cancer in a fairly advanced stage. But what can Zhu do? The Queen of the Underworld is no more a part of Zhu's Golden Nineties Project than Daniel. Jessie is just a local, an inhabitant of this spacetime with whom Zhu cannot trouble herself. Why should Zhu bother?

Because she's a Daughter of Compassion, that's why. Because she's a devotee of Kuan Yin, protector of women. Because if she ever sees Sally Chou again, she can say she did not fail the Cause in her day or in Jessie's. Zhu digs through her purse. She finds the little bottle marked "Montgomery Ward Quinine Pills," and shakes out a knockerblocker. Breaks the capsule in front of Jessie's nose. "Sniff," she says. Tenet Three be damned.

"You're always prepared, missy. But I don't take cocaine. I keep telling Mr. Watkins."

"This isn't cocaine, Miss Malone. Sniff. Quickly!"

Jessie does, her grimace of pain instantly transforming into something less disturbing. Suspiciously, "What is it, then?"

"Something from the future. Do you believe me?"

"Sure and why not?"

Zhu smiles. Daniel calls her a lunatic and loses no chance to belittle her whenever she admits her true nature and origin. But Jessie accepts her claim with a certain trusting forthrightness peculiar to this time. Zhu often wishes she had more to show Jessie. Of all people, Jessie would appreciate hearing from a guardian angel. Or from a spirit at a séance. Maybe she would stop drinking champagne for breakfast. But Muse will only deign to issue advice and project spectacular holoids to Donaldina Cameron. Which is a shame.

"Don't dawdle, missy," Jessie commands with new vigor. "You said walk. Let's walk."

They stroll down Dupont Avenue to Union Square, turn down the narrow lane. Only two blocks long, from Stockton to Kearny, and lined from start to finish with the most popular cribs in the city: Morton Alley. While the waking city streets are softly illuminated with rosy dawn light, this street is lit with a false dawn. Red lights shine over every door in flagrant disregard of the new ordinance. Though the rest of Union Square and surrounding streets are quiet and empty, save for a few sleepy-eyed tradesmen, Morton Alley seethes with humanity.

Alphanumerics flip in Zhu's peripheral vision as Muse opens a file and reviews it. "You're not from San Francisco, Z. Wong, so you don't know," Muse whispers in subaud.

"Don't know what?" Zhu whispers cautiously back. Jessie is too absorbed in scanning the crowd to notice.

"In the future, after the First Great Quake—the first big one the Archives have amply documented, anyway—this street will be renamed."

"Renamed?"

"There will be jewelry shops and leather shops, art galleries, and fancy cafés. They'll call it Maiden Lane, but no one will remember why."

Like a scene from a Bosch painting, the maidens lean from casement windows, naked to the waist. Shout prices, trill like creatures in heat, describe in detail certain acts to be performed, comment on the morning, belittle the anatomy, wealth, and intelligence of the mob below. Despite the freshness of the new day, Morton Alley reeks of whiskey, bile, tobacco smoke, sweat, urine, semen, blood. The street is thronged with drunken men who shout at the maidens. Shout at the pimps, the door maids, the bouncers, each other. Men stagger from crib to crib, peer in windows at the occupants as though viewing animals in a zoo, shout approval or disapproval, pinch flesh when they can reach it. Two fellows reel by locked in a violent embrace, bloodied from several rounds of fisticuffs.

Alarmed, Zhu seizes Jessie's arm.

"Don't worry," Jessie shouts in Zhu's ear, "the bulls won't bother anyone here unless there's a shooting."

A maiden spots Zhu. "There's a charity case!" Shouts to her through cupped hands, "Get some sense, bitch, stop giving it away for free."

Other maidens at their windows guffaw. Unlike the Parisian Mansion, where Jessie's girls are blond or red-haired and well-endowed, these women are of all different races. A panoply of nationalities. Every shape and size. All the colors of humanity—ivory white, golden yellow, fawn brown, ebony black.

Zhu gapes. For a weird moment, Morton Alley—one day, Maiden Lane—strikes her as vital, impressive, even wonderful. A manifestation of the modern American notion of integration, a concept that has been alternately embraced and rejected over the centuries. A prescient manifestation, like pirates on the high seas were one of the first equal opportunity employers welcoming Oriental, white, and black as long as one was sufficiently qualified with seamanship, avarice, and bloodthirstiness.

But as she and Jessie press into the crowd and draw nearer to the windows, Zhu sees the faces. Despite their variegated skin colors, hair colors, eye colors, their features fine or bold, their bodies robust or frail, these women have one thing in common. A look of deep despair behind the bawdy facade, the cruel grip of degradation. Cast over it all, the patina of poverty, makeup plastered over the taint of disease the way the buttery sauces concocted by the chefs of this day may drench tainted meat.

"Ten cents touch a titty, fifteen cents two titties, twenty-five cents fuck a Mexican, fifty cents Chink, Jap, or nigger, seventy-five cents a Frenchy, a dollar for an American beauty, all white meat!" shouts the pimp at the door leading up to a row of cribs.

A sign on the establishment: "The Cow Yard."

"My cribs are down the block," Jessie says, dragging Zhu through the crowd.

"Damn it, Jessie, how can you do business here?" Zhu demands, appalled.

"Missy, the biz is the biz." The madam is flushed. Feeling good, apparently, from her knockerblocker. "Won't you ever get that straight?"

"But Jessie . . ." Zhu calculates. The girls at the Parisian Mansion each get five dollars a john and up. "How can you clear a profit with that fee structure?"

Jessie turns with a smile. "Now you're thinking like a madam, missy. Each of my Morton Alley girls clears maybe eighty, a *hundred* a night."

"Eighty, a hundred—?"

"Johns," Jessie says.

"A hundred johns a night?" Zhu says.

"The Red Rooster has a reputation for the prettiest girls on this street. And Morton Alley is a port of call all its own. This way."

They find the Red Rooster. The cribs are also known by the bird's more succinct and common name among these denizens of Morton Alley. The Rooster is housed in a ramshackle commercial building aged for so many decades and of such crudity that Zhu is hard put even to call it Stick Victorian. With one hand, Jessie neatly slaps, pushes, shoves, and punches rowdies out of her way, resolutely pulling Zhu into the lair with the other.

"Bertha!" Jessie confers with the door maid, a black woman of tremendous height and girth. Not merely stalwart with the brawn of one who has performed hard physical labor for years, Bertha, in her new position, has eaten and drunk heartily. Bertha surveys Zhu with eyes of ice, a dour mouth.

"She the bitch askin' where that hundred went?" Bertha means an unaccountable monthly shortfall of a hundred dollars that Zhu discovered in the books for this place. Bertha extracts a cover charge of twenty-five cents from each john before he makes his choice inside; she takes the balance when he leaves. The bouncer inside also tabulates the number of johns for every twelve-hour period by logging in each visit to each prostitute. The system is meant to keep tabs on the women, how much traffic they attract. Zhu pointed out to Jessie the system served as a cross-check, too. Recorded the number of johns per period. Bertha was Zhu's first suspect. The shortfall is still unaccountable. But door maids like Bertha who will work Morton Alley are hard to find.

"Why doncha mind your own business?" Unmistakable smarm of guilt in the icy eyes.

Before Zhu can protest she was just doing her job, Jessie ushers her inside past the street mob into a hallway awash in dim red light. From a plain wood plank that functions as the bar, a wiry old man dispenses shots of whiskey and gin. Zhu notices a stove, a bubbling cauldron of water. A maid scoops hot water into a basin and hurries down the hall, dispensing water as each john finishes his business. More men, more windows, more cribs, more women leaning out, haranguing whoever stands there. A bouncer oversees the mob inside, announcing the fee scale in a loud monotone.

A drunken girl with slovenly blond hair, floppy breasts and arms, and bruises dappling her neck slumps over her window.

"Li'l Lucy," Zhu cries and hurries over. Columns of numbers on the books, that's what the Red Rooster has been to Zhu up till now. Each prostitute pays Jessie a basic rental charge for the privilege of working in one of these cribs. That covers Jessie's overhead. Out of earnings, each pays Jessie ninety percent. That covers protection from street violence, medical treatment, monthly civic contributions, the income opportunity guaranteed at this location, cash advances for clothes, booze, dope, food, children's expenses, and Jessie's profit. The biz is the biz.

Zhu peeks past Li'l Lucy. The crib is a little over six feet long, just as tall, and as wide as the span of a man's outspread arms. The amenities include a cot covered with a slick red cloth, a washbasin for the boiling water, a bottle of carbolic acid for douching. A framed placard on the wall over the cot reads "Li'l Lucy" romantically rendered in daisies.

"Hey, Zhu," Li'l Lucy says, holding herself up, both hands gripping the window. The ledge is padded with more of the slick red cloth. "Like my workshop?"

Zhu runs a finger over the cloth. "Oilcloth?"

"Yeah, on the bed, too. The johns don't never take their clothes off or their boots. Them's the rules. So the mud, an' shit? I can wipe it right off. See?" Li'l Lucy demonstrates with a stained rag she pulls from under the cot.

Suddenly Jessie looms behind Zhu, shoulders past her. "You're jagged again, Li'l Lucy." Seizes Li'l Lucy's face, turns her chin back and forth. Pulls her out into better light like yanking the head of a turtle out of its shell. "Smoking hop, too, aren't ya. Aren't ya?"

"No, Miss Malone, I would never . . ."

"Yeah, you are, I can see it in your eyes."

Li'l Lucy's eyes are all dark pupil, the flesh around them is dark, too, and mottled as though she has two black eyes. Zhu sees blood dappled down the back of Li'l Lucy's arm. "Jessie, what's this?"

Jessie looks and gestures to the maid, who runs over. To Li'l Lucy, "The creep in here again?"

Li'l Lucy nods. The maid comes. Jessie lets her into the crib with a key from the outside. The maid wipes Li'l Lucy down with hot water, a rag.

"'s okay, Zhu," Li'l Lucy says, smiling at Zhu's horror. "Some guy always comes here with a chicken. Cuts its throat right after he gets his. Likes to spray the blood around. What we call a creep."

"Let's go, missy." Jessie takes Zhu's arm and fairly drags her down the hall.

"You take care of yourself, Li'l Lucy," Zhu calls, feeling helpless, stupid. Outraged at Jessie.

Li'l Lucy has nearly two years left on her contract. "Oh, I ain't long for this world, Zhu," she calls back. " 's okay."

"How can you do this?" Zhu shouts at Jessie.

"The biz is the biz," Jessie says. Voice ragged.

"She was your girl at the mansion."

"She got the pox." Stops short, making Zhu careen into her.

"It's not her fault!"

"It *is* her fault." The Queen of the Underworld shakes a finger in her face. "I told you, Zhu. She didn't douche like I taught her. Always on a jag."

"What about you?" Low-down mean, Zhu knows. Says it anyway.

"I *never* smoked dope and I *never* got the pox, missy, and don't you forget it."

Jessie swipes a shot of gin from the maid's tray, knocks it back, and takes another. "Where's the new girl?"

"Number forty-two," the maid says, scurrying away. Steaming water splashes like a preparation for a baby's birth. "Got a boyfriend with her."

Jessie storms into the crib, Zhu following reluctantly. Loath to be here one moment longer. Protestations sputtering, then dying in her throat. The new girl turns.

Round face, pale gold skin, cheekbones deeper, defined by shadows. Dark eyes rimmed red, Zhu can hardly recognize her. Disheveled hair coming out of its braid. Apple green silk crinkled, embroidery unraveling, the fabric ruined by a scrubbing in hot water and soap. Raw hands, red knuckles, perhaps skinned by a washboard or brush. Straw sandals. Big knobby toes. Her feet, her feet . . .

"Wing Sing," Zhu says. Feet as big as the paddles on the end of a rowboat's oars. Is it really *her*? "Wing Sing, what are you *doing* here?"

" 'Lo, Jade Eyes." Imperturbable. Sharp edge; no longer the compliant parlor girl in her mask of makeup. Hard glint to the young eyes.

"You know this kid?" Jessie says. Takes the girl's face in her hand like she took Li'l Lucy's, turns it this way and that. Pries open her mouth, peers into her eyes. Pokes a finger into her ribs, pinches her breasts, her thighs.

"You're supposed to be at the home," Zhu says.

A tough young sailor with white blond hair lounges over the window of the crib. He turns. Handsome boy with bright green eyes and a deep sunburn. Wing Sing says to Zhu, "This my boyfriend, Rusty, from Selena's." To him, "This my friend Jade Eyes. See how I love your eyes, honey?"

"You. Scram," Jessie says to the sailor. He shrugs and slouches out.

"Bye-bye, Rusty honey," Wing Sing calls to him.

"Feed you pretty good there, do they, them Bible thumpers?" Jessie says, smiling. Calculating, calculating—Zhu can just see it. Perhaps worth more than fifty cents a john? Perhaps seventy-five?

"Damn it, Wing Sing," Zhu says. Sick feeling in her gut. *This is not supposed to happen, not supposed* . . . "Why aren't you at the home?"

"She make me wash, she make me sew, she make me scrub floor," Wing Sing says with supreme contempt. "She make me serve her table."

"Where were you working before, kid?" Jessie says.

"At Miss Selena's on Terrific Street," Wing Sing says. "I not go back there. Chee Song Tong kill me for sure." Glares at Zhu, accusation burning in her eyes: *You made me*. Leans close to Zhu and whispers in her ear, "I carry Rusty's child."

"You're *pregnant?*" Zhu whispers back. Horrified; what about her prenatal care? What about her diet? What about a hundred johns a day? Realizes instantly: of course, Wing Sing is pregnant. She's *supposed* to be pregnant. Green-eyed father; green-eyed daughter.

"Selena not take me back like this." Wing Sing furious at Zhu.

Jessie glances back and forth between the two of them,

nodding, a knowing look rising in her eyes. She guffaws. "Sure and I'll take you in, kid. Rent is five bucks a day. Your draw ten percent of take. Tips all yours." To Zhu, "I'm not greedy."

"I want new dress," Wing Sing says imperiously. "New underwear, stockings. New jewelry."

"Sure and they ruined your silk," Jessie says, picking at the frayed embroidery on her tunic. "I'll have Miss Wong draw up the contract today. Miss Wong? Make a note of that. And Miss Wong?" Rubbing it in. "Maybe you could lend the kid one of your dresses till she can get her own. You look like you're the same size. Give her that old gray rag of yours, you've worn it too much, anyway."

The same size. Zhu could strangle Jessie. "Wing Sing, you can't do this." *Not supposed to happen*. "You've got to go back to the home, you've *got* to."

"I not do nothing, Jade Eyes. I not wash, I not sew, I not scrub floor." Wing Sing spits on the floor of the crib. "I not serve *fahn quai*."

"I'll take you back," Zhu says. "I'll tell Cameron she's got to treat you better."

"She ruin my silk, she take my dowry. Take my good gold, my jade. I not go back to home. I not go."

"But you must!"

"No!" Her face is so cold, Zhu wants to weep. Where is the scruffy waif she found in the Japanese Tea Garden? Can this possibly be the same girl?

The crowd begins to twitter down the hall.

"Where is she?" an aristocratic voice calls out. "I do believe my girl is here. I just know it, Mr. Andrews. I shall find her if we have to tear this abomination down, board by board." Crash of glass, clatter of a washbasin, the maid's tray. Shrieks, laughter, roar of manly curses. "Out of my way, you filthy sinner."

Miss Donaldina Cameron stands at the door to the crib. All crisp gray cotton and scowling rage, policeman Andrews behind her, ax in hand. Sees Zhu. "So, Miss Wong? Relatives in Chee Song Tong?" Circles Wing Sing, who gazes back at Cameron rebelliously. Zhu cringes. Cameron doesn't need to articulate her accusation of treachery and deceit. Zhu knows exactly what she thinks.

Jessie is mightily amused. "You wanna go with Miss Cameron, kid?" she says with heavy sarcasm.

"I not go," says Wing Sing.

"Really?" Jessie says. Swipes at Cameron's shoulder aiming a friendly punch, but Cameron steps back, avoiding her touch. "I guess that's that, Bible lady. She ain't your girl. She's mine now."

Cameron turns her full fury on Zhu. "I thought you told me you were just the bookkeeper. I thought you were an educated young woman."

"I am," Zhu says. Humiliated.

"Then how can you let her take this girl to work in this place?"

"I hear you got *your* girls working, too," Jessie says. "Miss Holier-Than-Thou."

"*Working*," Cameron says, bristling. "Yes, work, real work. We teach our girls to love Jesus Christ and work. Work hard at fruitful tasks. Sewing, laundering, cleaning. Idle hands and idle heads lead to the path of wickedness. *Good* work is the way these young souls," beneficent gesture at Wing Sing, "can be saved from the heathen deviltry that enslaves them."

"Yeah, I hear," Jessie says, taking another shot of gin from the tray the trembling maid has brought in, "I hear your holy home resembles—what do they call it, Zhu?—a sweatshop." Sly glance. "Isn't that so? All them little orphan girls scrubbing and polishing and sewing and washing. Hey," she says, clapping Wing Sing on the shoulder, "ain't that so, missy? Just like a sweatshop in Tangrenbu."

"I not scrub floor," says Wing Sing.

"Come on, Miss Malone," Zhu says, finding her voice. "I never said any such thing."

"She ever pay you?" Jessie says to Wing Sing.

"Not one cent," Wing Sing says. "She ruin my silk. She take my dowry."

"This is outrageous," Cameron says. "We teach these girls how to run a decent Christian home. How to care for things. How to keep a house clean."

"How to be good little subservient wives, eh?" Jessie says. "Scrub them floors, wash them clothes. You know what I always say, Miss Cameron? I say if any of them wives would be more of a slut and less of a shrew, their husbands wouldn't all come to me."

Cameron sputters.

Zhu, warningly, "Jessie."

"But all that washing and sewing and polishing, Miss Holy." Jessie won't let it go. "Some of that's work from the outside, ain't it? Them Snob Hill mansions send down their dirty silver and clothes."

"We manage the girls' revenues for them," Cameron says, flushing deeply. "We depend on charity, Miss Malone. Charity often promised, seldom delivered, and stingily paid. Even our own churchgoers are recalcitrant. We must have some revenue. Revenue that pays for the home. For the girls' education and upkeep."

"Your upkeep, too, eh?" Jessie says, plucking at Cameron's sleeve.

"I am paid twenty-five dollars a month, plus room and board, madam," Cameron says. "Truly, I do not know how much longer I can continue." Significant glance at Zhu. "Yet continue I do. I devote myself to this thankless task for the sake of our Lord, Jesus Christ, who died for us so that we may be blessed with life everlasting."

"You believe in Jesus, kid?" Jessie asks Wing Sing.

"Jesus nice man," Wing Sing says. "But I honor the Lady of my people."

"Who's that?"

"Kuan Yin."

Now Zhu gapes at the girl.

"You know Kuan Yin, Jade Eyes?" Wing Sing says. "She see all, hear all."

"Of course," Zhu says. "She is the goddess of compassion."

"Com-pas-sion," Wing Sing says, trying out the word. "Maybe Kuan Yin bless me one day. I pray some more."

"Kuan Yin signifies the strength of women, Wing Sing," Zhu says. "You be strong, and Kuan Yin will bless you."

"There, you see, Bible lady?" Jessie says to Cameron triumphantly. "They got their own religion, their own culture. What makes you think yours is better?"

" 'Tis a religion and a culture that allows a little girl to be bought and sold, Miss Malone," Cameron says. "'Tis a religion and a culture that allows a girl's master to burn her with candle wax, beat her, starve her, force her into drudgery. And then, when she comes of age at thirteen, to sell her again to a crib in Tangrenbu where she will prostitute herself until she's dead at seventeen from disease, opium addiction, or sheer despair. So, yes, I say our Jesus Christ is the true Way and this Kuan Yin of theirs is heathen deviltry."

"Kuan Yin doesn't condone the exploitation of women, Miss Cameron," Zhu says. "Kuan Yin is a protector of women. She offers sanctuary . . . ."

"That's swell," says Jessie, interrupting. "We can all sit down one day and chat about whose god is better than whose. But, Miss Cameron, do you really think this fine culture of ours is any better when it comes to treating women? Stick your fine face out that door."

The high color drains from Cameron's face. She presses her lips together tightly. She doesn't need to stick her face out the door. The clamor of drunken men outside assessing the maidens in their cribs, bargaining with the bouncer, bragging of their exploits is only too clear.

"You've got yourself a family, don't you, Miss Cameron?" Jessie says, eyes sparkling with fury. "And a fiancé. Gonna get yourself a husband one day, isn't that right? What about us poor girls, huh? What if your folks died when you were a kid, and you got nothing? No money, no home, no property, no schooling, no nothing. What are you gonna do, huh? Go work in a sweatshop for eight dollars a week and the rent cost seven? Work in a factory and lose your hand to some machine? There's no room and board included. Take in piecework? Beg on the street? You know what them bosses at the fancy shops pay their girls? You know how many girls come to me because they can't make enough dough to live on working in a fancy jewelry store? You think this fine society don't wink at the buying and selling of female flesh?"

"The likes of you exist despite our best efforts to stamp you out," Cameron says. "Just like vermin will infect our storerooms even though we set traps."

"Yeah?" Jessie squares off with Cameron. The women look as if they are about to come to blows. Zhu steps between them. "The likes of me, lady, gives all them poor girls a chance. They get better pay than a goddamn sweatshop, a nicer life than a factory. My parlor gives 'em a taste of a fine life they'd never know otherwise."

"This is hardly a parlor," Cameron says.

The cribs are like nothing so much as cages in a zoo.

"They can earn more in one day even in this lousy crib than they would earn in a week at a fancy jewelry store. They can eat," Jessie says. "They're not walking the streets."

"You're a scourge upon our society," Cameron says.

"I'm the Queen of the Underworld, and don't you forget it," Jessie says.

"You won't last," Cameron says. "The drugs or the drink or sickness or some john will do you in in the end."

Jessie leaps and seizes Cameron's collar at the throat, tearing at Cameron's golden Art Nouveau brooch. "What would you know about johns?"

"Jessie!" Zhu grabs her. Jessie practically throttles Cameron.

"What would you know?" Jessie sobs. "My Betsy knew, but *you*? Miss Holier-Than-Thou, you don't know a damn thing about johns."

"Jessie, come on," Zhu says. Jessie releases Cameron and goes limp. Zhu leads her into the hallway, summons the maid, gets her a shot of gin. Goes back inside.

Donaldina Cameron and the cop stand over Wing Sing, who stares back defiantly. "Very well," Cameron says. "I will not force you if you will not go."

"Please go with her, Wing Sing," Zhu says. Knows in her heart the girl won't. *Never supposed to happen this way*. The Golden Nineties Project has irrevocably changed. The aurelia is nowhere to be found. The girl will not go back to the home. What now? Will Zhu become unborn and disappear? Catastrophe is implicit in violation of the tenets. If the past is changed, the future changes, doesn't it? Zhu waits, oddly disappointed when nothing happens to her.

Cameron regards Zhu curiously. "So. You did not incite her to leave us?"

"Certainly not," Zhu says.

"It's inevitable we'll lose some," Cameron says to Andrews, who stands impassively with his ax. To Wing Sing, "I must warn you, my dear girl, you will burn in hell."

"So I burn," says Wing Sing. Shrugs. "She will buy me dress; you ruin dress. She will buy me jewelry; you take my jewelry. Maybe you burn, too, *fahn quai*."

Zhu expects Cameron to be outraged at the girl's blasphemy, but she only nods. Took Wing Sing's jewelry? The little box of jade and gold that was supposed to have contained the aurelia? The box that keeps surfacing like a marked card?

"Why did you take her dowry?" Zhu says. "That's all she possessed of any value." Angry. "I told you she had it when I first found her."

"I did not take her jewelry out of ill will," Cameron says. "The madam she worked for, Miss Selena. She came by the home the day after the rescue with a warrant for Wing Sing's arrest. Claimed the girl stole the jewelry from her."

"But she didn't, I tell you!"

"And I believe you. I believe Wing Sing. But the madam would have had the girl arrested. I would have had no choice but to surrender her to the police. Before you know it, the highbinders would have bailed her out or Selena would have gone to the jail and dropped charges. Either way, the highbinders would have seized custody of her again. They would have taken her to another parlor or crib, perhaps even to a different city, and we'd never find her. It's a common ploy. Mrs. Culbertson lost many girls that way."

"I see. Then Selena has the jewelry?"

"I suppose so," Cameron says. "I'm truly sorry. I assumed it was better to surrender the jewelry than to lose her."

Zhu kneels before Wing Sing, takes her shoulders. "There, you see? Miss Cameron didn't want to steal from you. Listen to me, kiddo. I'm going to go to Selena and get your dowry.

If I do, will you think about going back to the home with Miss Cameron?"

"Why should I?" Wing Sing says. "I not scrub floor."

"Perhaps Miss Cameron could find something else for you to do. Isn't that right, Miss Cameron?" Cameron nods, chastened. Zhu thinks; how can she make this right? "Remember what I told you before, Wing Sing? You'll never find a husband and wear your dowry if you stay in this place."

The girl frowns but Zhu can see that she's listening, considering Zhu's plea. "Okay, Jade Eyes. You get my dowry, maybe I go." Fiercely to Cameron, "But I not wait table!"

"All right." Zhu rises. "Please take her back, if she'll come. I beg you."

Cameron nods again. "Good luck, Miss Wong." She sweeps out of the crib, Andrews trailing behind her like a bodyguard.

Jessie stands outside the door to the crib, another shot of gin in her hand. "I heard everything," she says.

"Then you know I'm not drawing up a contract for Wing Sing, Miss Malone. Not until I get back her dowry and Wing Sing decides what she wants to do."

"Why does that kid mean so much to you, missy?"

"Because I can't go home again," Zhu says, "until she does, too."

❜ ❜ ❜

Zhu strides up Montgomery to Terrific Street. The morning sun sears her skin. The Block's fine microderm will protect her from sunburn, won't it? Still, Zhu feels as though she's burning up. She idly slides her cuff up her arm. Stops dead. Her hand and wrist exposed below the cuff are darker than the skin covered by cloth.

"Muse," she says. "Why is my skin tanning?"

Flicker of alphanumerics. "Your skin is not tanning, Z. Wong," Muse whispers.

"Yes. Yes, it is. Does the patch of Block need replacing?"

"I show no indication that your Block needs replacing. I show no indication that your skin is tanning."

"I can see it with my own eyes!" Careful; a passing milkman swivels his head in her direction.

"Must be an illusion," Muse says. Bland synthetic voice in subaud mode. "You're tired."

"An illusion! Then everything must be an illusion."

"Perhaps it is."

"That doesn't help me, Muse. You're supposed to help me. You're supposed . . ."

"You're very tired," Muse says.

Yes, she's tired, rousted out of bed at dawn by Jessie. She leans against a streetlight, suddenly ill. Bile rises in her throat. Pulse pounds in her stomach beneath the corset. Her clothes feel too tight. Lend a dress to Wing Sing, she's the same size. Zhu is *not* the same size as Wing Sing. Zhu is not the same size *she* was months ago. Putting on fat from all the rich food. Some mornings she aches from gluttony.

One morning, as Zhu had retched in the toilet, Mariah had asked casually, "You in the family way, Miss Wong?"

"Certainly not," she had snapped, but she had fled to her bedroom and checked the contraceptive patch behind her knee. The patch was still bright red. Meaning still effective, though of course she had never planned on having an affair during the Golden Nineties Project. Never had an affair like this in her life. The contraceptive patch blocked the menstrual cycle completely. She had no menses at all; she has no menses still. But Mariah's question and her burgeoning body had sent a chill through her belly. She couldn't possibly . . . Didn't eat a bite that day, pleaded dyspepsia. Next day she felt fine, trimmed by fasting, restored.

"Muse," she whispers, "Muse, why are you doing this to me?"

"I am here to guide you, Z. Wong, and to monitor the progress of your project."

"Then advise regarding my attempt to regain the girl's dowry from Miss Selena."

"Proceed at once! Hurry!"

All right, hurry. Muse is defective, malfunctioning. Or did someone program Muse to confound her like this? Program Muse to oppose her, sabotage the Golden Nineties Project? She'll file a full report when she returns, absolutely. Six months behind her, a little under three months to go till the

Chinese New Year. She's still got time to bring Wing Sing back to Nine Twenty Sacramento Street, convince her to stay, make sure she's settled in. Nine months altogether, the duration of the project. Nine months, as long as it takes to bring a child to term.

No! The timing is a coincidence. She wasn't supposed to be with Daniel like this, wasn't supposed to fall in love. In love? She does not love him. He's horrible with his sadistic games. His cocaine habit out of control. No amount of lecturing moves him. She can't help him now even if she were allowed to under Tenet Three. He needs forcible restraint, hospitalization. His septum will perforate any day. He could have a stroke.

Daniel, oh Daniel.

Zhu trudges uphill to Terrific Street.

❙ ❙ ❙

The red light is burning bright at Miss Selena's. Front door flung open, music blaring. The parlor is crowded with white men. From snippets of conversation, a convention of distillery owners from Philadelphia come to view the wineries of Napa. Touring the restaurants and bagnios. Today it's Chinese. Miss Selena only too happy to accommodate.

Zhu slips through the party. Prostitutes lounge about in silk slips, their satin robes flung open, theatrical white makeup creating masks of their faces. Zhu considers whether she should take advantage of the diversion, break into Selena's room, rummage around. But the madam probably placed the rosewood box in her safe, and the safe is hidden. It could be anywhere. Better to confront her, get it over with.

"Miss Selena," Zhu says, tapping the madam on the shoulder. "I've come for Wing Sing's jade and gold."

The madam whirls, abandoning a sprightly conversation with a pock-faced gentleman. "Get out my house, you."

"Not till you give me the jewelry. You've no right to it, and you know it."

"No right! You got no right to take my girl. We pay gold for her. Mr. Gong!" she yells. "Mr. Gong, look who here. You don't got to look for her. She right here!"

The hatchet men stroll out of the kitchen, flush with drink, fingers oily from fried wontons, each with a woman hanging on his arm. The eyepatch wipes his hands on his companion's satin robe and shoves her away. The fat man throws the rest of his drink down his throat, the wiry fellow gobbles his wonton.

They surround Zhu.

The eyepatch thrusts his face in her face. "I think I like you better in rags, Jade Eyes." Runs his eagle eye over her cerulean dress. "I thought you a good girl. You say you go talk of family with little sister-friend. Not go to *fahn quai*, help her steal our girl. Then you come back here, looking for her gold? This not good, Jade Eyes. What can we do about this?"

"I say put *her* to work," Selena says. "Girl for girl. That fair."

"Mr. Chee want blood payment instead," the eyepatch says, as though this is a reasonable alternative. Reaches into his jacket, takes out a long curved knife. A butterfly knife, it's called. "Teach the people not to steal from Chee Song Tong."

The fat man and the wiry fellow grin, as though killing Zhu would be more gratifying than turning her out.

"Blood payment? Not enough Chinese ass in this town," Selena says. "I take *her*, girl for girl. I get one on Jessie Malone."

Zhu finds herself silently thanking the madam as the hatchet men circle around her, considering the possibilities. The eyepatch is as cold as ice, though. Any trace of a friendly connection between them has vanished.

But they're drunk, Zhu sober. She seizes a spittoon, dashes the foul contents on the eyepatch, his cohorts, Selena. The house maids and the bartender block the front door, the cook blocks the kitchen door. She dashes up the stairs. Think! What did Cameron say? "Muse," she whispers, "didn't Cameron say there's a trapdoor?"

"Southeast bedroom," Muse says. "Goes to the roof. Fire escape goes down from the next roof over; a butcher shop."

"Thank you, Muse."

"Any time, Z. Wong."

She dashes up the second flight, clatters down the hall. Dead end! Races down the other way. Third flight to a half story tucked around the corner. Finds the southeast bedroom, the door unlocked. Dashes in, locks the door behind her.

There, in the ceiling, a pull and a trapdoor like the entrance to an attic. That's it! Zhu slides a chair over, climbs up on the seat. Rickety thing, the chair wobbles with her frantic action, swishing skirts. Damn these skirts! Careful, don't break your neck! Good yank on the pull, and a cast-iron stepladder gracefully telescopes out. Bootheels pound down the hall outside the bedroom. She scrambles up the stepladder onto the roof, pulls the whole thing up after her, slams the trapdoor shut. In a corner of the roof, a barrel half-filled with dried-up tar. She rolls the barrel over the trapdoor.

Then heels sinking in the warm tar roof, she goes to the edge. A gap, maybe two feet, between the roofs. Still, it makes her dizzy to look. Pulls off the shoes, tosses them over. Lifts and gathers her skirts, works up a good run. She leaps over, skirts billowing, and tumbles onto the other side.

Stink of offal and blood from the butcher shop nearly makes her retch. She reclaims the shoes, finds the fire escape. Breath ragged in her throat, heartbeat pounding in her gut, she climbs down as quietly as she can. A butcher leans out of a window, his hands and apron smeared with blood and gobbets of flesh, knife dripping.

Finds herself in an alley a half block down from Broadway, bustling with traffic. The cries of ragpickers rise over the clatter of fine carriages.

"Take Broadway to Stockton," Muse whispers, "go through Tangrenbu. Hurry."

The invisible barrier around Tangrenbu, and she in her Western dress and ridiculous lady's button boots, the corset tearing at her lungs. She turns down Stockton as Muse advised, slows to a walk. The street is packed with anonymous slim men in denim *sahms*, fedoras pulled low, faces averted.

Zhu glances down the block, sees the hatchet men milling about on the sidewalk outside Selena's. The eyepatch spots her the moment she ventures across Pacific Avenue and scurries down Stockton on the other side. Well, of course. Who else in Tangrenbu is dressed in billowing cerulean silk today? What she'd give for her denim *sahm* and fedora now! She pushes men aside, scatters baskets of bok choy, kicks a cage of chickens.

"Turn left," Muse whispers, alphanumerics flickering, "down that alley, turn right. In there."

Elaborate gingerbread, a curving roof, gilt balconies—the joss house. Zhu ducks inside, kicks off her boots.

"Joss house," Muse whispers, "means god house. From the Portuguese 'deos.' Corrupted to 'joss.'"

She's still too visible. Under the billowing dress, she wears a slip, bloomers. Rips the dress off in front of the astonished priest, popping buttons. Wads the silk into a bundle and enters the shrine. If other worshippers notice her, they give no sign but continue their meditations. She finds a place in their midst, calms herself, and sits cross-legged, smoothing her slip. No lady of this time would ever sit like this. But what will the eyepatch see?

The hatchet men clatter in. She huddles next to a wizened old man. Instinctively, the old man pats her on the shoulder. She takes his arm, slings it across her shoulder, and huddles closer. The hush, the darkness, the flickering candlelight and choking incense, especially the large gilt deity reclining upon the shrine piled high with gifts from the pious—all these subdue the eyepatch and his cohorts. Tug of tradition. They glance about, jostle someone. Quickly leave, shamed by their intrusion.

Hand on her arm. Zhu starts, cries out. The priest gently asks her something, but she cannot understand his lilting words. She finds a coin in her feedbag purse, hands it to him. He nods and smiles.

Zhu catches her breath. Paper flowers spill from the ceiling to the floor in long sumptuous strands. Silk tassels, gold flags, loops of multicolored beads bedeck the shrine. The walls are paneled in carved ebony. The altarpiece is a huge piece of mottled green marble. Bronze bowls with the look of antiquity bear smoldering cones of incense.

Zhu crawls toward the altar in supplication. Thick yellow candles mounted in massive brass candlesticks send forth their scent and soft golden light. Hundreds of slim sticks of incense arranged like smoking fans flank the altarpiece. Supplicants have heaped fresh fruit, left steaming teas in cloisonne teapots. There is a huge tray with a whole roast pig, several clay-pot chickens, numerous bowls of rice. The smell of food and tea mingles with incense, candle smoke, an indefinable underscent.

The priest takes a strip of parchment scrawled with calligraphy, burns it in a brass bowl, scoops the ashes into a bowl of water, and sucks the water into his mouth. Takes a huge brass bell and, clanging the bell loudly, sprays ashy water from his mouth onto the floor as he whirls around like a dervish.

Devotees murmur in approval, "Cast demons out."

Zhu crawls closer, peers up at the impressive gilt deity. The deity reclines upon the altar, hands poised: Kuan Yin.

Here; in this joss house in San Francisco, 1895?

Of course! Bodhisattva of compassion, goddess of mercy. She who sacrifices that others may live. The virgin, the mother, the destroyer. Teacher of secrets. Kuan Yin has been worshipped for five thousand years.

Astonished, Zhu crawls closer to the altar, slipping through the worshippers. More fruit, trays of plum candies, more fans of incense sending wavering streams of smoke into the close air. Candlelight flickers on gold coins scattered in offering. There are cabochons of jade, lozenges of lapis lazuli, carved coral, a few strands of pearls. Kuan Yin gazes down serenely at the glittering bounty.

And there, amid the incense and candles, amid the coins and clay-pot chicken, is the aurelia.

A Premonition Is Just a Memory

Zhu picks it up, holds it for the first time: the aurelia.

The aurelia: surprisingly heavy for something so delicate.

Must be solid gold. Diamonds glimmer. Tiny tinted panes project spots of multicolored light like miniature stained glass windows. Zhu would know it anywhere. The aurelia. Feels alien in her hand, gold hot from proximity to the candles, the burning incense. So hot it feels like it will brand her, burn a cross-shaped stigmata into her palm.

Then suddenly feels so familiar, the way a ring you always wear feels familiar in your hand. A wedding ring, perhaps, familiar and terrible, from a marriage that's gone wrong. So familiar.

Like a premonition.

A premonition of disaster, of pain. Of unforgivable loss. Suddenly the Art Nouveau brooch, this meaningless bauble, an insect wrought in gold with an anonymous woman caught at its center, fills Zhu with such unreasonable fear that she kneels, whirls. Glances around the joss house.

The hatchet men; have they returned for a second look? Did they see her after all? Adrenaline soars through her blood. There they are! At the door, they've found her just like she knew they would, found her at last. They're pulling their knives . . .

She scrambles away, still on her knees, cringing before the eyepatch's knife.

But there's nothing in the semidarkness except the priest spewing ashy water on the ground and three men at the entrance. Three old Chinese men in denim *sahms*, devotees of Kuan Yin. They bow, slip off their shoes, drift in. Zhu has never seen them before.

She scurries away from the altar, praying no one saw her steal the offering. The worshippers only sit, heads bowed, eyes closed or gazing raptly at Kuan Yin. No one notices her transgression. She finds a smoke-choked corner and huddles in the dark, cross-legged, cradling the aurelia while sparkles of shock travel up her spine and down again. Who in Tangrenbu could have possessed a gold Art Nouveau brooch? Only fancy stores on Market Street would carry such a thing, not these shops.

The aurelia, at last,

—like a long-long friend—

—like a piece of plutonium tossed into her lap, radioactive and deadly—

"Muse," Zhu whispers. Sweat trickles down her temple. "What is happening to me?" *Never supposed to happen this way*. "This isn't the way the Golden Nineties Project is supposed to go. I'm just the chaperon for an anonymous Chinese girl. She's supposed to be saved, I'm supposed to go home. It's supposed to be easy, everything falling into place. *She's* supposed to have the aurelia, not me. Not *me*."

Shivering with fear, teeth chattering. Seemed so real for a moment that the hatchet men had come, wielding knives.

Muse silent. Only the priest's chanting monotone, people sighing and murmuring in the dark.

"Please, Muse. Please tell me."

Alphanumerics pulse in her peripheral vision. Muse displays the directory of her Archive, chooses a file.

Muse:\Archive\Zhu.doc

Thirty-five thousand three hundred and five bytes.

"No," Zhu whispers. "There must be some mistake."

Muse accesses the file effortlessly, downloading the holoid into her optic nerve.

A tiny holoid like a baseball made of light springs up before her face. Within: the room swathed like a cloud, her shoulder in prison blue, and Chiron Cat's Eye in Draco.

"Then why," she says in the holoid, "after all the technological breakthroughs, the expenditure of resources, did you cease tachyportation projects?" Her tone is wary, deferent, almost timid.

Zhu remembers how frightened she was. The red-haired man had filled her with nameless dread. The deal her lawyer struck stunk of cooptation, payoffs, illicit DNA experiments performed on political prisoners who had no one to defend them. Strange experiments.

Just to reduce the charges against her? But charges had not yet even been brought. She hadn't even had the chance to plea-bargain. There were extenuating circumstances, the lawyer had said so herself.

In the holoid, Chi says, "That's confidential." A drink in his hand, something clear with bubbles in a crystal glass.

Zhu blinks. A drink? A whiff of incense makes her head reel. Never liked incense, always made her dizzy. She had the right to know why they ceased tachyportation, didn't she?

"I have the right to know," she whispers in the holoid. "My lawyer said you would explain."

Tinkle of ice in his glass. "Remember I told you about the Save Betty Project?" Chi says.

"The project that polluted all of spacetime," Zhu replies dutifully, "permitting another reality to intrude."

"Yes. Naturally, there were those in the Luxon Institute for Superluminal Applications who felt they could control for pollution." Chi sighs. "Fortunately, Ariel Herbert and others in control of the majority interests of the institute persuaded the dissenters to concede. And they shut tachyportation down. Shut down perhaps the most exciting technological breakthrough since the silicon chip. The Save Betty Project? Betty died in the past; perhaps she even knew she was going to die."

"She had," Zhu says, "a premonition."

Chi nods. "You could say a premonition is just a memory. A memory of the future." He sips his drink. "But Betty *didn't* die in the past. We sent a t-porter and brought her back into her own timeline. And the Summer of Love Project? The girl was supposed to be pregnant; and then she aborted the fetus; and then she became pregnant again by another man. She *did* have her child."

"I'm right," Zhu whispers.

"So I'm right," Zhu says in the holoid, "you *did* do more than cocreate."

In the holoid, Chi inclines his head. "Tachyportation itself has become part of cosmology." He swirls his drink. "So how does tachyportation function in the multiverse if all reality is a process between the observer and the observed, a multitude of probabilities constantly collapsing into the timeline? A t-porter is another probability. His or her observation of and participation in reality becomes part of the process. And cosmicist philosophers could no longer account for tachyportation by denying its effect.

"In the aftermath of Save Betty and the Summer of Love

projects, philosophers set forth three theories of reality: superdeterminism, the multiverse theory, and the resiliency principle.

"Superdeterminism posits that everything already is the way it is in the One Day, the perpetuity that is spacetime. What we perceive as doubts, hesitation, shifts of position, accident, happenstance, paradox, tachyportation itself—all randomness and all acts of free will—are an illusion. Everything is.

"The multiverse theory suggests that reality is a set of probabilities. At each moment, these probable realities are collapsing into and out of the timeline. Tachyportation is dangerous because the technology may cause a probability to collapse out of the timeline."

"And the resiliency principle?" Zhu whispers as the joss house priest burns another strip of parchment and mixes the ashes in a bowl of water. "Chi himself had been frightened of the resiliency principle, Muse. Why?"

Muse silent.

"And the resiliency principle?" Zhu asks in the holoid.

Chiron sets down his drink. "Under the resiliency principle, anything goes. And everything stays the same, more or less. We witness *and* we make it so. We can change the details, and it doesn't matter. Tachyportation is freely permitted because the technology is part and parcel of the nature of reality itself. The past creates the future; the future also creates the past. I confess, Zhu, I am unhappy with that notion."

"Why are you unhappy?" Zhu says in the holoid.

"Because t-porting is *not* in the natural order of reality," Chi says in the holoid. Had he become a little drunk from whatever was in the glass? "T-porting may create probabilities that might otherwise never exist."

More worshippers enter the joss house. "Then you *did* create new realities," Zhu whispers, glancing down at the aurelia in the palm of her hand. "You *did* attempt to take over the Cosmic Mind." Aware that her heart is beating too fast.

"So I guess you could say you created new realities,"

she says in the holoid. Mocking tone. Perhaps she had not been so frightened, after all. "You wanted to *be* the Cosmic Mind."

In the holoid Chi stands, suddenly agitated. "Perhaps." He paces. "Who is to say what reality will be? Who is to govern all spacetime? Who is to make the creative decisions? Even cosmicists were not willing to assume that responsibility. Indeed, we'd already proven to ourselves just how wrong we could be even when our intentions were beyond reproach." He sits, looking exhausted. "No one could assume such responsibility. We did not want to tempt ourselves. And no one with intentions less altruistic than the cosmicists could be allowed to know what terrible power we had at our command. We shut the shuttles down. We vowed never to use tachyportation again."

Suddenly—and of all the strangeness of the session, this was the strangest thing of all—Chiron searches his pockets. Incongruously, like an old-timey magician pulling a dove from his sleeve, he produces something shiny and commands her. "Look at this."

The aurelia.

"A golden butterfly," Chiron whispers in the holoid.

Zhu's breath catches. The aurelia, the wings, the woman, hover before her in the holoid. The aurelia, the gold, the diamonds, lie heavily in the palm of her hand.

In the holoid Chi says, "The aurelia is a symbol. In Chinese mythology, the butterfly has two meanings: a dual meaning."

"A dual meaning," she whispers.

"A dual meaning?" she says in the holoid.

"The first meaning is beautiful," Chi says. "The butterfly is the symbol of love. Not platonic love, not the love of parent for child, sibling for sibling, not the love of friends. The love between a man and a woman. Imagine two golden butterflies, entwined with each other over new spring flowers."

"You mean sex," Zhu says in the holoid.

"Daniel," she whispers, dizzy from the incense.

In the holoid, Chi smiles. "The second meaning is darker, though not unconnected to the first. The butterfly also symbolizes everlasting life. Survival of the family through reproduction. Survival of the soul through love."

"You mean death," Zhu says in the holoid.

"Daniel," she whispers again.

"I mean survival," Chi says. "*She* will have it."

The holoid shrinks to a luminous pinpoint and disappears.

Zhu crouches in the joss house, clutching the aurelia, as the priest spews water from his mouth, casting demons out.

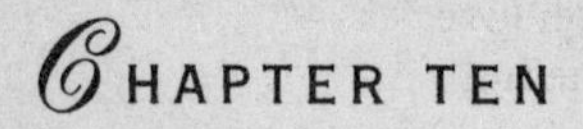

CHAPTER TEN

A Shindig on Snob Hill

"Where is she?" Daniel says. "Always disappearing when I need her." Dashes his glass against the baseboard in the smoking parlor, demonstrating his pique. Shards scatter across the Persian carpet. He seizes the bottle of Scotch Oats Essence from Mariah's tray, gulps nearly half while Mariah stands impassive, stern, judgmental. Always judging him with those black eyes of hers. As if she has any right.

"I don't know, Mr. Watkins." Polite, too. Always polite no matter how badly he behaves. She'll have to get down on her hands and knees, pick up the glass.

There, you see? a voice says inside his head. *You do know you're behaving badly*.

"She got up," Mariah says, "at the crack of dawn and went out with Miss Malone."

Runs fingers through his hair. He never heard voices in his head, not before he met *her*. His lunatic mistress from six hundred years in the future with her own voice that he can hear quite well though she never seems to hear his. Now his voices—there are more than one—cackle and sneer, admonish him every time he turns around, call him vile names, especially when there is a cacophonous sound, like the clatter of horses' hooves.

"I will not have that whore stealing my mistress away," he says.

"Miss Malone is her employer, Mr. Watkins," Mariah says. "Miss Malone may avail herself of Miss Wong's services whenever she's got a notion."

Holds out her hand for the medicine bottle. Belongs to Jessie, and the stuff's not cheap. Deliberately, defiantly, he tucks the Scotch Oats Essence into his jacket pocket. Smeared syrup will catch lint, tobacco crumbs.

Never mind. It's the only thing that seems to soothe his nerves, if only for a moment. Drink sends him into a worse rage. Anyway, controlling the drink is why he sniffs cocaine night and day. Definitely cutting down on the drink. Poor old Schultz should have given Dr. Mortimer's cure a try, but then poor old Schultz never was long on wits. Daniel has lost the paunch, too. Skinny as a kid again. Cannot understand this hellish anxiety, though. And his temper? The aftereffects of cutting down on drink, Dr. Mortimer assures him. Urges him to persist with the dipsomania cure. That'll be another five dollars, sir, ten dollars, fifteen.

"Got a notion," Daniel says, mocking the maid. "Since when does a woman get a notion?"

Mariah silent. She has a personal vendetta against him though he has never committed one single transgression against her. He addresses her roughly sometimes, perhaps, but not beyond the bounds proper for decorum toward servants.

"Anyway," he says, refusing to be shamed before her baleful glare, "my mistress has her own duties. She has no right to run off without consulting with me."

"Miss Wong," Mariah says, "has the right to do anything she wishes."

"Miss Wong has no right to do . . ."

Mariah turns on her heel and leaves without being dismissed.

"You're not dismissed," Daniel calls after her retreating

back. Got the back of a stevedore, that one does. "Hell with it," he mutters, taking out the Scotch Oats Essence. Zhu claims the stuff is loaded with whiskey, but it can't be the whiskey that soothes his fevered brow. No, it's the medicine, by God. He needs more of the same. Indeed, he needs something stronger.

Takes out his vial of cocaine and the spoon, snorts. Excruciating pain knifes through his sinuses. Numbs to nothing as soon as the cocaine settles into the flesh, but not quickly enough. Nosebleed worse. Zhu says the cocaine is eating a hole in his nose. To hell with what Zhu says. She's not a physician like Dr. Mortimer.

Daniel has got things to do before the shindig on Nob Hill tonight. Snob Hill, as Jessie calls the place. He was hoping to take Zhu with him to the courthouse. For a woman, she's awfully clever at paperwork. Just as well she doesn't accompany him to Mortimer's clinic, though. Preaching at him in that smart aleck way of hers—your smoking, your drinking, your cocaine, Daniel dear. In the future, we know better. Yes, in the future they know every damn thing, don't they? Perhaps he should send Zhu to London. Go meet Mr. H. G. Wells himself. That might put an end to her lunacy. Good thing she doesn't try to take his cocaine away. "I will kill you if you touch my cure," he has warned her.

Then off to the tailor to pick up his costume for the Mardi Gras at the art association. A costume party, of all things. As if this town doesn't celebrate enough. Some hoedown or other, complete with a parade, every month of the year. He's lost his taste for frivolity. People give him a bad case of nerves. He would never have allowed himself to be talked into accompanying Zhu and Jessie to this shindig on Snob Hill if he hadn't overheard at the Reception the other night that all the nabobs of the city will attend. In particular, a certain Mr. Jeremiah Duff will make his annual appearance. Mr. Duff has a reputation along the Cocktail Route of being a man well versed in narcotics. Dr. Mortimer has promised Daniel a letter of introduction.

By God, he's exhausted. If only he could sleep. Hasn't slept more than a couple hours at a time in weeks. Everything fragmented. Days and nights splinter into shards of consciousness as scattered as his glass on the Persian carpet. Sometimes when he's locked in his suite—lamp burning low, shades and drapes drawn, a bottle of good brandy, his vial and his spoon, sniffing, sniffing, sniffing—he doesn't know whether it's day or night. Doesn't care.

Daniel pauses, pain chasing across the backs of his eyes. Room suddenly spinning, bits and pieces of it swelling into and receding from his view. Chuckles, though he thinks he may be sick. Now, why can't he do that with his kinesis machine?

The kinesis machine, that's what he calls the device he has rigged up to experiment with moving photographs. A design not unlike his toy Zoetrope. He has mounted translucent sequential images on a large wheel. Has situated an electric lightbulb in the center. When he spins the wheel, the pictures whirl past the eye, illuminated from behind. It works, after a fashion. Still, the viewer cannot *enter* into the illusion the way he'd like. Even a peepshow is more engrossing. The apparatus is distancing, the photographs too small. He considers enlarging the photographs to the size of paintings, constructing a giant wheel on which to mount them, perhaps forty feet in diameter. He'd need an auditorium to show the illusion. Frustrated; it's a paltry simulation of what he can envision. He still encounters problems with continuous motion, can't quite determine the right acceleration. If he slows the action, the images jerk about; if he speeds it up, the images blur.

Blur like Zhu. Blur like Woman. He adores her, he abhors her.

"Where are you when I need you?" he yells in the empty parlor. His voice echoes strangely. Almost as if the reverberation preceded his cry.

By God, he's going mad.

❜ ❜ ❜

Daniel steps out onto Dupont Street and surveys the traffic with a shrewd eye. None of Harvey's thugs lurk about, though the evil way some of the streetwalkers glance at him merits fingertips ready on his Remington derringer, a hand poised for the Congress knife. Is that Fanny Spiggott crossing at the corner? She's been following him, too. He'll kill her if he ever catches her in an alley. For a moment he's sure he spies poor old Schultz, but it's just another portly German gentleman. Poor old Schultz is cold in his grave, Daniel reminds himself.

He sets out at an energetic clip for Stockton Street. Chinatown; they say the plague has struck here again. Smuggled coolies his mistress weeps about probably bring it from China, which suffered a dreadful dose in '94. There's the dump, 567 Stockton Street, which Mr. Ekberg has wept real tears over. Old man's got himself a hidey-hole in back, who knows or cares how many Chinese are crammed into the little rooms upstairs. Daniel knocks on the door, impatient, tapping his toe. Mr. Ekberg answers. Old prospector he is, face as ruined as the termite-riddled boards of this tumbledown place. Daniel will have to chastise Father; extending yet another loan on yet another piss poor property. Ekberg forks over thirty-five dollars in gold. That settles his account for another month, forget the arrears. What happens when old Ekberg cashes it in? Daniel sidesteps. A dead rat in the gutter writhes with maggots. Who will buy the dump at a price to cover the loan balance? He sees the wisdom of floating old Ekberg for as long as possible. Recalls the plague is spread by rats. Daniel clears out.

Mr. Harvey and his poolroom are another story. Mr. Harvey has been as intractable as a Hun and twice as dangerous. Resolution fills Daniel as he walks down to the county courthouse on Mission Street, a fine granite building rendered in a classical architecture worthy of this metropolis. Feeling very righteous, sir, as the crusading knight must have felt. Power and the might of the law on his side. Clicks across the marble floor, finds a clerk who assists him in filling out the documents. Doesn't need his clever mistress after all, well, he'll be sure to tell her so. Mr. Daniel J. Watkins hereby forecloses the mortgage held by Mr. Jonathan D. Watkins of Saint Louis on said property, 412 Water Street, Sausalito, California, occupied by Mr. Nicholas S. Harvey. He, Daniel J. Watkins, will not be intimidated by a barkeep. He pays an extra fee to have the notice delivered by messenger. Could be a handsome profit in Water Street as long as poolrooms stay legal in Sausalito. There's justice. Perhaps some rich gambler from the green cloth circuit will take an interest.

Feeling *much* better, money jingling in his pocket. Jogs back across Market, sprints three blocks to Montgomery Street, up four flights to the top floor of the Monkey Block and Dr. Mortimer's clinic. No more huffing and puffing for Daniel J. Watkins, sir, though his breath whistles in his nostrils, his lungs are on fire, his heart pounds like a drum. Taps out a ciggie to refresh himself. Drags on it deeply, relishing the sharp stab in his chest. There's a proper draw for a gentleman.

Knocks on the physician's door. No answer. Checks his pocket watch. Ten minutes late for his appointment. Dr. Mortimer not only promised him a letter of introduction to Mr. Jeremiah Duff, but hinted that a judicious use of the physician's new telephone might be in order, too. Splendid move. Daniel eagerly looks forward to speaking on the telephone with Mr. Duff. Even letters of introduction can be ticklish, rife with hesitation and awkwardness.

Still no answer. Not at all like Dr. Mortimer, who usually sprints to the door before Daniel can lay his knuckles on the glass. Tries the doorknob. Not locked. The door fans open with an eerie creak.

"Dr. Mortimer?" Daniel calls. Stiff feeling of intruding. Wouldn't like another man to barge into his suite this way. "Dr. Mortimer?"

First thing that leaps into Daniel's eyes: the bright blood spilling from Mortimer's nose onto pale green paper. The physician at his walnut desk, slumped, face canted against the pale green paper of his writing pad, and the blood, by God. One arm hanging limp, the other flung across the desk as though attempting to seize something or ward something off.

Murder. Shock explodes up and down Daniel's spine. He throws his hands into the air as though confronted by the criminal. Doesn't touch anything, he knows enough to know that. Circles in back of the physician, around the desk, completely confounded by this heinous crime. But why? Someone asking for the cocaine therapy? Wanting the cocaine, *needing* the cocaine? Perhaps without enough money, like poor old Schultz?

Then again, nothing seems disturbed besides the physician and his desk. The charts, the shelves filled with those dreadful decanters of preserved body parts, the side table where the physician kept his supplies. The mirrored tray, dusted with white powder and dappled with four stray stains, reddish brown. All of it quite the same.

Daniel pulls out the drawer, catches his breath. The drawer is positively stuffed with vials of cocaine, together with a good quantity of gold and silver coins.

Murder or . . . ? *This is what an aneurysm looks like, idiot*, says one of his voices. Splendid, now his voices are giving him medical advice. Why does this particular voice sound just like his mistress? "You're not a doctor, Zhu," he says out loud to the voice. *No, I'm not*, the voice says, *it's common knowledge about this drug in my day, Daniel*. "Please," he says. Struggling to remember. Did they actually have this conversation one tempestuous night? Seems familiar. Or just his mad imagination?

He takes ten vials from the drawer and tucks them in his pocket. Does not approve of thievery, sir. Thievery is a sin. Property is more durable than life, therefore possesses a sacramental quality. Daniel is no thief. He would never, for example, relieve Jessie Malone of the mermaid painting, cash it in for seven thousand, and blow town. No sir, he would not. He dutifully deposits five dollars into the drawer. The good physician would have required fifteen, but now that he's dead, Daniel thinks five is fair.

Go straight to the police, that's what he should do. *But if there's no foul play, sir*, says another voice, persuasive, confiding, *if it's not really murder but just the fellow's bad luck . . .*

Surely Dr. Mortimer has family and friends who will miss him, seek him out? Find him, of course. Why should Daniel pick up the pieces? Indeed, he does not particularly want his presence here today known by the police. Not that he's done anything wrong, certainly not. But he's got enough problems of his own. Mortimer is of no further use to him, is he? Goes back to the drawer. *A few more vials won't hurt poor old Mortimer; where are you going to get more?*

Daniel creeps out, closes the door. Damn bad luck, without his letter of introduction, without his telephone call to Jeremiah Duff. With an excellent supply of the Incan gift, true. But still without the means to ease his soul.

❜ ❜ ❜

The cable car on California Street climbs straight up Nob Hill, aiming its prow to stars whirling in heaven above. Truly the stars dance in Californ'. Daniel has never seen anything like it before, not even after his third glass of absinthe at La Nouvelle-Athènes. After his third glass of absinthe there, the stars would droop and smear, staining the night sky over Paris with blots of dull orange, and his fancy would soon turn to the enticements of Rochelle. But in this night sky the stars are frantic, sparking, wheeling, and dancing across a dark infinity.

He snuffles gently, nursing the juices in his nose. The cocaine he appropriated from Dr. Mortimer's clinic has elevated him to new heights of health and well-being. By God, the stars are dancing!

Gripping the pole, he leans off the platform as far as he can lean as they jolt up the hill to the art association.

"Careful, Daniel," Zhu calls to him. Proprietary, like a wife or a mother.

"Am I the only one in costume, then?" Daniel demands, ignoring her and flipping up his eyepatch.

Snares a chuckle from everyone on the car. *Everyone* is in costume, of course. There are nymphs and Romans, Buffalo Bills and winged fairies aplenty. An astonishing Egyptian pharaoh with his skin stained blue, a green-stained queen on his arm. The royal couple is loaded with gold and gems that look real. Can't get that gleam off a facet made of paste. There are several Dresden shepherdesses and their burly squires clad in varying degrees of authenticity and taste. An excellent mermaid with long silver hair, her lower limbs crippled by her gorgeous satin tail. She is carried aloft in the arms of two strapping bouncers adventurously clad as fishermen. One of Jessie's rivals? The madam can't keep her eyes off the gleaming scales. Revelers all, bound for the Artists' Ball.

Daniel is displeased, however, with the ladies he's escorting. He has stooped to this ridiculous swashbuckler getup with a real sword, a scarlet sash, a swooping hat, and an eyepatch. Not particularly original. Several pirates loll about the cable car in preliminary stages of inebriation. Yet he has been willing to engage in the pretense. His ladies have not.

Jessie Malone is Jessie Malone, Queen of the Underworld. All that gorgeous flesh pressed into a dress of extraordinary shape and texture. Sequins, loops of satin and lace. Her diamonds, by God, he had no idea. Took one look at her jewels before she stepped out of 263 Dupont Street and promptly went back to find Schultz's abandoned Smith and Wesson, which Daniel had discovered going through the deceased fellow's things. Daniel packed that along with his derringer, the Congress knife, and the real sword from the tailor. Jessie as Jessie. Rocks the size of knuckles sparkling on her knuckles. What they call a dog collar, bands of captive stars circling her neck above a bosom worthy of the Queen of Babylon, never mind the Queen of the Underworld. Earrings to knock your eye out dangling amid her riot of golden curls. And bracelets? He remembers his mother had a bracelet, a plain silver band. That was how a lady wore a bracelet: one plain band on a wrist as thin as the bone beneath the skin. Jessie has stacked each of her ample arms with bracelets, more bracelets than Daniel has ever witnessed on one arm, let alone two. Jessie's disguise? The Mask of Tragedy and Comedy, one side black and grieving, one side white and rejoicing, set upon an ivory and ebony handle. She intermittently places the mask over her exquisitely painted face.

Jessie will be Jessie. But his mistress?

They argued before he allowed her to board the cable car.

Zhu wears her denim *sahm*, the felt fedora, tinted spectacles, and straw sandals. Her long black braid trails down her spine like a queue, a peasant's queue. What kind of costume is that?

"What in hell are you doing?" he demanded.

"I'm going as a tachyporter," she said. "A time traveler, to use Mr. Wells's terminology. A woman of the future. Actually, I dress pretty much like this in my day."

"You cannot go to the Artists' Ball like that."

"But I can."

"You look like a goddamn coolie."

"Then I'll be your coolie."

His little lunatic. She says she likes the idea of being invisible in a crowd. Peculiar notion; Mr. Wells might make some hay of it. Daniel, however, would have liked to titillate the Smart Set by squiring the notorious madam on one arm, his lovely Chinese mistress on the other. Jessie as Jessie, perhaps, but Zhu as a royal concubine clad in gold and jade satin. But Zhu got her way. *She usually does*, says one of his voices.

Daniel squeezes onto the seat beside her. Irritated at her slumming when he knows she is capable of better.

"I am unhappy with your crude charade, mistress."

"I am unhappy with your cocaine, Daniel." Peers up into his face. "I am unhappy with your drinking."

Claps his hand to his forehead. "For the thousandth time, I am cured of drink."

Irritation spirals quickly into anger. She is as plain as a pretzel but for one small detail. Daniel spots it at once. So does Jessie.

"Say there, missy," Jessie says, craning her neck.

Pinned to Zhu's collar is the most charming bauble Daniel has ever seen. Art Nouveau style, rendered with dazzling genius. A golden butterfly, diamonds and bits of multicolored glass. A nude at the center, a lovely slim thing poised like a dancer. Something mesmerizing about her languid face. Daniel's hand collides with Jessie's grasping fingers.

Zhu shields her collar from them both.

"Let me see. What is that?" Jessie says, prying one of Zhu's hands away.

"It's called an aurelia," Zhu says.

Jessie stares. "Where'd you get that?"

"Like it?" Zhu coy. Not an attractive pose for her.

"It's blowed in the glass," Jessie says.

"Corking," Daniel says.

"Hardly goes with your little costume, though, missy," Jessie says, wheedling. "Let me wear it. Look, I've got a spot right here on my dress."

"No," Zhu says.

Jessie undeterred, as usual. Points out a prominence on her neckline. "I'll wear it just for you."

"No."

"You look like hell, Zhu," Jessie says, "if you want to know the truth."

"No, I can't let it out of my sight."

"You can look at me all night," Jessie offers.

"Why do you like the aurelia so much?" Zhu says. "The diamonds aren't much. Most of it is just glass."

"Why?" Jessie says. "You are forever asking why, missy. Why, why, why?"

"Why?" Zhu says.

"Because it's a nude, and I gotta have it."

"How about you, Daniel?" Zhu says. "You like it, too?"

"I do," he says and means it. "It's rather decadent."

"Decadent how?" Zhu says, turning to him urgently.

"Well, there she is"—he touches a fingertip to the tiny woman—"a human being borne away by an insect. The lowest creature on earth, though of course a butterfly is beautiful."

"Go on," Zhu says.

"This aurelia, as you call it," Daniel says, "is womankind herself being swept away by the brute force of destiny."

For a moment the cable car is silent but for the deep, metallic humming of the cables churning beneath them.

"That's all," Daniel says. Needs another spoonful of Mortimer's private mix.

"Please," Zhu says, "what else do you see?" Adds, "You've got a good eye."

"Well, all right," Daniel says. "She looks like *you*."

"She does not!" Zhu fairly tears the brooch off her collar. The pharaoh turns curiously. "She's white, Caucasian."

"No, look." Daniel brings Jessie in to bait his mistress, who really should have dressed better. "Look at the slant of her eyes. Her slender figure."

"Where did you get it?" Jessie asks again.

"I think a man sent it to me," Zhu replies. Dreamy; almost stunned. "That means it must be an enigma."

"An enigma?" Jessie says.

"A time enigma," Zhu says.

"A man?" Daniel says, blood flaring. She belongs to *him*. "By God, what man?"

"The red-haired man," she says to Jessie, who nods. Jessie has heard about this man, apparently. "From six hundred years in the future."

❙ ❙ ❙

The cable car grinds to the crest of California Street, finding level ground at the peak of Nob Hill. Daniel helps Jessie down. Zhu leaps off on her own. Daniel stands breathlessly and looks around. These astonishing mansions of the fabled rich—mining, railroads, banking, sugar, so much money it makes Daniel's teeth ache—are really only town houses. Half the time the houses are empty. The builders or builders' heirs are off to New York, Europe, or their country villas down the peninsula with acres of lawns for privacy. Not much privacy on top of Snob Hill. The mansions rub elbows with each other.

Daniel crosses the street to the Hopkins mansion. They say old man Hopkins never lived here at all, though he poured a fortune into the monstrous construction. Part cathedral, part Mansard, part Gothic, a dark moodiness like a German castle, a hint of Queen Anne with all the earnest excess and none of the frivolity. The place is atrocious, in Daniel's opinion. After the old man died, the widow moved East and took up with her interior decorator. Daniel's heard the rumors along the Cocktail Route. Young spunk. Knew which side his bread was buttered on. Widow died a couple of years ago. The decorator got everything. Good lad, though. Had another bigger, gaudier house built over in Massachusetts. No need to hang onto this one, apparently. Donated the whole caboodle to the San Francisco Art Association, which moved in like a flash.

Hence, the Mardi Gras, quite a show-off for the bohemian crowd. There's Mr. Ned Greenway, he of the twenty bottles of champagne a day, dressed like Puck, a wreath of laurel leaves crowning his sweaty pate, a tremendous white toga billowing about his girth. As though one should aspire to twenty bottles of champagne a day, Daniel sniffs. *Morality of the newly cured*, gloats one of his voices in a haughty tone not unlike Father's. Greenway a butterball. Good snort of the Incan gift might do the tastemaker a world of good.

They sweep into the foyer beneath candelabra all ablaze. Forests of asparagus fern sprout in every corner, smilax drapes the walls. Fresh flowers everywhere, from banks of orchids surrounding the polished dance floor to rose petals floating in champagne cocktails. The baroque ballroom is sheer cacophony. The orchestra strikes up a mazurka. Filters are rotated over the gaslights, sending a kaleidoscope of colors over the dancers. Jewels wink in abundance, masks bob with ostrich feathers, pale curves of flesh abandon modesty. Sideboards groan with punch bowls and platters of food rivaling the offerings along the Cocktail Route. Daniel smells terrapin in cream. Huge parlors converted into galleries are hung with a profusion of oil paintings, landscapes, portraits, still lifes, some sculpture. All rather dull to Daniel's eye but with the exciting scent of fresh oil paint, chalk, and newly cut stone. Revelers throng around the exhibitions and chatter like panicked monkeys.

A nabob dressed as Louis XIV strolls in, leading a donkey dyed green upon whose back the nabob's mistress perches costumed, so to speak, as Lady Godiva. Naked as a jaybird, for all Daniel can see, but for a pair of lady's riding boots fitted with spurs. The mistress's own ample golden locks are generously supplemented with fake curls. She does not look happy with her costume, which she desperately clutches to herself. Her wrists are bound and lashed to the donkey's cinch. Face livid with drink, the nabob announces, "She who spurs Green Jealousy, gentlemen. Take a good look."

Ladies of the Smart Set avert their eyes. "Really, Duncan," exclaims a leading social maven, "we'll not be a party to this disgraceful spectacle." She gathers up her chums and steers everyone away.

"Ah, but that's why they come to the Mardis Gras," Daniel says, laughing. "For disgraceful spectacles."

"My diamonds is bigger," Jessie murmurs, watching the maven sail off with her ladies.

Jessie turns heads, as much for her bejeweled bosom as her reputation. Zhu hovers behind like a shadow, her face drawn and dark. Suddenly Daniel is frazzled, claustrophobic. Panic wells in his throat like too much rotgut.

"Jessie." He takes her aside. Zhu huddles with them. "I was supposed to get a letter of introduction to a gentleman who's attending the ball tonight."

"Yeah?" Jessie says, grinning with delight as she recognizes her best clients, waving excitedly to other wealthy madams who promenade about the ballroom.

"He's a gentleman I need to meet," Daniel says urgently. Just like Mama, never paying attention.

"Why do you need to meet him?" Zhu asks.

"His name is Jeremiah Duff," Daniel says, ignoring his mistress.

"Jeremiah Duff?" Jessie says. "Jar me, you want to speak with Jeremiah Duff?"

"I do."

"Better gather your wits about you, Mr. Watkins. That dope fiend is no gentleman."

"He is prominent in society," Daniel says, "isn't he?"

"Prominent, hell!" Jessie says. "Jeremiah Duff made a killing in the silver mines. Never touched a shovel or a pick in his life. Trucked booze up into them hills, that's what Mr. Duff did. Married himself Elaine Hennessey, heiress to the dry goods fortune. A proper lady if I ever saw one, with her white cotton gloves and black cotton stockings. If she was more of a slut and less of a shrew, her husband wouldn't come to *me*."

"Dope fiend?" Zhu says.

Daniel waves her away. To Jessie, "My physician, Dr. Mortimer, was supposed to introduce me. Said Duff knows about the dipsomania cure."

"Daniel, what are you talking about?" Zhu demands.

"Don't you speak that way to me in public," Daniel says. "You're my coolie, remember?"

Fortunately, so many other revelers are yelling and laughing and drinking that no one pays them any attention. The orchestra strikes up a rousing waltz. The pharaoh and his queen wheel onto the dance floor.

"Then do you know Mr. Duff, Jessie?" Daniel says. "Do you know how I could meet him?"

"Do I know him?" Jessie says. "Darlin', Jeremiah Duff visits the Parisian Mansion every Thursday evening at seven. Used to ask for Li'l Lucy. Left that girl black and blue. Maybe left her with the pox, too. Well, she forgot to douche. He likes my new redhead well enough. At least she listens to me about douching."

Hope soars in Daniel's heart, which is beating a trifle too rapidly. "Could you introduce me?"

"Why not?" Jessie says. "Then you owe me a favor, Mr. Watkins."

"Whatever is fair," he says.

"What do you want from this man, Daniel?" Zhu says.

He is in no mood for her nagging. "Mistress, I shall truss *you* up and parade you naked if you don't leave me alone."

That shuts Zhu up. Daniel follows Jessie through the crowd. She moves fast for a woman of her size; sprightly despite the wasp waist imposed by her corset. Sashays straight up to a tall, gaunt man in an immaculate black tuxedo, a simple black satin mask tied over his eyes. Daniel feels like a fool. Should have had the sense to do the same as Duff. By God, a silly pirate. Remember next time. *If there is a next time*, sneers a voice in his head. "Stop it," he mutters to himself. "Pull yourself together, man." Before he knows it, he is being presented to Mr. Duff. Jessie knows how to be gracious when she wants to be.

Duff looks him up and down. Good thing Daniel lost the paunch. Duff has got the stringent look of someone who disapproves of the Greenway type. Gentlemanly salutations. They retire to a secluded corner buffered by three marble monoliths. An air of conspiracy about Mr. Duff. Splendid.

Zhu sidles up next to them. No graceful way to get rid of her. "My manservant," Daniel says. Hates explaining to Duff. "At my beck and call."

"Useful," says Duff. Whips off the mask. Looks Zhu up and down, the same blunt appraisal. Doesn't mind her looks, either. "A Chink could be useful. Pick up goods for you in Tangrenbu. I may have use for him, too." Receding hairline over a high forehead, skin like wax, pale brutal eyes. The kind of mouth that never smiles, the mustache drooping regretfully down the long, stern face. "Been taking Mortimer's cure, have you, sir?"

"Faithfully," Daniel says. "Puts me off the drink well enough, but I'm at wit's end about the nerves. Plus, the ticker goes too fast at times. Gives me a bit of a pain through the chest."

"Don't sleep much, either, eh?" Duff says. Scrutinizing him. Brutal eyes, yes, but thorough. Daniel likes the stringency, the conspiratorial huddle. Carries an aura of the chosen, of the cognoscente. Duff *knows*. "What did you say your age was, sir?"

"I'm nearly twenty-two," Daniel says. Catches a glass of champagne and a canapé from a tray sailing by on the shoulder of a harried waiter.

"Twenty-two," Duff says. "When I was twenty-two, sir, I trucked goods into the mountains. Even higher than the Gold Country, that's where the Comstock Lode was. Even higher, even harder, even crueler than the hills the forty-niners endured. I wore a burlap shirt, the denim of a coolie, padded cotton crawling with lice." Baleful glance at Daniel's satin eyepatch, scarlet vest, white silk sleeves, glossy gabardine jodhpurs, spit-and-polished black boots.

A bourgeois pirate. Daniel curses himself. What a dunce.

"We climbed rocks," Dunn says. "We slept on rocks. We ate stone soup when winter came to the mountains." Baleful glance at the champagne and canapé in Daniel's hands. Daniel sets his glass on a side table, gulps the canapé. "We ate squirrels when we could catch them. Have you ever tasted raw squirrel? Raw squirrel's brains, raw squirrel's intestines?"

"No, I have not," Daniel says, swallowing hard.

"You young men with your petty troubles, your women, your drink." Duff surveys the whirling party. "One day I fell, sir. Just a slip on some ice. I'd slipped many times before. But *this* slip did me in. I fell down that cliff like a son of a bitch. Shattered my goddamn leg forever."

Duff raises his right leg, showing Daniel his boot with the heel built up three inches high and a brace that disappears into the leg of his trousers. "That's when I started on the medicine, sir. Had to. Pain all the time."

Daniel murmurs, "I'm sorry."

"I took whiskey to the miners," Duff says, "God knows they needed it. I make no apology. My wife and her people"—spits this out—"enjoy chastising me for the source of my wealth. Well, sir, there are ways and ways."

"Real estate is hardly better," Daniel says.

"I took them whiskey," Duff says, ignoring him. "I took them whiskey, but I never touched a drop. No, sir, those were our goods. When we needed the fire of alcohol to warm us, we drank puma piss. Not a drink a fine young gentleman like yourself would know about."

"Puma piss," Daniel says. "Terrific rotgut. Homebrew, tobacco juice, and a dose of strychnine."

Duff finally cracks a smile. "Let us find the gentlemen's facilities, Mr. Watkins."

Duff leads the way, Daniel follows, Zhu trails. Daniel turns, "You *can't* come with us."

"I'm your manservant, sir," she says. Lowers the voice. By God, he could strangle her.

Duff turns. "Your manservant may attend us. He should

learn how this is done, Mr. Watkins. Like I said, he may be useful to you."

They find the gentlemen's urinal on the far side of the ballroom. Not too many fellows in here yet. The serious drinking has only just begun. They tour the gilt and scarlet antechamber set with spotless mirrors, marble tables and upholstered chairs, porcelain sinks and pitchers of water, trays with brushes and combs designed for a gentleman's special needs, freshly laundered towels, smelling salts, pots of mustache wax and hair tonics, colognes in cut crystal bottles.

Negro attendants descend like a flock of crows; Duff dismisses them. Finds a table and a mirror on the far side of the chamber. "Now look here." He takes a leather case from an inside pocket, unsnaps the top. Inside nestle several vials of powders, a steel spoon, a thick white rubber thong rather like an oversized rubber band, and a hypodermic needle.

Zhu expels a soft breath. Daniel knows that breath. The sound of her perpetual exasperation.

"Your manservant is impressed, eh?" Duff says, casting a keen look at his mistress, who, despite her attempt at this masquerade, cannot completely conceal her feminine charms.

But if Duff is nonplussed or distressed, he gives no indication but promptly sets about tapping a quantity of powder into the spoon. Carefully pours drops of water from the pitcher. Stirs the concoction with a silver toothpick over the hot tongue of a candle. Like an alchemist he sits, intently stirring. Says at last, "Take off your coat, Mr. Watkins, and roll up your sleeve. Lay down your arm; like this." Demonstrates. Rolls the thong up Daniel's arm. "You must cook it like a fine sauce. Like a fine sauce, it requires the right ingredients and attentive care."

Daniel sits and watches, enthralled. "This will help me sleep without drink?"

"Has drink helped you sleep?"

"Hardly." Asks again, hope soaring, "This will calm my nerves from the dipsomania cure? I will"—so tired, so overwrought, what he would give for relief!—"I will rest?"

"Rest," Duff says, and, tapping the inner aspect of Daniel's elbow, promptly jabs the needle right into his vein.

Pain! But not so much; and then—

—torn from his body, this pale wriggling worm, flung like a stone into the sea, waves of pressure, of sheer pleasure, pressing his very soul flat. Flat as death, dying without dying. A *rush*—by God!—the most incredible . . . Pleasure, pressure, pain so vast he is transformed into . . . sensation itself, mindless, nerveless, pleasure like the moment of sexual release but wrought a hundredfold, a thousandfold, tongues of pleasure caressing all over his body, and his brain, his poor sleepless harried haggard brain—

Rest, my son, says a voice in his head, a chorus of voices, discordant and beautiful, the way the sea smashing rocks is beautiful.

Like a dream, a distant dream, hazy and meaningless, the voice of his mistress, his stupid mistress with her nonsensical tales, is asking, "What did you give him?"

God's angel of light himself, Daniel's mentor, his rescuer, deliverer, savior, messiah. "You speakee English, boy?" Duff says.

"What did you give him, Mr. Duff?"

"I hope you followed how to do it. You can be of use to him. Yes, you can be very useful."

"What is it?"

"One of the most beneficent medicines God has granted us poor mortals."

"*What is it?*"

"Calm down, boy," Duff says, "or whatever you are. Keep your voice down." Packs up his leather bag, drifts back to the Artists' Ball. "It's only morphine."

❜ ❜ ❜

Daniel is sick, then, of course. Somehow that seems inevitable. The price of admission. Daniel retches, clutching his gut, over and over till there's nothing inside, nothing but his gut. Feels like the gut itself will come up, too.

Face filmed with tears and sweat and bile. By God, he

looks like hell in the mirror confronting him. "Poor mistress," he says as she leans over him with the basin, a washcloth, a pitcher of water, ice. Suddenly the sound of her breath, quick and close, thunders in his ears. She does not weep, but he can see the sorrow molding her face like the carved grief of an icon. "What I make you endure."

"There's nothing I can do, Daniel," Zhu says over and over. Catechism of despair.

Bloody sleeve, bloody face—nose going out on him again. "Do? Silly goose. What is it that you're supposed to do? You're not responsible for me, you know."

"Yes," she says.

"You're not my *mother*," he clarifies. And as soon as he says the word—mother—a cold draft blows over him like an exhalation of the dead.

Shivering, teeth chattering. Zhu summons an attendant. Handsome black fellow, all high cheeks, dark glancing eyes.

"She had a lover," he says.

"Who?" Zhu says. The attendant wraps a blanket over his shoulders. Someone brings tea. He can smell the bitter steam, waves it away.

"I know that now, though I didn't understand at the time. I was nine; ten, maybe. The lady had a lover."

Incipient summer, heat fecund and poisonous, winding like a serpent through the blackness of his heart. River black beneath the bending hickory, the cypress sighing, and the beautiful girl with deep sea eyes who married a cold scowling man found herself in love with a man who conducted a gambling business up and down the river. A quadroon. Daniel saw him once or twice. One of those quick-eyed men with charm, even Daniel could see the charm. *Mama crying, always crying, slap of flesh on flesh*. But she couldn't—wouldn't—give up her quadroon, her quick-eyed man with his high cheeks and crinkled hair, his clothes cut the way clothes should fit a masculine body, his laugh like the crack of a branch breaking. Like a woman's heart breaking.

Finally her quadroon left her. Plenty of iron tonic after that. Daniel watched his slender mother grow fat and luminous as the moon waxing full.

"I don't know when Father knew she was carrying the quadroon's child," Daniel says. Suddenly feels better. The antechamber hums with new activity. The pharaoh stumbles into the urinals. Louis XIV reels in, too. All manner of buffoons, pirates, kings, Pucks, an especially clever Pan clad in shearling chaps and goat's feet. "God knows she tried to hide it. But there was no hiding by the time she was well along."

"What did he do, your father?" Zhu tenderly wipes his face with the washcloth.

He slaps her hand away. "He beat her. What else could he do? He had position. He had a business, political pull, money, property. He had pride. He had his own child, a son. *Me.* When I think of it now, what else could he do?"

He beat her, kicked her, kicked her again when she was down, kicked her in the gut, over and over. *Slap of flesh on flesh.* Daniel crouching in the corner of Mama's dressing room, watching. Daniel at Mama's bedside when she lay tossing, blood in the bedpan. *I've been sick ever since you, Danny.*

"She lost the quadroon's baby."

Zhu pale, like pale gold marble, her strange green eyes dark with horror behind her tinted spectacles.

"Mama lost the baby," he says. "Lost her capacity ever to conceive again. Father could have killed her that night. Perhaps he should have. Instead, he only damaged her. Damaged her for the rest of her life. It must have been on that night when Dr. Dubose came and first administered morphine to my mother."

Zhu silent, staring.

"She was in a lot of pain."

Zhu still silent.

"And here I am. My mother's son. Sins of the mother, eh? Well, *say* something, mistress."

He cannot *stand* the pressure of Zhu's eyes, her silent rebuke. His temper flares. He wants to slap her, to kick the basin over, when Jeremiah Duff comes back. Dour Duff is jovial. Enjoys introducing a young gentleman to his medicine.

"Now, Mr. Watkins," Duff says, sitting down before him and taking his arm. "Let's try another shot at it, shall we?"

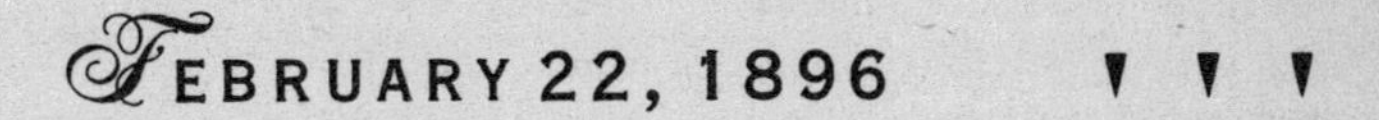

FEBRUARY 22, 1896

Chinese New Year

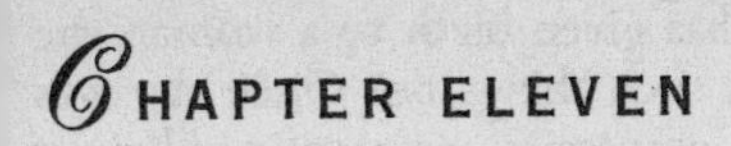

CHAPTER ELEVEN

Kelly's Shanghai Special

Clash of cymbals, brass on brass, and the high thin wail of a moon fiddle sounding like some tortured creature. *Bang, bang, bang!* Zhu runs to her bedroom window. Quite a hustle-bustle down on Dupont Street. New Year's Eve—Chinese New Year's Eve. Those are fireworks, of course. "Combustible explosives, not projectiles aimed at you," isn't that what Muse said? Was it only nine months ago that she stepped across the bridge over the brook in the Japanese Tea Garden? Only nine months since she last heard fireworks? What a thin, nervous woman she had been, cursing her skirts, dropping to her knees, a comrade dodging imagined gunfire.

Only nine months, and it is not her imagination: she is *not* pregnant. Muse has run a diagnostic and confirmed this. She has only grown stout from the bounty of Jessie Malone's table. Has dyspepsia because butter disagrees with her. Is lethargic because she has started to drink and champagne makes her sleepy. Has no menses because the contraceptive patch, the bright red square like a wound hidden behind her knee, next to the place where the black patch used to be, halts her cycle completely. That's all.

Yet although she is not pregnant, Zhu feels in a peculiar but very real way that she has given birth to a woman she hardly knows: herself. Can such things be? Once she was Zhu Wong, a Daughter of Compassion, an ascetic oblivious to her smallest comfort, a comrade dedicated to the Cause. Now she is Zhu Wong, bookkeeper for a madam, a servant to her own appetites, the mistress of a white man. Her very soul transfigured by this time, by the golden nineties, the way rich food and the corset have transfigured her body.

Stink of gunpowder from the fireworks. Like a pressed corsage, a sentimental memento, the acrid smell evokes sudden memories.

Gunpowder, smoke, the clamor of a street skirmish—there were skirmishes nearly every night in Changchi during the last days of the campaign. Memories? But how can she remember the future? Struggles to sort this out in her troubled mind: it is her *personal* past, though the events she remembers took place six centuries in the future.

You mean I have lived six centuries in the past? Then why don't I remember it?

A premonition is just a memory. A memory of what? *Of the future,* Chiron said.

So familiar this smoke, this clamor of revelers celebrating the Chinese New Year. The alleys of Tangrenbu are fragrant with new scents: blooming lilies, quince, almond and cherry branches heavy with aromatic spring flowers. The shops have set up stalls displaying a surprising bounty: platters of oranges and kumquats, bags of salted plums, trays of bean paste pastries, sugared coconut slices, litchi nuts, portly figs, candied strips of winter melon. Strings of gaudy paper flowers festoon the balconies and balustrades.

Yet Zhu can sense a dark sorrow beneath the festive air. The bachelors of Tangrenbu long for their homeland on this day. Long for families who are forbidden to come to Gold Mountain.

Space and time have plunged forward and crossed over the imaginary boundary humanity erects. According to the modern Western calendar, a new year: it is 1896. With the first new moon of the ancient lunar year, all San Francisco joins Tangrenbu in observing Tong Yan Sun Neen, the Chinese New Year. Under the lunar calendar, space and time don't just plunge forward, hurling over a demarcation. All spacetime changes, the energy transmutes. When Zhu first t-ported, it was 1895: Year of the Ram, in which ego, will, and domination prevail. Now the cycle has turned to the Year of the Monkey. The Year of the Trickster, he whose wily intelligence is not to be trusted.

Zhu does not trust the Trickster. Deep foreboding threads her waking moments, her dreams.

A premonition is just a memory.

Of the future? No! It's a lie. She does not remember the future. How can she? She has no special power. She is just an anonymous woman. She only remembers the past, like everyone.

She steps away from the window. Oscillation of alphanumerics in her peripheral vision.

"You're going home," Muse says, "to 2496. Tonight, at midnight."

"It's done, then?"

"It's done."

Muse clicks a file.

Muse:\Archive\Zhu.doc

Thirty-five thousand five hundred and fifty-three bytes.

"Go to the intersection of California and Mason streets," Muse says. "They've installed a tachyonic shuttle under the Grande Dome. The site has changed somewhat in physical characteristics, but the intersection is still the same. Much the same in character, despite the other changes." Muse amused. "You'll be all right."

"The Grande Dome?" Zhu says.

"You'll see," Muse says. "The private ecostructure over Nobhill Park. Quite mega. Four luxury hotels, the park, of course. Marvelous ecosystem—air, water, ground transportation, the works. Always was a fancy spot."

"Lovely," Zhu says. "Are the LISA techs arranging a room for me for the night?"

After all she's witnessed in San Francisco in the golden nineties, Zhu has seen nothing of San Francisco in the

PermaPlast nineties except the EM-Trans station and the institute's hydroplex bobbing in the bay. Feeling deprived. Feeling entitled.

"I doubt it," Muse says. "You're an accused felon. They'll debrief you at the institute. Then back to jail for you, Z. Wong. You'll be charged and stand trial within the week."

"Oh." Jolt of reality. Someone's reality, anyway. Cannot possibly be hers. An accused felon? Incredulity makes her heart flutter. Anxious, always this anxiety over the past nine months. Yet slowly, surely, anger touches her. Touches, catches. "You mean all this has been for nothing? I've earned no clemency? No credit?"

"Credit for what?" Muse says.

"For the Golden Nineties Project! That was part of the deal! I thought Chiron was arranging for a new lawyer, leniency, reduced charges."

"The Luxon Institute for Superluminal Applications made no promises," Muse says.

"Chiron did!"

"You must be mistaken."

"I'm not mistaken. Why would I t-port in the first place?"

"Because you were required to."

Anger catches, grips. "No, I was never *required* to. I volunteered. And I demand my rights after all I've done."

"And what have you done," Muse says, "for the Golden Nineties Project?"

"Well!" Anger tightens, but it's a delicate point. What *has* Zhu done? Bungle the project beyond repair? "I agreed to participate. I've fulfilled the object of the project as best I could. I've met people."

"You've associated yourself with a notorious madam," Muse says.

"She indentured me," Zhu says. "You advised me to cooperate with Jessie Malone."

"You've indulged yourself in a sadomasochistic relationship with a questionable young man who has turned out to be a drug addict," Muse says.

"Indulge! He brutalizes me, forces me . . ."

"You lusted for him."

"He wanted me," Zhu says. Reminds Muse, "He assaulted me. You could call it rape."

"I warned you he was stalking you."

"You did not." She paces back and forth. Wood planks squeak. The new boarder in the suite below bangs on his ceiling with a broom handle. "You never did, Muse."

"I most certainly did," Muse says.

"I don't remember."

Silent Muse. Subversive Muse. Zhu will file a full report.

Zhu bites her lip. "I've survived. I found the girl." Apparently Muse requires reminding. "I found the girl at the designated rendezvous. I stole her from the brothel, took her to the home."

"She's not at the home anymore," Muse reminds *her.*

"Yes, and she doesn't have the aurelia. She never had the aurelia, not that I can see. The Archivists were wrong about the aurelia. *You're* wrong."

Muse silent.

"I have the aurelia. *I* do. It's no accident that I found it in a joss house dedicated to Kuan Yin, is it? *He* knows I'm a devotee of Kuan Yin. That eventually I'd find that joss house. The aurelia. *He* sent the aurelia to me, didn't he?"

"Who?" Muse says.

"Chiron Cat's Eye in Draco," she says. Anger wraps around her in earnest now. "You know very well who I mean, Muse."

Muse silent.

"The aurelia is a time enigma, isn't it?" Zhu says. "The anonymous Chinese woman gives it to Chiron in 1967. He takes it with him to 2467. Then he sends it to me from 2495 to 1895 so I can give it to Wing Sing. Isn't that right?"

Muse silent.

"And Wing Sing will give it to her daughter. She *will* have a green-eyed daughter, won't she? The Archives support the existence of the baby, isn't that right? The child of Rusty, who is long gone, sailing to India. Doesn't matter if she's a child out of wedlock, the child of a prostitute, a child whose father will never know her. One way or another—the details don't matter—the daughter will possess the aurelia in 1967. She'll be seventy-one years old, and she'll give the aurelia to Chiron, who will take the aurelia to 2467. And then, in 2495, he will send the aurelia to me, to the joss house dedicated to Kuan Yin. But, Muse." Zhu hesitates, striving to find the right question. "Where does the aurelia come from? Where does it begin?"

"The aurelia is a fine hand-made brooch rendered in the Art Nouveau style of this period. The diamonds amount to two carats . . ." Muse says like an auctioneer placing the object on the block.

"*Damn* it, Muse!" Zhu tears at her neck where the hardware angles up into her skull. Finds the aurelia on her dressing table, carelessly tosses the precious object back and forth in her hands. "What is the purpose of the Golden Nineties Project? Can you tell me, Muse? Why spend all that money? Why assemble another tachyonic shuttle when the t-port program has been shut down for decades? Why undertake another project when the danger of spacetime pollution is so great? When there is so much potential for error, for a thousand violations of the Tenets of the Grandfather Principle? Why trap me into t-porting six centuries into the past with promises of leniency the LISA techs apparently have no intention of honoring when I return. *Why?*"

"The aurelia is the symbol of . . ." Muse starts, but Zhu interrupts.

"I'll tell you why." Her anger tightens into fury, fury like a vise on her heart. "I'm a courier for a goddamn enigma. That's all. Oh, how Chiron agonizes over his own tachyportation to 1967, to the Summer of Love. Forbidden food, forbidden love. But he made a mistake, didn't he? What happened, did he forget that he had tucked the aurelia into the pocket of his jacket? He wasn't supposed to bring the aurelia back to his day, was he? Because he created a Closed Time Loop. He *created* a new CTL and tossed in the aurelia."

"The aurelia symbolizes . . ." Muse starts again, then falls silent.

"Yes, and a CTL is an artifact of tachyportation, isn't that what Chiron was trying to tell me?" Holds this thought clear and steady: *the file, Muse:\Archive\Zhu.doc. The holoid is different. It's always different.* "A CTL always exists in the One Day of spacetime," Zhu says, "without beginning, without end. But it's artificial, a human construct. CTLs don't exist in nature, in the cosmos. Tachyportation isn't natural. What would happen, Muse, if a CTL, once *ascertained,* started to decompose, to unravel?"

Muse silent.

"A CTL is unstable, isn't it?"

Zhu tosses the aurelia onto her dressing table more vigorously than necessary. Delicate gold lands with a *thump,* but nothing breaks or loosens. Stronger than she appears, the tiny crucified woman of gold. Tonight's the night, then. It's over.

Zhu goes to her wardrobe, finds her pearl gray silk dress. She was going to give the dress to Wing Sing, as Jessie said, but the girl had already gone. Now the dress is much too tight for Zhu. How did she ever fit in it?

"Yes, I think I understand at last, Muse," Zhu says, shucking off the dress and relacing her corset more tightly. "The CTL causes instability up and down the timeline. That's why everything has been so mutable since I t-ported to this spacetime. Why things keep changing."

"What do you mean, 'mutable,' Z. Wong?" Muse solicitous. "What keeps changing?"

"The cigar wagon. Eleanor Olney's pince-nez. My tanned skin. Wing Sing's feet. Shadows, feelings, *me.* Your goddamn file, *Zhu.doc*!"

"You really are overwrought, Z. Wong."

"Oh, Muse," Zhu says. "How can you keep up this charade? You, yourself. Are you defective, are you damaged? I've even wondered whether someone programmed you to sabotage me, though I don't know why or who would want to. Sometimes I don't know why I'm here myself."

"Are you dipping into Daniel's cocaine, Z. Wong?" Muse says.

"Certainly not!" Ah, but she recalls the exhilaration of the black patch when the time-releasers fed stimulants into her veins. She has been tempted. Will never confess that to Muse, but she *has* been tempted by Daniel's spoon.

"You sound like you're taking cocaine." Muse accusatory. Good old Muse. Somehow that's better.

"Why do I sound like I'm taking cocaine?"

"You sound paranoid," Muse says. "Deluded. Crazy."

"You, too, Muse?" Zhu laughs coldly. "That's Daniel's line: Zhu the lunatic. Daniel; oh, Daniel." Sharp contraction of her soul whenever she contemplates Daniel. "He's part of the disintegrating CTL, too. One minute he's courteous, charming, tender, intelligent. The next, he's a monster. He loves me; he reviles me."

"Mr. Daniel J. Watkins is a shining example of the misogynist and racist views that overtly and covertly characterize the male intellectual of this period," Muse says. Harsh Muse. Even better. "He would call you a madwoman if you weren't a tachyporter."

"Views of this period," Zhu says, mulling over the enigma of Daniel. "It's as though the views of this period are a part of the CTL, too. Women are either angels or whores, neither and both. Women are powerful, all-consuming, and dangerous; and women are weak, objects to be consumed, and beneath contempt."

Muse impatient. "You had no business revealing your identity, Z. Wong. Your instructions were explicit. Don't blame me if these people think you're mad."

"Ah, but the truth is it doesn't matter if I've violated Tenet Five," Zhu says. "These people either believe me or they don't, and neither perception amounts to anything. Does it, Muse? Because of the resiliency principle. The LISA techs can create a new reality, if they want to."

"You are charged with observing the tenets," Muse says. "It is essential that you observe . . ." Falls silent.

"I thought my disorientation was tachyonic lag. But it is no such thing, Muse. The CTL within which the aurelia spins is disintegrating, disrupting the timeline. That's the secret the LISA techs have kept from me all this time. Isn't it?"

Breath stifled, nearly faint for a moment. Her gut throbs

beneath the relaced corset. She slips the pearl gray dress back on. The dress fits perfectly.

"And what will happen if the CTL falls apart?" Zhu says. Pulsing black dot in her peripheral vision; Muse discomforted. Good. "What will happen if the anonymous Chinese woman never gives the aurelia to Chiron in 1967? Will the impact pollute all of spacetime the way the Save Betty Project did? Will the disruption create a massive dim spot in the Archives? Will Chiron's Summer of Love Project be jeopardized? Will another alternate reality be unleashed, Muse? If I do not deliver the aurelia to Wing Sing, will I be the one who sets loose demons again?"

Alphanumerics race across her peripheral vision. "If that's what you believe, Z. Wong, then you should be honored to contribute your efforts to the preservation . . ."

"Preservation of *your* reality? Your cosmicist reality? A reality in which my skipparents abandon me? In which I eat millet gruel and sleep on a cot? In which I'm beaten and abused? And your people won't even put me up in a nice hotel room when I t-port back from six centuries in the past?"

Muse silent.

"No, Muse," Zhu says, slowly fastening each tiny mother-of-pearl button up the side of her dress. "I never gave a damn about tachyportation. I never knew about the resiliency principle. I am a Daughter of Compassion. I am dedicated to the Cause, *our* Cause in mother China. The cosmicists are elitists, and the elite still feel they can use the people."

"They asked you to go."

"Then you admit they asked me."

Muse undeterred. "You accepted."

"Then why do I feel used?" Zhu says. "Yes, the LISA techs used me to tidy up Chi's mistake. They don't give a damn about me or Wing Sing or Wing Sing's daughter. They never did. I'm an accused felon, she's a slave. And the daughter? Another kid without luck or a family. We're all just anonymous Chinese women, expendable . . ."

"You are *not* expendable, Z. Wong." Muse abrupt. "I have warned you of the CTL peril on several occasions. I have attempted to guide you according to the object of your project."

"We're expendable once we play out our parts." Zhu knows this. An abyss opens in her heart, and she *knows* this.

Muse silent.

She could weep with despair, but no tears come. The intersection of California and Mason streets? Very well. She cannot care about the project anymore. She's not some caretaker of Wing Sing, how could she be? The girl left Jessie's cribs of her own free will, just like she left the Presbyterian home. Zhu first heard about her departure from the new redhead at the Parisian Mansion, saw the notation in Jessie's ledger, and hurried down to Morton Alley with the pearl gray dress slung over her arm. Someone—Zhu didn't know who—must have told Wing Sing that the rosewood box and her dowry were gone for good. Or perhaps Bertha the door maid found out the girl was pregnant and evicted her. Perhaps her green-eyed sailor hung around her too often before he left for his next port of call.

When Zhu asked, Jessie protested. The madam didn't dismiss her girls for getting pregnant or for having boyfriends, not at the cribs. She merely added pregnancy leave to the term of their contracts. "Anyhow, the chit ran off with a hundred bucks worth of lingerie *I* paid for," Jessie complained.

Then Zhu saw Wing Sing herself, a retreating figure on Sutter Street, in the winter darkness, as Zhu was taking a cab back to the boardinghouse. A streetwalker. The most dangerous way to hook, prey to the worst kind of violence and degradation. Zhu has heard rumors that Wing Sing and Li'l Lucy are working the street together, sharing some dive on Pacific Street south of Broadway. The parlor girls are having a field day, gossip told in scandalized whispers, a smugness barely concealing their fear. *There but for the grace of God go I.* How long will the new redhead last? How long will any of the parlor girls last?

But Zhu doesn't care about that, either. How can she care? There is nothing she can do for Wing Sing and Li'l Lucy. There was never anything she could do, she sees that now.

"I'll go find Wing Sing and give her the aurelia," she tells Muse. She winds her braid around her head, pins on the Newport hat. "I'll be the courier, like I'm supposed to be. After that, it's not my problem. If Wing Sing sells the aurelia for dope or food or money, there's nothing I can do. It *is* over. Over for me."

"Correct," Muse says. Muse confirming; fine. Better than another argument.

"Midnight? I'll be there." Zhu knows the place. The intersection across from the Mark Hopkins mansion. "And not even a room at Nobhill Park for the night?"

"I doubt it, Z. Wong," Muse repeats. "Not after what you've done."

❙ ❙ ❙

What she had done. Sometimes Zhu had trouble remembering exactly what had happened. The door to the room. Which way had it opened, to the left or to the right? Had there been one sentry or two? A crowd or only a few people?

Changchi: there had been rain, summer rain, amazing rain, the first clean deluge they'd seen in three seasons of drought and poisonous hailstorms. The air was thick with humidity that filmed the skin and made her T-shirt stick. Ten thousand puddles pooled on mud like chocolate pudding. And it was so good, despite the sudden onslaught of mosquitoes, the healthy stink of fertilizer. The heat would have made Zhu sink into lethargy if she hadn't worn the black patch. Agriworkers slogged out into the fields, fighting weeds that choked the new corn, the tender rice, the peas, and the millet. Someone was trying to figure out what they could do with the weeds, which were bitter and stringy. Package them as herbal tea and sell them to Americans? There was talk of a large groundnut harvest, carrots, and onions. The people would eat, get fat, know happiness. Dusty pantries would be restocked, the storage bins would overflow. Each processing plant put on two new shifts. Despite the terrible poisonous spring, there was a chance Changchi would turn a profit this year. The children would get neckjacks and telelinks, new workstations for the schools. The promise of telespace was renewed.

The Society for the Rights of Parents pointed with glee to their new prosperity. "You see?" shouted the speaker in the civic center. "With technology and hard work, we will have plenty. Plenty! This campaign to force our people to give up having their own children is evil. A tool of international imperialists who have never flagged in their long effort to dominate the East, to dictate to China, to rule the world. The Daughters of Compassion are their pawns."

Sally Chou was infuriated, more by the glut than the Parents' rhetoric. For the rain, the tender green, the mud like pudding lulled people, even enlightened people, into thinking they didn't have to change for the future.

"This is a false promise," Sally said to the ranks assembled in the mess hall. Ranks noticeably thinned. "There is no respite from negative population growth when the earth still bears twelve billion people on her back. There is no exemption from the Generation-Skipping Law. There will be no relief when this boom ends."

"But, Sally," someone called out from the back. "Does this conflict produce a good result? A few more unlicensed babies aren't going to matter."

"Suppose you have a pond with water lilies," Sally said. "Each day the water lilies grow, covering double the area they covered the previous day. On what day do you face disaster?"

"On the day when the lilies cover half the pond," Zhu said. "Because on the next day they will cover all of it."

"A few more unlicensed babies?" Sally said to the backs of those who had risen from the benches and headed out the door. "We cannot face a few more babies. We must not expand the base for exponential growth! Not in lean times; not in fat times."

The World Birth Control Agency was of little help. The world lottery took up most of the agency's resources. Send police agents? *They* were the local police agents. There was no one to send. Still, Zhu knew Sally felt abandoned. There was nothing any of them could do but carry on. Carry on with the campaign to convince the people of Changchi only the law could provide them and their heirs with a viable future.

But who would believe it?

Because the rain brought greenery, damp heat, fresh smells. Even the insects taunted with their mating dances over new ponds. The ranks of the Daughters thinned again because who would believe it.

The ones who stayed, including Zhu, had been using the black patch since that awful spring. Zhu's bruises had healed almost at once after Sally got her hands on an all-purpose Australian nanofix. The lingering dysentery had faded with better food and water at the compound. But in her mind Zhu connected her whole return to health with the sheer relief from the black patch.

She began slapping a patch onto the back of her knee every two days, grinding its little teeth down into her skin, relishing the moment she could feel the first surge from the time releasers. She carefully saved spent patches, which could be redosed and recycled if they couldn't get fresh anymore. She since had learned the black patch was a combination of a bootleg Russian opiate and an illegal Vietnamese stimulant implemented by the time releasers, time-coded microbials that freed the active ingredients in a beautiful syncopation of rush and bliss. A downer and an upper. Speedball.

Didn't notice when the patch became a habit. Didn't notice she couldn't get by on the third day without it. Didn't notice how the combination of rush and bliss came to feel like normal, like everyday functioning, though it wasn't everyday functioning.

Just knew she felt *good.* Especially in that ugly spring when she was sick and wounded and dispirited.

Zhu especially didn't notice—no one noticed—when the Daughters of Compassion had transformed from Generation-Skipping activists into negative-growth fanatics.

Women of Changchi were defying the law, aided and abetted by the Society for the Rights of Parents. Skipmothers assigned to raise skipchildren were getting pregnant. Women who had one child were fat with number two. Teenagers who had no bearing rights at all were leaving school. All of them went down to illegal birth clinics provided by the Parents. "Dropping their spawn," Sally said, "like there's no tomorrow."

The Daughters of Compassion fell into a new routine. Frantic to avoid another contamination of their water supply or some worse assault, they set up shifts to watch the periphery of the compound and its infrastructure. Cadres of teachers went out in the afternoons with knuckletops, holoids, and contraceptive patches. In happier times, they had called their presentation the Sex Show, but the Daughters were not happy that summer. And in the night? The elite, the warrior women, the dedicated core of which Zhu was a principal member, spent the short hot nights searching for birth clinics.

Illegal birth clinics were strictly prohibited under the Generation-Skipping Law, yet they had sprouted in Changchi in the wet heat like . . . Like *what?* Zhu pondered as she fasted before the shrine of Kuan Yin at midnight. She slept even less than she ate those days. Like rabbits, rats, fleas, fungi, bacteria. Like human beings.

And like a domino striking another and that one striking the next, like the chain reaction in a nuclear power plant, like night follows day, like death follows life, one day Sally Chou announced that the Daughters of Compassion were going to stage a raid.

"We're going to go in there and seize contraband," Sally announced, gazing over her horde. Zhu passed rice liquor to a new comrade, a fierce teenage girl whose name she didn't even know, and pressed a black patch into the back of her knee.

A shout rose up, "Seize the contraband, the contraband, the contraband!"

Zhu gazed about the room, held her breath. She loved these women warriors. Wiry, lean, muscular. Some scrawny. Some sick and pale. All in blue or black denim. All slung with bandoliers, butterfly knives, little automatics called spitfires that could gut a bull in less than five seconds. The moment hung suspended like a teardrop that wouldn't fall. A thought struggled up out of her consciousness like a drowning swimmer: *What in hell are we doing?* Then flailed, failed, sunk down again into the roiling depths of a mindlessness that numbed her will. And then the moment leapt forward with hallucinogenic clarity. The room a tableau of irrationality, of incipient violence, of a bloodlust Zhu never thought any of them could be capable of, let alone herself. A supreme moment, too, a terrible victory. For the Daughters of Compassion decried violations of the law they swore to uphold. The only law that gave the world any hint of a viable future.

"What is the contraband?" someone said, but the shouts, the exultation, the impetus for *action* silenced all questions.

Everyone knew what the contraband was.

"Let's go!" Sally said.

And they swept into the night.

To the rice-processing plant where one of the day teachers had heard there was a birth clinic hidden in the basement. They had no trouble finding and breaking into the plant, a low concrete building squatting beneath a decrepit old dome stitched by a network of cracks in the PermaPlast. No trouble finding the basement, which turned out to be a utility room sunk below the loading dock, a construction of layered concrete slabs that, in the night lights, possessed the solemnity of an ancient temple. No trouble finding it because women brazenly climbed up and down the dock, unafraid in the shelter of half-lit darkness, laughing and jostling, fondling their own swollen breasts and bellies.

The last thing they expected: the Daughters of Compassion, heavily armed, as primed with wild righteousness as a posse seeking criminals.

Sally seized a girl by her wrist, flinging her against the concrete wall, shoving a spitfire under her chin. "Where's your birth license, bitch?"

The fierce teenager whose name Zhu didn't know kicked her, a knee thrust hard into the captive's belly. The girl doubled over, retching.

They stormed down the stairwell, boots clattering, women screaming and scattering before them like a flock of birds, eyes bright with terror.

The comrades exultant, flushed, surging with power.

"What did the fat old chairman say?" Zhu shouted at Sally. "You can't make an omelette without breaking some eggs!"

"That's too weak, Zhu," Sally shouted back, triumphant over her first victim's subjugation. "Effete, don't you think? Coming from the old soldier who stomped his boot on the neck of China half a millennium ago." They reached the door, Sally's boot smashing the jamb with a high sharp kick. "How about this, comrades: You can't achieve negative population growth without aborting some fetuses!"

They slammed through the door, which swung open to the right. The inside security brandished her stool at them like a tamer facing lions, but that's all she had. No other weapons. All she had was a whistle, which she jammed in her lips and blew. Piercing shriek, and a crowd of women cowered against the back wall. There was no other exit; it was only a utility room. Newborns wailed, toddlers and children who'd been brought along by their mothers screamed and cried. Stink of blood and baby shit and unwashed female bodies. Zhu remembered how that smell infuriated her: selfish greedy bitches, thinking with their cunts, oblivious of the future, of the deprivation, of the potential ruin that they unleashed by the act of illicit procreation. All in the name of tradition.

A voice—hers—shouted, "You want tradition? We are here to uphold an old tradition: infanticide!"

Zhu pulled the handgun from beneath her right arm as a woman nine months pregnant and her young son quailed on the concrete floor before her. The astonished look on the woman's face: that Zhu would pull a gun on an unarmed woman and a two-year-old boy, or that Zhu was left-handed?

She didn't shoot, a bullet would have been too easy. She flipped the gun over, taking the barrel in her fist. Slammed the grip on the woman's shoulders, her back, her kidneys, aiming for the belly, the obscenely swollen belly, while the woman crouched, wrapping her arms around her knees, protecting herself and her unborn. Her little boy cried and clung to his mother while the grip of the gun went *whump,*

whump, whump. And then she was hitting the kid, smacking the kid, *whump, whump, whump,* his little hands, his neck, his soft round skull, his face canting back to look at her with wide green eyes, opaque with incomprehension, his mouth an O of surprise.

❜ ❜ ❜

Is he alive or dead?

That's all Zhu kept asking, all she wanted to know, after they arrested her, Sally Chou, and the cadre.

Police assailed the clinic. Everything was chaos. Zhu couldn't remember much after that except the screams, the blood, the stink. The shock of the boy's eyes, like emerald cabochons. Of course they beat her on the way to jail, ripped off the black patch, forced her into detox. Didn't feel the trauma till she lay in the cell in the central women's prison facility at Beijing, semicomatose for nearly five days while the interrogator asked her "What is your name?" over and over. And then the guilt, the horror, the shame. *Is he alive or dead?*

The media called it the Night of Broken Blossoms. Her face was featured in telespace: the abandoned skipchild. Didn't know what happened to Sally. No one would say. It was late June 2495, when her lawyer barged into the prison facility, roused her from an exhausted sleep, and said, "Listen up, Wong, I've got a deal."

Bang, bang, bang in the street.

"I am not a murderer," Zhu says, collecting her feedbag purse. "Not even for the Cause. A lot of things had happened before that night. I was not myself."

"You are always yourself." Muse unsympathetic.

"I never meant to kill a child, Muse."

"But you attempted to do so." Muse noncommittal.

"In support of a law your cosmicists dreamed up."

"Overpopulation of the earth has been the most serious problem facing global renewal since the brown ages."

"Then why is his life so important?"

Muse silent.

"You don't want to say, do you? What *is* the value of a

life in a world burdened with twelve billion people? Under True Value, human beings are no more important than an endangered butterfly, isn't that what the cosmicists believe? Who is to be the arbiter of True Value? Who is to be my judge?"

Zhu studies herself in the watery reflection of her mirror. *Is he alive or dead?* She'll find out tonight at midnight. The t-port is instantaneous. The ME3 Event flings her from this Now to her Now. There isn't even movement, not really. Tachyportation is a transmutation, not a traveling. There is no duration. A second seems to pass, but that is only subjective. The subjective second and the void.

Shudders when she thinks of the void.

She pins the aurelia to her collar. The final touch. Stands at the threshold of her bedroom for the last time, nostalgia already leaking into her heart. *I'll never see this place again.* She *knows* this is true.

Hurries through Mariah's parlor, into the hall, downstairs.

She knows where to find Wing Sing. Where the most desperate streetwalkers ply their trade: the Barbary Coast.

ꜝ ꜝ ꜝ

Shouts in the foyer, Jessie and Daniel. Zhu creeps to the bottom of the stairs, tries to sneak past them to the kitchen and out the back door. Daniel fastens his glittering red-rimmed eyes upon her at once, seizes her wrist, and drags her back.

"She'll stand me for the month, won't you, mistress?"

"I'll be goddamned if you'll take the wage I pay to my employee to pay *me*," Jessie says.

"It's her money, isn't it?"

"She belongs to me." Jessie sallow, bloated, mouth pinched with pain. Won't listen to Zhu about the corset. Won't stop guzzling Scotch Oats Essence and champagne all day. Muse says Scotch Oats Essence is not only loaded with whiskey, but with morphine, as well. Muse says Jessie is one drink away from the grave.

"Let's hear what Zhu has to say."

"Mr. Watkins," Jessie says, "you've got money rolling in from your Chinese slum, you sold your Western Addition lot, you're gonna get the goods on Harvey. . . ."

"The lawyers are breaking my back," Daniel says, "and we haven't even gone to court."

"If you want to blow your wad on dope, that's your business," Jessie says, "but I'll not be stiffed by the likes of you."

"I'm not stiffing you, madam." His sarcasm doesn't help just now. "My mistress will tide me over till next month, won't you, Zhu?"

He draws her into the smoking parlor for a private conference. "Now, listen, I know she's paying you your wage, all I need . . ."

Zhu closes her eyes. Choking; air in the parlor is putrid with old smoke. His feverish whisper becomes a jumble in her ear, incomprehensible. Daniel, oh Daniel. His father kicking the mother till she aborted, kicking her into a permanent hell of pain and guilt. In the end, is that the attraction? Why Zhu was drawn together with him? That's how cosmicists think: correlations and correspondences are not random, not merely synchronicity, but indicative of patterns, the vast underlying patterns of space and time that imply the guiding force of the Cosmic Mind. Has she ever believed cosmicist cosmology? Maybe not, but how else to account for their mutual attraction, dreadful as it is, except to point to a vast unseen pattern of pain, of atrocity?

"Just fifty dollars," he is saying. "What do you say?"

"I say you're killing yourself, Daniel," Zhu says quietly. "You'll be dead before the turn of this year." *Knows this.* "And there's nothing I can do for you."

"Hell, I might as well be dead," he says. From his vest pocket he pulls a clutch of thin papers, scrawled and blotched with ink. "I missed it. I missed it, goddamn it."

"Missed what?"

"The Lumière brothers; they did it. They figured it out. I should never have left Paris, *damn* Father and his troubles. By God, I am such an idiot!"

"Daniel . . ."

"They've made a machine that shows moving pictures." Shakes the letter. "Rochelle wrote. The bastards showed their moving pictures. 'A train charging into the station' "—stabs the letter with a finger yellowed with nicotine—"'smoke-stack spewing like the wrath of God.' As if Rochelle could ever wax so eloquent. Probably got that fairy poet to write this for her."

"When?"

"After Christmas, she says, in the Salon Indien of the Grand Café on the Boulevard des Capucines." Slaps his palm to his forehead. "How many hours I wasted at the Grand, sipping rainbow cups."

"There, you see?" Zhu says. "And you're wasting more . . ."

"Don't go temperance on me, mistress." He paces across the parlor, growing more and more feverish. "The Lumières are rich capitalists. They threw money at it, there was no contest." He examines the letter as though the ungainly scrawl will reveal something more, something he overlooked. "Rochelle says their box takes the pictures *and* projects them. By God, why didn't I think of that?" Whirls on her. "Why didn't *you*?"

"Me?"

"Not so clever after all, are you, mistress? Well, of course, you're a woman. The longer the hair, the smaller the brain, as good old Swinburne says." He pauses, musing. "I must see their machine. I shall go to Paris at once!"

"Not before you pay me for all the back rent you owe me, buster," Jessie says, standing on the threshold, tapping her toe.

"Pay you," Daniel says. "I'll pay you. Take it out of my hide, madam. All you whores ever think about is the filthy lucre."

"And all you gentlemen ever do is try to rook us out of it," Jessie says.

Suddenly Zhu cannot tolerate either one of them. There's nothing she can do for them, *nothing*. Without a word, she flees from the smoking parlor before Daniel can latch onto her arm again. She pulls the veil down from the brim of her Newport hat.

"Hurry," Muse whispers.

Zhu sweeps into the night.

▼ ▼ ▼

"Missy," Jessie yells after her, "where in hell are you going?"

Daniel pleading, "Just fifty dollars, mistress."

"Lose them," Muse commands.

Zhu picks up her skirts, dashes north on Dupont, crosses over at the Monkey Block, and strides up the long incline of Montgomery Street, which looks gentle but in fact is slow and cruel, making her breath catch and her legs ache. Four bruisers in fishermen's togs and caps who have been tramping along the sidewalk on the opposite side of the street turn the corner when she does. *Nymphes du pavé* stroll about, flutter fans, take out makeup cases and pat powder on their sores, smooth rouge on blistered lips, spread gap-toothed smiles as inviting as a medusa's cave. Music and song spill from a multitude of open doors, along with rowdy shouts and the laughter of oblivion.

The golden nineties look gentle, too: the polite speech and the genteel manners, long silk dresses and the golden glow of gaslight, champagne and terrapin in sweet cream. A slower time, before cars and shuttles and telespace. But the golden nineties are cruel, Zhu knows that now. The rhetoric of social Darwinism lurks beneath the polite speech, bigotry behind genteel manners. Crippling corsets bind women's bodies beneath the pretty dresses; you can barely see the bruises in the dimness of gaslight. Gentlemen eat and drink themselves into early graves, and a blend of whiskey and morphine is a medicine freely swilled from a bottle with pink cupids on the label.

Muse whispers, "Hurry."

A hand on her shoulder, a hand pulling on the strap of her feedbag purse. Jessie and Daniel flank her, breathless.

"Missy."

"Mistress."

"What?" she cries.

"Looking for Wing Sing?" Jessie says. Her face is weary, swollen, her eyes hard in the lamplight. "I knew it. Well, all right. I'd like to find that chit, too. She owes me money."

"For*get* the money, Jessie."

"Yeah, I know you, Zhu." The hard eyes search her face. *Do you, Jessie?* "You got mush for a heart. You're gonna give her the gimcrack, aren't you?" Touches the aurelia on Zhu's collar. "Feel bad about her dowry? Forget it, it was them tongs. Wasn't your fault." Jessie shakes Zhu's shoulder. "Don't give good diamonds to that whore. She'll only blow it on dope."

"Indeed, give the aurelia to me," Daniel says. The nagging pleas of addiction. Sends shivers down Zhu's spine. *Nothing she can do.*

Jessie slaps him. "Shut your trap, you dope fiend. You'll only pawn it yourself. She'll give the gold to me, won't you, darlin'?"

"Hurry," Muse whispers.

Something snaps inside. Zhu is cold, determined, purposeful. Something inside her has already crossed over six centuries. "No! I'm giving the aurelia to Wing Sing. It belongs to her. It's her birthright. And neither one of you had better interfere." She shakes loose of them, strides away, and turns. "You can help me find her. That's the one last thing you can do for me. I'm leaving tonight."

She feels strange pleasure at the look of despair on each of their faces. Daniel J. Watkins and Jessie Malone. Such completely different people and yet sharing the serendipity of meeting her, Zhu Wong, in the golden nineties.

THERE IS A PROSPECT OF A THRILLING TIME AHEAD FOR YOU

That was her fortune in the Japanese Tea Garden. A thrilling time? Or a vast unseen pattern of pain, of atrocity, and everyone—Jessie, Daniel, Chiron, the LISA techs, even Sally Chou—has used her, exploited her, *tricked* her.

She turns up Pacific Street; Jessie and Daniel follow. So do the four bruisers. And so do three shadows stalking out of Tangrenbu into the open zone of the Barbary Coast.

The Barbary Coast: the infamous sink of iniquity. Music blares from bawdy bars, bagnios and brothels beckon, the gambling dens and opium dens for people of all races never close. On the grimy sidewalk an entrepreneur has set up a peepshow. "See the mermaid; see the live mermaid."

Zhu peers around the moth-eaten satin curtain. The live mermaid is only a very dead female monkey, its little teats unevenly enhanced by stuffing. The dismembered torso is stitched to a large tuna tail. The monstrosity is preserved in a smeary aquarium reeking of formaldehyde.

Jessie's sallow face goes white at the sight.

"You freak!" she screams at the entrepreneur. "You're the goddamn freak!"

"Ah, go blow, lady," the entrepreneur says.

"A poor little fake, that's all it is," Zhu says, nonplussed by her vehemence. She takes Jessie's elbow and steers her away.

"Don't you make fun of mermaids, buster." Jessie is nearly weeping.

The broken streets are slippery, gutters ripe with raw sewage and mud. Sailors throng the saloons, emaciated fellows with terrible teeth, sick with drink, complaisant victims of the great shipping companies that press them into the hard labor of crewing transoceanic ships.

"Watch out for that Muldoon," Jessie says in Zhu's ear, pointing out a short man in a scarlet cutaway. "He's a crimp." Wiry and quick, Muldoon yammers at a gang of drunks like a tobacco auctioneer. A gold earring flashes against his neck. "A slaver for them clipper ships. Kidnaps crew right off these streets."

Daniel slings his arm around Zhu's shoulders and grins at her. She smells whiskey on his breath. He must have ducked in somewhere and downed a quick shot. Zhu smiles back anyway, lips trembling. Daniel; even now he's so beautiful, his hair spilling over his high starched collar. Pale skin stretched over his bones, glazed eyes bright with drink, deep with dope. *He's going to die.* And there's nothing she can do.

They pass by the Lively Flea. Zhu runs to the swinging doors, peeks in. Where is Wing Sing? On the stage lies a brown-skinned woman, naked, her face a painted mask. Standing over her, a stud pony. On the next stage, another woman, equally unclothed, equally masked, and a huge dog, its tongue lolling. An ivory-skinned woman and a man the color of onyx writhe upon a podium next to a white woman grappling with a brown woman. A woman and a bull calf; a woman and another dog; a woman and what looks like a fresh corpse contorted in rigor mortis.

Men guffaw or watch, transfixed. Zhu stands on the threshold, stunned. Someone lurches toward her. She backs off, backs away, fingers pressed to her throat. Darts out into the street, darts down toward the wharves where the surf sprays bars built out over the water.

Alphanumerics flicker in her peripheral vision. "Heads up, Z. Wong." Muse dispassionate.

Wing Sing. There, along the waterfront. Zhu would know that moon face anywhere, the delicate cheekbones, the slope of a nose, the curious mouth, her slim, tall figure in apple green silk, a new tunic and trousers. Big broad feet, Zhu can see them from here. Unbound feet in pink silk stockings, slipped into sandals on platforms of straw. A green satin bandeau binds her forehead, the shiny black braid swings down her back. A blond woman sashays next to her. Could it possibly be Li'l Lucy? No, the blond is much too thin. Wing Sing and her companion duck into a Stick cantilevered precariously over the water: Kelly's Saloon & The Eye-Wink Ballroom.

Jessie's hand grips her elbow like a vise. "Let's don't go in here, missy."

"Why not?"

Jessie's bleary face looms so close, Zhu can smell her foul breath. "Nothing but trouble in Kelly's."

"But I need to see Wing Sing."

"That's right, let's go in, mistress." Daniel sweeps past them through the swinging doors. "I need another nip. Just a tiny one, of course. I don't need the drink when I've got the Inca's gift."

But Jessie balks, her face taut with tension.

"Don't tell me the Queen of the Underworld is shy tonight," Daniel says. He comes back out and impatiently holds the door open for them.

"I got a feeling," Jessie says. "Missy, please. Let's wait for her to come out."

"Wait?" Zhu says. She glances in at the clock behind the bar in Kelly's. Nine minutes after eleven. She has less than an hour to get back downtown, catch the cable car up California Street, and find the intersection at Mason. She cannot miss her rendezvous, not this one. "I can't wait, Miss Malone."

"In a hurry?" Jessie says.

"Yes! I told you. I'm leaving tonight."

"Leaving for where?" Daniel demands.

"For the future. For my time in the future."

"Damn it, missy," Jessie says. "Enough is enough."

"I thought you believed me."

"Sure I do," Jessie says. "Like I believe in Santa Claus and the tooth fairy. And I always got gifts for Christmas and a penny under my pillow."

"What about everything I've told you?"

Stubborn Jessie. "Tall tales."

"What about my mollie knife?"

"I was drinking absinthe that night. So were you."

Zhu is silent. What if Jessie insists on a version of reality that's different from what she remembers?

"Come, my poor little lunatic," Daniel says, laughing, "let's have a drink. Miss Malone? It's on me."

"On you," Jessie says. "What about my rent, buster?"

"Let's discuss the rent over a shot of rye."

"Get in there, Z. Wong," Muse whispers in her ear. "Find Wing Sing *now.*"

"Yes, let's," Zhu says, sweeping Jessie and Daniel into Kelly's.

The bar stinks of cheap beer and rotgut. The air is fogged with tobacco smoke, the clotted sawdust ankle deep. Games of faro are conducted here and there and a sizable crowd crouches around dice, but the prime activity at Kelly's is drinking. There is no ballroom dancing, despite the sign, but plenty of fornication transacted in a series of little plywood booths set across the back. The place is mobbed with sailors.

And there. There! Posing before a table, sandal propped on the seat of a chair, arms akimbo, giggling, bantering: Wing Sing. She negotiates with sailors who wear the grizzled, famished look of months at sea. An anomalous sight she is, too. A young Chinese woman in apple green silk walking the Barbary Coast, imprisoned neither in crib nor in parlor. And although she is degraded by her trade, robbed of her future, denied the simple comforts of ordinary life other women either savor or endure, for a moment Wing Sing stands triumphant before Zhu: a free woman.

Zhu takes her arm. Wing Sing shrugs her off. The sailors guffaw.

The four bruisers sashay through the swinging doors. A small man accompanies them. Black hair, black beard, black pools for eyes. Harvey walks arm in arm with Muldoon, the crimp. Harvey and his entourage saunter up to the bar, exchange ribald greetings with the bartender, Mr. Kelly himself. Harvey spots Daniel, tips his top hat. Jessie tugs on Daniel's sleeve, but Daniel ignores both her and his debtor's greeting.

"Please," Zhu says to Wing Sing. "I have something to give you."

Three Chinese men in black slouch hats drift into Kelley's. The eyepatch and his hatchet men step up to the bar.

"You give me something?" Wing Sing arches her eyebrows and arranges her face in a caricature of surprise. Says to the sailors, "Excuse please, gentlemen."

She marches indignantly to the table where the skinny blond sits nursing a drink. Not Li'l Lucy. Dark blotches rim both women's eyes. Their skin possesses that sallow cast Zhu has seen on the faces of opium addicts in Tangrenbu. "What you want, Jade Eyes, huh?"

"Like I said, I want to give you something."

"No, no, I not take nothing from you."

"Something nice."

"You bad luck to me, Jade Eyes."

"Please." Zhu unpins the aurelia. The gold and diamonds

linger in her fingers. The tiny golden woman is impassive, lifeless, a sacrifice on the cross of destiny. Zhu hands the aurelia to Wing Sing.

Wing Sing's mouth hangs open. She gapes at the aurelia, turning it over and over. "What this?"

"This is real gold." Zhu takes and pins the brooch on Wing Sing's collar. "You take. You keep. To make up for your dowry. For you and your daughter. Rusty's baby."

Wing Sing shrugs. "If my baby is girl, I sell her to Chee Song Tong. Clear my debt."

Protest swells on Zhu's tongue but she is silent. There is nothing she can say, nothing she can do. She will step across six centuries tonight, never to return. She only smiles and says, "Ah, but you won't. You'll love her. You'll keep her."

Wing Sing vigorously shakes her head. "I not keep girl."

"She'll look just like you," Zhu says. "You can name her Wing Sing, too."

"I not name girl for *me*," Wing Sing says contemptuously. "You so smart, Jade Eyes, have explanation for everything. You know what 'Wing Sing' mean in the tongue of my village?"

"What does 'Wing Sing' mean?"

"It mean 'everlasting life.' You think I want to live forever? Like this? Huh. Forget it, Jade Eyes."

Daniel comes to Zhu's side. Cold glance for Wing Sing, the aurelia pinned to her collar. "You're supposed to come and have a drink with us, mistress."

Zhu turns to go. Muse whispers, "The aurelia." Dizzy suddenly, a sick feeling in her gut. Alphanumerics skitter and swirl, a wind whistles in her ear. Voices scramble into nonsense, laughter clatters. The eyepatch scans the crowd, his eye piercing the smoke, lighting upon Zhu and Wing Sing. His hand whips out like a snake striking, tugging at the wiry fellow and the fat man.

Jessie comes to Zhu's side. "What's going on here, missy?"

Muse whispers, "The aurelia, Z. Wong."

An odd gleam shoots from the curve of the aurelia's wing.

Zhu looks around, confused. Suddenly Harvey, Muldoon, Kelly, and the four bruisers surround Daniel. Harvey smiles appeasingly, though the expression doesn't fit on his face. He holds two drinks in tall tumblers. "So you're takin' me to court, are you, Mr. Watkins?"

"That I am, Harvey," Daniel says. The teeth, the charming smile, he will never lose them. "You'll get what's coming."

Daniel, oh Daniel. Fear wells in Zhu's chest, her heart skips.

"Have a drink with me first." Harvey smiling; but Harvey never smiles. "Then we'll see who gets his."

"Daniel," Zhu says.

"The aurelia," Muse repeats. Is the monitor jammed?

Daniel takes the tumbler Harvey offers. Zhu sees his arm lift, his hand reach out, his long fingers curl around the tumbler. He knocks the rim against Harvey's. The glass shimmers as he raises it to his lips, and he downs half, takes a breath, downs the next half. Harvey watches, not smiling, not drinking.

"Oh, Daniel," Zhu says.

The eyepatch and his hatchet men cross Kelly's. Kelly guffaws.

Daniel's tumbler drops to the floor, tipping top over bottom, and shatters when it strikes the wood floor. Muffled sound in the sawdust, but ineluctable. Irreversible. The cracking sound of death.

Harvey spills coins into Muldoon's open palm.

Daniel's eyes roll back, and he collapses. Harvey's thugs seize him, drag his crumpled body through the sawdust. Jessie whips the thugs with her handbag and screams, "Knockout drops in his drink, you bastards!" Kelly finds a handle in the floor, flips open a trapdoor. Zhu smells the stink of the harbor, of things rotting in the water. Someone reaches up from a boat bobbing below the trapdoor.

"He'll be halfway to Shanghai 'fore he wakes up," Muldoon says to Harvey. "*If* he wakes up."

"My Shanghai Special," Kelly says. "Works like a charm."

Harvey laughs. "Teach that boy to sue me."

"The aurelia," Muse whispers, "the aurelia, the aurelia."

"No!" Zhu rushes for the trapdoor, seizes Daniel's coattails. "No, you can't shanghai him!"

Harvey's thugs guffaw and push her away.

"*Do* something, you deadbeats!" Jessie implores the sailors. "You gonna let a goddamn crimp take a man?"

Someone seizes Zhu, lifts her, and spins her around. For a moment Zhu sees Wing Sing, an inexplicable look on her face, the aurelia gleaming on her collar.

"Aurelia, aurelia, aurelia," says Muse.

The eyepatch shakes Zhu like a rag doll. "No one cross Chee Song Tong."

"I never crossed you," Zhu says. Her breath catches in her throat.

"You cross us. You steal from us."

"Then get the law. Have me arrested." *Never supposed to happen this way.*

"This our law, Jade Eyes."

Flash of silver. The eyepatch whips out a knife and cuts her throat.

Harvey's thugs throw Daniel into the boat below the trapdoor.

Jessie screams, "No, no, no, no!"

Sharp sting, but the blood loss from her severed jugular vein sends Zhu into shock so sudden and intense, dying almost feels like pleasure.

Muse says forlornly, "The aurelia, the aurelia, the aurelia . . ." Then silence.

❘ ❘ ❘

Jessie seizes Wing Sing and backs away from the awful scene. A couple of beat cops wander in to investigate the cries of murder. But this is the Barbary Coast and the fresh corpse is only a woman. Only a poor Chinese woman in ladies' clothes without any station in life. The black wagon of the morgue arrives and takes the body away.

"She's dead, Mother of God," Jessie says, crossing herself. "Betsy, my sweet innocent angel, you look out for that girl, you hear me? I loved her, too."

"Poor Jade Eyes," Wing Sing says, clasping her hand to her throat. She covers the gold thing, what Zhu had called an aurelia.

The cops look around. The sergeant takes a drink from Kelly. Harvey saunters away with a waitress. Harvey's thugs secure the trapdoor and cover it with sawdust. The boat bearing Daniel J. Watkins is halfway to a clipper ship bound for the far East. When Mr. Watkins wakes from the laudanum, the ship will be well out to sea. If morphine withdrawal doesn't kill him first, the hard labor will.

Jessie drags Wing Sing out of Kelly's. Rips the aurelia off her collar.

"That mine!" Wing Sing cries.

"You're just gonna sell it for dope," Jessie says.

"No, Jade Eyes say it for me. For me and my daughter."

Jessie slaps the girl's flat belly. "Liar; you're not pregnant."

"I am, Miss Malone. I not get monthlies."

"That's just the opium, you fool."

"No, I make little girl. Jade Eyes say."

Jessie's fingers curl around the gold, the diamonds. The bauble feels hot, but she will not drop it, will not hand such a valuable thing over to a whore like Wing Sing. It's too beautiful for the likes of her.

"I'll keep it for you," Jessie says.

In July of 1896, Wing Sing gives birth to an underweight female infant and dies three days later of internal hemorrhaging. Jessie takes the infant to Donaldina Cameron. It's the least she can do in memory of Zhu Wong, who had cared so much for the baby's pathetic mother. Not that Jessie likes the Bible thumper, but who else will raise a Chinese girl with nothing but the clothes on her back in anything like decency?

Chee Song Tong becomes embroiled in a war with Hop Sing Tong. On Bastille Day, the eyepatch is hacked to death in Bartlett Alley by an assassin. Mr. Heald suffers a heart attack and dies in the hospital. Jessie's new connection to the mayor's office quadruples her civic contributions.

In September of 1896, Mariah invites Jessie to go with her to the National American Woman Suffrage Association meeting. It turns out that Mariah has been stealing away from the Dupont Street boardinghouse over the years to attend meetings of the local woman suffrage chapter. Jessie declines the invitation. Mariah works every spare moment on the committee supporting the state referendum for woman suffrage in California, but, to her bitter disappointment, the measure is defeated. In the spring of 1897, Mariah leaves San Francisco, having hoarded her salary in a savings account at Wells Fargo Bank. She goes back to her family in Boston—Jessie never knew Mariah was from Boston—opens up her own boardinghouse, and begins to write for *The Woman's Era.* She is appointed by Josephine St. Pierre Ruffin to be treasurer of the National Federation of Afro-American Women, which merges into the National Association of Colored Women.

Short on cash in July of 1897, Jessie takes the aurelia down to Andrews' Diamond Palace, contemplating pawning the thing. Colonel Andrews, supercilious as ever in his immaculate tuxedo and top hat, tells her the piece is old-fashioned and tenders a ridiculously low offer. Jessie tosses the aurelia into her handbag and stalks out.

On Columbus Day, 1897, the police call Jessie down to the morgue to identify a blond prostitute who has been beaten to death outside of Kelly's. Jessie cannot positively tell if the thin, poxy corpse is that of Li'l Lucy. The face is too disfigured, the arms riddled with needle tracks. If it is, Li'l Lucy didn't live to see her twenty-first birthday.

Eight years after the turn of the century and endless trouble with the police, the johns, the whores, and her unflagging appetites, Jessie learns she is ill with cancer of the liver. It's bad. Her doctor tells her she has a month or two left.

At last Miss Jessie Malone, face and bosom fallen, waist excruciating beneath the corsets that are still in style, deeply in debt, deeply in drink, and unable to rest at night, goes up to Nine Twenty Sacramento Street.

The red brick edifice looks exactly the same.

Donaldina Cameron, as stern as ever, much grayer and more gaunt, answers the door.

"I have something," Jessie says, breathing hard, "for the kid."

"You'll not come near her," Cameron says. "Not after what you did to her mother."

"Miss Cameron," Jessie says, "it's her goddamn inheritance. I was keeping it for her mother. Sure and I don't need it anymore, I'm about to kick the bucket myself."

Cameron reluctantly lets the old whore in. And that's when Jessie gives the aurelia to Wing Sing's daughter.

"I know it's old-fashioned, but it meant something to the girl I got it from," Jessie says, handing over the jewelry. "Maybe one day you'll know what. She often told me about a red-haired man who gave it to her. Jar me, what a story. Said he was from six hundred years in the future, can you beat that? Maybe one day you'll meet a man with red hair. Maybe that's who the aurelia really belongs to."

Wing Sing's daughter is a sturdy girl with wide green eyes from a father she never knew, a moon face, and black hair chopped in a modern style. She takes the piece of old-fashioned golden jewelry. Her hands are chapped from washing dishes. Prim in her gray wool dress, disdainful, a touch frightened of the ugly old woman, she says, "Thank you. Good-bye."

JUNE 21, 2495

A Premonition Is Just a Memory of the Future

"And Donaldina Cameron? She died in 1968. Lived to be ninety-eight years old," says the Chief Archivist. "Good Scotch genes. No DNA tweaking in those days." The Chief Archivist herself is nearly as old. She's got an elastic bandage wrapped around her ankle, the ankle propped on a stool. Twisted it playing racquetball with her skipdaughter, a sprightly kid of thirty-eight. The Chief Archivist is grumpy today. She has snapped at Chi twice during their conference.

Chiron Cat's Eye in Draco sighs. "You're sure that's her."

"No doubt about it."

Chi clicks the viewer and closes the file. The holoid of the old woman in the wheelchair and her elderly Chinese companion fades into a field of gleaming blue. The field shrinks to the size of a luminous blue ping-pong ball and winks off, leaving Chi and the Chief Archivist sitting in the soft golden light of the conference room. The room rocks gently back and forth. The bay is rough from a summer storm, whitecaps slapping against the hydroplex of Luxon Institute for Superluminal Applications.

"By the way, happy anniversary," says the Chief Archivist, breaking open a neurobic and sniffing greedily. "June 21, the summer solstice. It's been twenty-eight years since we sent you on the Summer of Love Project. And look at you. Red hair down to your butt."

Chi grins. "I decided I liked the hair, after all."

He can't help himself. He turns on the viewer, clicks to the holoid for the tenth time, and studies the trampled grass of Golden Gate Park, the woman in the wheelchair, the companion.

The holoid had been retrieved by Chi's knuckletop during the Summer of Love. He had taken plenty of holoids for the Archives, collected a lot of data about the dim spot. The Archivists easily identified Cameron. The Archives contain dozens of photographs and abundant documentation about Lo Mo, the Mother. Rescuer of Chinese slave girls. A female hero; a modern saint. Chi can barely remember that afternoon himself. It had been the day before he was to t-port back to 2467 and he had walked through the park with the girl while four musicians sat on the grass, jamming. Two acoustic guitars, a banjo, a tambourine. A knot of people had gathered to listen, along with Chiron and the girl, the old woman in the wheelchair, her companion. The old woman had smiled. The companion had stared and slowly unpinned something from her collar, walking across the grass to hand a piece of jewelry to him. That was the Summer of Love; people were always giving him things. He had thought it was charming that two old women would get into the spirit of the Haight-Ashbury. He had thought no more of the incident than that.

"And the companion who gave me the aurelia?"

"We don't know. It's a dim spot," the Chief Archivist snaps. She *hates* lack of information. "Whatever motivated her occurred before we sent you on the Summer of Love Project. We can't trace her. She's a classic Jane Doe."

"But there was part of a fingerprint on the gold."

"If you want to call less than a millimeter a 'part.' You must remember people weren't routinely d-based in those days. We don't have prints for these people."

"And a couple of skin cells."

"From which we can generate a scanty DNA profile. Basic characteristics: race, sex, approximate age. We already knew all that from you and the holoid."

"Yes." Chiron clicks onto the companion, blows up the holoid. Short gray hair, still threaded with black, sunlight full on a round little face. The surprise of green eyes. "About seventy years old?"

"We estimate seventy-one from the profile. Like I said, no DNA tweaking in those days."

"So she would have been born in 1896. We assume in San Francisco?"

"Yes." The Chief Archivist stands restlessly and paces a bit, limping painfully on the ankle. She sits down again, annoyed. "If the profile is right, she was part Caucasian. Which makes things dicey. A baby of mixed race in 1896 who wound up at Cameron's place? You have to understand, the Chinese were strictly segregated in San Francisco then, except for certain brothels employing Chinese girls exclusively for a white clientele. You see? That's the most probable way the baby would have been conceived."

"Do the Archives support the existence of this baby in 1896?"

"They do. Cameron took in a number of Chinese infants. Some of them were left on her doorstep. No data on where they came from. Many left the home when they came of age, married, and had their own families, but kept in touch with Cameron. Donaldina was well loved by her girls."

"All right." Chi closes the file with an air of finality. The holoid snaps off; the blue field hovers before them. "And the child at the birth clinic in Changchi?"

"His mother immigrated to Chihli Province ten years ago. Lives and works on one of the agricultural communes. Part of the Motherland Movement. The way American Jews went to live on kibbutzim in what, the late twentieth century? And some stayed, became citizens of Israel. Same situation with the Motherland Movement in China."

"The mother is American?"

"From an old San Franciscan family, dating back to the nineteenth century. And, yes, there's some Caucasian blood in the family tree."

"The child's eyes."

"The green eyes are avatistic. Crop up every other generation or so." The Chief Archivist slips another holoid into the viewer. "The mother married a local guy. Bore the child in '93. Now she's pregnant with number two."

"Is she going to be okay?" Chi says.

"Oh, sure. She got roughed up a bit by the Daughters of Compassion, but she'll be all right."

"And the child: *Is he alive or dead?*"

The Chief Archivist clicks on the new holoid. The Night of Broken Blossoms received a burst of international attention, especially since the conflict highlighted the thorny problems of the Generation-Skipping Law. A fresh and virulent debate between opponents and proponents of the law raged in telespace, in every medium. Chiron leans forward.

The hospital at Changchi: pale lime green walls, gray-green linoleum, halogen lights casting a green tinge on grim faces of the staff. A brilliantly lit hall leads up to a door. As Chi watches, little bright white flashes flicker over the door.

"Poor resolution," he says, reaching for the viewer.

"Watch," says the Chief Archivist.

From the opposite side of the door dart sharp black flashes like a rain of tiny ebony daggers piercing the white. A doctor gingerly takes the door handle, cracks open the door, left to right. Suddenly the doctor is thrown by some invisible force that rams her across the waist. The doctor doubles over in pain, staggering into the arms of her staff. All of them tumble backwards, pushed by the force. The focus goes wild for a moment. Shots of the ceiling, the walls, people's terrified faces whirl by in confusion.

"We should cut that," mutters the Chief Archivist.

"No, leave it in," Chi says.

The focus reestablishes on the door. The door handle is on the right side of the door.

"See that?" whispers the Chief Archivist.

"It's switched!" Chi says. "Wasn't the handle on the left?"

Before their astonished eyes, the door handle appears and disappears, like the illusion of a stage magician, now on the left, now on the right, even once protruding from the middle.

The intrepid doctor darts forward, tries again. She manages to seize the handle and kicks open the door.

The room—just an ordinary hospital room with a cot, IV apparatus, a monitor beeping softly—swirls with a grainy gray fog or smoke. On the cot, the child. Now so badly bruised, Chi can hardly bear to look at his disfigured little face, next healed as though he'd never been pistol-whipped, next lying in a pool of coagulated blood, his green eyes wide open, dead. Clearly dead, flat line on the monitor.

And yet again, the child stirs, cries, blinks up at the monitor. Or laughs, waving his tiny fists, reaching for a stuffed panda.

The doctor says, "What can we do for him? We don't know what to do."

"A Prime Probability," Chiron says. Whistles.

"A Prime Probability that won't collapse," says the Chief Archivist, clicking the holoid off. "In or out of the timeline, the probability won't collapse. We don't even know which way we *want* the probability to go."

"Careful," Chi says. "We're talking about a little boy's life."

"We're talking about another Crisis," snaps the Chief Archivist. "The LISA techs are calling the child a quantum probability: a Prime Probability that won't collapse."

"A quantum probability?"

"You know the discredited Schrödinger's cat metaphor used to demonstrate the probable nature of reality. The cat in the gas chamber, alive and dead at the same time until someone opens the chamber and observes the result."

"Of course."

"The quantum probability won't collapse one way or the other because some event connected to that child has become unresolved, uncertain, *jeopardized*, in the past. There's only one way that could happen: it must be an event connected to tachyportation."

Chi stands, paces across the conference room. "Well, the fact that the companion gave me the aurelia is directly connected to my Summer of Love Project. But what does the aurelia have to do with the child?"

"The child is the descendant of an old San Francisco family, Chinese mixed with Caucasian. The anonymous companion of Cameron was Chinese mixed with Caucasian, and it's likely she was born in the late 1890s. The aurelia itself in style and workmanship dates from that period." The Chief Archivist shrugs. "All we have is a theory. That's all we ever have whenever we undertake a tachyportation project. That's why we shut t-porting down. Too risky. Too tricky. Too bloody *theoretical*."

"And your theory is?"

"The child has become a quantum probability because the birth of his probable ancestor, Cameron's companion, is in jeopardy. If that green-eyed woman is never born, she'll never give you the aurelia."

"But the aurelia was never a part of my project! I'm sorry I took the damn thing. I didn't mean to. I *never* meant to. I certainly never meant to bring it to our day. I put it in my pocket and forgot I had it, plain and simple." He kneels before the Chief Archivist. "It's just a detail. A small mistake. I'm *sorry*."

"Your apology is accepted, but it doesn't help."

"Are you suggesting that because I inadvertantly took the aurelia to the future, I've affected events in a past I know nothing about?"

"I'm suggesting there's a link," the Chief Archivist says,

"between the quantum probability the boy has become and *you*, Chi. That link is the anonymous woman and the aurelia."

"But you're suggesting that the future affects the past!"

"Chi," says the Chief Archivist, "we don't know what will happen if the anonymous Chinese woman is never born. Is the child her descendant? There's a probability that he is. If that's true and she's never born, the child will die. We'll all be sorry; his death will be a tragedy. But it's more than that: if the woman never gives you the aurelia, your tachyportation to 1967 will be changed. Your return to our day will be changed. We don't know what will happen then. Nothing? Or another massive hole in the Archives? The collapse of our spacetime out of this timeline? The destruction of all reality as we know it?"

Chi rises, staring down at the Chief Archivist. "You're more concerned about an insignificant piece of jewelry than the child's life!"

"I am concerned about the preservation of reality as we know it," the Chief Archivist says coldly. "It is *essential* that the woman give the aurelia to you in 1967."

Chi shakes his head, disgusted. "When do I go?"

"We're not sending you. We need to send someone who can get close to the companion's mother. Close enough to protect her life and her unborn baby. Close enough to impress her with the importance of keeping the piece in the family. We need a woman, a Chinese woman."

"Li Chut is a fine technician."

"I thought of Li," the Chief Archivist says. "And I agree, Li would be a good choice. But we wanted to find another connection, another link to the configuration of data."

"What about the boy's mother?"

"Another good choice, but she's due to deliver any day now."

"Well, is there any other woman sufficiently connected to the child? Another descendant of the family, maybe?"

"There is, but she's not a descendant." The Chief Archivist smiles for the first time that afternoon. "She's got a neckjack, so we can install a monitor, throw in some Archives, subaud and voice projection, holoid capability. We won't have to worry about a knuckletop. And she's gene-tweaked, so she'll be resistant to bacteria, viruses, minor injury."

"Chinese?"

"Oh, yes. A skipchild. No skipfamily, but that's another story."

"All right." Chi smiles, too, though he still doesn't feel much better about the quantum probability. That is, the child. "Who is this mystery woman?"

"She's one of the Daughters of Compassion. A real fanatic, strung out on a bootleg speedball patch. After she goes through detox, she'll be as strong as an ox. Knows karate, can handle a gun. I think we can work with her, I really do. She's not stupid."

"Daughters of Compassion—but that's who raided the birth clinic!"

"Yes. As a matter of fact, she's the woman who tried to kill the kid."

Chi's jaw drops. "You want to t-port a woman who attempted murder?"

"Sure," says the Chief Archivist. "She's got green eyes."

FEBRUARY 22, 1896 ▼ ▼ ▼

Tong Yan Sun Neen

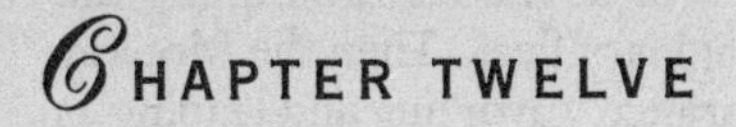

Gung Hay Fat Choy

Clash of cymbals, brass on brass, and the high thin wail of a moon fiddle sounding like some creature in heat. Zhu runs to her bedroom window. *Bang, bang, bang!* Fireworks, of course. Was it nine months ago when she last heard fireworks? Oh, marvelous, that means the parade is coming. The parade for the New Year—Chinese New Year—wends its way on Dupont Street below her window. Quite a hustle-bustle. What a sight! She's seen New Years' parades two dozen times in Changchi, but never like this, in the golden nineties.

Never like this.

The great dragon—Gum Lum—bows, snorts, and undulates, the long puppet carried aloft on poles borne by exuberant bachelors. His tremendous papier-mâché head is bright with gold leaf, red silk streamers, black and yellow spangles, little mirrors that reflect the gaslight like jewels. Gum Lum snaps his hinged jaws at the pearl of everlasting life and virtue, a huge paper lantern carried by three joyful boys. The Eight Immortals stalk by on stilts, twice as tall as a man. Acrobats turn handsprings, flipping over, leaping high. The shaggy lions, also called fu dogs—puppets manned by two fellows, one the head, one the tail—roar at the children lining the street and scratch at their imaginary fleas. Then the Monkey himself makes his royal appearance, cavorting and leaping as the crowd roars. For this, 1896, is the Year of the Monkey, the Trickster.

Zhu does not know if she trusts the Trickster. The Trickster is clever. The Monkey with his quick intelligence can outwit the gods themselves.

"Gung hay fat choy!" Zhu calls from her window. "Happy New Year!"

Still there's a dark sorrow beneath the festive air, Zhu can sense it. A darkness tumbling, roiling in her heart . . .

A premonition is just a memory. . . .

A memory of what? A memory of the future?

It is done. Tonight's the night. Muse recites her instructions.

"California and Mason streets?" she says. "Of course, I know the spot. I know that's where the rendezvous will be."

Muse scoffs. "How do you know?"

"You told me."

"I did not tell you, Z. Wong."

"Of course you did."

Alphanumerics flicker. "I never told you, Z. Wong."

"The private ecostructure over Nobhill Park, of *course* you told me. Will they arrange a room for me at the Grande Dome when I get back?"

"I doubt it. Back to jail for you, Z. Wong." Muse noncommittal. "You'll be charged and stand trial within the week."

Grief strikes her like a blow. Everything she has done for the Golden Nineties Project, everything she has sacrificed. Does it all amount to nothing? She argues with Muse. She always argues with Muse. They argue like an old married couple whose love is long dead.

"I've been used," she says. *That's* why she resented Chiron, why she hated him, feared him. She *knew* right from the start. She's been used by the Luxon Institute for Superluminal

Applications as a courier for an enigma whirling in a CTL. A pawn used to patch up the mistake made by one of their elite. The CTL is an artifact of tachyportation, unstable, destablizing to all of spacetime. The aurelia is more important than Wing Sing or Wing Sing's daughter or Zhu or whoever the anonymous Chinese woman is who gives the aurelia to Chiron Cat's Eye in Draco in Golden Gate Park, in the summer of 1967.

She goes to the wardrobe. The pearl gray dress, of course. The cosmicists love symbolic gestures. She will return as she went, in the pearl gray dress. From jail to jail, from this when to that when, dust to dust, ashes to ashes. She sorts through her fragrant silk dresses. So pretty: the cerulean blue, the turquoise, the mauve.

"Muse, where is my gray dress?"

"You gave it to Wing Sing. You took the dress down to Morton Alley. Jessie asked you to. The girl is just your size. Remember?"

"I did no such thing," Zhu snaps. "She was gone by the time I got there."

"You could hardly fit into that dress, Z. Wong." Muse prim. "Considering your condition."

She goes and stands before the watery glass of her mirror. Swollen bosom, swollen belly, even the corset tightly laced cannot conceal her bulges. Shock reverberates through her blood.

"What condition? I've just grown fat. All that rich food Jessie serves," Zhu says. "Plus, I've started to drink. The dyspepsia is awful."

"You're pregnant, Z. Wong." Muse frank. "You've indulged yourself in a sadomasochistic relationship with a questionable young man who has turned out to be a drug addict."

"Indulge! I *love* Daniel."

"You lusted for him."

"He loves me, and I love him. I wanted to help him."

"And now you're pregnant."

Zhu paces back and forth. Wood planks squeak. The new boarder in the suite below bangs on his ceiling with a broom handle. An odd buoyant feeling rises in her lungs like the first rush of the black patch or a breath of fresh air. She goes back to the wardrobe.

There, in the wardrobe, is a *sahm* of apple green silk. A lovely new tunic and trousers, a green silk bandeau. At the bottom of the wardrobe, green-threaded sandals with platforms of straw.

"That's better, Z. Wong." Muse solicitous. "The *samh* will conceal your condition. Much more comfortable for you, too. Anyway, it's Chinese New Year. Gung hay fat choy."

"Gung hay fat choy," Zhu whispers and slips on the *sahm*, which fits her perfectly despite her burgeoning pregnancy. She finds the aurelia on her dressing table, pins the brooch on her collar.

Stands at the threshold of her bedroom for the last time. Nostalgia leaks into her heart. *I'll never see this place again.* She *knows* this is true. *A premonition is just a memory of the future.*

"Hurry," Muse whispers.

▾ ▾ ▾

Zhu flees into the night, Jessie and Daniel dogging her heels. Four bruisers follow them up Montgomery Street to the Barbary Coast. A hand on her shoulder, a hand on her purse. She stops, whirls, facing Daniel J. Watkins and Jessie Malone. "I'm leaving you tonight," she tells them, pleased at their look of despair. How on earth did she ever get involved with these people?

YOU WILL ALWAYS BE SURROUNDED BY
LOVING FRIENDS

That was her fortune in the Japanese Tea Garden. Daniel and Jessie, loving friends? Yet seeing their despair at her announced departure, she knows it's true. Jessie took her away from the hatchet men, took her into the boardinghouse, gave her a chance to survive. And Daniel? He is her lover, the most compelling lover she ever had.

Zhu loves the golden nineties, how can she deny it? The

pleasures and debaucheries of this ancient night are beautiful, wild and free, free in a way Zhu never knew freedom before. She was not free as a Daughter of Compassion. She was empty, emaciated, filled with the blind yearning to belong to *something*. Gripped always, ever since she could remember, with the need to numb the deep apprehension of incipient disaster. Burdened with the presentiment of doom, a *premonition*. She was brutalized; and became brutal.

Jessie and Daniel love her, she knows this. She has always known this. Why did she stay in the employ of the Queen of the Underworld? Why did she have an affair with Daniel? This is the final, irrational answer. They've always loved her, and she has always loved them.

Not a pattern of pain, of atrocity. No, Zhu will not accept that.

"Don't you make fun of mermaids, buster," Jessie shouts at the peepshow entrepreneur, who mutters, "Sorry, lady. It's just a joke."

"Watch out for that Muldoon," Jessie says in Zhu's ear, pointing out a short man in a scarlet cutaway. "He's a crimp."

Daniel slings his arm around Zhu's shoulders and grins at her. She smells brandy on his breath. He must have ducked in somewhere and downed a quick shot. Zhu smiles back. Daniel; he's so beautiful, his hair spilling over his collar. Pale skin stretched over his bones, glazed eyes bright with drink, deep with dope. *He's going to die.*

And there's nothing she can do.

But why? Why must that be? Are they all like the aurelia, human beings slung upon the cross of destiny? Zhu *will not* accept that. Daniel had a life before the Luxon Institute for Superluminal Applications decided to t-port her six centuries into the past. He must have a life now. He must go to Paris to see the Lumière brothers' moving picture machine. Perhaps he'll work with Thomas Edison. Perhaps he'll come back to California, to Los Angeles next time. He'll know the work of another Charles Chaplin, not the misogynist painter of broken-backed nymphs, but an actor who goes by Charlie and will make people laugh.

They pass by the Lively Flea, the most debased showcase

on the Barbary Coast. Zhu stares at the shows, live on stage. Women copulating with animals, with men of different races, with other women, with corpses. She presses her fingers to her throat.

A group of temperance women stand outside the doors of the Lively Flea and commence a song, ring brass bells, bang on a drum. "Shall we gather by the river, the beautiful, beautiful river? Shall we gather by the river . . ."

A temperance woman approaches Zhu, hands her a leaflet. "Turn away from sin, my child. Turn away from the degradation of women and children. Turn away from the oppression of the colored races. Turn away from cruelty to God's creatures."

Zhu hands the leaflet to Jessie. Alphanumerics flicker in her peripheral vision. "Heads up, Z. Wong," Muse says urgently.

Wing Sing. There, along the waterfront. Zhu would know that moon face anywhere, the delicate cheekbones, the slope of a nose, the curious mouth, her slim, tall figure in the pearl gray dress, a straw boater pinned over the shiny black braid that swings down her back. Wing Sing totters painfully in button boots small enough to fit a child. Are her feet bound or unbound? Zhu cannot tell. Wing Sing leans on the shoulder of a blond woman. Li'l Lucy? No, the blond is much too thin. Wing Sing and her companion duck into Kelly's Saloon & the Eye-Wink Ballroom.

"Let's have a drink!" Daniel declares. "Just a nip. I don't need the drink when I've got the Inca's gift."

Jessie's hand grips Zhu's elbow. Her face is taut and pale. "I got a feeling, missy. Let's don't go in here."

Everything is exactly the way it's supposed to be. Of course Zhu gave the pearl gray dress to Wing Sing. Of course Zhu wears a *sahm* of apple green silk. She had it custom-made for her at Lucky Gold Trading Company so she can be comfortable during her pregnancy. It is nine minutes after eleven. Zhu has less than an hour to get all the way downtown, catch the cable car up California Street. She cannot miss her rendezvous, not this one.

Everything slows down for a moment. Alphanumerics

skitter and swirl across her eyes, a wind whistles in her ear. Voices scramble into nonsense, laughter clatters.

"Why?" Zhu says.

"Why, why, *why*?" Jessie cries. "Always *why* with you, missy."

"Why don't you want to go in?" Zhu says.

"Because I got a *feeling*. What do you call it: a premonition."

"Hurry," Muse whispers.

"I can't wait," Zhu says.

"Come, my poor little lunatic," Daniel says, laughing and sweeping them into Kelly's. "Let's have a drink."

Crummy bar, smoke and sawdust. The four bruisers sashay through the swinging doors. Harvey walks in with Muldoon the crimp, and they all exchange ribaldries with Mr. Kelly himself. Three hatchet men in black drift through the swinging doors, too. The eyepatch turns his glittering eye on the crowd.

Zhu takes Wing Sing's arm and leads her away from a table of sailors, who shout prices and what they'd like her to do.

They go to the table where the skinny blonde sits.

"Li'l Lucy?" Zhu says.

"I know, I'm so ugly now," Li'l Lucy says, hiding her bony face and black-rimmed eyes behind a silk fan. "It's the hop."

Wing Sing whirls. "Look at you, Jade Eyes. Fat with your baby, huh?"

Zhu studies Wing Sing's slim belly. "You will be, too. Fat with your new daughter."

Li'l Lucy giggles but Wing Sing is furious, her eyes slicked with tears. "No, no, I not make baby. I lose Rusty's baby. Monthlies stop, that all. Hop stop monthlies, that why singsong girls smoke. Maybe hop make me lose baby, too. Anyway, good for business."

Wing Sing reaches over and slaps Li'l Lucy squarely on her cheek. Li'l Lucy stops giggling.

"You so smart, Jade Eyes," Wing Sing says, "have fancy explanation for everything." She leans over the table. Zhu can smell the sickly sweet reek of opium. "You know what 'Wing Sing' mean in the tongue of my village?"

"What does 'Wing Sing' mean?"

"It mean 'everlasting life.' You think I want to live forever? Like this? Huh." Wing Sing's face is a mask of sorrow. "Huh, forget it, Jade Eyes. I'd rather die."

Daniel comes to Zhu's side. Cold glance for Wing Sing. "You're supposed to come and have a drink with us, mistress."

"So what you want, Jade Eyes, huh?" Wing Sing says.

This is when Zhu is supposed to give the aurelia to Wing Sing. For the future; for Wing Sing's daughter. Wing Sing will get pregnant again; she *must.*

"The aurelia," Muse whispers.

But Zhu turns aside from all of them and bows her head. "Why, Muse?" she whispers. "Why should I? Wing Sing never had the aurelia; I have it. Wing Sing isn't pregnant; I am. If the aurelia is an enigma, an anomaly of time with no beginning and no end, what difference does it make who gives the aurelia to Chiron in 1967?"

"The aurelia," Muse whispers.

"What difference does it make under the resiliency principle? The resiliency principle that Chiron is so afraid of? If, under the resiliency principle, *we* can make reality then *I,* Zhu Wong, choose. I'll be one hundred and one years old in 1967. With my gene-tweaking, I'll easily live that long. *That* is my sacrifice; to stay."

Muse silent. Daniel shakes her arm. "Let's go, my little lunatic."

"I want you to take care, Wing Sing," Zhu says, a deep foreboding rising in her chest. "I'm sorry."

"Sorry for what, Jade Eyes?" Wing Sing says and shrugs. "You bad luck to me."

"I'm sorry, I'm so sorry. . . ."

Muse whispers, "The aurelia."

The aurelia. Zhu covers the gold brooch with her hand. This is Kelly's. The place is thick with thieves, cutpurses, desperadoes, crimps. A tightly corseted small woman conspicuously faints in back near the cooch booths. Fanny Spiggot is working the crowd.

Zhu rises. She's got to get out of this place!

But Harvey, Muldoon, Kelly, the four bruisers surround

her and Daniel. Harvey holds two drinks in tall tumblers. "So you're taking me to court, Mr. Watkins?"

Daniel takes the drink. Kelly guffaws. The eyepatch and the hatchet men cross Kelly's. Daniel raises the drink to his lips.

Zhu kicks, moving easily in the *sahm*. She plants a hard heel in the gut of one of Harvey's thugs before she whips her fist like a snake striking and knocks the doped drink from Daniel's hand. The tumbler falls to the floor and shatters. The trapdoor flips open, waiting like a grave. Kelly's confederates wait in a boat below, ready to catch the next man to crew the clipper ship bound for Shanghai.

Jessie yells, "*Do* something, you deadbeats! You gonna let them crimps take a man?"

Someone seizes Zhu, but she whirls and strikes. Gasps at the sharp sting of a knife slicing the skin of her arm.

"No one cross Chee Song Tong," the eyepatch says. "No woman cross me, Jade Eyes."

"I never crossed you," Zhu says. Her breath catches in her throat.

"You cross us. You steal from us. Steal from *me*."

Daniel yells and seizes a shard of glass from the shattered tumbler. Harvey's thugs descend on him, fists flying, the awful thud of skin on skin. Daniel falls to the filthy sawdust, blood pooling on his lip. Two thugs drag him by his ankles to the trapdoor. Harvey brandishes a hypodermic needle. A narcotic squirts from its gleaming tip.

Jessie screams, "No, no, no, no!"

Zhu leaps at the eyepatch, in spite of his knife, and whips the side of her hand across his throat. The shock makes him crumble, and she seizes a gun—a Smith and Wesson revolver—from his waistband, fires off two rounds. Harvey disappears like a counterfeit coin. Harvey's thugs drop Daniel's legs and slink away into the smoke and confusion.

Shriek of police whistles. Jessie yanks Daniel to his feet, slings his arm over her shoulder. The trapdoor flips shut, a grave denied its corpse.

The eyepatch stares at Zhu, his face a mask of malice of one betrayed on an inexplicable level of loyalty Zhu didn't know they shared. She trains the Smith and Wesson on him. He looks wildly around, determined to satisfy Zhu's debt. He seizes Wing Sing, who screams and staggers, ungainly in her dress and too-small boots. Zhu squeezes the trigger, but there's nothing, the gun needs reloading. She flips the grip into her palm, but before she can launch another attack, the eyepatch whips the knife and cuts Wing Sing's throat from ear to ear. Blood sprays all over the pearl gray dress. Wing Sing falls to the floor and dies.

Muse says, "Hurry."

MARCH 17, 1896

Saint Patrick's Day

CHAPTER THIRTEEN ▼ ▼ ▼

Woodward's Dancing Bears

On her way back from Mr. Chang's pharmacy bearing powdered willow bark in a white paper packet, Zhu hears Old Father Elphich announcing the news as he tends his newsstand on Market Street. He holds aloft a copy of the Examiner, brandishing the headlines in a hand clawed by arthritis.

TONG WARS RAGE: MURDER IN CHINATOWN

HATCHET MEN HACK AS COPS WATCH

"Oh, newsboy, gimme a *Call*," says a rotund man bursting out of his chartreuse velvet waistcoat, emerald studs the size of dice winking on his cuffs. The gentlemen of the golden nineties call Old Father Elphich a newsboy despite the fact Old Father Elphich's chalk-white hair falls to his waist and he must be over seventy.

Zhu jostles her way to the newsstand amid men crashing steins of green-tinted beer, downing shots of green-tinted gin or whiskey the color of old copper infused with liquid patina. Everyone in San Francisco is Irish on Saint Patrick's

Day. People need some cheer this cold rainy spring. Despite the morning drizzle, celebrants quaff their libations out on the sidewalk, hoping to sight a rainbow in the blustery skies. The saloons along the Cocktail Route serve up great steaming platters of cabbage and corned beef, pots of freshly ground mustard and horseradish, boiled potatoes and carrots, black loaves of rye bread, pound cake laced with butter, tart San Joaquin strawberries, pale green whipped cream.

A parade careens down Market Street, white horses, grays, and piebalds all dyed a rusty green. Plenty of crepe paper shamrocks, streamers, and rosettes as bright as new grass, a tipsy brass band in kelly green top hats.

A gaggle of blond and red-haired Irish prostitutes has rented a phaeton with a gypsy top. The prostitutes are well oiled, rouged, and whiskeyed. They wave and cheer, kick up their legs revealing green garters, pull down their bodices showing green lace along the tops of their corsets. One hooker boasts a shiny emerald beauty spot on her abundant breast. Gentlemen cheer. Ladies glare, scandalized. Someone will have a word with the mayor's staff, who are likely to be found at the Irish parlor tonight.

"Saint Patrick's Day," Muse says, "is generally observed despite its ethnic and religious origin because people intuitively want to celebrate the vernal equinox, the rebirth of life after winter, the joyful fertility of spring, the commencement of a new cycle of . . ."

"Thank you, Muse." Zhu curt. She is not feeling joyful. No, though she could very well call her miraculous escape on the night of Tong Yan Sun Neen a rebirth, the commencement of a new cycle, she is left with confusion, fear, and Daniel. Daniel dying.

Zhu buys an *Examiner* from Old Father Elphich, slips into the shelter of a flower stand in front of the Metropolitan Market, and scans the front-page article. The usual righteous rant against criminal activities in Tangrenbu although the white community does not really give a damn about the tongs and their activities except to the extent that bloodshed is bad for the tourist trade, of which Tangrenbu is a prime attraction. The bloody skirmish—a man beheaded, another gutted—was apparently a dispute over a girl. A Chinese slave girl. Another pretty girl kidnapped, duped into a false marriage, or simply sold by her father and smuggled through the coolie trade.

"Wing Sing, I'm sorry, I'm so sorry," Zhu whispers. The grief, the guilt tug hard at her heart.

Alphanumerics scroll across her peripheral vision. "An anonymous Chinese woman in a gray silk dress got her throat cut the night of Tong Yan Sun Neen." Muse dispassionate. But the monitor opens the file that Zhu has studied over and over, a morgue of newspaper clippings and articles not much different from the one she holds in her hands. Muse highlights the relevant text. "She dies; she always dies. No one knows who she was. There was nothing you could do."

"My throat aches, Muse."

Muse silent.

"The sacrifice was supposed to be mine."

"You have made other sacrifices. You will make more."

"I survived the Closed Time Loop."

"You survived that *particular* CTL, the Prime Probability that collapsed on the Chinese New Year." Muse glum. "Permit me to remind you, we're still here. Still in this Now." Muse accusatory. What will happen to the AI when she dies and is buried in an anonymous grave five hundred years before the monitor was manufactured? The steelyn ultrawire and microchips will not disintegrate the way her brain and nerve cells will. Is there more than one Muse? Is Muse unique? Is Muse afraid? "You never made the rendezvous," Muse says.

A man whose blond muttonchops have been rendered a variegated green pours his beer over the head of a swarthy, dark-eyed fellow. The men grapple, tumble, knocking over buckets of green carnations. Green water pools on the macadam. A crowd gathers, cheering them on, the mood turning tense with violence.

Never made the rendezvous at California and Mason streets? No, Zhu did not, and what was she to do? A squad of local bulls had dragged Daniel, Jessie, and Zhu out of Kelly's and down to the precinct station to file a statement while Harvey, his thugs, and the eyepatch with his hatchet men had faded swiftly into the night. The morgue had collected Wing Sing's body, listing her as a Jane Doe. No identification, no immigration documents, no next of kin. Her death was not only meaningless, but an embarrassment. That's the Barbary Coast. Nob Hill swells clucked their tongues and mothers pleaded with sons to stay away from that wicked place.

When the bulls had finally released them, Jessie caught a cab and spirited Zhu and Daniel away to the south o' the slot. Jessie prevailed upon a distant cousin working as the concierge in a seedy Tehama Street boardinghouse to put the couple up.

"Jar me, you can't come back to my house," Jessie had said as they fled in the dawn. "I run a class joint."

"We've done nothing wrong." Zhu had been furious, exhausted, and scared. By then, Daniel had become unconscious.

Jessie had softened. "Missy, Harvey's thugs will be looking for you there."

Zhu has not seen her bedroom at 263 Dupont Street again. *Knew* she wouldn't.

Two beat cops descend upon the grappling men and separate them, escorting them in opposite directions down Market Street. Zhu's belly flutters. She ducks out of the flower stand, finds a corner in the Metropolitan Market where she can sit down.

"What will happen now, Muse? Will all of spacetime be polluted? Have I unleashed another reality?"

"I don't know." Muse honest for once.

"The aurelia is still an enigma."

"That it is."

"And I'm a more reliable courier than the LISA techs bargained for."

"You are not the anonymous Chinese woman who gives the aurelia to Chiron in 1967, Z. Wong."

"Who else? I've got green eyes."

"No, no." Muse adamant. "The Archivists would have certainly identified you."

"Wise up, Muse. Do you really believe Chiron and the institute would have told me that they were sending me into the past to die? And if Wing Sing didn't survive, that I could take her place? Wasn't that their secret plan?"

"No, *I* would have been informed."

"What difference does it make under the resiliency principle?"

Muse silent.

"Without Block and mouth swathe and neurobics, I'll look like an old woman at one hundred and one years old. But I'll make it. Without a new contraceptive patch, I may even have more children."

Muse silent. Then, "You're creating a new reality, Z. Wong. *You* are."

"Muse, I'm the only one who knows exactly what to do."

Zhu cups her hand on her belly. Five months pregnant, that's what Jessie Malone's doctor says. So hungry, but whenever she eats, her stomach squeezes against the baby and then she can't eat. Jessie's doctor cannot tell the gender of her baby. That technology won't be available for nearly another century. Technology? The contraceptive patch behind her knee is still bright red. Defective technology.

Zhu opens up her paper, anxiety clumping in her throat, and reads:

> **A notorious hatchet man who wears a black eyepatch like a pirate on the high seas, is employed by the notorious Chee Song Tong, and is well known for his nefarious and vicious acts of murder, mayhem, and violence contracted and commissioned for substantial sums of gold, was among the casualties at the Bartlett Alley massacre yesterday afternoon.**

"The eyepatch," Zhu whispers, "he's dead." *We are all strangers here.* She grips her forehead, expels a breath.

A shop clerk bends over her. "You all right, miss? Can I get you something?"

She looks up, sees the startlement in his eyes at the sight of her features. Doesn't have to tell him to leave her alone. He backs away. She rises and braces herself for the crowd on Market Street.

Yet her relief that the hatchet man can no longer seek her for the blood debt called by Chee Song Tong is pierced with a certain sadness. *You pretty girl, too, Jade Eyes.* How had the eyepatch become a tong enforcer? Could they have talked? Wasn't he just another traveler to Gold Mountain? Another traveler to the cruel golden nineties of San Francisco? Or was her sense of a fragile connection with the man a delusion?

Notorious hatchet man hatcheted. Newspaper fodder and sighs of relief from the Chinatown Squad. Till the next assassin immigrates to Tangrenbu ready, willing, and able to carry out the next contract. Zhu abandons her *Examiner* on Old Father Elphich's newsstand. She's got to get back to Daniel. She fights the throng on Market Street, heading for Fifth Street.

"You still need to worry about Harvey." Alert Muse. "Heads up, Z. Wong."

Two bad eggs circulate through the Saint Patrick's Day crowd, not participating in the drunken revelry or gratuitous violence but watching, searching, checking out faces. Checking out Chinese; the women.

Every tough bird merits Zhu's attention. Since that awful night, Harvey has circulated the word through the underworld that he means to kill Daniel. Jessie heard the rumor from a john at Morton Alley. Jessie's distant cousin turned out to be a terrible gossip. "You kids better move on," Jessie told Zhu. Zhu found a room at another humble boardinghouse south o' the slot. Daniel's lawyers are still pursuing the foreclosure action against Harvey's Sausalito poolroom. Dressed in her denim *sahm*, wielding Daniel's power of attorney, Zhu has appeared and signed several petitions in Daniel's behalf, keeping both the foreclosure action and Harvey's vendetta alive. Harvey's spies know she may dress as a lady, a Chinese whore, or a coolie. Harvey's spies know she is Jade Eyes.

Harvey means to kill Daniel, all right, but Daniel may oblige Harvey by dying all on his own. *He's going to die.*

No!

Zhu cannot abandon Daniel. She cannot let him die. There must be something Zhu can do right in the golden nineties.

Old Father Elphich's cry soars above the din of the crowd, "Missy, missy, you left your paper, missy!"

The two bad eggs turn and crane their necks.

Zhu flees.

❜ ❜ ❜

To south o' the slot where the humble people live, the ones who sweep streets and stitch boots and scrub floors. Jessie's neighborhood is a glossier place, despite the saloon on every corner, plump with gold and silver coins that tumble carelessly in and out of every pocket. South o' the slot—south of Mission Street, a stone's throw from elegant Market Street and the grand hotels—reflects its own dingy economy. Not Tangrenbu, which despite its degradation, colorful filth, and occasional plague is cherished as a tourist attraction. Not North Beach or the Latin Quarter, which with their handsome swarthy people, thick red wines, odoriferous cheeses and fish, and bay views also attract the moneyed. No, south o' the slot is just plain poor with no extra zest or exotic quality to attract anything other than thousands of penniless new immigrants from Britain, Ireland, Scotland, Wales, Germany, France, Belgium, and everywhere else in America. Stick saloons, laundries, tiny groceries with wilting produce and day-old bread stand side by side with boardinghouses, warehouses, whiskey distilleries, and sugar refineries. The stink of tanneries and butcher shops mingles with the bitter clean smell of hops and bleach. Saloons are as plentiful as in the tenderloin and along the Cocktail Route, but these are cheap beer halls or wine dumps where the wine is raw alcohol colored and flavored with cherry extract.

Zhu circles the boardinghouse twice, watching for signs of anyone following. She finally darts in, climbs the stairs, and examines the three deadbolts she installed top, middle, and bottom. An old trick from the compound where the Daughters of Compassion lived. Thugs can't crowbar open a door with deadbolts top to bottom without a lot of work.

You will hear them first, step out onto the fire escape. Get your gun.

Harvey's thugs had beaten Daniel badly on the night of Tong Yan Sun Neen. In the freezing dawn as Zhu had taken a room at the Tehama Street boardinghouse, he had slipped in and out of consciousness and cried for morphine. Could Zhu refuse him? She herself had once lain like this, leaking blood, ready to die if it hadn't been for the black patch. She found his works in his jacket pocket: a smart brass Parke-Davis emergency kit custom-fitted with a hypodermic needle and vials of cocaine, morphine, atropine, and strychnine.

The atropine, even the strychnine, she could use. Keep his ticker pumping. She hid the narcotics in her feedbag purse.

It was bad enough Harvey's thugs had beaten him so severely that night, worse that the bulls had detained them when Daniel should have been taken to the hospital at once. Worse still the condition to which he had brought himself. Daniel's heart, liver, lungs, skin, nasal passages, throat, and most likely his brain were severely traumatized from his alcohol, cocaine, nicotine, and morphine habits.

She would not give him morphine.

The worst came, though, when she imposed withdrawal and tried to guide Daniel through detoxification. Nothing prepared her for the violence of his reaction. Withdrawal from the complex of highly addictive substances promptly sent his body into shock and a condition that resembled a severe case of dysentery, together with cardiac arrhythmia, infection of his needle tracks, and hemorrhaging in his nose. She was terrified he would have a stroke.

"Oh, Kuan Yin," Zhu cried one night. "I'm not a doctor. This isn't a hospital."

"Sure and we once saw a bird as bad off as this." Jessie brought hot water, clean sheets, blankets, food. "At the mansion, too, so don't be ashamed of him. Fine gentlemen get themselves in a fix from time to time. They go take the water cure for the summer season at San Rafael and bring their fancy doctors with them. Jar me," Jessie said, sniffing indignantly, "if there ain't more dope fiends on Snob Hill than in all of Tangrenbu."

Muse perused the Archives. "Poor water quality control. Massive problems with dysentery throughout the nineteenth century. That's why morphine therapy is so popular in this day."

"What do I *do?*" Zhu wailed as her lover lay writhing on a cot. She hoisted him up at least every quarter hour and led him to the toilet down the hall where fluid gushed out of him again and again.

"Go get some paregoric," Muse said. "But don't let him get his hands on it. It's got a little opium in it." And, "You may try a neurobic." The paregoric helped. The neurobic conferred no benefit at all.

The specter of the CTL loomed before her, unstable, destabilizing, an unnatural consequence of tachyportation. She had become conscious within this CTL, she knew that now. She would eternally become conscious to face this hell, die, be reborn, face this hell again and again. Would she die, sometimes, on the night of Tong Yan Sun Neen, would she *know* for sure next time she was going to die? Her throat ached.

Jessie brought Scotch Oats Essence, which Zhu waved away. Muse concocted a mix she could make out of her stock of pharmaceuticals for the Golden Nineties Project. Jessie couldn't find the mortar and pestle Zhu had left behind at 263 Dupont Street. Zhu bought another set. After two intensive weeks of grinding tiny pills and breaking open capsules, she discovered that all her antibacterials were gone. There was nothing left for her if she got sick.

"I don't care," Zhu whispered to Muse. "I lost Wing Sing; I cannot lose Daniel."

And still Daniel lay, semicomatose. Dying.

"He needs nourishment through the blood," Muse said. "His digestive system can't sustain him. He needs sugar, salts, fluids. Especially fluids. And a general nontoxic anodyne and restorative. Safe synthetic aspirin is a few years away, but you can get powdered willow bark at one of the better Chinese pharmacies."

Mr. Chang's pharmacy did stock willow bark. Zhu boiled water, prepared strange soups for the blood, rigged rubber tubing with Daniel's hypodermic needle, and constructed a crude intravenous apparatus. She cleaned the needle with isopropyl alcohol. She worked the mollie knife up Daniel's nostrils until the punctured cartilage of his tortured septum healed. She ran the mollie knife up and down his arms where abscesses festered, and slowly the needle wounds healed.

One night he flailed on the cot, crying softly.

"Get him cigarettes," Muse advised. "Go on. Won't kill him for a couple of decades, anyway."

Zhu ran to the Devil's Acre Saloon on Tehama Street, looking for cigarettes for Daniel.

Click-click-click; she unlocks the three deadbolts. Steps into their room.

Daniel lies quietly where she left him, smoking.

"You look better."

He stares at the smoke spiraling up to the ceiling like the spirit is leaving his flesh.

"Eat something?"

The bowl of millet soup is cold, untouched.

"Drink something?"

Half the orange juice is gone.

"Good." She checks his pulse, his forehead, the insides of his arms.

"Daniel?"

He offers his limbs to her lifelessly.

"Daniel?"

He raises his eyes, opaque pools whose depths are denied to her. Have been denied for so many long gray days that Zhu has lost track of time.

"*Daniel?*"

Something is broken inside him, and she doesn't know how to mend it. The mollie knife cannot touch it, and neither can her love.

She sinks to the floor and begins to weep. For Wing Sing, for Daniel, for the little green-eyed boy she nearly killed six centuries in the future. She has not wept in years, not since summer camp when someone flew a kite shaped like a fish.

His hand squeezes on her shoulder, stronger than she thought possible. "Don't cry, angel," he says. His first words since the awful night of Tong Yan Sun Neen. His face, when she looks up, is etched again with life, the opaque surface of the eyes broken at last.

She wipes her eyes at once and leaps to her feet. Her first impulse is to scold him. "I'm not an angel." She helps him back into bed, but he will not lie down. He sits next to her, comforting her against her small outburst of self-pity.

"But you are. Who else would save the life of a sinner like me?" He reaches for his ciggie.

"You're not a sinner." A painful shudder she can only call joy squeezes her chest. "But you *still* smoke too much." She finds her Patent Dust Protector, pulls the mask over her face.

"What the devil are you doing?"

"I'm pregnant. I don't want to breathe your smoke."

"A little smoke won't hurt you."

"That smoke could harm the baby. *Our* baby."

He stubs the ciggie out. "But I am a sinner, condemned to hell itself."

Through the dust protector, "Why do you think you're a sinner?"

"Because I'm a failure, like Father. I've no head for business."

"You didn't do so badly, Daniel. I don't believe you believe that."

"All right; because the dope got the best of me."

"Daniel, Dr. Mortimer prescribed the cocaine. The Scotch Oats Essence Jessie guzzles as 'medicine' is morphine and whiskey. You've made some wrong decisions, and you've *got* to start making right ones, but I don't blame you. Besides, look at your own mother."

"My mother." His face, empty for so long, twists with a sharp sudden anger. "Such a fine lady. An angel of purity. Do you know that when I went to London and Paris, I didn't care if I ever saw her face again? I was furious when my father called me home in time to watch her die. Pale and beautiful, as always. Her deep sea eyes beseeching me."

"Deep sea eyes?"

"Not emeralds like yours, angel. Just . . . green, green eyes. Her question, always her question, even on her death bed, 'Danny, haven't I been good to you? Haven't I always been good?' I answered, I always gave same answer. 'Yes, Mama,' I said. 'Of course, Mama. I love you, too, Mama.' My God!"

Zhu pulls the dust protector off. "But, Daniel," she says, puzzled, "I thought you did love her. I thought you understood about her addiction. I thought you were angry with your father."

"I can't stand my father's self-righteousness, the morality he preaches, the sin he decries, all while he was an adulterer and a cheat. Yes, he beat my mother and aborted her bastard child. He should go to jail for what he's done. She suffered too much."

Zhu cringes. What is the value of a life when the world is burdened with twelve billion people?

Daniel does not notice. He rubs his forehead, remembering. "But she? By God, Zhu, she was a drunk and a dope fiend. An adulterer, too. Yes, she suffered. But she was hardly innocent. All her pretensions, all her hypocrisy. She was no lady."

"You told me," Zhu says, "she was prescribed alcohol and morphine by doctors."

"Certainly! She became an expert on booze and narcotics. And when I was an unruly child, when I ran about too much or shouted or simply annoyed her, she knew just what dosage to give me. 'Haven't I been good to you? Haven't I always been good?' She dosed me up with 'soothing syrup.' 'Time for your medicine, Danny.'"

"She gave you alcohol and morphine," Zhu says carefully, "when you were a child?"

Daniel paces about the room, a little unsteadily, but he's up, he's moving! Pale face flushed with anger, eyes alive. "I've been a dope fiend for all my life, and that's the truth." He lights another ciggie. "By God, I could use a drink."

"Daniel."

"All right, angel. I could use some fresh air."

Zhu says, "Look, the sun has come out."

❙ ❙ ❙

They help each other dress. Daniel is still weak, pale, and much too thin but looks wonderful in his three-piece gabardine suit that Jessie brought from Dupont Street. Zhu is tired with the pregnancy and the stress of the past weeks but looks fine in the new maternity dress Jessie bought her. Jessie produced an undergarment called an abdominal corset constructed expressly for pregnant women. Zhu took one look, cupped her hand on her belly, and said, "I'd rather be fat."

Daniel examines the abdominal corset with a peculiar look.

"*No*," Zhu says.

She's nervous as they stroll downstairs, gripping each other like an elderly couple. She should have bought Daniel a cane. The stink of whiskey and beer is overwhelming when they get down to the street.

"Daniel," she says warningly.

He glances hungrily at the celebrants, who take the sudden sunshine as a portent that must be toasted with renewed vigor. Cries ring out, "A rainbow, sir! I see 'un!" Guffaws, "Have another shot o' Irish."

Zhu turns and faces him. "You cannot drink, Daniel. Do you hear me? You *must* not."

He licks his lips, loosens his collar. Despite the chilly spring air, sweat trickles down his temple.

"You wanted to make moving pictures," Zhu says. "You wanted to be the first, remember?"

He looks at her as though she's slapped his face.

"You can still make moving pictures, Daniel. But you'll never do it, you'll never fulfill your dream, if you drink yourself to death by the time you're twenty-two."

A gentleman staggers into them, raising his shot glass. "To your health, mate!"

"Daniel? Do you hear me?"

He turns to her angrily. "Then why did you bring me out here?"

"Take him to Woodward's Gardens," Muse whispers, projecting its voice over Zhu's left shoulder.

"We're going to Woodward's Gardens," Zhu says, "for some fresh air."

"My little lunatic," he says. "Still the voices. And I thought it was all the dope I was taking."

"That's not a hallucination, *that's* an angel," Zhu says. "Right, Muse?"

Muse pleased with the charade. "I am her guardian angel," whispers the monitor. "Not that she deserves me."

▼ ▼ ▼

They take the train to Mission and Fourteenth where the amusement park called Woodward's Gardens stretches over several huge city blocks from Thirteenth Street to Fifteenth Street, Mission to Valencia. The entrance is grand. Snapping flags, banks of ivy spilling over the wrought iron fence, colorful posters announcing events and attractions. They enter a lush labyrinth, stroll meandering paths amid little lakes and streams. Admire sculptures, fountains, and monuments, visit the glass-paned conservatory with its tropical flowers and trees, tour the art museum where Virgil Williams, founder of the School of Design, has hung a new exhibition. The former residence of Mr. Woodward, who made his fortune with a hotel called What Cheer House, shelters a natural history museum. Zhu is amazed by the zoological garden, which boasts small but nicely appointed cages and yards for curious lamas, shy deer, shouting peacocks, twittering birds from South America with wings of emerald, ruby, and gold. California sea lions cavort and beg for fish at the seal pond.

"I've never seen anything like it," Zhu says. "Like a billionaire's preserve. I'm amazed the public is allowed in."

"Of course, the public is allowed in," Daniel says. "Why wouldn't they be?" A skeptical look. "What, angel? Are you going to insist on your tall tales again?"

"Never mind."

"Let's hear it then. Are you going to tell me that six hundred years in the future people won't have amusement parks anymore?"

"Oh, there are disneylands and playplexes and metaworlds. Plenty of zoos in telespace for the masses to jack into. When I was a kid, I used to think dinosaurs and dodos, elephants and lynxes all lived in America at the turn of the millennium, and how lucky people were to see them." At his quizzical look, adds, "Cheap virtual zoo of extinct species; didn't distinguish between epochs. Or maybe I just didn't pay attention." Zhu sighs and sniffs the air, which smells like new grass and eucalyptus leaves. "But nothing like this. Only the very rich and very rich private foundations like the Luxon Institute for Superluminal Applications can afford to maintain natural habitats like this. New Golden Gate Preserve is one. And the public is not allowed in."

"Then you're very rich here with me," Daniel says.

"So I am." To Muse, "Does this beautiful place last a long time?"

Muse searches the Archives and posts a file in Zhu's peripheral vision. "Woodward's Gardens will be torn down at the turn of this century." Muse whispers. "The site will be paved and filled in with industrial warehouses and low-cost multifamily housing. Where the grand entrance stands now will be the on-ramp to a major elevated freeway. In the earthquake of 2129, the elevation will collapse, killing two hundred commuters at the height of the rush hour. In 2254 . . ."

"Muse off," Zhu says, unexpected tears welling in her throat. "I don't want to hear anymore."

Daniel takes her hand. He is somber, pale. "By God, angel, is the future that terrible?"

"You're beginning to believe me?"

His hand trembles in hers. "How can we bear it?"

"We bear it because we must." She cannot stand to see him sink into depression again. "Listen," she says. A pipe organ strikes up a lively tune.

They stroll to a stage set up outside the zoological garden. The stage is caged. The back wall is set with a door leading into another cage on the inside of the zoo.

A dapper fellow in tails and a top hat steps up, equipped with a crop and a bucket of chopped apples. "Ladies and gentlemen-ah, we now-ah present Woodward's famous dancing bears-ah!"

The back door opens and four brown bears amble onto the stage. Each wears a silly hat and costume. A bellboy's hat and a necktie; a sailor's cap and a life preserver; a lady's straw boater and an apron; a lace bonnet and a ballerina's tutu.

"Hah, hup, hup!" says the dapper fellow, snapping his crop, but mostly tossing bits of apple.

The bears whirl, roll over, climb up onto pedestals. Stand on their hind legs, paws batting the air, turn slow shuffling pirouettes. They snuffle and bleat with strange goatlike cries, bend and lunge to catch apple chunks in their jaws.

With each burst of applause, the dapper fellow winks and sends his charges into another frenzy of gesticulation and posture. "Woodward's dancing bears-ah!"

"That's probably bear abuse," Zhu says, enchanted, "but I don't care."

"Bear abuse? I suppose you're going to tell me next that people in future worry about whether bears have feelings."

"Not just whether bears have feelings," Zhu says, "but whether they're *happy*."

"By God," he murmurs. "I feel just like that fellow in the bellboy's cap."

"Muse," Zhu whispers, suddenly inspired, "holoid this. Do it for him. Can you do it?"

Alphanumerics flicker in her peripheral vision.

But as they watch Woodward's dancing bears, Daniel's smile fades. A wistful mood falls over him. That awful wooden look steals into his face. His eyes seem to sink, the surface of the pools ices over. His hand is cold in hers.

"Daniel," she calls gaily, "you've gotten much too thin. Let me buy you a squarer. I know how you love oysters."

"No, no." Distracted, distant. "I'm not hungry."

Zhu insistent. "You haven't had your oysters for too long. We'll picnic by the lake." Tantalizing, "I want to show you something." She's so inept at flirting. It's not a behavior pattern that ever made sense to her in Changchi. "I'll be right back."

He sits weakly on a bench set along the path. Has she pushed him too far today? He's got to eat. She hurries to a food stall manned by a hardy Chinese cook with a huge smile, quick intelligence sparkling in his eyes.

"Make me an oyster loaf, please." Hands him one silver bit.

"Missy mean a squarer?"

"A squarer, please."

"Snack for sick gentleman friend?"

She turns in surprise. "Does he look that bad?"

The cook gives her a look of sympathy. "I make good." The huge smile. "For you, missy."

He seizes a loaf of fresh milk bread, slashes off the top with a huge steel knife. Scoops out a hollow, slathers top and bottom with sweet butter, pops the bottom half into an oven to toast. Next he tosses a bowl of coppery bay oysters into a shiny copper saute pan with a huge scoop of butter. Pinches coarse salt and black pepper onto the shellfish, which sizzle, turning up at the edges. Takes the toasted bread shell from the oven, spoons the oysters inside, clamps the thickly buttered lid on top, and wraps the fragrant concoction in crisp white paper.

"Squarer for you, missy," says the cook. "San Francisco style."

Zhu hurries back to Daniel. He sits slumped and shivering, face fallen, arms folded like the limbs of a puppet. "Muse?" she says, panicked.

"Give him a neurobic," Muse says. "Have you any left? Two if you've got them."

She finds the last half dozen neurobics in her feedbag purse, takes out two without a second thought. Breaks one under Daniel's nose. His eyes flicker, a little color filters into his cheeks. She breaks another. He smiles wanly.

"What have you got there, angel? Smells wonderful."

She leads him to the picnic tables set beneath whispering willow trees. They sit and munch on the squarer. After the first two enthusiastic bites, Daniel pauses, becoming pensive.

"I loathe the real estate business," he says. "Never was cut out for it."

"Tell your father. Give it up."

"But what else can I do? I wasn't the first," he says heavily, "to make pictures move."

"You don't have to be the first," Zhu says. "Believe me, this is only the beginning. You can make pictures move in all sorts of new ways."

"I wish I had a drink," he says.

"You're going to have to fight for your sobriety your whole life," Zhu says. "If your mother fed you whiskey and morphine to keep you quiet, you're going to have to fight every day, Daniel. But it will be worth it."

"Why?" he says, throwing down the food. "Oysters taste so much better with champagne. Eat, drink, and be merry. We *do* die, tomorrow, don't we, my little lunatic? As life follows birth. As death follows life."

Zhu wonders. If she dies in the past, then her birth and life are still to follow. And she has become conscious; how many times has she made this loop, thought these thoughts? A deep chill rises up inside her. Eat, drink, and be merry? How *will* she bear the rest of her life?

"I can't see the stars dance," Daniel says.

"The stars dance?"

"In the sky above marvelous Californ'. There was a time I could look up and see the stars dance." Voice flat. "Not anymore."

"Muse?" Zhu whispers. "Help me."

Scratchy feeling in her left eye. Muse downloads the data through her optic nerve and projects a holoid field above the picnic table opposite their own. The field is a translucent wall of blue light hovering over the grass, in front of a willow tree.

Daniel gasps. He leaps to his feet—with only the slightest glance at Zhu—and circles the wall of blue light. He thrusts his hands into the field, marveling at the lack of resistance. Well, of course, this is how the future would do it. Guffaws with delight. His cheeks bloom with color. He glances back at her, imperiously. "Go on, what's next?"

She blinks. Muse's holoid of Woodward's dancing bears pops up amid the swishing leaves of the willow tree.

And there they are, hats, costumes, yelping for apple chunks. The holoid is nothing special to Zhu, just an electronic recapitulation of a previously recorded reality. But Daniel drops to his knees, ruining his trousers crawling all around the holoid, studying the three-dimensional images of Woodward's dancing bears from every angle.

To Zhu's surprise, Muse goes on, delving into the Archives it holds in its memory, retrieving holoids of megalopolises, the Mars terraformation, the EM-Trans, the huge infrastructure of stations orbiting the Earth. A hodgepodge of epochs. Then holocausts, conquests, visions of apocalypse. The adjustments age not very far from Daniel's time. The brown ages that last for terrible centuries. And restoration of the atmosphere, the New Renaissance. A stampede of virtual gazelles leaps over a blind where a man and woman lie hidden together.

"I will be able to do this?" he says at last.

"Not all, not yet," Zhu says. "But look, Daniel. Look, and learn. Perhaps you'll tell the story of civilization with your moving pictures."

❙ ❙ ❙

Zhu hails a cab back to their Mission hidey-hole as the afternoon slips into evening. The driver cajoles the young bay gelding that rolls its eyes at every drunken whoop and bellow. The first celebrants of Saint Patrick's Day have staggered off to their favorite brothels or cribs, passed out in the backs of saloons, or gone home. Another shift streams into the saloons, fresh from factories, warehouses, sweatshops, the docks.

"Did you see the rainbow, miss?" the vegetable vendor cries as she and Daniel make their way back to the boardinghouse. "Ah, you should have seen. Too bad you missed it."

Missed it. A sharp foreboding pierces her; Zhu hesitates. "Let's circle the block, Daniel."

"I can't, angel," Daniel says. "So tired . . ."

Boom boom boom! Fiery debris sprays from their room on the second floor. People scream, jump back, run from the blast. A knot of five men stand impassively on the corner, watching. One dangles a can of fuel boldly in one hand.

"Stay here," Zhu commands. Cupping her hand to her belly, she runs toward the boardinghouse, intent on identifying those men.

A small dark man with a mane of greasy black hair. Harvey laughs, holding a match to his cigar. Before he and his thugs even notice her, Zhu chops him in the kidneys, in the neck. He turns, grips his fists, but cannot bring himself to slug a pregnant woman. She hoists her skirts and lets him have it with a kick in the kneecaps. Harvey crumbles. People start running, the local bulls and local guys, the bartender at the Devil's Acre, the landlady's very nice son, Old Father Elphich's cadre of street newsboys.

"You bastard, you bastard," Zhu yells, kicking Harvey as he falls. She can smell the whiskey on him.

The local guys seize Harvey's thugs, including the one with the can of fuel. The landlady's son pulls out a pistol and trains it on them. "I'll blast your friggin' heads off!" he warns them. The newsboys descend on Harvey, gleefully pummeling him with their fists before the bulls pull them off and handcuff Harvey. A paddy wagon gallops up to the scene and hauls Harvey and his thugs to the cooler.

▼ ▼ ▼

"We don't have to hide anymore?" Daniel says.

"Muse, is there anyone else Daniel must hide from?" Zhu whispers.

Muse posts a string of statistics in her peripheral vision. "Negative. My analysis indicates his opponents have been disposed of."

"We don't have to hide anymore," she says.

"The luck of the Irish has smiled on us today!" Daniel crows. "I'm going to get us a room at Lucky Baldwin's hotel! We're going to eat, drink . . . Well, we'll eat and be merry, by God."

He hails a cab. A smart black brougham halts for them. They board and collapse, laughing, on the plush leather seat.

"My angel," he says, cradling her.

"I'm not an angel, Daniel."

"Yes, you are."

"No! I'm not an angel and I'm not a whore. I have intelligence and passion, strength and perseverance. I am capable of abstract thought, intellectual accomplishment, and artistic expression just like you, sir."

He ponders that as the brougham trots up Fifth Street to Market. "What shall I call you, then?"

Zhu smiles. "You may call me a woman."

Chapter Fourteen

High Tea with Miss Anthony

When Zhu and Daniel step down from the brougham at Market and Powell and stroll to the entrance of the magnificent Baldwin Hotel, Zhu sees Jessie Malone walking into the lobby. Actually, Jessie isn't walking. She is being alternately led, pushed, and pulled by Madame De Cassin and an adamant, smiling Mariah. Mariah smiling? Zhu cannot remember the last time she saw Mariah smile. Or if she's *ever* seen Mariah smile.

"Jar me," Jessie says to her persuasive companions, "if women go into politics, they'll wind up as bad as men."

"You don't want some man telling you how to run your business," Madame De Cassin says. As always, the spiritualist is dressed in her dashing black riding habit.

"So why do you want men deciding the laws that govern you?" Mariah says. Mariah looks like a different person. Zhu blinks, wary, afraid for a moment that she'll suddenly see Mariah unsmiling and stern in her customary maid's uniform. But when she looks again, Mariah is still smiling. Still wearing a blue French-cut jacket with silk braid and fancy geegaws like a general's decorations, matching blue boots, a blue Caroline hat, and a sweeping burgundy skirt.

"We'll all wind up in Napa Asylum," Jessie says. "We'll all start smoking cigars and growing beards."

"Hello, Miss Wong," Mariah calls. "Mr. Watkins, good to see you. We've been worried about you."

"You have?" Daniel says.

"We're delighted you're coming to the meeting," Madame De Cassin says. "We welcome gentlemen; of course, you'll have to keep quiet."

"Meeting?" Daniel says.

"The meeting of the National American Woman Suffrage Association," Mariah says. "I've been attending the meetings of our local chapter for years."

"I persuaded Mariah to go," Madame De Cassin says. "We spiritualist brothers and sisters support woman suffrage, along with equal opportunities for all our American brothers and sisters."

"You do?" Daniel says.

"Certainly," Madame De Cassin says. "Our souls are all equal in the Summerland."

Jessie turns to the spiritualist in surprise. "Is that so?"

"Yes, indeed," Madame De Cassin says.

"So that's where Mariah was always sneaking off to," Daniel says to Zhu.

"Miss Anthony has honored our town with a visit to raise support for the state referendum."

"What referendum is that?" Zhu says.

"The constitutional amendment permitting woman suffrage in California," Mariah says, beaming with excitement.

"The measure will be on the ballot this November," Madame De Cassin says. "Perhaps you will persuade your gentlemen friends to vote for it, Mr. Watkins."

"Perhaps I will," he says.

"Miss Anthony?" Zhu says.

"Susan B. Anthony," Mariah says. "President of the National American Woman Suffrage Association."

"We'll all start lying, cheating, and stealing," Jessie says. "We'll dishonor the sanctity of the family."

"Jessie, you do that now," Madame De Cassin says.

Jessie indignant. "I do not lie, cheat, or steal."

Zhu and Daniel join the throng of women sweeping into a downstairs salon, which is set with dining tables and chairs. The sideboard offers hot tea, cream, sugar, scones, bread pudding, candied violets, and a large shamrock fashioned out of Lady Baltimore cake and iced with green butter frosting.

"What, no champagne?" Jessie complains.

"Thank God, no booze," Daniel says to Zhu.

"Doesn't the temperance movement support woman suffrage?" Zhu says, trying a candied violet. The candy tastes exactly like purple sugar. "I don't think they'd approve of sherry at this high tea."

"That's so," Madame De Cassin says, overhearing her. "Although Miss Anthony asked the WCTU not to meet in California this year like they planned. The liquor interests are keen on defeating the referendum; they're investing oodles of money into the campaign against it. The liquor interests exploit the link between temperance and woman suffrage when they get half a chance. What drinking man whose wife hates his habit wants to let her have a say-so in government? Let alone a vote to go dry?"

Zhu collects her tea and joins Daniel at a table. They are joined by Jessie, Madame De Cassin, and Mariah.

A plump young blond woman sits next to Zhu.

"Li'l Lucy?" Zhu says.

"Just Lucy is fine, Miss Wong," she says. She looks radiant and fresh, with neatly combed hair, a scrubbed face, a high-collared blue dress. "I met this wonderful fellow. He's in shipping. He helped me get over the dope and the booze. I'll never go back to the sportin' life. We got married last week and bought a house in the Western Addition." She glances at Zhu's belly. "With luck, I'll look like you come autumn."

As Zhu congratulates Lucy, a tiny, tightly corseted and veiled lady sits tentatively next to Mariah. Fanny Spiggot smiles nervously at the company, avoiding Daniel's eyes. Mariah says, "Welcome." Smiles; switches her purse to her other arm.

A tall elegant lady in a pompadour streaked with white sweeps into the salon and sits next to Lucy. "Good afternoon, ladies," Donaldina Cameron says with a dour look at Jessie and Zhu. She hesitates, too, pondering whether she should be seen in such company, but the other tables have filled up with attendees. Cameron shrugs. She studies Daniel for a moment. "Haven't we met before, sir?"

Zhu glances at Daniel as he coughs into his napkin. "I believe you must be mistaken, miss," he says. "That's Dolly," he whispers to Zhu in an insinuating tone.

Zhu punches his shoulder. "How do you know?"

Suddenly Mariah cries out and leaps to her feet. She ushers a stately woman into their midst, bidding her to sit in the last seat at their table.

The stately woman joins them. White hair pulled back in a severe bun, a pince-nez planted on her nose, her stern face ravaged by sun and age, a stout figure in stiff black silk. But despite her austere appearance, the woman's eyes sparkle with warmth, deep compassion, a keen intelligence.

Zhu catches her breath. Susan B. Anthony is a formidable woman, but her love for her fellow woman is the most striking thing about her. Miss Anthony studies the table, smiling at them all.

Zhu glances at the table, too: a notorious Irish madam, a German former hooker, a cockney pickpocket, a black housemaid, a French spiritualist, a Scotch missionary, and a Chinese bookkeeper. A Chinese bookkeeper from six centuries in the future who is pregnant by and unmarried to the young American gentleman seated next to her who will go on to make movies in the next two decades. What a motley crew! From the astute look on Miss Anthony's face as Mariah makes introductions, Zhu does not doubt Miss Anthony appreciates their multifarious composition, too, though she cannot know the full extent of their diversity.

"Sure and we'll all be growing mustaches, Miss Anthony," says Jessie. Tart look at Miss Anthony's face and figure. Jessie is resplendent in a tightly corseted green silk gown and enormous Colombian emeralds. There will be a bash for Saint Paddy's at the mansion tonight. Ah Chong must make wonderful corned beef.

Miss Anthony turns to her quizzically. "Are you a working woman, Miss Malone?"

"Ha! You bet." Jessie juts an elbow into Mariah's ribs.

"And what sort of work do you do?"

"I own whorehouses, Miss Anthony. A parlor and some cribs." Jessie tosses her blond curls defiantly, eagerly seeking a shocked look on Miss Anthony's craggy face. "I'm what you call a madam." She raises her voice in case the elderly suffragist is hard of hearing. "A whore, Miss Anthony."

Everyone at the table coughs, cringes, or blushes, but no shocked look comes from Miss Anthony. On the contrary, Miss Anthony leans forward, eyes sparkling with interest. "And how did you get started in that line of work, may I ask?"

Donaldina Cameron rolls her eyes. Madame De Cassin reaches over and pats Cameron's hand sympathetically. Daniel circles his arm around Zhu's shoulders protectively.

"Line of work! The biz is the biz." Jessie blares with laughter. "You really want to know, Miss Anthony?"

"Indeed, I do," the suffragist says.

Jessie pulls a flask from her purse. Zhu smells brandy. The madam takes a long pull.

"Once I was a little girl," she says sarcastically.

But the table hushes, the brandy works its chemistry, and Jessie's eyes glisten.

"I was a little girl with a littler girl, my own sweet innocent Betsy. She was younger than me by a year and a half, but Mum liked to say we was twins because we looked so much alike. 'My sweet angels,' Mum called us. 'My mermaids.' We lived at Lily Lake on the Oregon side of the border, sure and we swam in that lake every chance we got from the time we could walk. That's the way I thought about us. *We* walked, *we* swam, *we* ate, *we* slept. Betsy and me, like one. She was younger but wilder and stronger. Betsy could hold her breath and dive down deep and swim near halfway across that lake, under the water! Her skinny arms and legs went pumping like a frog. And Mum and me, we'd get scared. 'Betsy, Betsy,' we'd call and hug each other. 'She ain't comin' up this time, Mum,' I'd cry. And then she would. She would pop up from the water, gasping and laughing, and wipe the water from her eyes. She'd yell, 'Are you cryin' for me, Jessie? You thought I ain't comin' up this time, huh? Didn't you?'"

Jessie tips her flask again.

"And then your mommy died, didn't she?" Miss Anthony says.

"Mum died," Jessie says, with a look of surprise. "Pater, too. Fever going around that winter. Pater was a smithy, that's where I get my touch with the nags. Business had been slow, the house was cold, and they both got the fever, him from tending to her, and her from wherever fevers come from. I was ten years old, Betsy eight going on nine. There must have been some money. Pater had owned our house and stables. But a lawyer came in to settle their accounts and sent me and Betsy to an orphanage in Portland. Maybe some money went with us for our keep, I don't know. All I know is we never saw a dime of it.

"Sure and we hated that place! I remember I came to believe that the orphanage had somehow killed Mum and Pater. Mum and Pater would never have gone off and left me and Betsy like that. So we turned bad. We ran away every chance we got. We went down to the river. There's this river that winds through Portland like a great big old snake. And down to the river we'd go to swim. We missed our Lily Lake.

"One hot summer day we'd run away and gone down to the river to swim. Betsy was swimming underwater the way she did, diving, spouting water from her mouth, kicking up her legs. Showing off she was. And me crying and wringing my hands and begging her to come up, come back. My sweet innocent Betsy, she was all I had.

"Suddenly a strange gentleman with silver hair stood next to me on the riverbank.

"I was never shy, but I stood dripping wet in my cotton shift, and I remember how his black eyes went up and down. I think that must have been the first time I got an inkling about the lust of men. I remember how I found my crumpled dress on the bank and clutched it to myself as though a dusty wad of cotton could hide my body from him.

"But it wasn't me he wanted; he wanted Betsy. He made small talk. 'Can you swim, too?' he said. 'Sure can,' I said.

I think I even got mad when I realized it was Betsy who had grabbed his eye. 'We grew up at Lily Lake,' I said. 'We've swum like mermaids since we could walk.' 'Mermaids,' he said. 'Charming.'

"Like a fool I spilled our whole story. 'Orphans?' he said. 'How would you like to get out of that orphanage, young lady?' 'How?' I said. 'Come with me,' he said. 'I own a circus.'"

"You joined the circus, Miss Malone?" Lucy says incredulously.

"But that's wonderful!" says Zhu. After her skipparents had abandoned her and she'd gone to live at the barracks, Zhu had often fantasized about just such an escape from the cruelties of her young life. Jessie Malone ran off to join the circus?

Jessie smiles wanly and pulls at her flask again. "Yeah, well, what seems wonderful ain't always so wonderful.

"We joined the circus, Betsy and me. Mr. Girabaldi—he was the silver-haired gentleman with the black eyes—billed us as 'The Water Princesses—See the Little Living Mermaids!' Betsy at nine was not so little; she shot up taller than me. And at eleven, I was not so little, either. After the cheap grease and grits they fed us, I developed my bosom and hips, you bet. Neither of us was such little girls anymore.

"Oh, but you should have seen our act! Mr. Girabaldi put us in silver and green sateen bathing suits. That was for starters. Then he had a glass tank made; it was as big as a whole room. And he filled that tank with water, and tinted the water blue, and in we'd slip, the Living Mermaids. I could hold my breath, too, but Betsy was best. She could spin, she could roll, she could turn loop-the-loops in that tank. Oh, we was grand! The audience loved us."

"Then you must have made a lot of money," Miss Anthony asks.

"Mr. Girabaldi made a lot of money," Jessie says.

"I thought so," Miss Anthony says.

Jessie's look at the craggy suffragist is not so tart. "Yeah, *he* made the money, and *we* worked like slaves." To her maid, "Beg pardon, Mariah."

"Don't apologize to me, Miss Malone," Mariah says. "I have

never been a slave. You've always paid me fair and square. I have saved ten thousand dollars in the bank."

Zhu shoots a look at Cameron, who returns a grudging nod.

Jessie dabs at her eyes with her fingertips. Madame De Cassin hands her a napkin.

"So you traveled with the circus, Miss Malone?" Miss Anthony says. "Did Mr. Garibaldi treat you well?"

"Oh, he was swell," Jessie says. "We traveled all over the West in a horse-and-wagon caravan. Mr. Garibaldi wasn't exactly like our Pater, he didn't much care about anything but his money, but he fed us, clothed us, and gave us our own little wagon and a big gray gelding. The company was very good to us. Betsy had a sweetheart, the son of an acrobat. Me, I didn't care about boys at that time. And then everything changed.

"We toured through San Francisco. A lady named Miss Hester saw our act. Somehow she found her way backstage. Sure and wasn't she agog over us. 'Mermaids,' Miss Hester would say as she dried Betsy's hair with a thick cotton towel. 'So beautiful.' I guess we both was still missing our Mum. Miss Hester came to see us every night after that. She brought us little gifts and fancy things to eat. Roasted quail, chocolate truffles. She bought me my first diamond, a silly worthless chip, but at the time I thought it was the queen's own jewel.

"It turned out Miss Hester was a madam. She owned a parlor on Terrific Street. A class joint. One night after the show, she asked us out to dinner. No, she didn't take us to her parlor at first. She took us to the Poodle Dog. The Dog was such a naughty place, them Snob Hill ladies wouldn't be caught dead even on the first floor in those days. Sure and we went up to a suite on the third floor. Oh, the wicked third floor. I was twelve by then, Betsy going on eleven, as skinny as a stick but developing her bosom. After the circus, we was *not* stupid chits. Still, we was pretty young kids, and the circus folk had coddled us. We was the Little Mermaids.

"So we did not expect to find several fine Snob Hill gentlemen waiting for us in that suite on the third floor of the Poodle Dog. Gentlemen who wanted to meet the Little Mermaids. Who wanted to see us perform. In private, you see.

One Mr. Heald, a young up-and-comer in town, had taken it upon himself to make up the same sort of tank we swam in for our act. He had the water tinted blue, and everything. And our Miss Hester urged us—no, she insisted—that we perform as true mermaids do. Without our green and silver sateen bathing suits."

"So you swam in the nude for these gentlemen, you and your Betsy," Miss Anthony says.

"We did." Jessie sniffs.

"And what happened after that?" Miss Anthony says.

"Ah, come on, Miss Anthony. You know. We went to work as parlor gals for Miss Hester, we did," Jessie says.

"You were eleven and thirteen at the time?"

Jessie nods.

Miss Anthony nods as if she has heard Jessie's mermaid tale a thousand times.

"Ah," Donaldina Cameron says softly. Big dark eyes cast down.

"We all have a path," Zhu says, "don't we, Miss Cameron? And you; you have your Cause."

Cameron blinks up at Jessie with sympathy.

"Hester tricked us out," Jessie says wearily. "Betsy and me. She set up a tank in her Terrific Street parlor and dyed the water blue. And we swam. After our act, we went upstairs with the best gentlemen in town. Sure and we were the toast of the parlor. The toast of San Francisco! Made money for Miss Hester *and* ourselves. Made the other girls sick with jealousy. I learned most of what I know about the biz today before I celebrated my fifteenth birthday. I was good with money. I didn't blow it in. I started a bank account and bought real estate."

"But Betsy is on the Other Side, isn't she, Miss Malone?" says Madame De Cassin. "She's the one you always call. She's the one who always comes to you."

"She was so beautiful at thirteen," Jessie says. "The toast of San Francisco. The highest paid girl in town. My sweet innocent angel, my Betsy. Sure and she was bad, though. She loved to pit her gentlemen against one another. Made them jealous the way she loved to make me afraid when she swam beneath the water at Lily Lake. When I told her she was bad, making the johns angry like that, she only laughed at me. 'Make them pay, darlin', she would say, 'make them pay.' She didn't just mean gold. She demanded passion. It became a game for her. Who would come calling Sunday morning before church. Who would bring the best diamonds. Who would surprise her with a mare or a boat or a dress from Paris.

"Then Sergeant Franklin Morrisey blew into town. He'd served under General Grant as a teenager. A fighting cock, that one. He'd gambled his way across the West, played poker in Tombstone, killed two men in Cheyenne. Still proud and handsome by the time he got to San Francisco, but getting on in his years. No longer such a young man. Wanting a wife equal to *his* passion.

"He went sweet for Betsy from the moment he laid his pale blue eyes on her. He demanded her hand. She would have none of it. Wild as a cat she was. What would Betsy do, being married? She'd acquired a taste for the sporting life. One night she consented to dine with him at the Poodle Dog. A third-floor suite, a closed door, and plenty of champagne. He must have proposed to her for the tenth time; she surely must have mocked him. Morrisey never did have a sunny temper, but Betsy made him crazy. So he beat her. They found her in that suite, on the third floor of the Poodle Dog. Her neck was broke. Morrisey never hung for it, either. He blew town. I never heard about him again. And the police? Well, she was just a hooker."

Everyone is struck with silence. "Thank you for sharing your story, Miss Malone," Miss Anthony says.

Jessie sniffs, but her face is as hard as stone. "And that's how my Betsy crossed over to the Summerland."

"Poverty," Miss Anthony says, stroking her chin. "No protection for children's legal rights. No decent child labor laws. No decent wage laws at all. No decent educational opportunities for women. Few decent employment opportunities for women except in menial jobs that don't pay a wage that a single person needs to live on. Prostitution has little to do with morality, and everything to do with poverty. That's why," Miss Anthony says, "we must have woman suffrage.

Because if men don't care to address these issues with their vote, women will. Women will."

"Miss Wong says she knows about the future," Jessie says. "Tell us, Zhu. Mr. H. G. Wells doesn't say. Do women get the vote? Do women go into politics?"

"Women will get the vote," Zhu says, and everyone applauds and cheers. She doesn't want to say women won't get the vote for another quarter century. The Nineteenth Amendment will be passed in 1920, long after Miss Anthony has gone to her grave. "And women will serve in government. Women will be elected to every important office, including the office of President of the United States." She doesn't want to say the first woman American president will not be elected until 2093, nearly two centuries after this time.

"That's grand!" Donaldina Cameron says cheerfully. "Then women will also outlaw prostitution. We'll drive Miss Malone and her loathsome flesh trade out of business."

Zhu also doesn't want to say that the flesh trade will last for at least another six hundred years.

Jessie glares. "Sure and we'll look into your own private sweatshop while we're at it, Miss Cameron."

"Sweatshop!" Cameron says, rising from her chair. "And what, pray tell, are you calling a sweatshop?"

"Your mission, that's what I'm calling a sweatshop," Jessie says, rising too. She tosses a bit of shamrock cake at Cameron. "What sort of wage do you pay your little prisoners?"

"Prisoners!" Cameron says, heaving her tea at Jessie.

Jessie hops out of the way, saving her green silk from ruin. "Sure and maybe your so-called rescues are really kidnapping, Miss Holier-Than-Thou."

"Kidnapping!" Cameron advances menacingly. "I'll have you arrested for slander, you sinful wretch!"

"Wretch. Look who's slandering who!" Jessie steps forward, shoves her face in Cameron's face.

Zhu and Mariah leap to their feet, each restraining a combatant.

"Ladies," Miss Anthony says. "Miss Wong says we're going to get the vote; we're going to run for office. So sit down. Let's talk about the future. Have some tea with me."

JULY 14, 1896 ▼ ▼ ▼

Bastille Day

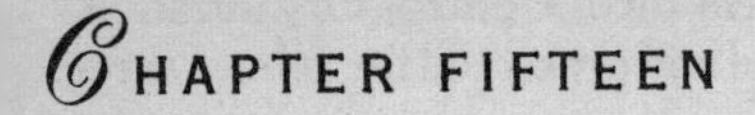

The View from the Cliff House

A cold bottle and a hot bird," says Jessie Malone, tucking into the traditional Cliff House breakfast. Roast turkey, a saddle of venison, a ham baked in plum preserves, and champagne. Jessie insists on ordering two turkeys so she and Zhu and Daniel won't quarrel over who gets the choicest cuts. "Viva la Bastille Day! Here's to you, Mr. Watkins, and good luck."

"Good luck to us all, Miss Malone," Daniel says, sipping his first glass of champagne. Darts a guilty look at Zhu. Sets his glass down.

"And especially to our beautiful Hope," Jessie says, raising another toast with a wicked look. Likes to taunt the newly reformed. "May she enjoy a long and happy life."

Daniel raises his glass again. "To Hope," he says.

Zhu cradles their newborn daughter, Hope, and tries not to judge as she gazes out at the view from the Cliff House. How she wishes Daniel and Jessie would change their ways. Wishes Daniel would settle down, stop drinking and smoking. Wishes Jessie would give up the biz, for her own health and safety, not out of any spurious morality. The international sex industry, which is alive and well in Zhu's day and covertly supported by the World Birth Control Organization, will not be properly regulated and protected for at least three centuries.

But this is the golden nineties. Of course Jessie and Daniel are going to eat, drink, and be merry. They're going to guzzle champagne for breakfast, lunch on grizzly bear steak, sup on lobster in butter. They're going to drink and smoke and carry on, nip on morphine and snort cocaine till such drugs are deemed illegal. They're not going to change just because Zhu—their little lunatic telling tall tales about the future—tells them they've got risky health habits. Mr. H. G. Wells is entertaining, too, and he doesn't tell them to give up smoking and drinking. Nor does Mr. Wells say when the cures for syphilis and cancer are discovered.

Oh, Jessie and Daniel *have* changed. Zhu has made *some* difference. But this is their world, not hers. In the days since giving birth to Hope, Zhu has felt an alienation blooming inside her like a dark flower. A disengagement; a turning away from this world. Away from the golden nineties.

From the Cliff House she can see the shifting Pacific Ocean unmarred by drilling rigs, hydroplexes, seaworld domes, megatankers, the sea wall erected when coastlines flooded during the brown ages in the 2200s and already timeworn in her day. Pale gray in the late morning light, the sea stretches out to the azure horizon, empty and pure. Just the sea, gulls wheeling, a colony of sea lions frolicking on the rocks, and the good fresh smell of brine unsullied by toxin. The timeless view fills her with melancholy, a sense of her own insignificance.

The Cliff House, newly rebuilt after a catastrophic fire and reopened by Mayor Sutro in February of this year, boasts this fine view from every one of its five stories. Tourist concessions selling hot peanuts and trinkets for a penny line the first floor. An art gallery graces the third floor; how San Franciscans love their art galleries. Every amusement park, tourist attraction, saloon, and brothel offers art, high and low, for the citizenry's contemplation. The rest of the stories are devoted to eating, drinking, and dallying. Plenty of private suites and decks. A paradise for idle gazing and amorous affairs. The turreted chateau was to be styled after San Diego's Hotel del Coronado, but the architects, Mr. Lemme and Mr. Colley, have imbued the edifice with its very own rococo character. Mr. Ambrose Bierce has pronounced the new Cliff House a monstrosity, but diners celebrating Bastille Day find the view and food and drink very fine indeed.

Change; things always change moment to moment. Isn't that what Zhu pondered from the very start of the Golden Nineties Project? At the most basic quantum level, reality is no static thing, but a flux, an incessancy, a great trembling. Spacetime spins; it ebbs and flows. In cosmicist theory, reality is One Day, existing for all eternity. Yet the multiverse is like a beam of light, swirling with realities.

Change: the first Cliff House burned to the ground. Where Zhu sits now is its second incarnation. When Muse whispers in her ear that this too will be annihilated by fire in just a few years, she asks the monitor to keep silent.

Another change: Jessie finally went to a doctor who told her what she already knew from Zhu: cut down on the drinking or her liver will bust. Jessie proudly claims she has reduced her intake of champagne from twenty bottles a day to three, plus a brandy nightcap. Well, two brandy nightcaps. As a result, and much to her delight, Jessie has slimmed down precipitously in a mere three months. "Mr. Worth is showing the cinched waist," Jessie says, "it's a good thing I dropped some of that lard."

And more change: Daniel has started drinking again. He says he can control himself. So far, he takes a bottle of wine with his dinner and that's all. Still. Zhu shifts Hope to her other arm, displeased with Jessie's toasts. Champagne for breakfast; that's a throwback to Dupont Street. Daniel really should stay sober for breakfast.

But it is Bastille Day, and Daniel is leaving for Paris.

Their private dining room, as well as the adjoining restaurant on the second floor of the Cliff House, is draped with red, white, and blue bunting, sprays of white and red carnations, bowers of smilax, and hundreds of French,

Californian, and American flags. On the deck outside, a string quartet plays the waltz from Tchaikovsky's *Sleeping Beauty.*

"The fall of the Bastille is France's Independence Day," Jessie explains to Hope as though the newborn will understand her perfectly. Getting drunk already. When the baby squeals at her, Jessie asks, "Let me hold her, missy."

Zhu sighs and hands over the baby. Hope still has the scrunched, ancient look of a newborn, her pale head streaked with fine black hair. Her eyes, when she opens them, are green. Though still hard to tell, not gene-green, yet bright and sparkling as emeralds. While it's possible Zhu could have passed on the tweak to her child, the odds are against it. Gene-tweaks are resilient in the recipient, but weak in genetic descent. No, Hope's green eyes probably come from the deep sea eyes of Daniel's mother, from the atavistic gene running through the maternal side of his family. From Hope's Caucasian ancestors.

The ambiguity is not lost on Zhu: whose green eyes? Hers? Daniel's mother's? *Under the resiliency principle, we could become the Cosmic Mind. We could change the details, and it didn't matter.*

A baby; unreal that Zhu should have a baby. The birth was easy and quick, over almost as soon as her labor began. She never planned to have a baby, not in her own time. Certainly not during the Golden Nineties Project. She is a Daughter of Compassion. She is not permitted to have a child. Never wanted one, really. Never had that need. The Cause sustained her. Kuan Yin nourished her devotion.

At the mere sight of her baby, a shudder of joy ripples up Zhu's spine so intense it's painful. But the joy—the pain—is abstract and distancing. Like contemplating the Mars terraformation through a telescope. Intense pride for an accomplishment that has little to do with her. She feels a peculiar disengagement from the child. Hope is not *her* baby, not really. Hope does not belong to her. Zhu is merely the means through which Hope could manifest, an instrument, a medium. Not the guiding principle of Hope's life to come.

Daniel lights a cigarette, stubs it out at Zhu's glance. He promises he'll cut the smoking down, too. He promises they will marry when he returns from Paris.

He loves her, she knows he loves her. Also *knows* their marriage is never to be. That is not Daniel J. Watkins's destiny. He wrote to the Lumière brothers, who were delighted to welcome a young American interested in their moving pictures. He *will* work with Thomas Edison, he *will* go to Los Angeles, he *will* meet Charlie Chaplin one day. He will make the moving pictures he loves. Zhu has a premonition.

Daniel knows it, too. He has left the Stockton Street boardinghouse in a trust for Hope, together with the proceeds from the foreclosure sale of Harvey's poolroom. "Just in case," he says. He will take with him only the proceeds from the sale of the undeveloped lots in the Western Addition. "I'll be back in two months," he says.

But he won't. He doesn't see it yet; Zhu does. Daniel J. Watkins has settled his affairs in San Francisco.

"So the old man is finally giving you some respect," Jessie says to Daniel, carving meat from the turkey.

"Father thinks the moving picture business has potential. Mr. Edison isn't so sure, but Father is nuts about the notion." Another guilty look for Zhu. She has witnessed his condemnation of his father, heard all about his father's abundant flaws. Yet the tug of blood is powerful. Zhu—a skipchild—has never known that tug for herself, though she can see it plainly in Daniel. The son still craves the father's respect. Welcomes the most degraded reprobate with open arms if only he can win that respect.

Zhu pats Daniel's hand. "If your father decides to invest in the moving picture business, he won't regret it. Mr. Edison's loss will be his gain."

Jessie and Daniel both lean forward, hanging on her words. Do they believe she knows a thing or two about the future, after all? Would they take investment advice from Mr. H. G. Wells? Or has Zhu proven a higher degree of reliability? The thought makes her smile.

A sudden twitter like a flock of gulls descending on a shoal of buttered popcorn tossed by tourists. Donaldina Cameron sweeps into the restaurant with Eleanor Olney and a bevy of her girls. The girls, neatly dressed in gray cotton smocks, black hair and black eyes shining, are ecstatic about their outing. They seldom see such luxury, plus a view of the ocean. Nine Twenty Sacramento Street depends on charity. The mission does not have a lot of money. Nine Twenty Sacramento Street will never have much money—Zhu knows that from the Archives—but Cameron will manage, survive, and thrive for all the ninety-eight years of her life. She will never waver from her Cause again.

"Here, Miss Cameron," Jessie says. Just can't turn off the sarcasm. "I got another kid for you." She holds out Hope.

Cameron and her girls eagerly crowd forward. Cameron takes the baby from Jessie's arms. Her stern Scotch face is transformed. Despite the streak of white hair and her austerity, Donaldina Cameron is not yet thirty. She is younger than Zhu.

"Ah, another one of my daughters," Cameron says, "that's what she is."

"Your daughters?" Jessie says.

"All these girls are my daughters," Cameron says as the girls hover around their Lo Mo. She gazes at the baby. "Sweet heavens, she is beautiful. Those eyes."

Jessie rolls her eyes at Daniel. "Let's go outside; I need some fresh air. Sure and I think she's about to kidnap another one right from her mother's arms."

Daniel rises, takes Jessie's elbow. "I do believe I need a smoke." They stroll out onto the deck.

"Miss Donaldina Cameron?" Muse's whisper hovers over Cameron and Hope.

"Good heavens, the guardian angel?" Cameron whispers.

"I guess so," Zhu says. Good old Muse.

"This is your Cause, Donaldina," Muse says in a high, clear voice. "And your Cause, Z. Wong."

Muse downloads the file:

Muse:\Archive\Zhu.doc

Alphanumerics flicker. The directory flashes across in her peripheral vision. Over forty thousand bytes? Another five thousand bytes in the file? A trickle of dread spills down Zhu's spine. Another reality in the multiverse manifesting before her eyes?

Eyes scratchy. In less than a second, Muse downloads the file, sends the data through her optic nerve, and projects a holoid. The luminous blue field pops up in the corner of the private dining room.

The little girls and Miss Olney stare, goggle-eyed, but Cameron watches calmly, rocking Hope in her arms.

The scene in Golden Gate Park unfolds: the young man with the painted face, the barefoot girl. The anonymous Chinese woman pushing the wheelchair, Cameron smiling at the park, at the people, at Chiron Cat's Eye in Draco. Cameron waves to him. Her companion reaches up to her collar and unpins the aurelia.

Zhu unpins the aurelia from her collar and cups the brooch in her palm. The tiny golden woman with jeweled butterfly wings poises as though ready to fly away.

The holoid shifts, the park fades, and Chi sits before them in the room like a cloud, gazing steadily at his unseen audience.

"He's alive," Chi says.

Is he alive or dead?

Zhu's heart begins to hammer, her breath catches. "Muse?"

"The new bytes spontaneously appeared in my directory, Z. Wong," Muse says.

"The little green-eyed boy is alive," Chi says in the holoid. "The Night of Broken Blossoms is over. The Prime Probability has collapsed into the timeline. He was a quantum probability, and Zhu was the one who tipped the probabilities, like balancing a coin on its rim. The Golden Nineties Project has always been about Zhu, not some piece of gold. Zhu has opened one Closed Time Loop, and secured another. The past affects the future, but the future also affects the past. We have witnessed, and we have made it so.

"Is the boy related to Zhu?" Chi continues. "Is she his great-great-grandmother?

"He has green eyes; his lineage is from old San Francisco. Is he a descendant of Zhu's daughter? We can't say for sure, I'm sorry. That information is lost to the Archives.

"Come back, Zhu. You are not the woman I will meet in Golden Gate Park. You belong here, now. We have installed a tachyonic shuttle at Point Lobos, on the rocks below the old site of the Cliff House. It's the last tachyonic shuttle we'll ever use. Come back. You have work to do. You have the Cause. You probably do have a family. You probably do have a great-great-grandson. We cosmicists are chastened, Zhu Wong. You have shown us that the great principle of the Cosmic Mind is love. You were never destined to murder your own descendant."

The holoid vanishes. The luminous blue field hovers for a moment, shrinks to a point of light, and disappears.

"But how can I leave my baby?" Zhu whispers. "How can I leave Daniel? How can I leave when there is a task to be done seven decades from now?"

Muse says, "Hurry."

Donaldina Cameron takes the aurelia. "I'll keep this for her," she says. "The man with red hair. I won't forget. I know exactly what to do."

Out on the deck, Jessie laughs at some joke Daniel has told.

Cameron takes Zhu's hand. "Do you want to say goodbye?"

Zhu shakes her head.

"Then hurry," Cameron says.

Zhu turns and walks away, taking the stairs. She steps out of the Cliff House into a cold sea breeze. Life follows birth, death follows life. The past affects the future, that is the natural order of the multiverse. Yet in the One Day that is reality, sometimes the future creates the past and life follows death. Zhu climbs down the rocks, searching for the portal that will take her home.

About the Author

A Phi Beta Kappa scholar and a graduate of the University of Michigan Law School, LISA MASON is the author of four novels: *Arachne* and *Cyberweb*, which are cyberpunk tales taking place in a future California; *Summer of Love* (a 1994 Philip K. Dick Award finalist) and *The Golden Nineties*, published by Bantam Spectra, which are time travel tales.

Mason published her first short story, "Arachne," in *Omni* and has since published acclaimed short fiction in numerous publications and anthologies, including *Omni, Year's Best Fantasy and Horror, Full Spectrum, Asimov's Science Fiction Magazine, Magazine of Fantasy and Science Fiction, Universe, Unique, Transcendental Tales, Unter Die Haut, Echtzeit, Immortal Unicorn, David Copperfield's Tales of the Impossible, Desire Burn, Fantastic Alice,* and *Sorceries: Magicks Old and New.* Her novels and short stories have been translated into French, German, Italian, Japanese, Portugese, Spanish, and Swedish. She optioned her 1989 *Omni* story, "Tomorrow's Child," to Helpern-Melzer Film Productions. Mason is currently working on a major sf novel for Bantam Spectra, *Pangaea.* She lives in the San Francisco Bay area with the artist and jeweler Tom Robinson.